— BOOK I —

THUMOS RISING

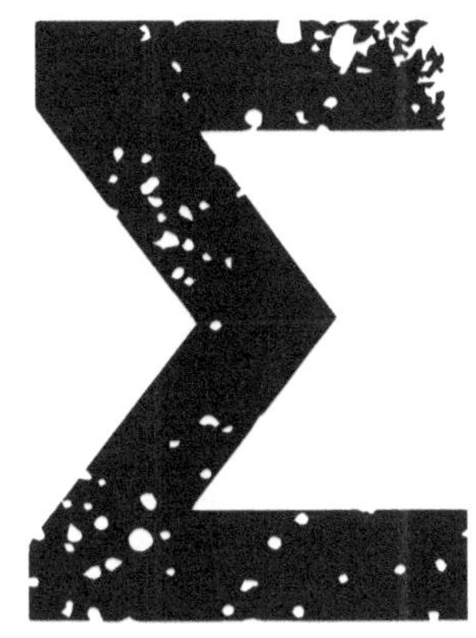

— BOOK I —

THUMOS RISING

Demitrios Lopez

atmosphere press

Ουτος βιβλιος εστι Ελορα μου. παντα α ειμι αει
εσονται σοι

"And they made it clear to everyone, not least of all to that same king, that there are many males, but few men."

— Herodotus 7.210

Land of Giants
Northern Ice Cap
Lumen Ocean
Proto-Aner Gulf
Dragon Territory
Troll Territory
Cliaza
Cyclopoi
Grey Peaks Mts.
Eastern Steppes
Attiloi Centaurs
The Wall of Zan
Sun River
Zan Sea
Zan
Katzamoto Sea
Udor Andros Ocean
Taedemaru
Xhiputzec
(Submarine Kingdom)
Ximon Ocean
Southern Ice Cap

Polluted Wastelands
Namer Canal
Osaeria
Trails of Ka
Enkadu Jungle
Pharonic Sound
Tyra
Jungle Peoples
Elora Ocean
Unclaimed Southern Islands
Ignis Rex Volcano

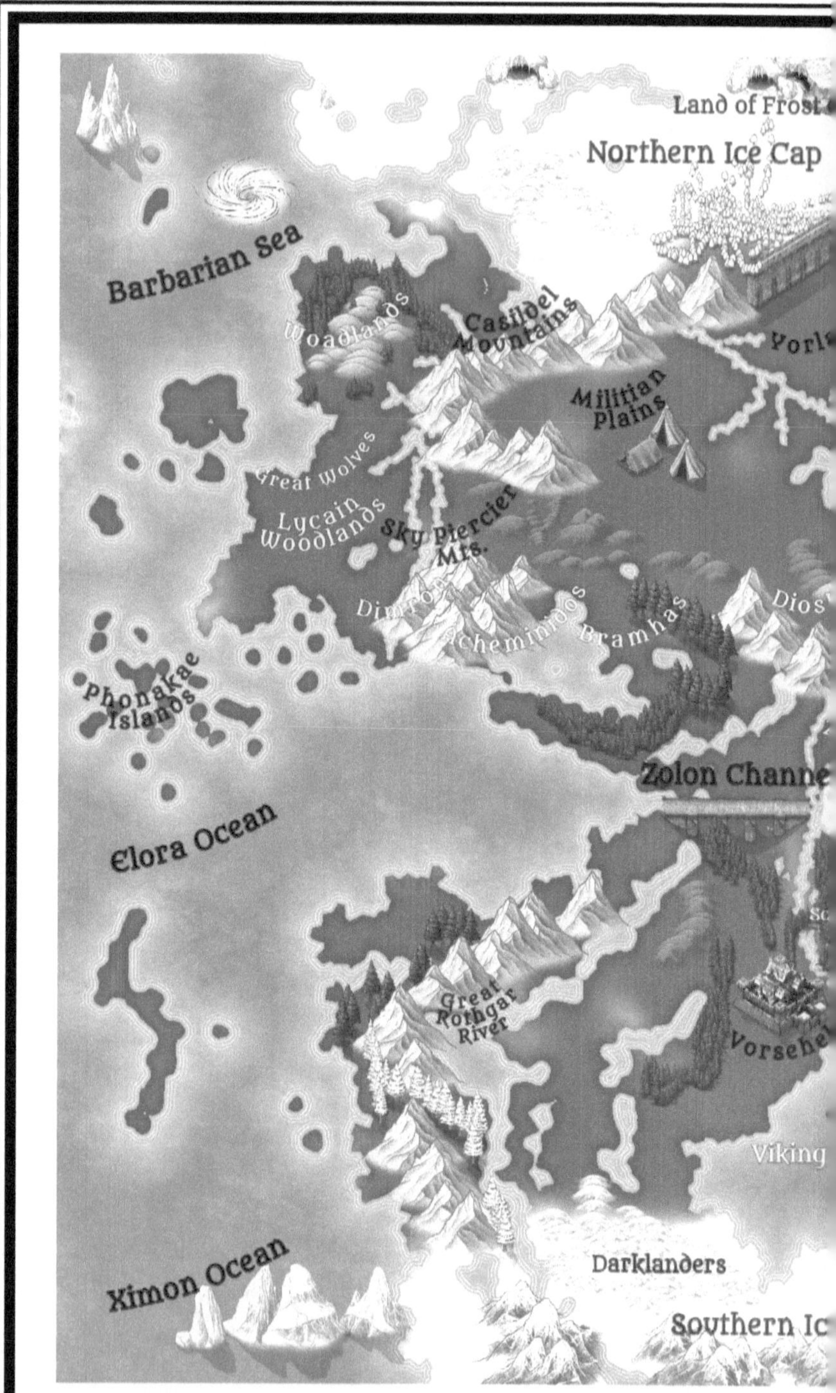
Land of Frost
Northern Ice Cap
Barbarian Sea
Woodlands
Casildel Mountains
Yorl
Militian Plains
Great Wolves
Lycain Wooolands
Sky Piercier Mts.
Dimron
Scheminros
Bramhas
Dios
Phonakae Islands
Zolon Channe
Elora Ocean
Sc
Great Rothgar River
Vorsehe
Viking
Ximon Ocean
Darklanders
Southern Ic

ll
Jona
Lumen Ocean
Aixonian Gulf
Sarpdadon
Isthmus of Sarpadon
Adalfi Sea
Hipperos
Udor Andros Ocean
Igolids

CHAPTER I
ZENO

Zeno came to Sarpedon, haunted by ghosts of his past.

The past was Alexandra. He remembered the day he and Alexandra's father, Lysandros, learned of her death. Nine days after the sack of Dioskuria, they came upon a band of refugees fleeing Ying-Chau, the underground capital of Zan, where the Dioskurian refugees fled, Alexandra among them. There were twenty-three Zan, mostly men and older boys between the ages of fifteen and thirty-five. There were few women, even fewer girls, and one old man. They were exhausted, hungry, and covered in blood and dirt.

"What happened?" Lysandros asked the lone senior of the group.

"The Vampire arrived with a small fraction of his forces eight days after he took Dioskuria," the old man narrated. "At first, we were not concerned. We thought it a vanguard, nothing more. There were only three thousand of them, and we did not expect an assault so quickly. But then we learned that the Vampire himself was among them, as well as his witch, Lana Tarquinia.

"The following day, the Xhiputzec Mermen arrived and set up a blockade on the Zan Sea. Lord Nikolaus of the house Polymaxes organized the defenders and manned the gates as best he could. But an attack never came. That's when we realized the Vampire had no intention of taking the city. He only meant to keep us within it."

The old man paused to catch his breath. He had been shot through the shoulder and had a nasty gash on his leg. Wounds he had suffered in his escape. Neither lethal on their own but inflicted on one so aged and under such emotional and physical distress, they were practically fatal. Zeno dressed the wounds as best he could with the supplies still left in his kit. The old man was clearly the patriarch of the family, and everyone was concerned for him. He took a drink of water from one of his grandchildren's canteens and continued.

"The Remani pitched camp in front of the main gate. Sorcerers advanced from the army in rank. The Vampire himself emerged from them, accompanied by Lana and her father, Tarquinius Augustus. Lana and Tarquinius entered a trance and began chanting quietly under their breath, as if they were possessed. The Vampire raised his hands, and the sky filled with clouds." The man again lost his breath, so engrossed was he telling his tale. His grandson gave him another swig of water, and he continued. "Lightning flashed. Thunder rolled. The earth rumbled gently at first. But the Vampire continued. He began chanting in some language; none of our linguists could make it out. The tremors continued, magnified. Then the gates began to crumble. Our guards abandoned their positions atop the walls, running across the crumbling ramparts, trying to find safety. The Vampire meant to destroy the gates and bury the people alive in the underground city.

"Thousands of us, stricken with panic like rats on a sinking ship, ran out the only exits available, the northern and southern gates. But the Vampire was ready. He had stationed gunships there, as well as Remani snipers. He already had the mermen in the harbor. They mowed down many of those trying to escape. We were some of the few who managed to get through the barrage. Many of my own family didn't make it." The old man's eyes began to water as he recalled the harrowing experience just days earlier. "Any men of Ying-Chau who did not die trying to escape were sealed in the dark city, forty feet beneath the ground. The Vampire buried them alive, all of them." The old man shook his head.

Zeno shot a look at Lysandros. Both fear and rage erupted from his eyes. He rushed off away from the group, his face animated with rage and heartbreak. Zeno, leaning against a tree with his face buried in the bark, cried silently and pounded his fist into the trunk.

"You're going to break your hand like that. The tree has no give," Lysandros began.

Zeno didn't turn around. "She's dead. God damn... She's dead. Why did you send her away? She could have come with us! She would still be alive, and we'd all be together! We'd be homeless, helpless, hunted all our lives, but at least we would be together. Dark Gods! She was in there when the gates came down! Trapped in the dark, starving, scared..."

"Keep your voice down. We're both wanted men."

"You think I care if we live or die now?" Zeno turned to face the man who had for so many years been his surrogate father.

Lysandros walked over to Zeno, unholstered his ion pistol, and offered him the handle.

Zeno was not sure how Lysandros meant this gesture and if he was serious or not—Lysandros was a Ranger, and Rangers were known for their nonchalant attitudes about suicide—but Zeno was in no such mood.

"Fuck off," he growled. "You sent her to her death."

"We should have died at Dioskuria," Lysandros answered. "She should have lived at Ying-Chau. At least a little longer than we would have. Everyone who fought the Vampire at Dioskuria is either dead or dying. We made it out only by chance, or fate, or by the Dark Gods' cruel trick. For whatever reason, it's just war, Zeno. We don't get to choose who lives or dies. All we can do is try to protect those we love based on the information we have. That's what I did. That's why I sent her away."

Zeno wiped the tears from his eyes. "I understand why you did it. But I'll never forgive you for it."

Lysandros re-holstered the gun and sat on a felled tree trunk.

"She was my daughter," Lysandros said, as if in a trance. "I loved her too."

Zeno never forgave Lysandros, but he did accompany him to the Woadlands, where they lived and fought with the Woadish tribes for the next ten years before he finally understood the real reason why Lysandros had sent Alexandra away all those years ago. When he learned the truth, Zeno abandoned his friend and mentor. He fled to Sarpedon.

For Zeno, Sarpedon was the ideal place to settle. The Sarpedonians were an Elledic people, ethnic brothers to his own Dioskurians. He felt at home around them and blended in well. Zeno knew he could find work as a mercenary or smuggler, but wanted to avoid violence as much as possible. He eventually became the apprentice to the royal historian under the Sarpedonian Emperor, Glaucon. The job paid fair wages, provided free room and board, and, most importantly, gave him ample hours for reading, solitude, and reflection.

Despite his best efforts to live a normal life, Zeno was haunted by nightmares of his future. His future was the Stokian spacecraft, the Theomorphosis chamber, its uncanny Priestess, and the great power she had offered him. As soon as he drifted into sleep, Zeno opened his eyes to see the Sofia Forest around him. He feared turning around. He knew it would be there. Then, as if pulled by an invisible hand, he spun around. There was the crashed starship, the ark by which the once mighty Stokians had first come to the planet Ninivon, escaping a war that had spanned throughout the galaxy. A war they could only win by creating a godman. The very thing that made their godman, the Theomorphosis Chamber, Zeno knew to rest deep inside the walls of the crashed ship. He knew that if he remained outside its walls, he would be safe. In the dream, Zeno took great solace in this. Then, again involuntarily, Zeno was inside the ship. The Theomorphosis Chamber was before him. He felt her presence behind him. Zeno turned. The Priestess of

Sofia gazed at him with her cold, dark eyes.

"By the Gods, lady," Zeno begged. "Will you not let me be? Can I not escape you even in my dreams?"

"It's not me you seek to escape, Zeno. It's the call of the All Fire. The blood of Thumos cries for its heir to take up his claim."

"I don't want to be the heir! I will not assume this power! I will kill myself before I do. I swear to the Dark Gods, if you and your sorceries do not leave me in peace, I'll take my own life to be rid of you."

Zeno raised a dagger and pressed it to his heart. He meant to end it right there. No more mourning for Alexandra, no more rage for Lysandros for taking Alexandra from him, no more fear of the alien presence and the alien ship.

Zeno stared down the Priestess. She seemed unconvinced. He had had enough. He would take back his autonomy. He would take his life and show her and whatever other otherworldly consciousness had invaded his dreams. He pressed the dagger forward into his heart. But no blood spewed forth. Rather, a voice came from the cavity he had opened in his chest. Her voice. Alexandra's voice, screaming his name. And then simply screaming. Her cries grew in volume until they became deafening. Zeno pressed his hands over his ears and fell to his knees.

"Let me go, witch! It's my life. I can take it if I want. I will take it! I will not become what you want me to be!"

The screams dissipated.

"Oh, Zeno," the Priestess muttered. "It is not your life to take. You will answer the call. You know it. I know it. Thumos knows it."

That name... that cursed name... Thumos... the godman of the alien Stokians...

Zeno awoke and shot up from the bed. Beads of sweat flowed down from his head and over his bare chest. He balled up his knees and wrapped his arms around them. He placed his head down against them. For a moment, he sat there in an upright fetal position and rocked, soothing himself.

Then, he sensed a presence. He was not alone. He looked up. A dark silhouette. Tall. It opened its mouth, and Zeno could see the glimmer of sharp fangs. Then the thing opened its eyes. Purple, pupil-less, elliptical spheres bored down into him, looking into his soul.

A primal fear gripped Zeno. Then he awoke. A dream within a dream. He would have no sleep, no peace.

That name... those purple eyes...

Zeno slept as little as possible to avoid the nightmares. Then, the visions started.

"We must be careful," Thucoditus, the senior librarian and historian, told Zeno as they worked in the royal library. "These are not the sycophantic books you'll find in the main stacks of the library, the ones that hail the Vampire as a liberator. No, these tell the truth about the Great Terror: The war that ripped our world apart. Here," Thucoditus opened one folio and began reading. "*Strategically, Sarpedon was paramount, for whoever controlled the city controlled the Isthmus of Sarpedon, the only passage to the west. The city submitted to the Vampire's eastern allies when they invaded, opening up the western passage. In return for its cooperation, the Vampire allowed Sarpedon to retain a fraction of her independence, provided she sent him child hostages from among the aristocracy. The Vampire also permanently stationed a large occupying Joni regiment there to help maintain and defend the city.*" The old man closed the book. "And that leads us up to where we are today."

Zeno pulled out a volume and opened it.

After he seized the capital, the Vampire immediately called all kings, leaders, and aristocrats to Dioskuria. They were required to bring their oldest child with them. Those who did not have children brought siblings or next of kin. The leaders of the nations who fought against him were crucified in Acropolis Square. As they were crucified, they watched as the Rapti sucked the blood from their children; many of them survived long enough to watch their children turn. The bodies were never removed from the crosses. The children of those nations that had initially declared neutrality but later joined the Vampire were held as hostages. They would be trained and, as adults, serve as the Vampire's elite corps of knights: the Equitati. They were treated very well and, as they grew, were given every reason to obey their master and carry out his wishes to the best of their abilities. This had the additional benefit of ensuring the loyalty of their parents as well, for if they spoke out against the Vampire, he would kill their children. Finally, the leaders of those nations that had supported the Vampire from the beginning were given wealth, land, and a promise of protection and relative freedom, so long as they submitted to his commands. They were also given the right to take a certain percentage of the population of those nations that had fought against the Vampire as slaves. Those who supported the Vampire were the Joni, Remani, Osaerians, Karthagoi, and the Hipperi. Of the humanoid races, the angels of Dimron, the mermen of Itzel, the centaurs, and cyclopes served him. Additionally, the Vampire and his blood-drinking spawn would only feed from the conquered nations, not his allies.

"You wrote this one yourself. Did you not, sir?" Zeno asked.

"I did," Thucoditus answered. "But life for a historian is difficult under a tyrant. More than getting published, one must worry not to lose one's head. I had to write something to demonstrate my loyalty to the new regime as well." The old man pulled several books from the shelf. They were dusty and appeared to have been unused for a while. "But these books are relatively unbiased histories. Here you can find a factual narrative of what happened during the conflict. Some are written in languages I cannot read, but you can."

In order to acquire this job Zeno made no small matter of the fact that he could read four languages, not including the common tongue. When asked from whence he had acquired these skills, he simply reported that his father had paid good money for the best tutors before he fell ill and died. A lie. But necessary to protect his true background and training.

The old librarian handed Zeno another text. "You'll need to translate this before we can upload them to our private queue. It's Anchillian."

"The tongue of angels," Zeno acknowledged, taking the book. He opened this text as well. He stared at it for several moments.

"The Vampire disbanded the egoga. Practically all of the Rangers were dead, and those who were not confirmed dead had a price placed on their heads. They were forced to go into hiding. The Vampire saw the surviving Rangers as the greatest threat to his rule. The hunting down and murder of these defenders, these men and women who had given up their lives to serve the Republic and its citizens, was met with applause across all of Ninivon. Indeed, to not applaud would have risked incurring the wrath of the Vampire himself."

"The Vampire established an ethnic hierarchy," Thucoditus interrupted. "He built schools in his preferred kingdoms where he indoctrinated the young. The Vampire was the liberating hero in their histories; the Republic, the Archons who directed it, and the Rangers who defended it, were seen as imperialistic oppressors. Young children learned to hate and see other races as inferior. Most of these nations already had their own prejudices. The Vampire built on these. The lofty status, along with financial gains for the elevated nations, quickly won the Vampire a loyal populace to rule, and the brutality and lack of civil rights and education for the lower nations likewise effectively suppressed any opposition against him. The Equitati became the most feared warriors in all of Ninivon..." The old man squinted his face. He was trying hard to remember.

"I thought you couldn't read it."

"I can't," Thucoditus replied. "But my older sister could. She was trying to memorize several of these texts before they were discovered and destroyed. She made me memorize several passages as well."

"What happened to her?" Zeno inquired.

"They found out what she was doing, and she was taken to the feeding camps."

The *feeding camps*: the darkest dungeons under Dioskuria, where the Vampire kept his ultimate weapon: the Rapti. They needed blood; those who went to the camps provided it. The Vampire partook as well, quenching his ungodly thirst in the darkness of his royal quarters.

"I'm sorry." Zeno closed the book and handed it back to Thucoditus. He truly was. The text had brought back as many painful memories for him as it had for his employer. But Zeno was not at liberty to share.

Zeno turned his head to look for some other books. Peering at him from between the folios were a set of purple eyes. He knew them instantly. They were the eyes of the Rapti. Zeno jumped back and nearly fell into the bookcase behind him.

Thucoditus immediately turned. "Are you all right, Zeno?"

"Yes. I just thought I saw…" Zeno franticly whispered.

"Saw what?"

"Saw something. Or someone."

The old man rose and looked in the direction where Zeno's eyes were fixed. "There is no one else here. Few people at the library even know of this room. You must be seeing things, son." Thucoditus bent back over and went back about his work. "These old stacks can play tricks on old eyes, young ones too." He smiled.

Zeno now saw no one. He calmed his breathing and continued his work. There were other visions, some more disturbing than others. The visions during waking hours and the nightmares while he slept made it impossible for Zeno to get any rest. He retreated into his mind as best he could. He was sleeping less and less and feeling more and more detached from reality.

When he returned to his room that evening, Zeno sat on his bed. An owl, large and black with streaks of white down its feathers, landed on his window sill. Zeno slowly turned to face the creature. He pulled a loaded ion-revolver he had hidden between his mattresses. He extended the weapon towards the bird, who gazed back at him. Zeno wasn't sure this owl was real. But if it was, it was surely some sorcery the Priestess sent to torment him. Then Zeno turned the gun to his own head.

"Don't." A voice, soft and familiar. Alexandra.

Zeno turned. He knew now that he was hallucinating. Alexandra stood on the other side of the bed, her eyes fixed on him, sympathetic and mournful.

"I don't know how much longer I can do this," Zeno began. "My joy died when you did. I knew the day I heard about what happened at Ying-Chau, I would never be happy again. I chose to live because your father ordered me to. He said he needed me. I thought he needed me to be his son because he lost his daughter. I had no idea what his true intentions were. When I discovered them, I ran."

"Because you blamed my father for my death?"

"No. Because I blamed myself. He sacrificed you to save me."

"Put the gun down, Zeno. To Tartarus with my father and with Thumos too. Live for me."

Zeno lowered the weapon and his head. The owl took off into the night. Was this reality, or just another dream? Zeno was certain he was devolving into madness.

CHAPTER II
ALEXANDRA

"Who are you?" the medicine woman asked.

"Alexandra of the Menimu," the little girl responded, standing at attention in the dark tent, her head down in a show of respect to her elder.

"Who are the Menimu?"

"Women of the Red Sky."

They were called the Militae by the rest of Ninivon. They called themselves *da'kumbra danasou kikinou*. In the common tongue, Women of the Red Sky.

The old woman continued her probe of the eleven-year-old girl. This questioning was part of a purification ritual known as the Releasing. Before one of the Militae was asked to take on a grave personal challenge, they would submit to the questioning of a medicine woman to free their souls from any personal encumbrances that might hinder them in their allotted task.

"Are the Menimu all the Women of the Red Sky?"

"No. There are many tribes who embrace the Way. But we are Menimu. I am my people's, and my people are mine."

Seventeen tribes in all lived the lives of hunters and nomads in the Militian Planes.

"What do our people most value?"

"The horse, as is pleasing to Xaimera. And the ion gun, as is pleasing to Belitor, the warrior and Ultor, the avenger."

"Do our people believe the gods take pleasure in material things only?"

"No. Neither of these artifacts would mean anything to Xaimera or the others were it not for the courage of our warrioresses."

"Not courage only. What else?"

"Loyalty, medicine woman."

"Are you loyal to the Menimu, Alexandra?"

"I am, wise woman."

"You will do as you are commanded? For the good of the tribe? According to the Way?"

Alexandra hesitated. She was young, but she knew enough to know what would follow such questions. The last time she had been asked such a question, it was by the War Mother herself. She was sparring with tomahawk axes—blades covered for safety—with her best friend, Diana. Alexandra landed a blow across the back of the neck. It hurt Diana. But Diana was a stubborn and tough girl, like Alexandra. Spurred on by their shared honor culture, which despised luxury and worshiped bravery, Diana wouldn't submit but struggled to her feet.

Alexandra hesitated then as well. She knew what those watching wanted, both younger girls as well as girls of their same cycle, as well as older warrioresses. But Diana was like a sister to her. Alexandra didn't want to hurt her friend. Immediately there was a chorus of jeers and outrage. Then, silence. Alexandra turned. The War Mother, the chief warrioress who directed all military affairs, including training of the next generation of warriors, raised her hand, calling for silence. Their eyes met for but a moment. The War Mother asked, "Will you spare your friend at the expense of the people? Will you follow the Way?"

By *the Way*, Alexandra knew that she meant the hard way of life of her people, who had studied war for generations and had retained their cultural practices of living and dying on the horse hundreds of years after the rest of Ninivon had adopted solar-powered motor vehicles. The way was brutal, but it allowed a society of only women to successfully defend themselves against armies of men who had more advanced technology.

Diana rose to her feet. Alexandra slammed the blade of the tomahawk into her friend's face in an uppercut blow. Diana fell immediately. She would be okay. But she would not rise again this fight.

Alexandra now wondered what she would be asked to do following this line of questioning.

"Alexandra?" the medicine woman again asked.

"Yes. I will do as commanded. I will follow our Mothers, and the Way, while there is life in me, to whatever end."

The medicine woman smiled. She seemed satisfied.

"The warrioresses are returning from the Genion. Your grandmother among them. She will give you an order you will not like, Alexandra. When you hear it, and you feel the resistance rise within you, remember, you took an oath."

Alexandra didn't have much use for oaths. They seemed a social coercion to force people to do things they didn't want to do. It was not the feature of her people she most loved. That was the emphasis on freedom. To live on the planes was to be free. She was one with the red sky. She could do and say what she wanted. If someone said or did something she didn't like, she could fight them. If she won, which she often did—Alexandra was the best fighter of her cycle—they would not do or say that thing again, not around her anyway. And when she was old enough, she could take lovers from among the tribe for however long they wished to be together. It was a far better life than what she understood girls her age in the Republic of Eighteen had to look forward to.

Then again, Alexandra also understood that all freedom came at a price. The freedom of the Militae would not have been possible had it not been for the Way. Though it chaffed her, Alexandra knew part of the Way was bending self-will to do what was best for the tribe. She would do her part, whatever the request. Besides, she was only eleven cycles old; what great sacrifice could the Great Mother ask her to make?

"Go to her then." The medicine woman nodded.

Alexandra left the tent and looked out on the Menimu camp, bustling with activity. The warrioresses had indeed returned from the Genion, their yearly sojourn in the world of men to seek pregnancy, and were settling back into their tents.

"What was that all about?" a voice came from behind the tent. It was Diana.

"I'm not sure yet. My grandmother wants to see me."

"She's been away for two weeks. Of course, she wants to see you."

"It's not that," Alexandra replied. "She doesn't want to see me as my grandmother. She wants to see me as the Great Mother."

Diana's face contorted. Alexandra's words accurately communicated the potential gravity of the upcoming meeting. The Great Mother was the head of the entire tribe.

"Well," Diana began. "She'll need a few moments. Let's ride."

Alexandra and Diana thundered across the open grassland atop two mustangs. In the Republic, some people had never ridden a horse their entire life. She felt so rich in these moments. Like all Militian girls, she was atop a horse as soon as her legs were long enough to grip its belly and her hands strong enough to grasp its back. The Militae did not use reigns. They did not need them. They had evolved a magical bond with the animals. Mature Militae warrioresses could communicate and control their horses through telepathy. They called this *ho ippeus*: the bond. It was for this reason they rode mustangs. The Militae did not keep their horses in captivity; it was, in fact, prohibited in their religion, the cult of Xaimera, to do so. The feral herds tended to orbit the camp for easy access to food and care. When a warrioress needed her horse, she made the request in her mind, and her horse answered. Alexandra had not fully developed these skills yet. But she had a lifetime to live among her people. She both looked forward to the warrioress she would become and appreciated the childhood the Way afforded her.

As the sun began to dip in the red sky, the two girls made

their way back to camp. Diana walked with Alexandra up to the entrance of the Great Mother's tent. The tension built between them as they came ever closer. Finally, the girls stopped.

"Maybe she's finally ready to tell you what happened to your mother," Diana suggested.

"I already know everything anyone is going to tell me about that. She was a great warrioress, and she died defending the people. Grandmother will never let me know anything more."

"You will tell me what this is all about as soon as you are out?" Diana commanded more than inquired.

"If I can. I might be sworn to secrecy."

"You're not that important," Diana protested.

Alexandra smirked. It was a joke. But found herself hoping Diana was right. She had an uneasy feeling about this.

The girls hugged. Then, with a nod, Diana stood back.

Alexandra was grateful for Diana. Aside from being a good friend, she was the most mature and disciplined of all the girls in their cycle. She was also the best rider. Alexandra often thought they might both rise to leadership one day. She could see herself as the War Mother and Diana as the Great Mother. What a team they would make. They would lead the tribe respectively in peace and war. They would take the Genion together, have children together—hopefully daughters—and perhaps even be lovers one day. Whatever her grandmother had to tell her, Diana would be the first to whom she would share.

Alexandra entered the tent to find her grandmother talking with the War Mother and two other high-ranking leaders. It was a tense conversation; Alexandra could tell that. All words ceased, and all eyes shifted to her when Alexandra entered.

Xaimera. Surely, they're not arguing about me.

The group broke, and the visitors turned to leave. The War Mother looked particularly irritated, angry even. The Great Mother had her back turned to Alexandra.

Once alone with her grandmother. Alexandra bowed, "Matriarch, I have come at your command."

"You have," her grandmother answered without turning around.

"Was your Genion fruitful? Are you with child?"

"May Xaimera grant it. May it be a girl strong and fearless." She finally turned. Her eyes, tender, met those of Alexandra. "Like you."

"May a child ask with what people you mingled?" It was small talk. Alexandra was nervous.

"I went with the matriarchal guard to Dioskuria."

Dioskuria: The capital of the Republic of Eighteen, the source of the corrupting ways of the entitled. Also, rather far for a warrioress to travel for the Genion. Most women went to border towns in Yorland to the east and Bramhas to the south.

"Are the breeders good there?"

"Dioskuria is the home of the Rangers. The best fighters the entitled world has to offer."

"But not better than our warrioresses, surely, Matriarch?" For some reason, Alexandra needed her grandmother to affirm this. She needed the Way affirmed. Though rare, there were instances when warrioresses would venture into the entitled lands for the Genion, find mates, and become infected with the Inversion. This was the Militian term when a warrioress fell in love with their male breeders and decided to abandon the Way to live with them. It was called the Inversion because it inverted the natural way. Surely, her grandmother had not become inverted?

The Great Mother's face turned hard. "You are an excellent fighter for your age, Alexandra. You will be a great warrioress one day. But you are rebellious. Too peer-oriented are you. It leads you to question the Way. Do you know what the older women say of you?"

"I do not, Matriarch."

"They say you have too much of the world of men in you. Too much of their curiosity. Perhaps it was because your own mother died in combat when you were so young. Perhaps because I had not the time as Great Mother to give you the attachment that you needed. Whatever the cause, you have grown to distrust the Way."

"No one in my cycle loves the planes, or the mustang, or our people as much as I, Matriarch." There was more desperation than defensiveness in Alexandra's voice.

"You are devoted. No one questions that. But you have an intrinsic questioning that your devotion must always overcome."

"Is it wrong to question, Matriarch?"

"It is not our way, girl. Those are the ways of the scientists and philosophers of the Republic."

Alexandra was scared now and slightly hurt.

"Because of this, what I ask of you now, I ask as your Great Mother. You are bound by our laws to obey. Do you understand?"

"I do."

"But know that once I have given my order, I will embrace you as your grandmother. You will have a chance to cry in my arms. I will comfort you. Will you rest in this?"

Alexandra took a deep breath. "Yes, Matriarch."

"In four days' time, you will leave with a small band of warrioresses. You will go to Dioskuria, where you will meet your father."

Outrage.

Male babies were always given to their fathers to do with as they wished. But girls born to Militae warrioresses never met their fathers. They had no need.

"Your father is a Ranger among the peoples of the Republic. He is the greatest Ranger. He is what they call High Strategos. Like our War Mother. He does not command one tribe only, but the entirety of the Republic's armies. He is also the leader of the egoga. You have heard of the egoga?"

Alexandra nodded. Even on the Militian Planes, everyone had heard of the ferocity and excellence of the training program that took children from all over the Republic and turned them into Rangers. It was often debated among the younger girls who would win in a fight: A Militae warrioress or a Ranger.

"He has arranged for you to enter the egoga," her grandmother continued. "It is a great honor, girl. No one of our people has ever been invited to join the training."

Tears now welled in Alexandra's eyes.

"You do not see it for the honor it is."

"Why, Grandma?" At that moment, the hard veneer the Way had engendered in her vanished. Alexandra was a child again; she was deeply wounded. She cried freely. She was losing her home and family.

Her grandmother stretched out her arms. The girl rushed into her embrace, which immediately closed around her. "I told you I would hold you," she whispered. "Even us Women of the Red Sky are human. We feel when we lose. It's okay to cry."

"But I don't understand. Why?"

"Your father is a very powerful man. He needs you."

"He *needs* me?"

"There is much I myself do not understand, Alex. But a great war is coming. Not just to the Republic, but to our people as well, to all of Ninivon. The Rangers will be the tip of the spear in our defense. Your father needs the strength of the Women of the Red Sky. I am sending him you."

"But would the Republic not be better served to make an alliance with our people? Would the tribe not be better served with me among them?"

"Apparently not. Apparently, you can best protect our people among the entitled. I am losing too, Alex. I do not wish to give up my granddaughter. But I must follow the Way, as you swore earlier that you would do in the Releasing."

"I don't want to do it." There was ire in Alexandra's voice. Pain was quickly giving way to anger.

Moments later, Alexandra burst from her grandmother's tent. The sun had set. The night was growing. But Alexandra could still see Diana sitting on the ground. She had waited for her friend. Alexandra was not interested in talking. She need-ed her horse. She sprinted past Diana, who jumped to her feet.

"Alex?" she called out in the darkness. "Alex!"

The journey from the Militian Planes to the borders of Dio-skuria and then to the capital city of the same name took two weeks. Alexandra hardly said a word that whole time. They arrived at the outer gates of the city on the seventeenth day of the journey. Alexandra had long wondered what the allure of the Republic with their entitled lifestyle was. It seemed little better than slavery to her. Particularly for women who were encouraged to be submissive in most of the eighteen nations that made up the Republic, particularly when compared to the majesty of the open planes. But when she saw the outer walls, stretching nearly a hundred feet into the sky, etched with low relief sculptures of dragons, centaurs, trolls, cyclopes, the winged angels, the finned Mer-peoples, as well as Rangers in combat, magicians in sorcery, scientists in discovery, and politicians in debate, Alexandra was awestruck. The wall was no less a work of art than a military defense, which it also very much was. Constructed of Ninivonium, the strongest steel in Ninivon, the walls could withstand both missiles and dragon fire.

The city itself was no less magnificent, filled with countless temples, baths, amphitheaters, roads, agoras, gardens, an ad-vanced aerial train system for public transportation, and defensive works. Beneath the city was an intricate maze of sewer and drainage systems. Millions of citizens commuted daily across the city in the aerial tramcars, which hung from a rail suspended above the city proper.

The small band of eight Militae seemed no less a wonder to the entitled peoples than the city was to Alexandra. Most of the citizenry cleared before them, ducking into their homes, local businesses, or into alleys. Most were scared. Some spat insults and jeers, all in the common tongue, which neither Al-exandra nor the other warrioresses understood. Some of the police guards in the city paid special attention as they passed by. But none encumbered them.

It seemed to Alexandra that the city stretched on forever. She had never seen such a mass of humanity before. They finally reached a second wall, shorter than the outer wall but still tall. A group of soldiers met them there. Each wore a single-piece metal breastplate with greaves and battle skirt. Rifles hung across their backs, and short swords at their sides. They were Elledic hoplites. So magnificent had been the wonders of the city that Alexandra had nearly forgotten how much she didn't want to be there. The sight of the soldiers' armor reminded her. *How can their horses carry so much weight?* Then she remembered: hoplites fight on foot and mostly use air travel to go to and from the battlefield. *How foolish.* The Way was clearly superior.

Alexandra was intrigued by the blades. The Militae did not use swords. Only ion guns, knives, and the tomahawk. Alexandra found the weapon symmetrical, beautiful even. As soon as she saw one, she wanted to hold it.

The Militae stopped. This was clearly intended to be the exchange point. The senior warrioress looked down to Alexandra and nodded. Alexandra knew that meant she was to dismount and continue with the soldiers.

"These men are Rangers," the warrioress said. "Follow them. They will take you to your progenitor."

"Vortex?" Alexandra asked.

"Don't worry about your horse, girl. She will follow us back to the planes. The city is no place for a mustang."

Alexandra smiled. Vortex had selected her as his rider when she was five. She knew the Militian magic would keep him with the warrioress until they were home.

"Do not disgrace your people among the entitled," the woman said. "Xaimera guide you, daughter of the Red Sky." With that, the Militae turned and rode away, leaving Alexandra in the hands of the entitled.

Alexandra entered the gates and walked up a long and

wide ramp leading up to the acropolis, the heart of the city: a large public square with three monolithic towers situated to the rear. To the east, a tower that was built of green limestone and stretched one hundred and sixty feet high. To the west, a tower with a sharp, daggerlike rock facing, essentially a steep mountain. But at the very top rested the head of a sphinx with a woman's head in the Dioskurian style.

In between the two smaller towers was the most wondrous sight Alexandra had ever seen. A third tower, two hundred feet tall and made of pure blue marble. It shined like a jewel in the sun. Its entrance was a great temple complex, twelve columns across, thirty-three deep. The temple had both triglyphs and metopes, as well as a monumental pediment and decorative frieze. The east pediment showed the Light Gods celebrating the birth of the goddess Sofia, goddess of wisdom among the entitled, whose statue was twenty feet tall and stood in the very center. It was into this tower the soldiers were taking Alexandra.

The inside was no less magnificent, with marble staircases, columns, vaulted ceilings, and various niches for artwork. It was also no less crowded. Alexandra felt a tinge of claustrophobia, such hordes of people were going and coming around her.

The Rangers seemed to be walking Alexandra into a wall. Then, perhaps by magic, the wall opened. Alexandra now noticed there were many such openings. They were doors that automatically slid back into the wall when people approached. They entered a small room, and the doors closed again. Then, something she did not expect: the floor quickly moved. Alexandra could feel the entire room rise, but how? Where were they going? She was nearing the point of panic. But the Rangers seemed completely at ease, bored even. Alexandra decided if there was anything to fear, these men and women would do something. Also, she didn't want to dishonor her people by seeming fearful.

The room continued to rise for many seconds. Then, it stopped. The doors opened, and they were in another part of the tower, one far less crowded. They exited into an atrium which opened into a long hall. A few people and soldiers walked up and down the hall, some conversing. One side of the wall had windows through which Alexandra could see the entire city. She had never been so high up before.

Finally, they reached two large, wooden double doors. The guards at the doors opened them before the group. Alexandra entered the room to see a man standing before them, a smile on his face. His skin was olive, not as dark as hers, but close. He was clearly an Elled. He had a short beard that covered part of his face. He wore a simple shirt under a pelops garment. He seemed to be about thirty years of age, though Alexandra was not good at guessing the ages of men due to her lack of exposure to them.

The Rangers said something to the man in the common tongue, and he responded. The Rangers then turned and left. Alexandra was alone with whom she presumed to be her father. She could tell underneath his clothes that his body was well-muscled, and his hands and face both bore scars. He was indeed a fighting man.

"Welcome to Dioskuria, Alexandra of the Menimu," he began in flawless Militian.

"You speak my language?"

"I do. And you must learn mine soon. Both Elledic and the common tongue. I am Lysandros of House Polymaxes. I am your father."

Silence. Alexandra wasn't sure what to say, what formalities were expected, if any. Given the fact that she had been taken from her people and forced to come here, she wasn't sure she wanted to give much respect.

"I can't imagine how hard this must be for you. You have questions. And I will try to answer what I can. Perhaps the most important thing for you to know right now is that I cannot tell you everything you're wondering. Some of which I know, but it is not my place to tell. Much is unknown even to me. What I do know is that you are already a respected fighter in your cycle among the Militae. I would continue your training here at Dioskuria. You are to be both a Militae warrioress and a Ranger. No one has ever done that before. Do you believe yourself strong enough to accomplish this?"

A challenge. She liked this man's way, even though she still harbored resentment against him. "I can... sir? Is that what people like you are called?"

Lysandros smiled. "It is. And you will have to address me as such in your training. But here, behind closed doors, where it is just you and me, I hope you will eventually call me father when you're ready. I want you to know that there are two major breaks from the training. One in winter and one in summer. You will be allowed to go visit the Militae and your grandmother if you wish. But again, I hope you will come to see this place as your home."

Alexandra looked around. The floor had some weird red grass growing from it in some places; in others, it was stone. There were odd machines she recognized as instruments. Something she had seen photographs of, called a computer. And books, lots of books. The place reeked of entitlement. On the far back wall were two large swords hanging crossed. Alexandra walked towards the great weapons. She estimated they were nearly as long as her.

Lysandros saw her interest and took one of the blades down. He handed it to Alexandra. She wrapped her hands around the handle instinctually. As soon as Lysandros let go of the blade, it fell to the ground. Alexandra looked up at her father.

"This cannot be a real weapon. It's too heavy to swing."

"This is a ceremonial blade. That is true. But we do use swords like this. It's not too heavy to swing. You are still young and too weak to wield it right now."

"I have not been called weak among my people. Sometimes impulsive and undisciplined."

"You are very self-aware for one so young. And for a stranger in a strange land, no less. You do remind me of your mother."

Alexandra turned to Lysandros. He had her full attention now. Her grandmother had never said much about her mother, nor had any of the other matriarchs or the Menimu in general. In fact, it had always seemed to be a taboo subject. This only fired her curiosity more. But in a parochial culture like the Militae, Alexandra learned not to ask too many questions. Perhaps she had asked one too many, and that was why she was here now. She wanted Lysandros to say more. But rather, she said, "I wish to learn to use such weapons."

Lysandros lowered to his knees and took the sword. He now looked at Alexandra eye to eye. "You will. You will be a master of war by the time I am done with you. Not all children in the Republic enter the egoga. Only those who pass the Trials when they are of nine years of age. Cycles in the Militae way. Those who pass begin the training at eleven. You will be competing with and training beside the most gifted children in the world. Many who begin do not finish. You will receive no special graces from me, only that you do not have to take the Trials. I have arranged for your automatic acceptance. Many will envy you this. Others will see you as a barbarian and bastard. Some, both. You will receive hate from all sides. You will need to make them see who you are. You will have to prove yourself worthy. And you will need to make allies." Lysandros rose. "You will have the remaining summer to acclimate yourself to life in the Republic, begin learning our languages, and get used to me. Then you begin."

The challenge would be greater than she had ever anticipated, and she already missed Diana, Vortex, her grandmother, and the freedom of the planes. But at that moment, something snapped into place inside of Alexandra. She would do what had never been done. She would be the first of her people to complete the egoga. She would become one of the greatest warriors in Ninivon. She would show them all, her father included. If the entitled could do it, she could do it.

Then a voice behind her asked some questions. Alexandra

turned. She saw a young boy coming from one of the back rooms. He seemed about her age. Like Lysandros, he had the olive skin and black hair and eyes of the Elleds. The boy was tall, skinny, and rather sheepish as well. But he had a kind face and a piercing gaze. Though she could not say why, she liked this boy. He relaxed her.

Lysandros addressed the boy in either Elledic or the common tongue. Then he turned to his daughter. "Alexandra, I want you to meet one of your fellow initiates with whom you will begin the egoga in the Fall. Like you, he is also leaving behind the only home and family he has ever known for the good of the Republic and all of Ninivon. I have been tutoring him in Militian. I would have you practice the common tongue with him. He will help you around the city as well. Perhaps, you will be placed together when the new initiates are sorted into Commons. His name is Zenosthenes Andrea. You may call him Zeno."

CHAPTER III
ZENO

Days became months and finally a year. Zeno had not seen or heard from Lysandros. But even in faraway Sarpedon, Zeno heard about the Brown Chieftain, the name by which Lysandros was known among the barbaric Woads. The Brown Chieftain had indeed led a coalition of Woadish tribes, now known throughout Ninivon as the Woadish League, over the Casildel mountains and formed an alliance with their ancestral enemies, the Militae. The combined forces attacked Western Yorland, driving the Joni out of villages, towns, and some small cities. There had even been a major battle: twelve thousand Woadish infantry and six thousand Militae cavalry surrounded and massacred a force of eight thousand Joni at the Yordic Pass. After eleven years of oppression under the Vampire, revolution returned to Ninivon.

The success of the northern revolt emboldened would-be rebels and freedom fighters all over the planet. Uprisings sprung up in a half dozen places, including Sarpedon. Zeno had heard rumors before of armed gangs of men in the northeastern section of the Sofia Forest. He even heard whispers of an organization known as the Blue Order.

It was the ninth day of the second month, in the eleventh year of the reign of the Vampire: Terror and Woe of Ninivon. Zeno and Thucoditus were walking through the crowded streets of Sarpedon. Zeno observed, "There is a larger Jonish presence than normal. Everyone looks nervous, trepidatious, as if they are expecting an attack. Is something going on?"

"Why yes! You haven't heard the reports? A rebellion," Thucoditus responded.

"I know about the rebellion in Yorland and Acheminidos. I even heard talk of rebellions in Vorsehelgda and Zutaera."

"Yes, but this is here," Thucoditus said, eyeing the crowd, trying to observe who might be listening over the roar of the market. "You have heard of the Blue Order, have you not?"

"Yes, thugs trying to carve out a black market under the Vampire's heavy hand. Organized crime isn't the same as a rebellion."

"They're not just thugs or criminals anymore. Now they are rebels. They carried out an attack on the airfield last night. They hit an airdrop that was transporting ion rifles, ammunition, and bombs. Likely did it to arm their own men. The Blue Order has taken credit for the attack, as has their leader, a man who calls himself Ghost."

"Ghost?" Zeno repeated. "How did they get through the perimeter of the airfield?"

"Suicide bombers," Thucoditus said. "I'm surprised you didn't hear the blasts last night yourself."

"I heard them. I ignored them."

"What kind of man ignores ion blasts?"

One who wants to hide from more than bombs.

"This Ghost claims he was a Ranger," Thucoditus continued.

The Rangers were the elite warrior class of the Republic of Eighteen before the dark times, before the Vampire. If that were true, Zeno would have known him, or at least known of him. "What else do you know about him?" Zeno probed.

"I know he is using the poor young lads of Sarpedon to run weapons for his guerrillas."

"That's tactically sound," Zeno said. "Any real rebellion must start with arming the people, and the Vampire has issued strict arms control laws. But using children..."

"Yes, one would be sympathetic to his cause, even supportive, were it not for his readiness to put children in danger and sew explosive devices into men's chests before sending them into large crowds," Thucoditus angrily agreed. "This Ghost has little regard for human life. Several children have been caught with arms and ammunition already. Glaucon ordered both them and their parents skinned alive."

The situation became more violent in Sarpedon, as well as throughout all of Ninivon. Ghost continued his guerrilla operations from his base in the Sofia Forest. No one knew who he was, but he had managed to turn every young orphan or poor child in Sarpedon into a weapons smuggler. Actual attacks were few and far between. But when they did happen, they were violent, terrible, and unexpected. Twelve Joni knights were gunned down in a public latrine. Sarpedonian hoplites were stabbed to death while sleeping with prostitutes in a brothel. Bombs detonated in temples during religious services. The Blue Order sought to kill their enemies by any means necessary, and they considered not only the Joni and the Sarpedonian aristocrats who had sided with the Vampire their enemies, but every citizen who would not support their cause. Gangs of street boys would form and recruit other boys to run weapons and supplies to the rebels. If the family refused to surrender its sons, it became a target for the Blue Order as well. In time, the citizens of Sarpedon, already so oppressed by Glaucon and his regime, came to fear the Blue Order as much as the Joni and their own government.

In turn, Glaucon and the Joni regiment stationed in Sarpedon, pressed down upon the people with even more brutal methods. They had no idea who was or was not a member of the Blue Order. They would raid the homes of suspected rebels, beat any male old enough to fight and imprison them, then sell the women and children of the family into slavery. Often the Joni would venture into the Sofia Forest looking for the Order. But each time, they came back empty-handed, often with fewer men. The Order would strike and disappear into the dark woods. The Joni would chase; if it was a small enough unit, the rebels would attack. If the Joni were too numerous, the Order disappeared. With each successive attack, the fever pitch and ice-cold grasp of fear on the people caught in the middle tightened. By the beginning of spring, the city seemed ready to explode into all-out civil war.

On the twelfth day of the sixth month of the eleventh year of the reign of the Vampire: Terror and Woe of Ninivon, Zeno was walking along the various booths of the vendors who sold in the valley outside the city walls. He enjoyed walking along the aisles of booths and seeing the various merchants, some of whom he had grown quite close to, selling their goods. Zeno quickly became a favorite among the children of the merchants who traveled with their parents to market. This gave him a few moments of peace in an otherwise tortured life.

The sun was beginning to set, and the crowds, what crowds there were, began to wane. Many booths were closing. Business had not been good since the Blue Order had taken up arms against the Sarpedonian army and the Joni soldiers who supported them. Zeno talked with the adults and played with the children, who were bound to their parents' tents. Glaucon had degreed that any child caught after dark without adult supervision be killed. All children were subject to search and arrest, even if they were with adults.

A number of the children centered around Zeno. Just as they gave him a respite from his nightmares and visions, his company helped calm their nerves and distract them. Zeno had never met his father, so he relished the opportunity to play a paternal role in these children's lives. As an adult who worked inside the Sarpedonian government, the parents trusted Zeno with their children. In reality, if he were stopped by soldiers, he doubted his lowly role as a royal historian would save them from a search. Moreover, although unknown to all but him, Zeno was a graduate of the egoga. Zeno carried himself with the confidence of a man who had once been among the most skilled warriors in Ninivon. This confidence made those around him more at ease. Zeno walked with five boys along the isles of the valley market.

"Tell us the story about the dragons again," one boy asked Zeno

"We've only heard that one a hundred times," another responded.

"So? I want to hear it one hundred and one," the first child shot back.

Zeno felt torn. On the one hand, he genuinely hated talking about the Great Terror. He grew nervous whenever he did so, as if saying the names of the ghosts from the past would make them manifest, and he was here to avoid such memories. On the other hand, he couldn't help but feel pity for these children. Zeno had grown up in a world of dragons and science and magic. A world unified in relative peace, where one could travel from one end of the Republic to the other. These children had known only the rigid world of the Vampire, where any mystery that could challenge his rule had been snuffed out. These children had no idea how much they had lost when the Republic of Eighteen fell. Besides, they needed to be entertained.

"There was a time when dragons filled the skies above Grey Peaks and ruled the skies all across Ninivon," Zeno began, with the children walking beside him. "That was the way things were for thousands of years.

"Then came the age of the machine, and later the computer. Men learned to make jets with turbo-fan engines and great wings, aerial vehicles which enabled them to venture into the forbidden lair of the skies, the lair of dragons. The dragons saw the threat immediately. Mages developed techniques for communicating with the most intelligent of the creatures. No dragon understood this communication better than Likavitos.

"The Archons swore to never use military aircraft, never to develop large capacity bombers, and never to fly over the air space of Grey Peaks if the dragons would not attack transport air vehicles. Both parties upheld their word for some six hundred years.

"Then came the Vampire. He bewitched Likavitos with his sorcery. Because he controlled Likavitos, he controlled all the dragons. They were his first air force. But Likavitos' will was strong. The Vampire feared the old dragon would break his spell. So, he secretly developed a fleet of warplanes. Once completed, he unleashed these on the very dragons who served him. He hunted the dragons to the point of extinction. In fact, no one has seen one since the air battle of Grey Peaks."

"Will the dragons ever return?" a six-year-old named Diomedes asked.

"I don't know."

"How do you know so much about this stuff, Zeno?" Patroklos inquired.

Because I once visited Grey Peaks. I was once in the egoga, and a Ranger. I saw the dragon pit with my own eyes.

"I work in a library." Zeno frowned. "I read a lot of books."

Four Sarpedonian hoplites turned the corner of the next aisle over and approached from the far end. Zeno saw them before they saw the group. He tried to steer the children into a different alley, but the lead guard made eye contact, and Zeno knew they would be searched. To dodge into another alley now would only confirm their guilt in the eyes of the soldiers. Zeno was calm. He knew all of these children well and their families. They were poor but not desperate. He knew that none of them were running weapons for the Blue Order. He just hoped that fact would make a difference to the hoplites.

Zeno pulled the boys in and leaned down. Already he could see the fear in their eyes and trepidation on their faces. They knew what could happen next. The boys ranged in age from eight to twelve. But each understood the gravity of a possible interview with the soldiers, all of whom now saw every child as a prospective smuggler and were all too eager to strike first if they thought a particular child was serving the Blue Order. Only a certain kind of man could see children as potential military opponents. Many such men now populated the files of the Sarpedonian army; such men were given to abuse the power entrusted to them.

"Okay," Zeno began. "Those soldiers are going to want to talk with us. They may even want to search some or all of us. Do what they say. Let me do the talking. If they address you directly, respond with 'yes sir' and 'no sir.' Nothing else. Do you all understand?" All nodded. The two youngest seemed on the verge of tears. Zeno felt the need to calm their nerves. "And Patroklos," Zeno turned to a particularly chubby young boy. "Don't fart. If you do that, they'll surely arrest you for assaulting an imperial soldier," Patroklos chuckled. Zeno grinned. The boys smiled briefly. It was a bad joke, but it was the best Zeno could do. He desperately needed these boys to act relaxed and natural, at least for a few moments.

"Good evening, men." Zeno turned and addressed the Sarpedonians. "Are the gods treating you well this..."

"Are all these children with you?" the sergeant asked, cutting Zeno off. He was armed with a sword and an ion handgun with a shield on his back, as was another; a third had no sword but a spear, another a rifle but no handgun. Each wore orange tunics with embroidery under ion-proof plate mail and hoplite helmets.

"They are sir," Zeno answered.

"But they're not all yours?" the sergeant again asked.

"No, my lord, I'm afraid my woman doesn't have that kind of stamina." Again, a poor joke. Soldiers normally appreciated crass humor, but none of the Sarpedonians cracked a smile.

"Looks suspicious," the soldier with the rifle said. "One man with five little brats. The Blue fucking Order has imps like these running weapons and supplies to the forest."

"I can assure my lord these children are engaged in no such activities. Their parents are all merchants who sell goods in this very market. You can go and speak with them now if you like. I can personally vouch for each and every one of them…"

"Who are you?" The sergeant again cut him off.

"My name is Zenosthenes Andrea. I am the apprentice historian under Thucoditus. I represent the same government you do and have no love for the Blue Order."

"You're a goddamned book peddler," the sergeant barked in Zeno's face. Zeno smelled ale on his breath, and not just his, but his three companions as well. They were drunk. They locked eyes for a while. It seemed like an eternity to Zeno. How long must that moment have seemed for the children? Zeno sought to communicate submission. He knew instinctively that the leader was as drunk on authority as ale and would not respond well to confrontation. He would humble himself, humiliate himself if he had to. Anything to avoid violence.

"That one there!" The sergeant pointed to Diomedes. "Search him. And this one." He pointed next to a nine-year-old.

Both boys looked tepidly at Zeno. Their eyes asked what they should do. Zeno could practically reach out and grab their fear, so tangible it seemed. He worried for the boys; he knew they carried no arms. But he worried their fear would cause them to do something rash, which in turn would spur the hoplites to do something even more rash. Still, he nodded.

The soldier with the rifle and the other one carrying a pistol and sword both frisked the young boys. The experience itself was harrowing. The younger boy began to blubber.

"Shut up, or I'll give you a reason to cry, you little shit."

Diomedes fought to maintain his composure, but tears began to silently fall down his cheek as well. The men were rough and thorough, but they found nothing.

"Ah, they have nothing, Petras," the hoplite with the rifle reported to his superior.

Sergeant Petras eyed Zeno suspiciously. Then he turned to a lad of eleven, nicknamed Pole due to his unusual height and slender frame.

Pole's eyes immediately went to Zeno. There was something exceptionally panicked in Pole's face. Both soldiers frisked the boy. One of the soldiers pulled a large ion revolver from under Pole's shirt. The sergeant's face lit up like a candle.

"I'm sorry, my lord!" Pole began to wail. "They forced me. Said my family would pay if I didn't help them."

The soldier with the rifle wrenched Pole's arm behind his back. "You know the penalty for this, you little cum spot?" Petras spat as the other soldier handed the gun to the soldier with the spear.

Zeno couldn't let them take Pole. Could he talk his way out of this?

The sergeant approached the terrified boy. "You're serving the Order. They killed my cousin."

"I, I meant no harm, my lord! I..."

"Shut up, boy!"

"My lord!" Zeno stepped forward. "It's not the boy's fault. The gun is mine. With the Blue Order afoot, not even the markets are safe. I panicked when I saw you approaching and passed the gun to this boy, gambling that you would search anyone but him."

"Then you are a fool," the sergeant shot back at Zeno. By now, the confrontation was attracting many spectators. All conversations stopped. All eyes turned to Zeno, the terrified boys, and the soldiers.

"Indeed, Sir," Zeno politely replied. "A great fool. But not a criminal, and neither is the boy. Please, have mercy, my lord." Zeno's eyes begged to be believed. He was a talented liar. He had been lying about who he was for eleven years now, and the egoga taught one to lie as a survival skill.

"Gods of Tartarus!" the hoplite with a spear replied after inspecting the chambers of the gun. "The damn thing isn't even loaded, Petras. Let it go."

"Less than ten days ago, the Blue Order attacked one of our platoons," Petras fired back. "Some are dead, and others lay bleeding in the infirmary right now. I'm not going to let it go. These bastards must learn the price for supporting rebels and terrorists."

"Fine," said the other. "Then let's beat this man." He motioned to Zeno. "Or the child, or both. But then we let them go. It's not worth the trouble. We're starting to draw attention."

Sergeant Petras stared into Zeno's eyes, then Pole's, and Zeno's again. Zeno knew that Petras knew the eyes of everyone were upon him. An insecure man would respond with a demonstrative show of force. What kind of man was this soldier? Zeno caught a whiff of ale and remembered the man was drunk.

"No mercy to the Blue Order," Petras said. "No mercy to those who support them. Take the child," he roared to the other two soldiers who had performed the frisk, one of which still held Pole in an arm bar. The soldier began to walk away.

"No! Please!" Pole cried. "Zeno, help me! Don't let them take me!"

Pole's parents came, and Pole's mother threw herself at the feet of the sergeant begging for clemency. He kicked her away, and the soldier who found the gun snatched her from the ground kicking and screaming and threw her back a good five yards. She got up and yelled out again, "Mercy, my lord! He is our only child!" The soldier who had thrown her back stepped forward and knocked her off her feet with a slap to the face.

Zeno watched this comedy of errors transpire before him. There were only four, and they were inebriated. He was a Ranger and had spent the ten years prior to his self-imposed exile in Sarpedon fighting alongside Lysandros in the Woadlands, where warriors wagered their souls on their swords. Plus, he had the element of surprise. They didn't know about his talents. Zeno felt confident he could defeat them, but to what end? The valley seethed with armed troops, many of which would soon rush to the source of the conflict. Neither he nor Pole could get away.

As these thoughts flooded Zeno's mind, the boy's father, enraged and overtaken by emotion, charged the soldier and pushed him away from his wife. The Sarpedonian retreated a few steps and drew his ion pistol.

"Now you'll learn!" the soldier yelled.

"No! Please! Someone help us! Help us!" the mother screamed.

Pole fought and kicked but was knocked senseless in the back of the head by his captor. The soldier with the spear raised his weapon to the crowd, who was watching in horror. A few brave men shouted curses at the soldiers, but no one dared step forward. Other troops were pouring into the area.

It is an odd thing, those seconds before a fight. Lysandros had always taught Zeno that killing was harder than it seemed. Most people didn't have the psychological makeup for it. For them, in these moments, everything sped up; they lost control of their bodies, not in an overt way, but in subtle ways. It was the difference between a man who takes the time to aim his shot before he fires and the one who just fires in his target's direction. The egoga had taught Zeno that the best soldiers do the little things right when it matters most. It was a details game. He who kept his head and got the details right normally won. Remembering this, Zeno found some solace in the fact that, despite having not once raised his hand to another human being since coming to Sarpedon, things began to slow down for him, not speed up. His warrior senses had not dulled.

Zeno rushed the hoplite who held a pistol at Pole's father. He snapped the soldier's arm at the elbow just as the ill-aimed shot was fired past the father. There was no time for half-measures now. Zeno drew the Sarpedonian's sword from his belt and stabbed the man up under his armor and through his belly. This all happened before the other three Sarpedonians could react. Zeno wrested the gun from the wounded hoplite. But by the time he had possession of it, the soldier holding Pole had tossed the boy aside and drew his rifle; the sergeant likewise had his handgun drawn and ready. They fired. One shot went high, and the other sliced into Zeno's hip. Pain seared through Zeno's body as he pulled the trigger twice. Both soldiers fell to the ground, the sergeant dead, the other wounded. Now the fourth soldier charged Zeno with his spear extended. Zeno had no time to turn and fire. He parried the thrust with the blade he had taken from the first soldier and sliced it into the meat of the soldier's upper chest. Zeno plunged the sword deep into his back. Hot blood gushed from the wound and covered Zeno's hand. The soldier roared, but the sound was soon drowned out as his throat filled with blood. Zeno cast him down, his flesh being cut even more as his body slid off the blade. The other soldier whom Zeno had wounded rose to one knee and aimed his rifle at Zeno's exposed back. Zeno, almost instinctively, turned and fired his pistol. The ion round found its resting place between the Sarpedonian's eyes and exploded out the back of his skull. Just like that, Zeno had killed four men.

The Rangers believed that when a man fought, he was possessed by the *furens*: war madness. This spirit animated the soldier's body and put him into a trance. The deeper the union between the warrior and the furens, the deeper the trance, the better he fought. Zeno had not sensed his furens in some time. But it came back to him like the hungry caresses of a forgotten lover.

All around, soldiers were closing in, weapons drawn, shouting. The spectators were all silent. Most rushed for cover; a few just stared frozen at Zeno.

Zeno turned to Pole and yelled, "Run! Run!" The boy and his parents ran behind Zeno and down an alleyway of booths. Zeno grabbed the ion rifle from the soldier whom he had just shot. "Run!" he yelled again at the bystanders. "All of you." The people scattered; the scene was chaos. Zeno ducked behind a wooden booth for cover and planned to put up what fight he could. He wished Lysandros and Alexandra were with him.

Joni knights and Sarpedonian hoplites bore down on Zeno, firing. One Joni fell with a scream, then another, and a Sarpedonian. How? Zeno hadn't fired his rifle. Were the other citizens helping him? They didn't have firearms. The questions ceased when an ion blast incinerated the wooden board above Zeno's head. The furens took preeminence. Aim, fire. Aim again, fire. Zeno shot those closest to him. But others were falling as well. Bystanders were hit in the crossfire. The Joni and the Sarpedonians stopped charging and looked for cover themselves. Then Zeno knew someone was attacking the soldiers. An all-out firefight ensued. Zeno heard a horse running upon him from behind. He had been flanked! He turned and raised his rifle. But the mounted man he saw was no Joni knight or Sarpedonian cavalry. He was heavily bearded, had thick, mane-like black hair, and olive skin. His face was scarred. He wore a breastplate overlaid with streaks of blue paint horizontally across his chest. On his back hung the blue cape of a Ranger.

"Unless you want to die here, mount up!" the bearded man roared. Zeno obeyed. He leaped behind the man, and he spurred his horse out into the fray, thundering down the aisle for the woods at the far north side of the valley. It was a good six hundred paces to the tree line, and they were running into crossfire.

We'll never make it, Zeno thought. But everywhere he looked, Joni and Sarpedonians were falling. He smelt the stench of burning flesh in the air. He saw bodies fall before them. And, of course, there were the screams. On three occasions, Zeno saw enemy soldiers aim directly at him and the bearded man. Each time Zeno knew the shot would find its mark. But before the soldiers could fire, counterfire brought them low. Someone was covering them and doing it well.

"Can you shoot atop a horse?" the man yelled back to Zeno.

"Yes!" Zeno responded

"Then, by Andrea, do it!" Zeno tightened his leg muscles around the massive lower body of the horse, practicing the same technique as the Militae and Hipperi horse warriors, lifted his rifle, and began to fire.

Four hundred paces away.

Zeno shot at enemy troops directly in their path when whoever was covering them missed. He didn't need to hit them, just force them out of the way and prevent them from getting off an aimed shot at close range.

Three hundred paces away.

Now the bearded man drew a revolver from his tunic and fired as well.

Two hundred paces away.

The horse shimmied. It had been hit. How bad? It continued to run. They were past the booths now and had an open plain before them to the forest. Zeno could now see dozens of merchants with guns falling back to continue to provide them cover. This was the force clearing the way for them. Whoever they were, they were not merchants; they were just using their dress as a disguise, and they were well-trained. They moved with stealth and urgency. Zeno could see some of them had been shot as well. They mounted their dead and wounded on horses and followed the path Zeno and the bearded man had taken. As the cover fire began to wane, enemy fire intensified. The horse was hit again. Explosions flooded the air with light, heat, and noise across the fields and along the alleys of booths.

One hundred paces away.

They wouldn't make it. The horse sprawled to the ground, throwing both riders forward. Zeno was up first. He ran to the bearded man. He was unconscious or dead. One of the mounted fighters pulled up next to him. Zeno knew his intent. He lifted the bearded man onto the soldier's horse, and the rider flew away. Zeno turned and sprinted for the woods, ion fire singeing his hair and nipping his boots.

He made it. As soon as Zeno passed the tree line, he saw a host of armed men and women in a line. One row on their knees and the other standing above them, rifles at the ready. As the last of the fighters cleared the tree line, a woman gave the command to fire. Her voice sounded familiar.

No. It couldn't be her.

It was nerves from the fight, the effect of the furens, perhaps.

The troops obeyed. Sarpedonians and Joni, both mounted and on foot, fell to the earth, most wounded, some dead. Those who were not hit fell to the ground for cover; others turned and ran. Another command was given. They fired again. More Joni and Sarpedonians fell. They broke off the pursuit. Zeno could scarcely believe it, but he would live another day.

A hand grabbed Zeno by the shoulder and spun him around. Zeno turned to see a man dressed in blue wearing a helmet splattered with blood and rifle grease. He, too, had black hair and olive skin. He was an Elled for certain, of which nation, Sarpedon or Dioskuria, Zeno could not say.

"They will regroup at Sarpedon and come after us," the young man said. "You. They'll be after you too. You better come with us. Besides, you're wounded. We can mend you at our camp."

Zeno nodded. He had no idea where they were going, but he was sure that these men and women were the infamous Blue Order. He was also sure that, regardless of his personal feelings for their tactics, he had no choice but to accompany them.

CHAPTER IV

LYSANDROS

The emblem of a bear adorned the crest of the house of Poly-maxes, one of the most distinguished houses of the Dioskurian aristocracy. It was said that Polymaxes had stood next to the last king of Dioskuria, Tyanus, when he killed his own sons and established the Republic.

The bear that adorned Lysandros' breastplate was covered in blood and soot. He had fought hard and lost. He stared now at another bear, one that rested on the breastplate of his younger brother, Nikolaus, who held an ion handgun poised to kill his older sibling.

"Why?" Lysandros asked, betrayal echoing in his voice.

"You know why," Nikolaus answered.

"You swore an oath. As a Ranger, you swore an oath!"

"From my perspective, the Archons swore an oath and broke it."

"The Baroquistas are lying, Nikolaus," Lysandros pleaded.

"I know."

Lysandros looked puzzled. "You *know*?"

"Just because they're lying doesn't mean they're wrong. Just because they're lying about the election doesn't mean they're not telling the truth about the Republic. Our democracy is no longer functional, Lysandros. Too many aristocrats like us telling too many commoners that live on the other side of the planet how to live their lives. Had the Archons listened, there wouldn't have been an uprising."

"They were standing up for the rule of the people: democracy."

"Funny how only those in power get to define democracy. See the problem?"

Until now, Lysandros had hoped to reason with his younger brother, the man with whom he had endured the egoga, became a Ranger, and had now fought beside in numerous battles. He knew his brother to be an emotional man. He knew he harbored Baroquista sentimentalities. He knew he had a liking for the woman who led the Baroquista uprising, the daughter of the Emperor of Rema, Lana Tarquinia. Perhaps they had even slept together. But Lysandros never thought his brother would betray the Republic of Eighteen. Now he realized how lost his little brother was. He stood a little straighter.

"I stand with the Republic. If you plan to assassinate the Archons, you'll have to kill me first."

"I expected no less from you."

Nikolaus pulled the trigger.

Lysandros awoke in a sweat, breathing as if he had just sprinted a quarter mile. What were these dreams that had plagued him? They had haunted his nights since his unit had deployed to the Sofia Forest nearly three weeks ago.

Lysandros rose from the ground and looked around. Everything seemed in order. His unit lay scattered about, including his brother Nikolaus, all sleeping soundly. Lysandros looked to the left and right. The sentries stood guard. He looked to the center of the camp. One solitary tent stood. Inside was the unit commander, Ode. The Rangers were a multi-ethnic, multi-race, multi-gendered unit comprised of people from all across Ninivon. Ode was Zutaeran, the ebony-skinned people to the south. But his second in command was Bella, a pale-skinned Joni from her island in the north. This was intentional to ensure each Ranger's highest loyalties were to the Republic rather than their ancestral home. But the Baroquista uprising had strained these relations. Five of the eighteen nations that made up the Republic rebelled under the rule of the dual Archons that guided the global government from the capital: Dioskuria. In response to this rebellion, Lysandros' unit had been deployed deep within this ancient forest to protect the Zolon Channel, which the Baroquistas desperately needed.

"Whooooo…"

Lysandros turned. The owl. A large black owl with streaks of white along its feathers. Lysandros was a soldier and not easily scared. But something about this creature rattled him. Every time he awoke from a nightmare, it was there. Was he going mad?

The great bird now sat perched on a tree branch a good fifteen feet above him. It peered down at him as if he were the only thing in the world the creature cared for.

"What are you?" Lysandros whispered into the night.

Then a voice. Not audible, but in his head, clear yet alien, both inviting and terrifying.

Come and see.

Lysandros looked at the Owl. The creature sat there, a blank yet probing gaze.

Magic, or he was truly going mad? Lysandros chose to believe it was magic. Not surprising. Lysandros recalled the stories he had heard around campfires about these woods. Some said a witch of terrible power lived in the western part of the forest. Others said it was not one witch but a coven that led men to their temple, bewitched them into becoming their slaves, and then ate them when they had outlived their use. Regardless of the source, magic made him uneasy. The Rangers were masters of the physical; the metaphysical lay beyond them. Such otherworldly powers made the greatest soldiers in Ninivon as children.

Come. Again the voice.

Lysandros looked around. Sleep was like death on his unit. Somehow, he knew the sentries would not see him leave. Though terrified, he knew he had to obey. He took the first step, and the Owl took off into the night. Every step thereafter was a foregone conclusion.

Lysandros hiked for nearly forty minutes. The Owl led him deep into the Sofia Forest. With every step, the foliage grew thicker until he finally stepped into a wide-open clearing. Fifty yards before him was a crashed spaceship. He knew instinctively that it was alien. It was not part of any contemporary air force of the nations which made up the Republic of Eighteen, and none of the tribal peoples outside of the Republic had aircraft. The ship was long and ovular. It was at least three hundred feet in length and nearly a hundred in height. It wasn't aerodynamic at all, but rather had several smaller oval-shaped compartments jutting out of the main body of the ship. This would have been a great hindrance for any vessel flying within the atmosphere, but not for one traveling through deep space.

Lysandros could also see it was old, very old. The forest had grown around it. Vines and vegetation crept up the archaic walls. They almost seemed to pulsate, like blood vessels in the arms of an athlete exercising. The place seemed alive, not like a man, but like a phantom. Because of the denseness of the forest, it would have been completely hidden from the casual wanderer through the woods. The only way someone would catch a glimpse of this monolithic spacecraft would be if they walked into the clearing in which Lysandros now stood. But enough of it was visible to see alien runes and hieroglyphs along the exterior, neither of which Lysandros had ever seen before. The ship also looked like it had been through absolute hell. There were giant holes in various parts of the hull, large sections of the fuselage were bent or dented, and every visible part of the ship betrayed evidence of both burning and freezing. Remarkably, there appeared to be no rust anywhere.

There had long been myths about the Sofia Forest, some of which said it hid some artifact of another world. Many explorers and treasure hunters had spent their lives searching for this mysterious thing. No one had ever found anything. Some never returned. Those who did were crazed and insane. They babbled of witches, demons, and ghosts.

Lysandros pulled out his ion handgun and checked it to ensure the magazine was properly loaded and a round was in the chamber. He often did this when he was anxious. The owl flew without hesitation and disappeared somewhere around the ship. Lysandros approached with caution. As he approached, a door opened along the outer hull. This gave him pause. Lysandros stood there paralyzed for several moments. The interior of the ship was a pit of blackness. Then another screech. The owl had not vanished, though he could not see the bird. Lysandros pulled out his mini-ion torch, lit it, swallowed down his inhibitions and progressed.

Uncanny hieroglyphs were carved into the walls: carvings of warriors in combat. Lysandros saw other creatures as well. Men with fangs protruding from their lips, strange species, men with four arms, monolithic flying star ships, far more advanced than anything that now existed on Ninivon, monstrous creatures that looked similar to bats, the size of dragons, and a naked woman with the head of the bat-like monsters.

Lysandros walked for several minutes until he saw a large set of double doors in front of him. They were made of wood and, like the walls, were engraved with detailed images of warriors in combat. The central figure in the scene was a great warrior holding a large sword above his head and preparing to strike down some humanoid creature with long fangs. Above the battle was the only image Lysandros recognized, a "Σ," which on Ninivon was the emblem of the Light Goddess Sofia.

As Lysandros reached the doors, they opened on cue before him as the outer doors had. Now he knew what his intuition had already told him; not only was he being watched, but someone or something was inviting him deeper within the ship. He felt both fear and wonder grow inside of him, each competing for supremacy.

As the doors opened, a ghoulish soft blue light illuminated

the dark hall. The doors opened into a great room lined with dozens of lights on each side. A great staircase stood thirty feet high directly in front of him at the back of the room. Atop the staircase was a chair surrounded by various panels, all of which glowed a soft blue light and various alien symbols. Sitting in the chair was a woman, elegant and lovely. It was hard to tell in the scarce light, but she seemed to wear a faded black dress with white streaks that covered both arms and stretched down the sides. On her head was a golden headdress adorned with black feathers, in the center of which was the totem of Sofia: the Σ. Her face was fine, oval in shape, with large brown eyes, small lips, and the dark brown skin of the Women of the Red Sky. Long black hair hung down behind the headdress. She looked to be perhaps forty. She was breathtaking. The woman rose and began to descend the staircase.

"You will not be needing that, Ranger." Her voice was soft yet alien and jarring.

Lysandros had not realized that he had held his ion handgun poised and at the ready this whole time. He put his weapon away.

The woman stopped in front of Lysandros. "You need not worry about time. Your unit and commander will sleep soundly until you return."

Lysandros was bewildered.

"You're wondering if this is due to my magic or if I have just foreseen it. Of course, the answer is both."

Again, trepidatious silence.

"And now the real question: why are you here? You'll feel better once you ask it yourself. Go ahead, Lysandros, ask me."

She knows my name. This shook Lysandros. Yet, given the fact that this sorceress, or witch, or whatever she was, had occupied his dreams for weeks and clearly knew the future, why should this be so shocking?

"Because it's so personal, of course." The woman smiled.

With this, all of Lysandros' military bearing, as well as his fear, finally gave way. He shook his head and began groaning in disgusted agitation.

She reached out and wrapped her arms around him. This shocked Lysandros. But the moment she touched him, all his fear and doubt melted. He felt safe, warm, protected. He felt like a baby in its mother's arms. *What sorcery is this?* Lysandros' last thought before he surrendered.

"Good," she said. "A fighting man is a man of the physical. He perceives the world through touch. It is for this reason that the more war-like people are given to great sexual licenses. One of your ancient philosophers said that."

This woman knew the ancient Elledic philosopher Letotsira. Lysandros found this quaint, almost comical. They released the embrace, but she did not let him go, perhaps for fear that she would again lose him to his fear. The woman held him at his forearms with both hands.

"Do you know the purpose of the Baroquista uprising?"

Now she wants to talk politics?

"Lana Tarquinia of Rema refused to acknowledge that she lost the election for junior Archon and rallied the dissident nations to rebel against the lawfully elected government."

"No. That is the cause of the war but not its purpose. Not its *telos*."

Telos was old Elledic for the meaningful end of a thing. Not just soldiers, the Rangers were well-trained in languages, history, and rhetoric. This woman was speaking Lysandros' language on many levels.

"What is the telos of the war, lady?"

"That the house of Polymaxes might rise."

"My grandmother sits on the Assembly that advises the Archons, as does my father and uncles."

"Yes. But it has been centuries since your house has sat in the seats of the Archons. This must come to pass. You, Lysandros, will be named Archon."

Now Lysandros was confused. "To what telos, lady?"

"A direct and wise question. The only real question that matters. There is a child yet unborn. His name will be Zeno. You need not search him out. He will come to you. You will become dean of the egoga. Zeno will pass the Trials. You must be mindful of his training. He must learn the skills of a soldier. But more still, he must develop the heart of a leader and champion. He must be both warrior and sage, philosopher and politician. A great and terrible war is coming. A threat far greater than anything you could possibly imagine."

"After tonight, lady, I can imagine quite a lot."

The woman smiled. "Your wit returns. A good sign. For you must grow comfortable within these walls. This will not be the last time you are here. You must grow comfortable with me as well. When the great war comes, this boy will be the key to our victory. He will save our people. But none of this can happen in a vacuum. We both, and many others, must play our parts. My part was to bring you here tonight and give you this warning. Yours must be to protect and train Zeno. There will come a time when your loyalties are questioned. You will be asked to sacrifice both your family and the Republic itself to protect this boy. When you grow weary in your vow, remember: your greatest loyalty must be to Zeno and to me."

"With respect, lady, I have taken no such vow to you and could not. I am a son of the Bear and a child of the Republic. I could never betray either the Archons or my house."

The woman now released Lysandros and took a step back. Her look was coy.

"You will, Lysandros. Before you leave this forest, your soul will be mine, and you will be happy for it."

Lysandros didn't like the sound of that. He liked the confidence with which she said it even less. He turned and began to leave.

"There is one other thing you must know."

Lysandros stopped and turned.

"Your dreams are warnings of things that will be if you do

not stop them. Your brother doesn't know it yet, but he will betray the Republic and side with the Tarquinii. The young princess will seduce him. She will take him to her bed and secure his allegiance."

"Through sorcery?" It was more a protest than a question. Nikolaus was impulsive, and he liked his women. But to betray the Republic would mean not only that Nikolaus broke his vow as a Ranger but that he took the sword against his own house.

"Only the sorcery that is common to all women. *Charis*, your people call it."

Charis was the Elledic word for female sexual power and the weaponization of that power. It was also the name of the goddess of love and sex: the only deity among the Ninivonian pantheon who was both a Light and Dark Goddess, depending on whether she was sowing unity or chaos through her power.

Lysandros turned again to walk away.

"He will attempt to assassinate the Archons," the woman called out behind him. "When this comes to pass, you will remember what I said tonight. Long before that, you will return to me."

CHAPTER V
THE VAMPIRE

He was something else once. A homo sapiens, like all homo sapiens who evolved on planets orbited by stars like his. He had a name but had long forgotten it. The Erīeds called him Ze-Vadak Dur. But he would never speak that name again; it was cursed for him.

He was not sure how long his ship had lain there, buried in the snow of the south. He was weak from lack of human blood. He drifted in and out of consciousness. He did know that he had landed on Ninivon. In his delirious state, thoughts of his life among the Erīeds danced in his thoughts. Mostly he remembered her face, young and beautiful, perhaps the only face he had ever loved with no thought for himself. Kara Dox-ana once accused him of being a narcissist. Perhaps she was right. But if he was, he was never more selfless than he had been with his daughter.

Then the pain. The searing, heart-wrenching agony of know-ing he would spend the rest of his life, which for the Erīeds lasted eons, without ever seeing his child again. He considered doing nothing. Just feeling the pain until lack of blood eventu-ally ended his unnaturally long life, then he would have peace.

But as soon as the thought came, he rebuffed it. He was not one for peace. Even before, he was a conqueror who bent the world to his will and relished in his power. Having been once a slave in his home world, he had plenty of reason to hate. But even if he had not, he would have hated for hate's sake. Now, the face of his little girl gave him all the reason he would ever need. He remembered why he risked his life to come to Ninivon in the first place. He should be dead already, but now he only lived to make his enemies suffer.

He reached up to release the straps that held him into the seat. Then fought his way up and to the hatch and finally out the door. As he exited, the cold struck him like a blow. A cold-blooded creature, he was sensitive to the chill. The wind blew hard. He struggled to breathe. He knew it would take time to adapt to the new atmosphere. But he also knew neither this nor the cold would kill him. They would just hurt. He could endure pain. Lack of blood, on the other hand, could take his life. The instruments on his spacecraft informed him that there were homo sapiens on the planet, but where? Could he find them before he expired?

He trudged forward in the snow, clothes tattered, body gaunt. How far had he traveled, a few steps or a few miles? He could not tell. Only onward he pushed, driven by a deep rage and determination within.

Do not die yet. There are so many left to kill.

Then he finally collapsed. Before he closed his eyes, he could have sworn he saw the face of his daughter.

He awoke in a warm bed, weak but regaining his strength. He was in a small room. There was a fire on the far side and light coming from a small lamp that stood next to the bed. There was something in his left arm. He reached over to find a needle connected to a tube, which itself hung from a bag. Inside the bag was a thick red liquid. It was blood.

A woman entered the room and said something to him that he did not understand. She was human, or at least this planet's version thereof. He could tell that from her scent. She awoke a deep hunger in him. But he was still weak and was connected to the life-giving liquid his kind needed to survive. He could wait. Moreover, he sensed this woman had more to offer than just her blood.

She was short and petite but walked with authority. Her black hair rested in a bun atop her head, and makeup covered her olive skin and large eyes. Her heartbeat accelerated a bit. She was scared, as she should be in his presence, but the fear rather excited her than held her back. She walked forward and sat on the bed beside him. She said a few more words that were babble. He had always hated the language barrier. Traveling from planet to planet, learning new languages so that the Erīeds could convert as many as possible had worn on him. He much preferred to kill and eat the native populations.

A boy came in. Prepubescent but impossible to tell how old he was. He didn't know how long a year was on this planet.

The boy brought a cup to the woman, who took it and drank. She glanced over and saw him hungrily staring at the child. The intensity coming from his eyes burned like a summer sun.

The boy turned to leave, but the woman reached out and stopped him. She said a few words, and the child, shaking, crawled into bed with him. He gripped the boy by his hair, gentle at first, but his hold grew painful, inescapable. The child now violently shook and began to cry openly, but he did not fight back. He pressed his face deep within the crevice of the child's neck. More than the blood, he so loved the taste of fear.

The woman did not turn away as the boy screamed. Rather, she smiled. Some of the boy's blood spurted on her thick white coat.

It did not take long to drain the child, so hungry he was. The infusion was a lifeline, not full satiation. He felt like himself now. He leaped from the bed. This did cause the woman to jump back, but she was too slow. He was upon her, but he did not attack her. He gripped her at her waist and sucked the blood stains from the crotch of her coat. He could tell the woman was both aroused and terrified.

Then he heard the boy reviving behind him. The child thrashed and wailed. It bent its body over into uncanny contortions. It finally rose to its knees and vomited. An inhuman growl came from the child as it raised its head. Its pupils were gone, its eyes were purple, its mouth was rowed with sharp fangs. Its skin was pale and gaunt. It seemed to be wasting away before their eyes. The child rose and lunged at the woman, who fell back in horror.

Then, just as quickly as the boy attacked, it halted. It sat on the floor, breathing heavily, no less inhuman and monstrous but subdued. The woman looked to see him now standing on his feet, his hand extended and eyes fixed on the creature that had moments earlier been a human child. He turned his eyes to meet hers, likewise purple and pupil-less. She saw that he could control the creature. The woman whispered the first word in the Ninivonian common tongue he understood.

"Vampire."

In the ninth month of the fourth year of the archonship of Asha of Zutaera and in the third month of the second year of the archonship of Xi Juntao of Zan, Archons of the Republic of Eighteen, the Vampire attacked.

He first came to the city of Vorsehelgda, the capital of the Vorse Southmen, just north of the Southern Ice Cap. Dark Landers preceded him. They came to the city in droves, starving, exhausted, wounded, and insane. They spoke of a being with unspeakable magical powers. They said his body was lean and muscular. His flesh was pale, almost ivory. They said he was handsome but with alien features, purple, pupil-less eyes and grey hair that hung just below his pointed ears, all of which he hid beneath a black hood and cassock. His grin betrayed two long canine fangs, and his skin was cold to the touch. He had superhuman strength and stamina. No weapon could slay him, for his wounds healed within seconds. He drank human blood, and those from whom he drank rose behind him and fought at his side, consuming the blood of anyone before them. Those from whom they drank also rose with the ungodly thirst, devoid of any powers of speech or reason. They were animals—no, they were worse than animals. And they were spreading.

The king of the Vorse Southmen ordered troops to be sent into the Dark Lands to investigate. They did not return. Then the attack came. A force of one hundred thousand strong: all Dark Landers who had been turned by either their demonic leader or by their fellow creatures.

Fear spread across Ninivon. The Vampire and his demonic forces moved north and attacked the nations of Acheminidos; Zutaera, home of Asha; and Sarpedon, all members of the Republic. Every day, another city fell. All were slain; their blood sucked from their bodies. These regenerated. The Ninivonians called them the *Rapti*, or *the taken*. Those who were bitten but survived the initial encounter remained human until the poison of the bite claimed their lives. Then, they were taken. Only those who were killed by something other than the bite were spared this fate. The Vampire filled dungeons and citadels with prisoners. Then he released a few Rapti among them. The dark army grew. The Rapti did not attack like a regular army but like a pack of hyenas, charging through spears and gunfire to tear at their victims with their hands and teeth.

As for the Vampire, his power seemed almost limitless. He would lead his ungodly followers into battle, slashing with his sword. No warrior could match him. With every swing, men died. Many times he was wounded. These attacks clearly hurt him. But his composition was not like that of other men. Blows that would have easily killed others barely hindered him. Explosives that should have vaporized his body simply burned him. Even these wounds healed within seconds, minutes at most. The Vampire reveled in the pain; he rejoiced in the Ninivonians' desperate attempts to kill him. He laughed and mockingly called his enemies' names. He beat them with his bare hands and then left them to watch as he dismantled their armies. He told them that he would drink the blood of their spouses and that once they were taken, he would watch in pleasure as their unholy hunger caused them to drink the blood of their children, and they would be forced to slay their husbands and wives in defense of their sons and daughters.

The Vampire also had allies. Several of the nations that had long spurned the rule of the Republic rallied to his cause, including those that had rebelled twenty years earlier in the Baroquista Uprising. Other nations heard about his terrible power and joined the devil to avoid his wrath. Jona was the first. The Jonish were an Angolid people who lived on a great island in the Lumen Ocean. As soon as the Vampire attacked Vorsehelgda, they crossed the Yorish Gulf and attacked Yorland, inhabited by their Angolid cousins with whom they were often in dispute. The Vampire learned that the woman who had found and saved him in the icy cold of the south was Lana Tarquinia, whose father was the Emperor of Rema. She soon brought her father and all of his forces over to the Vampire's side.

Rema was one of the leading nations in the East. The Remani produced the Vampire's war machines and provided him with artillery, tanks, and infantry. They were followed by the Osaerians and the Karthagoi, both powerful neighbors to the Remani. With their combined might, they practically gave the Vampire the entire eastern hemisphere.

Aside from providing men and money for the Vampire's war effort, these nations produced and manned his aerial armada of transport ships. They also made warplanes for him: fighters and bombers fitted with ion missiles. The Republic had troop transports but no offensive military aircraft because of the dragons who would suffer no air machine equipped with guns or bombs to take to the skies. With virtually the entire world under the Republic of Eighteen, there was little use for them anyway.

But the Vampire used dark magic to control the dragons. He used them to rain death from the skies until he built an aerial armada. Once he had warplanes, he attacked the ancient beasts who had served him. The great old race of dragons who, for so long, had ruled the skies of Ninivon was hunted to the point of extinction. With the dragons dead, the Vampire accelerated the production of military aircraft and took control of the skies.

Next to cross over to the Vampire were the Xhiputzecs, the mermen who lived at the bottom of the Udorandreos Ocean. Their sorcerers called on hideous monsters from the depths of the ocean to attack Republican ships and naval bases. The Hipperi, a nomadic people from the Tempus Desert, provided the Vampire with mounted riflemen and spearmen. The centaurs of the eastern steppes provided heavy cavalry. The cyclopes, guardians of the dragons of Grey Peaks, contributed twenty thousand infantry. As his personal bodyguards, the Vampire called upon the ferocious great wolves from the Lycian Woadlands: monstrous beasts the size of bears.

These nations collectively did the jobs and fought the battles that the mindless Rapti could not, and they were successful. Over a third of the Republic was in open rebellion. The Vampire's forces engaged the Republic of Eighteen in the skies and on the seas. His soldiers and sorcerers met theirs in open combat. In all places, he conquered. There was no neutrality. The Vampire killed all who did not swear allegiance to him. The Great Terror consumed all of Ninivon.

The Vampire moved west. Dimron capitulated. Acheminidos fell, as did Yorland, trapped with the Jonish to their east and the Vampire and his soulless hordes to their south. Even the Militae were hammered. A second army of Rapti crossed the Lumen Ocean in the east on Remani ships and made the impossible journey over the Northern Ice Cap—no army of mortal men could have survived the cold. They attacked the Woadish Barbarians north of the Casildel Mountains, as did Bramhas from the south once the Bramhai surrendered their navy and army to fight for the Vampire. To the east, the Katanas of Taedemaru Island, named after the swords they used, were conquered. Only the Zan, behind their vast defensive wall and isolated in their immense underground capital of Ying-Chau, were able to hold out. Finally, with all the world conquered save for Ying-Chau, the Vampire brought his great army to Dioskuria.

The aerial battle began first. The skies shrieked and howled as jet fighters raced above the battlefield and over the city. Ion cannons, mounted from the outer defensive walls, fired in support of the Republican air force. Then the Vampire unleashed his bombers and gunships. They flooded the sky and rained down fire on the defenses. The sound of the machines as they crashed, added to the canon fire, equaled an unholy symphony of horror.

In the valley before the city, the last army of the Republic stood ready to meet the Vampire's ground assault.

"Are they fools or suicidal?" Lana asked in the tent with the rulers of the individual nations that had sworn allegiance to the Vampire. "Why wouldn't they hide behind their walls?"

"In truth, I'm not sure," her father, Tarquinius, answered. "It's not a wise tactical decision."

"Archon Asha is no longer thinking like a general who wants to win a war," the Vampire announced, not taking his eyes off the capital city and the army assembled to defend it, some three hundred yards to his north. He turned to face his cabinet. "She knows she cannot win this battle. She intends to give her defenders a glorious death, heroes' deaths."

"Our reports say the remaining Rangers have amassed in Acropolis Square before the Three Towers. They say Asha is among them," added Ravi Zachaves, King of Bramhas.

"Good," the Vampire replied. "We have already killed one Archon. The other will not escape. It is important that we kill both; we must crush any hope those we have enslaved have that a hero will rise to save them. What of the High Strategos? Lysandros?"

"He remains with the Archon, my lord," Lana replied.

The Vampire smiled and turned. "Move the Rapti into position. We will attack with them first both to test their mettle and tire them out before the cavalry attacks. Have the centaurs ready to attack next, then the small two-man motorized chariots of the Osaerians and the light cavalry of the Hipperi. You may accompany your armies in the final wave or not, whatever you wish."

With that, the Vampire turned to leave, as did the individual generals, to return to their forces.

"Will you lay back and attack with us, my lord?" Lana asked the Vampire before he left the command tent.

"No. I will go with my children. They are hungry. As a good father, I must see them fed."

CHAPTER VI
ALEXANDRA

The footage had traveled around Ninivon like cancer, from computer screen to computer screen, spreading fear in its wake. If the invasion of the Vampire could be capsulated in twelve seconds of video, this was it. The video was taken by a senior Ranger who had been part of the army that responded to the distress call of the Vorse King. By the time the army arrived, they found the city abandoned, ransacked, and blood-soaked. There were no bodies save one: a child, a boy, chained down in the city square, naked, with the snow piling atop his body.

He was not a zombie by any means. His heart was beating. There was no muscle or skin deterioration save for some gangrene on his extremities which was brought on by the extreme cold. But this didn't seem to bother him. When they first found him, reports said he was docile, lethargic. But when he saw the troops, he came alive and writhed like a bear in a trap to free himself. All attempts to communicate with the child failed. While the troops were around him, he howled and wailed and fought to reach them. When they backed off, he returned to his passive state. He seemed to be, as the previous reports had said, completely devoid of any consciousness or reason. A holy man might say the child was bereft of a soul. Carved into the child's chest were the words "I am coming." That was when everyone knew the rumors were true: The Vampire was real.

Alexandra now stared at her computer, watching the footage over and over. It had been nearly eighteen months since the video was taken. Now, almost all of Ninivon had fallen beneath the sword of the Vampire. Only two cities remained: Ying-Chau, the underground capital of the Zan, and Dioskuria. Her city. Her home. The place to which the Vampire was now marching.

Alexandra was in her sixth year of the egoga, a member of the Ursae—bears—age grade. Fitting, considering her family's crest. When she first came to the city from the Militian Plains, she never thought she would ever call Dioskuria home. Now, a young woman of seventeen and halfway through the egoga, there was no place for which she would more readily fight and die. Her father quickly won her respect and love. She excelled in the physical elements of the egoga. For the academic elements where she found herself lacking, she had Zeno.

Zeno had taught her to both speak and read the common tongue. Often when she didn't understand what was being asked of her in class, he would help. One day, not more than a week into her new life in the capital, another initiate made fun of her because she couldn't speak the language and because of her Militian heritage.

"The only reason you're here is because of who your dad is, freak!" the boy shouted.

He was thirteen, had already been training for two years, and was a far larger specimen than Zeno. Alexandra didn't know what he was saying or even that it was an insult at first. But Zeno did.

"Shut your mouth, or I'll shut it up for you!" Zeno barked back, she later learned.

The boys fought. It was quickly obvious the boy would break Zeno. Alexandra jumped on the older boy's back. His friends then joined the fray as well. Both Alexandra and Zeno were beaten up, but neither was seriously injured. Between the two of them—thanks mostly to her—they managed to pummel the upperclassmen as well. Alexandra and Zeno were never bullied again.

But they were never accepted either. Despite her martial

prowess and who her father was, Alexandra was always seen as an outsider and a barbarian, particularly by the girls of the Archonical Court.

"My father abandoned us shortly after I was born," Zeno told her one evening in their dormitory after a long day of training. "My mother never remarried. She raised me by herself, and my uncles and grandmother contributed as best they could, but my family was a poor one living in Limnae, the most notorious ghetto in Dioskuria. When I passed the Trials, I became not only their pride and joy but their bright shining hope to become part of the aristocracy." Every Ranger was granted lands that would remain in their family, as well as a generous salary and retirement, more than enough to change a poor family into a landed house.

A knock at the door. Alexandra shut off her computer, and the screen vanished. "What is it?" she yelled through the door to her single room.

"Your father wants to see us both." It was Zeno.

"Do you know what's going on?" Alexandra asked Zeno as they rushed through the busy halls of the Tower of the Sphinx, the military headquarters of Dioskuria and where all initiates of the egoga were housed.

"Just that our world is burning."

"Where has he been? The High Strategos doesn't just up and abandon the capital when we've got the fight of our lives ahead of us."

"Not even I know. It may have been some secret mission from Archon Asha."

This surprised Alexandra. Lysandros had taken Zeno as his personal squire two years earlier. A high honor, even if Zeno was the unlikely choice for it.

"I do know there is an announcement coming to the initiates," Zeno continued. "Soon. Possibly tonight. But he wants to talk to us first."

"I don't like the sound of that." A deep emptiness grew in

Alexandra's stomach. She had not felt this uneasy since her fateful talk with her grandmother six years ago.

The two arrived at Lysandros' office and stood at attention. Lysandros sent out the throng of generals and intelligence officers and closed the door behind them.

"Stand at ease. Both of you."

The youths relaxed.

Lysandros sat on his desk. He looked tired, desperate. His eyes bulged from lack of sleep, and he had lost weight. He had engaged the Vampire in a dozen battles. Only twice had he been victorious, and even those times were questionable.

"The Vampire is coming. He will be here within the week."

Both teenagers met the intensity of Lysandros' eyes. They knew this was coming. But now, having a timetable, it seemed all too real.

"Archon Asha has made the following proclamations. First, all civilians in the city will be evacuated to Ying Chau. Nikolaus is leading the caravan."

"But the people will be trapped there," Alexandra protested. "There is no way out of the underground city."

"There are also only four ways in, each of which can be easily defended. It's the best chance they have, Alex."

"And what of us, my lord?" Zeno asked. As initiates, they were neither military nor civilians.

"That is the second proclamation. The initiates will be sent back to their families. The Archon wishes them to spend their last days with and defending their kin."

"Many have no kin left," Alexandra added. She meant Zeno; his mother had died before the Great Terror, and the rest of his family died in the famine and riots the Great Terror caused.

"You do," Lysandros answered. "You are to accompany your uncle to Ying Chau."

"What?" Alexandra burst out.

Lysandros rose and turned his back to the two initiates. "You will accompany your uncle."

"What are you going to do?" she demanded.

"I will stay here and defend the capital and the Archon."

"Then I stay with you."

"You can't." Lysandros' voice grew forceful.

"What do you mean *I can't*?"

"I mean, you can't!" Lysandros turned. "You are a soldier, and soldiers follow orders. I am your highest commanding officer, and I have given an order. You will accompany your uncle."

"I am your daughter! I came to this city because you took me away from my people and brought me here six years ago. I was told you brought me here to help you prepare for a great war. What war could that be if not this? I refuse your order. I am staying."

"Alexandra." Tears were beginning to form in Lysandros' eyes. Alexandra had never seen him cry before. "I love you more than I love life. I would sacrifice anything for you. I did not expect you to receive this news happily. I know what I have taken from you. And I know what I am asking you to give up now. But going to Ying Chau, though also treacherous, is the best chance I can give you to live."

"I don't want to live without you, Father." Alexandra was now crying as well. She did not give way to tears easily. "I've already lost my people. I lost my mother."

Lysandros sighed. He seemed on the brink of despair. Alexandra knew her words had cut deep. At one point, she had hoped to learn more about her mother from her father. But as they grew to know each other, Alexandra realized that he was even more hesitant to discuss her mother than her grandmother had been. In all their years together, Alexandra had never known her father to have another woman. She was certain he still loved her.

Zeno took Alexandra's hand. "I'll go with Alex."

"No, you won't," Lysandros informed them. Now it was Zeno's turn for outrage.

"You must remain here with me, Zeno. You are my squire.

You know me and my methods as well as any of the generals in our army. I may need you to convey vital information. I need you here, son."

"I'm not leaving her, Lysandros!"

"And I'm not leaving him," Alexandra added. "Or you."

"My brave, brave young soldiers. You both honor me. The egoga has worked its magic well in you both. The Republic is soon to be destroyed, and yet here you are, willing to defend it and each other with your lives." Lysandros sat back on his desk. "Remember the first day we met, Alex? I told you I could not give you all the answers you were seeking. I told you I didn't know them all. I still don't. I do know that I love you both. I can't save you, Zeno. I wish I could. But I can't, not without putting the rest of the Rangers and our army at risk. But you I can save, Alex. Please, we have two days before the caravan departs. I will have precious few moments with you both together while preparing for the attack. I would have us pass those moments as a family. Would you obey me? Will you grant this last request from a man about to die?"

Alexandra was not able to grant her father's request. She hated what he was doing. Furthermore, he spent most of the next forty-eight hours preparing for the attack, and Alexandra spent them preparing for her departure and with Zeno. Right up until the moment the refugees left, they were together.

Alexandra sat atop a horse next to a tank that housed her uncle outside the gates of the city. Behind them stretched a column of civilians over two miles long. They would be crowded once they arrived at the underground city.

"I still don't understand why he can't send you back to the Militae," Zeno said, speaking to Alexandra from the ground.

"The Vampire has all but wiped out the Menimu. My tribe is gone. My grandmother is dead and what Militae remain are being hunted to the point of extinction. He can't send me back to the plains. He shouldn't be sending me away at all."

Zeno said nothing, just averted his eyes.

Alexandra turned to him. "You're glad he's sending me away, aren't you?"

"Alex…"

"Don't lie to me, Zeno."

"Yes. I'm glad. And you know why I'm glad. So why talk about it?"

Alexandra turned her head forward again and thought if she should let it end there. She decided since Zeno was her best friend and she would never see him again, that she should be honest.

"I understand too. I understand why he's sending me to Ying-Chau. If I were him, I'd do the same thing." Then she looked back down at Zeno. "But if he were me, he'd feel betrayed as I do. So would you. I was already asked to leave behind the people I loved once. Now they are gone. I was told I had no say in where I lived and with whom I lived. I was given no choice over my life. My life. No one will tell him what he can and can't die for. I want that same freedom, Zeno. I think I've earned it."

Zeno took her hand. "You have. I don't agree with it. But I understand. Since we're giving confessions, I should confess something to you."

"What?"

Zeno turned away for a moment, then back to Alexandra. She could see how difficult it was to say what was in his heart.

"Are you going to tell me that you love me?"

Zeno's face flushed. "Is it that obvious?"

"It has been for years." Alexandra smiled. "Come here."

Zeno obeyed. Alexandra bent down and gave him a kiss. Not the passionate kiss of a lover, but still moving, as an old couple might kiss as a show of mutual affection and respect more than sexual desire.

Nikolaus arose from the tank. "All right. Roll out!" He lowered himself back into the tank and closed the hatch. The tank revved up and began to roll forward.

Alexandra broke off the kiss and looked down at her friend. His eyes were still closed, but he opened them slowly. They looked into each other's eyes for a moment. She wanted to memorize his face, kind and welcoming, the friendliest face she had ever known. She hoped the kiss would give him something to remember her by.

The emotions were rolling within Alexandra. She didn't want to cry.

Go. Alexandra spoke to the animal through the Bond. The horse took off.

She looked back only once. When she did, she saw that Zeno had not moved but remained, watching her leave. She knew he would. Alexandra turned forward and, for the second time in her life, let go of her home.

CHAPTER VII
LYSANDROS

It rained the night of the final battle. Most civilians had already evacuated to Ying-Chau. Archon Asha, knowing the inevitable outcome of the battle—and no longer needing to think of protecting women, children, and the elderly—ordered that the hoplites and cavalry be stationed outside the walls of Dioskuria. The army would die in glorious battle like the warriors they were. They would not prolong their agony fighting house to house or die of hunger in a long siege. They positioned the artillery along the walls of the city. As the Rapti came into view on the Hills of Panton to the west of Dioskuria, led by the Vampire himself riding a menacing white mare, a cold chill came barreling down the plain.

Before the battle began, Lysandros was summoned to meet Archon Asha in the throne room in Ninivon Tower, the middle of the Three Towers. Her husband, Abayomi, a high-ranking Ranger who would command the artillery, was there, along with Casandra, the Elledic queen of Dioskuria, who would command the infantry. Although the Archons' official residence was in Dioskuria, they only ruled over matters of the Republic. The Dioskurian monarchs ruled the nation-state.

Lysandros entered. He saw the Archon and her husband together, clutching each other's hands and sitting on the white marble steps leading up to the throne. Casandra was just leaving. Their eyes met for a long second as she walked past Lysandros down the staircase leading into the throne room. They had known and served alongside each other for years.

"Don't argue with her, Lysandros," Casandra told him as she walked by.

Lysandros said nothing in response. He just stood and watched the Archon and her husband. There was no crying; the couple simply held each other intentionally, sorrowfully. They seemed broken and were completely unaware of his presence, so much were they lost in each other's touch. Finally, Lysandros walked forward and showed himself to the archon. Archon Asha stood and walked forward to address him.

"Lysandros," she began, leading him away from her husband. "How did you feel when you watched Alexandra ride away with your brother, knowing you would never see her again?"

He could not answer. His body tensed up. The Archon studied his face.

"Yes," she continued, "helpless. We feel helpless when we cannot defend the ones we love. When we realize their best chance for life lies apart from us, part of us dies. I hope those venturing to Ying-Chau now have a kinder fate than awaits us. I hope Alexandra makes it."

The Archon and Lysandros looked out the great window at the back end of the throne room. The chamber was long but simple. It was made of glimmering blue marble and stretched over a hundred meters from the back wall where they stood to the white marble steps leading up to the two thrones, one for each Archon. From the ceiling hung eighteen huge banners, nine on each side, representing the eighteen nations that made up the Republic of Eighteen. This was the only window in the room. It, too, was monolithic. Four grown men could stand up on its sill. The throne room was the top story of Ninivon Tower. Above it was the roof of the tower, which served as a landing pad for the Archons' personal aircraft.

From the throne room window, the Archon and Lysandros could see well over the entire city and out onto the Valley of Wisdom, where most of their army was camped. Occasionally they would see missiles explode, lighting up the valley like fire-flies. Farther west were the Hills of Panton, where the enemy could also be seen. Overlooking all of this, Archon Asha began:

"I have had weeks to think about this moment, to think about my death. I have ruled the world for the last five years, and I can tell you I never found joy in it. I was always working, trying to live up to the expectations of my office. I tried to build a world but never took the time to live in it. I loved my husband but rarely made time for him." She motioned to Abayomi. "I was always here in Dioskuria, he was often in Zutaera, and even when I was home with him, I was always on official business.

"Now the Vampire is going to destroy our city and what is left of our army. He is going to destroy a republic that has lasted for eight hundred years. Then he is going to take my husband and, finally, my life. I wish I had more time."

"My lady," Lysandros pleaded, ready to replay the argument he had had with the Archon dozens of times leading up to this moment. "We can still get you out. We can get you to Ying Chau."

"No," the Archon shook her head, "I will not be that kind of ruler. I will not run to refuge while my most faithful soldiers die."

"My lady, you are all that's left of the Republic. It is our duty to sacrifice our lives so you can live and Ninivon with you."

"And you expect me to sacrifice less than the common soldier on that battlefield?" she asked, motioning to the valley and armies outside the window.

"May I speak my heart?" Lysandros asked.

"You always do."

"You're not thinking clearly. It's not just about you. What future will our people, our civilization, have after you die tonight?"

"Our Republic is bigger than any one man, even an Archon. Did you think I had changed my mind, Lysandros? That

I would run now, and that is why I called you?"

"I had hoped."

"Will you serve your Archon and honor the request of your friend who is soon to die?"

"You know I will, my lady."

"There are three jets fueled and ready for takeoff on the royal launchpad. Two of the fighters will serve as your escorts." Her voice quaked with desperation. "Take the jet. Go to Ying-Chau."

In all his years of knowing Archon Asha, he had only seen her cry once, at the death of her son, slain in a battle against the Vampire. But as she made this desperate request, he could see the tears well up in her eyes.

"There is more," she continued, "Archon Juntao is dead. In times of national emergency, our laws allow for the normal process of electing an Archon to be suspended. Rather, the sitting Archon may name a replacement. The lawyers and witnesses are on their way to the throne room now. I am naming you the Co-Archon of the Republic. You will carry on the fight against the Vampire wherever you can, in whatever way you can. You will be the spark that starts the fire of rebellion."

Lysandros stood a bit straighter, the anxiety of the moment building up within him. He remembered the words of prophecy spoken to him so long ago. He was beginning to think they had been false. "Archon, my place is with the men preparing to die in defense of Dioskuria. I will not abandon them. I will not abandon you."

"I hear your daughter said a similar thing to you when you informed her she would be traveling to Ying-Chau."

Lysandros stood rebuffed. There wasn't much he could say in his defense.

"You said it yourself, if both Archons are dead, the Republic dies with it. You came here, hoping to persuade me to flee, preserving my life and the archonship and thus the Republic. Would you not follow the same admonition you gave me?"

"I did hope to persuade you, and you refused to go. Now you say I must? Why is this action fit for me, my lady, but not you?"

"Because right now, I am still Archon, and you are not," she snapped. "You have sworn to follow my orders, not the other way around."

Lysandros relaxed, realizing this was her plan all along. She never meant for him to lead the defenses. "If you had named me Archon and sent me with the refugees, the Vampire would have followed and wiped them out to get to me. Rather than ignore them, and focus his attentions here, on you."

Asha smiled. Even in the face of death, the woman was always a general.

"As you wish, Archon," was all Lysandros could reply. He knew there were other forces at work here that were beyond even the Archon's comprehension.

"Your squire Zeno is waiting for you at the jets," the Archon added.

The royal cabinet all took their places. Lysandros bowed before Archon Asha. Someone spoke an oath. He repeated it. Lysandros didn't remember much about the ceremony. In the moments that followed, all noises around him began to fade out. Even the guns and explosions of the battle raging beneath them became inaudible. All he could think of was his fighter jet and the path he would take. He knew just where to go.

The ceremony was over. Lysandros was the new Archon of the Republic of Eighteen. Soon to be the only living Archon of the Republic. Asha rushed to her husband. They stared into each other's eyes for some moments as if wanting to memorize each other's faces, knowing they would never see them again. The Archon's eyes welled with tears, and her face bloomed with the bitterness known only by women who have lost virtuous men whom they loved to a violent end.

Four pilots had now emerged to fly the other two fighter jets. Archon Asha turned and nodded to Lysandros. Then the slow motion ended; from that point forward, everything sped up. The four pilots ran up the stairs on the sides of the throne room to the royal launchpad above. Lysandros ran behind them down the length of the throne room and then up the stairs.

In seconds, they reached the platform. Lysandros ran to the fighter and confirmed with the maintainers that they were ready for takeoff. Below them was a scene of utter chaos. From the height of Ninivon Tower, even the aerial battle was happening beneath them. Warships flew among firing artillery guns. Everywhere munitions could be seen bombarding the city.

Lysandros jumped into the main pilot seat and looked back to the gunner's chair. There sat Zeno, already a hardened soldier in many ways, but scared. Lysandros put his hand on his shoulder to reassure him. In spite of his great fear, Lysandros saw something of the warrior in his eyes. The egoga made men of seventeen-year-old boys. Around them, there were six heavy ion cannons on the platform, raining down hell on the enemy below. They ceased their fire and reset their trajectory to cover the path of escape. Within seconds, the engines of the fighters were on and at max power. The first rose slowly and took off. He would be the point man. Lysandros and Zeno were next, and the third pulled up the rear.

They were all airborne and drawing fire from the Vampire's fighters. Their ion cannons returned the favor. They lost the rear fighter almost immediately. The forward fighter fired and destroyed one of the enemy ships. Two more replaced it. Lysandros felt a jolt shove the ship forward in the air and heard an explosion behind them. Zeno had shot down another jet. Soon they would be out of range of the ion cannons and would be on their own. Another jet joined the pursuit. The new Archon and his squire would not get far. In seconds, six enemy aircraft were behind them. Lysandros and Zeno continued to fire and destroyed two ships. The remaining jets retaliated, and Lysandros saw a brilliant explosion to his right as the last of their escort was blown away.

Then they were hit. Not hard, but it was a solid blast on the aft engine; the solar-powered motor began to give way. It slowed down, and the enemy gained speed. For a moment, Lysandros thought perhaps they would die after all. "Use every round!" he yelled back to Zeno. "Make them count!"

The clouds grew thick around the fighter. They had flown for hours. Lysandros and Zeno's jet, as well as those of their pursuers, had exhausted all ammunition. But the Vampire's fighters flew close behind and were joined by an Osaerian C-70 troop transport. They meant to follow them until they landed or ran out of power and hunt them down. Lysandros heard the sound of thunder and saw a flash of lightning. It would be extremely difficult to fly in such a storm. With their weak engine struggling against the wind, the fighter could take no more, and they were thrown toward the earth. But it didn't matter. They had arrived at their destination.

The crash was broken by a thick cluster of trees in the Sofia Forest. Before Lysandros even knew for sure that he had survived the crash, he yelled back to Zeno, "You alive?"

"For now!" Zeno shouted. They ran into the thick of the woods. The fighters flew on, but the C-70 stopped and hovered forty feet in the air. Thirty-two Osaerian troops rappelled to the ground and began pursuit.

Within seconds, the Osaerians were firing on the fugitives. "Follow me!" Lysandros barked to Zeno. They took off, running as fast as they could amid enemy fire.

Lysandros and Zeno burst through the tree line and finally reached their destination: the crashed spaceship buried deep in the Sofia Forest.

"What the hell?" Zeno shouted.

"Just follow me," Lysandros roared.

They sprinted up the steps and ran through the great entrance doors that stood wide open. It was almost pitch black. The night sky seemed bright in comparison. Lysandros and

Zeno took cover behind two columns. Within a few seconds, the Osaerians appeared at the entrance, silhouetted by the light from outside. They had only handguns, not rifles, as the Osaerians did. If they had charged, they would have over-whelmed Lysandros and Zeno through their numbers. If they had laid back, the Osaerians surely would have gunned them down with their superior firepower. She was their only hope.

The ship's doors slammed shut. It was completely dark. Lysandros and Zeno couldn't see anything. The thud of the door echoed through the hallway. Then a light arose: a strange, eerie, blue light. It seemed unworldly and caused an irrational fear to rise within even Lysandros, who had been inside the ship many times since his first encounter nineteen years ago. They could see the Osaerians, and the Osaerians could see them, but they didn't fire. Zeno looked to Lysandros as if to ask, what's going on? Lysandros couldn't answer, but he knew who was behind the magic. For a moment, they were all spectators together, waiting for what would happen next. A burst of cold wind blew through the hall. Lysandros could see the Osaerians frown in confusion. Where did it come from? He knew.

Then something happened. Lysandros had seen war and death, fought sorcerers and dragons; he fought the Vampire himself. He knew he and Zeno had nothing to fear in that ship, but this moment was pure unworldly, irrational terror. In that blue light, Lysandros saw a damnable thing, accursed by even the Dark Gods. The Osaerians screamed. Zeno's eyes widened in fear and disbelief. Lysandros knew she was powerful within the walls of this ship, but he never fully understood how pow-erful she was until that moment.

When it was over, the Osaerians were gone, and all was quiet. Lysandros had not fully regained his composure when he heard footsteps behind them. He and Zeno both turned. Then they saw her.

CHAPTER VIII
ZENO

Zeno and the guerilla soldiers of the Blue Order hiked two miles west until they reached the Xor River, a tributary that fed into the Sofia, and then turned south for another two. Zeno had been down this part of the river once when he followed it to Sarpedon. It was the widest and deepest point, useful for quick transportation. The moon had risen now and reflected silver veins of light off the tranquil waters. It was a beautiful sight, and it helped calm Zeno's nerves. Zeno was "purging." He had been lectured about this in the egoga many times. When a man was possessed by the furens, he was compelled by the spirit to action. But when the furens left, and eventually it always did, the soldier had to contemplate what he had done, the lives he had taken, how close he himself had been to death. Even if the homicides occurred in a just cause, it was no different. Lysandros always said the human soul did not distinguish between just and unjust killing; human life was human life, and once the spark left a man's eyes and returned to the All Fire, it could never be rekindled. These thoughts humbled the warrior and crushed his soul, and so he must "purge," he must give his soul an opportunity to come to grips with this emotionally. No two warriors purged the same way; some screamed, some cried, some drank until they passed out, some had sex rougher than normal. Zeno just shook.

The Blue Order was well-trained. Zeno was wrong about them being street thugs and organized criminals. They were far more than that. They demonstrated the discipline and stamina of drilled battle troops. They covered the forested ground before them quickly with nothing but the slim streaks of moonlight that came through the branches and shone off the river to guide them. More importantly, they did this quietly. After a battle, some men love to talk. These always would embellish their valor and the danger they were in. The man who killed one enemy said he killed two. The man who was almost stabbed through the leg was almost stabbed through the heart. These warriors did this as well, but only in whispers; Zeno could scarcely make out more than a few words. They were more numerous than Zeno had originally thought. At Sarpedon, he couldn't have seen more than forty. But now he could tell the total force was closer to one hundred and fifty. They had blended in among the merchants and managed to steal into the market right under the noses of the Sarpedonians and Joni. They must have planned to hit the market that night. Zeno's misadventures provided them with the perfect cover for their attack, and in return, they saved his life.

They eventually came to a waterfall, dropping sheaths of water from forty-nine feet above. This was not the Balendria waterfall but a lesser structure known as the Nalena Falls. Zeno knew the area well. Young lovers in Sarpedon would retreat here to make love free from the prying eyes of their parents. Or at least they used to before the Blue Order. What he did not know was that beneath the fall was a series of caves in the rock face. The men disappeared one by one behind the waterfall and into the cave. The entrance opened up into a huge internal chamber. The top of the cave had to be thirty feet up; it was covered in bats. A shallow but wide stream of water flowed from the falls and into the interior floor. The men waded through the water, which came up to their knees. Along the walls, ion lamps were hung, giving a plethora of light. There were many men and women there to welcome the force back.

They must be the support staff.

These searched the lines of those entering with trepidation. When they found the one special soldier for whom they waited, their eyes lit up. Hugs were given, and tears of joy added to the stream on the cavern floor. For a few, that moment of relief never came.

The men continued into another cavern in the back of the cave. This opened into an even larger room with even more people. Everywhere someone was doing something; collecting weapons, tending to the wounded, cooking food, washing clothes. This was the embodiment of quiet industry. On the side walls, Zeno could see many other tunnels leading into a multitude of different labyrinths. Perhaps a few of those tunnels even led to another exit somewhere in the woods. If so, this was the perfect place from which to wage a guerrilla war.

"You," said the same man who had ordered Zeno to come with them. "Sit over there," he barked, pointing to a ledge along the side of the cave. "Someone will dress your wound." This man was clearly a lieutenant of some kind. Zeno suspected that the lieutenant was younger than him, possibly in his late twenties.

Zeno found a seat among the men seeking care. In a few moments, a young lady in military trousers and an overcoat came to him. "Pull your pants down," she commanded.

"I'm sorry?" Zeno asked.

The woman looked annoyed. "Not all the way. Just enough to let me clean and plug your wound."

Zeno obeyed, and she went to work.

"I haven't seen you before. Did you just join up?" the girl asked.

"Yeah."

"What's your name?"

"Zeno."

"Well, Zeno," she said. "The Light Gods must love you. It stopped bleeding on its own. I should still bandage it."

"How long have you been here?" Zeno inquired.

The girl stopped her work and eyed Zeno with suspicion.

"I mean, how long ago did you join the Order?"

She lowered her gaze and bandaged the wound with gauze. "Ten months." She stood up and looked Zeno in the eye. "Since the Joni killed my husband."

Zeno looked down. He tensed up and pulled back in fear. On the girl's arm was a tattoo, a "Σ." The totem of Sofia.

"What is that?" Zeno cried.

"It's a bloody scab," the girl answered, perplexed and annoyed.

Zeno looked again; there was no tattoo. Just a scabbed-over piece of flesh. Zeno rested his head in his hands in frustration.

"You're a jumpy one," the girl smirked.

"Reina!" It was the same young lieutenant. "Finish up with that one! The commander wants to see him!"

"He's all done!" the girl yelled back.

"I'm sorry about your husband," Zeno said as she walked away.

"You!" yelled the young commander at Zeno. "Let's go!"

Zeno followed the young man through one of the openings shooting off from the main cavern. The cave hall was narrow but well-lit. The pathway ended at what was obviously a private chamber with a hung curtain blocking it off from the tunnel.

"Are you armed?" the young guerilla asked.

"Yes. I have an ion pistol in my belt."

"Hand it over."

Zeno reached for the pistol and gave it to the young man handle first, pointing the lethal muzzle back towards himself. This was how the egoga had taught Zeno to hand over his weapon. It was good manners.

The soldier pulled back the curtain, and Zeno walked in. It opened into a smaller room furnished with a table and a bed (Zeno had seen many cots in the caverns and passageways leading to this corridor, but this was the first actual bed). Sitting crouched down in a chair on the right side of the room was the bearded warrior who had saved him. He held a cloth on the right side of his head and raised his eyes to Zeno.

"Thank you, Vultus," the man said. "You may leave us."

The soldier left, and Zeno was alone with the man he presumed was Ghost. The room was dimly lit by a battery-powered lamp in the far corner. Although Zeno was now only a few feet away from Ghost, he had a hard time making out his features. His thick beard ate up most of his face. But there was something hauntingly familiar about this man. Zeno was certain he had met him before.

"Sit down, son," Ghost instructed as he poured wine into an earthen cup. "Have some wine."

Zeno immediately felt like a fool. How could he have been so blind? It was obvious that Ghost was none other than Nikolaus, of the house of Polymaxes, Lysandros' younger brother who had led the refugees to Ying-Chau almost twelve years ago. Zeno was shocked. He believed this man, along with all the other Dioskurian refugees, to be dead. "Lord Nikolaus?"

"No, Zeno, don't call me *lord*. I'm not the lord of anything, not anymore. The title never fit me, anyway. My prick of a brother was always far better suited for it."

Zeno's head was a whirlwind of thoughts. But one question burst forth from deep within where he had buried it for the last ten years. Now it seemed to be the only question in the world that mattered.

"Alexandra?"

Before Nikolaus could answer, the curtain flew back, and a girl entered. Her hair was long, slightly curled, and black. It was up in a ponytail but still extended a third of the way down her back. Her skin was sun-kissed. Her face was a perfectly symmetrical oval. She wore tall brown hunting boots that came almost to her kneecap. Her legs were bare, cut, and muscled. She wore a short battle skirt that stretched just below the top of her thigh. She wore a sleeveless white blouse and a leather breastplate on top, both of which clung to her body, revealing every curve and contour. Her arms were slender but strong. Zeno could see she had scars on her shoulders. An ion rifle was slung across her back. She had a belt that hung over her hip with a large pistol on one side and a tomahawk on the other. But most striking were her eyes: they were the most magnificent brown. Her eyes were haunting, deep, both angelic and terrifying. It was Alexandra. "Zeno?" she softly asked.

Zeno leaped from his seat and rushed to Alexandra, who met him in the center of the small cavern. They embraced, wrapping their arms tightly around each other and burying their faces in the cleft of one another's necks. For a few moments, they were children again. They hugged as family, as soul mates would who had been separated not just by time and distance but by belief as well.

Alexandra eventually pulled up enough to look at Zeno's face. "I never thought I'd see you again," she whispered. "I thought you were dead."

"I almost was. But the Archon sent your father away just before the attack came. I went with him as his squire. We weren't even in Dioskuria when the battle happened."

"What? My father is alive?"

"I haven't seen or spoken to him for over eighteen months. But he was alive and well last I saw him. We heard how the Vampire buried Ying Chau. Then we headed north into the Woadlands. He's made himself a king among the Woads."

"We fled Ying-Chau before the Vampire brought the gates down," Alexandra interjected.

Zeno began to choke up. Tears softly fell down his cheek. "Had I known you were alive... had I known... I would have run to you. You know I would have run to you. I thought you were dead. Your father said we had to leave the past behind us and make a new life. I would have run to you..."

Alexandra again wrapped her strong arms around Zeno and fixed her hands in his long black hair.

"It's all right. It's all right, Zeno. You were young and scared. I was young and scared. We both thought my father to be superhuman. We both trusted him with our lives. He was right to tell you that. You were right to follow. You did as you were told. I would have done the same. But none of that matters. We're together now. And I'm not letting your gullible ass out of my sight again."

Ghost finished his wine and rose from his seat. "Ah, my older brother; he always was the driven type. You said he was king among the Woads. Is he this *Brown Chieftain* we keep hearing about?"

Zeno nodded.

"And the *Brown Warrior*. His second in command, whose skill with the two-handed claymore was so notorious. That was you?"

"It was."

"You helped him unite the Woads and the Militae." Alexandra seemed surprised and impressed. "My people hate the Woads."

"I wasn't with Lysandros when he invaded the Militian Plains. But I was there during the final battle that consolidated the Woads under his leadership."

"That's impressive, Zeno," Ghost added. "But you said that you haven't seen my brother for a year and a half. Why are you not with him in the Woadlands now?"

"We had a disagreement." Zeno wished to say no more. He hoped Nikolaus would drop it.

"Must have been a hell of a disagreement."

Zeno said nothing but kept his eyes down.

"Well, my brother can have that effect on people. I never could stand the prick. But you're a free man now and a well-trained one at that. The Archons are dead, the Republic is dead, and my brother is the king of nothing save for an army of savages. You are not bound to him anymore." Ghost stepped toward Zeno. "I know you just got here. And I know a whirlwind must be going through your head. But we are at war. We need soldiers. You would be a great asset to us."

Zeno looked down for a second and then raised his eyes

to Ghost's. "I thought you were both dead ten minutes ago. I came to Sarpedon to find peace."

"Doesn't look like you've found it." Ghost smirked. "But the war has found you."

Zeno thought hard. His head was flush with emotions. *You're more terrorists than rebels. But I'm not leaving Alex again.* What he needed was time. Time to think, time to talk with Alexandra. He turned to her. Her face was beaming.

"Well," Ghost interrupted his train of thought. "You don't have to work all of that out now. The Sarpedonians will be looking for you for a few days. Stay with us in the safety of the cave until things cool down. Alex will show you around. You can decide if you'd like to stay later. You will stay for a few days, though, won't you?"

Zeno looked at Ghost. He knew Nikolaus was no fool. He knew he wanted him, much as Lysandros did, and for the same reason. If he turned down Lysandros' rebellion, he wanted no part of Nikolaus'. But Nikolaus had a secret weapon: Alexandra. Zeno looked back at her; affection and admiration were all over his face. *He's betting she'll convince me to stay. But I bet he isn't worried that I can convince her to leave.*

Alexandra's eyes flashed. She threw her arms around Zeno yet again. Ghost smiled as well. He approached and placed his right hand on Zeno's shoulder. "You fought very well tonight. Worthy of a Ranger." Ghost smiled. "Alexandra, I am placing our guest in your custody. See that he is fed and given a proper place to sleep. Can I trust you with him?"

Alexandra grinned from ear to ear. Ghost pulled back the curtain. Zeno and Alexandra disappeared together into the corridor.

CHAPTER IX
ALEXANDRA

Alexandra led Zeno out into the main cave, explaining the intricate labyrinth and the work that was done in each section. Nikolaus' forces had made the cave their base, and the cave functioned as an active military base would. One section was for storage. That section was then divided into sub-sections for food, batteries, garments, and weapons. Another section was for training.

"We've been here for three years now," Alexandra told Zeno. "Some of the tunnels and caverns we hewed out with laser drills. We have sleeping quarters and even private chambers."

"What about alternate exits? If you were tracked and there is no other way out, you'd be trapped."

"We have nine different exits, all leading to rallying points in the Sofia Forest. But none of us know all of them. That way, no one will ever leak out all of our exit points to the enemy." Alexandra took Zeno by the arm and leaned over to whisper to him, "I have one last thing to show you. But this is a secret only between you and me."

Alexandra led Zeno down a twisting cavern that seemed to go down forever. There were no torches, and everything was pitch-black save for the small light on Alexandra's rifle, which she now used as a flashlight. Eventually, they stopped. Alexandra turned to face him.

"Ready?" she asked.

"Sure."

Alexandra removed the flashlight from her rifle and threw it down in front of them. It hit a pool of water that splashed on their feet. Soft blue light exploded from a deep pool of water. The light had made the water glow. It lit up everything. The walls of the cave rippled in the glow.

"Don't ask me to explain it. You know I always hated science," Alexandra began. "But it has something to do with the algae. When you put the light in, the algae in the pool reflects it back a hundred-fold. I found this place last year. No one knows about it, not even Uncle. This is my special place. I come here to get away."

"It's beautiful." Zeno smiled. "But if this is your place to escape from everyone, why did you bring me here?"

Alexandra smiled. "To swim!" With that, she grabbed Zeno by his shirt and wheeled him over her back into the water. Her form was perfect. She easily manhandled him even though he outweighed her by a good sixty pounds. The pool was deep. By the time Zeno popped his head up, Alexandra was undressing. Already she had shed both weapons and breastplate and was pulling her battle skirt down to her feet. When Alexandra had stripped down to her undergarments, she plunged into the water.

Alexandra pulled Zeno by his legs beneath the surface and pushed him back. She smiled in front of him, mouthing the words, "Fight back." They wrestled underwater for a few seconds, returned to the surface for a breath, and submerged again to continue their playful struggle. Alexandra was relaxed, perhaps for the first time since her father sent her to Ying Chau twelve years ago. She had mourned Zeno. When she buried him in her heart, she had not realized how much of herself she had buried with his memory. All of that came flooding back now. It embraced her as the water in the pool.

Zeno seemed lost in his own way. Even underwater, she noticed how he gazed at her body. He looked at her as one might look at a majestic canyon or a beautiful work of art that silently demands to be noticed and appreciated for the wonder it is. She felt like Charis herself under his gaze. Alexandra would use this to convince Zeno to stay if she had to.

After a half hour of playful swimming, the two emerged from the water and sat on a rock leading into the pool. There they talked for what seemed like minutes, but in actuality was hours. They reminisced on common memories before the war, laughing and smiling, and told detailed accounts of what their lives had been like since last they saw each other.

"We were only in Ying-Chau three weeks before things got bad," Alexandra began. "With all the extra mouths to feed from Dioskuria, food became scarce. Almost immediately, Emperor Watanbu blamed Uncle for the starvation of his people, but there was nothing Nikolaus could have done. Factions started forming in the city: foreigners against Zan and sub-factions of those. It was only a matter of time before violence broke out. Pretty soon, Uncle had to use the Republic troops under his command to keep the peace and defend one group from the other. When the Remani appeared in the valley, many tried to escape by boat, but the Xhiputzecs sunk every ship that left the harbor, big or small. Things were bad, really bad.

"So, one night, Uncle pulled me from my bed and explained that we were leaving and that I was not to ask any questions until we made it out. I was to obey orders only. We made for the harbor and climbed down to the ocean. We swam along the rock line for what seemed like hours. We passed Xhiputzec submarines undetected. The mermen had individual scouting parties swimming in the ocean, killing anyone they found. I grew so tired. My muscles felt like they would explode if I took one more stroke. I was taking in salt water in big gulps. We had one canteen of water between us. I drank half of it those first few hours. By the Dark Gods, it seemed as if we were in the water forever! Our skin felt so wilted that I thought it would fall off. Our hair was soaked in the brine, and our lips burst, they were chapped so badly. Then we pulled up to a cliff, and Uncle told me that once we climbed to the top, we would see the hill country of Taedemaru before us, and we would be safe. That climb was brutal, but after all I had been through, I wasn't about to die being so close to deliverance. When I reached the top, I saw three horses, one mounted by a Katana. The Vampire had already taken the island, but the Taedemaru were strong and resilient. Pockets of resistance carried on the fight from the Yokota Mountains. This particular Katana was Uncle's friend. They had fought against the Vampire together when he first took the island. He had food and water. We mounted up and rode into the mountains."

"Gods... what a story." Zeno sighed. "Your father and I rushed towards Ying Chau as soon as we escaped Dioskuria. We met some Zan refugees along the way who told us the Vampire and his corps of sorcerers used their magic to bring down the four gates of the city. They said it took them twenty hours to perform the spells, but by the end, the entire city was buried alive." Zeno looked away for a moment. Alexandra could tell it was hard for him to retell the story. He turned back to her. "That was the worst day of my life, Alex. The day I heard you died."

Alexandra reached up and cupped his face in her hand. "I'm sorry you had to carry that around all these years. I carried your loss as well. Sometimes I willed myself to believe you had escaped. I couldn't bear the thought that you died in combat and I wasn't there to fight by your side. We've both had to carry survivors' guilt."

"How did you make it from Taedemaru to here?"

"We lived with the Katanas," Alexandra continued. "Fought and killed beside them. Life was hard; we were always on the run. We attacked from mountain strongholds, then retreated before our enemies could counter. The Rapti could never catch us. We outmaneuvered the Vampire's motorized jeeps and tanks. We scattered every time we saw his gunships. But eventually, the Vampire caught up with us. Centaurs pushed us into a ravine. But rather than attack, they blocked the exit. Then we heard the engines of the gunships overhead. They shot down on us without mercy. Uncle and I dismounted in the chaos and began to climb out of the ravine. For the second time in my life, I was certain I would die. Only a handful of us made it out alive. We crawled out on hands and knees, drenched in our own blood and that of the friends we'd lost and the enemies we'd killed. That was the end of the Katana resistance.

"We headed west with a few Taedemaru, foraging, stealing, doing what we had to in order to survive. We drifted from city to city until we made it to Tena, a Sarpedonian city just west of the capital. Being thieves, we ran with thieves. There wasn't much of an organized crime ring. The Vampire's draconian policies had effectively stamped out street crime. What thugs dare fight the government when the government is crueler than thugs? Only suicidal people would do that; only desperate people. We were very desperate. Within a year, Nikolaus was the crime lord of the underground. The poor, young, and angry flocked to us. By the time we made it to the Sofia Forest, we had collected a hundred rogues. We came to the waterfall here and found this cave. At first, we planned to just stay here only a few months and move into the city. But we soon found the advantage of having a central command away from the city streets in which we were operating. We stole everything we could from the Sarpedonians; we stole the gold teeth from their mouths while they slept. Uncle always justified this by saying that they had allied with the devil and so deserved to be robbed of whatever fortune their unholy pact with evil had won them. We kept some but gave much more away. We didn't do it for the money."

"No. You did it to kill the Vampire's agents," Zeno cut in. "You couldn't fight him on the battlefield, so you fought him in the alleys. You gave the money away to keep the common folk happy. You needed to win their loyalty. But that wasn't enough. You quickly found that fear shuts more mouths than generosity. So, you threatened them."

"We didn't just threaten them. We still offered them money. Credits if they helped us. If they did not, then we strongly encouraged them to." Zeno seemed disturbed by Alexandra's nonchalant way of saying it. But these were textbook population control tactics.

"How'd he get the nickname *Ghost*?" Zeno changed the subject.

"Ah," Alexandra smiled. "He got that from our first attack on a Joni platoon. A column of knights was riding through the Sofia Forest. There were only twenty-eight of us at the time. We were outnumbered nearly two to one. We loaded rifles and sat them at intervals behind trees on both sides of the road. We hid them in the trees and bushes and took positions. When the column came through, I gave the signal. We all began to fire. As soon as our clips were empty, we jumped from our positions and ran to the other rifles, picked them up, took cover, and continued to fire until the clips were out again. But not Uncle. He drew his katana and darted through the fray, running from one tree to the next, hopefully killing one or two of the knights with each pass. I was so scared one of our men would hit him. But we couldn't catch him; the Joni couldn't catch him either. All they saw was the flash of his armor, followed by a spray of blood. I don't think I've ever seen him fight so well. He was like one of the Dark Gods that day.

"There was only one survivor; he said the unit was attacked by a ghost. A ghost who was everywhere at once, behind them, in front of them, among them, to both the left and right. The nickname stuck." Alexandra, whose eyes had danced between the pool and her audience, now focused completely on Zeno. "What about you? What of your time among the Woads?"

"As soon as I heard about Ying-Chau, I broke. I think your father did, too, in his own way. I think he wanted to go to the Woadlands to forget. And to fight. To have someone to take out his sorrow on. We lived among the Chimmerian clan. Started fighting with Claymores. Wore kilts. Tattooed ourselves."

"I noticed." Alexandra smiled, looking at the sleeve of Woadish looms stretching from Zeno's shoulder. She also noticed how well-muscled he was. His eighteen months of living in Sarpedon had done nothing to whither his warrior's body.

"Your father grew his beard even longer. They called him the Brown Chieftain and me the Brown Warrior because we were the darkest-skinned people the Woads had ever seen. Well, seen and not tried to kill. We fought the Joni pushing west and the other Woads in the east. We eventually consolidated all seventeen clans under our rule."

"Why did you leave him?" Alexandra asked.

Zeno looked away.

"Secrets? Between us?" Alexandra teased. "It didn't use to be so."

Zeno turned back to her. "Alex, I am so grateful to be here with you. But things cannot be as they were."

"I don't like the sound of that." Alexandra's words went from playful to serious.

"Whatever your intentions were in the beginning, the Blue Order has devolved into a gang of murderers."

"Every army is a gang of murderers, Zeno," Alexandra snapped back.

"That's a dodge, and you know it. The Order has kidnapped homeless men and women, poor people whom the Vampire's policies have left out on the streets, and sewed bombs into their bellies before sending them out in crowded streets and markets. They have recruited children as young as eight to smuggle weapons and supplies for them. They have attacked innocent families and forced them to donate their goods, money, and children to the cause. I even heard one of your boys took an old woman for a human shield once. These are the very people the Order should protect. Yet, now the common people fear you as much as they fear Glaucon."

"Oh, and you know the plight of the common people from your tower in the royal palace where you read your fucking books?"

"I knew the boy who had that pistol, Alex. Knew him well

and his family. He's a good kid. He wouldn't go looking for trouble unless he had no other choice. He could have died tonight."

"And how many more boys like him will die if the Vampire continues to rule?" Alexandra leaned away from Zeno. Her eyes burned with the fire of righteous anger. "I don't like some of our methods either, Zeno. But there is no other way."

"*Our methods*? Were you the one who thought up forming street gangs to force children to help you? Or was that your uncle?"

"Because I love you and because you don't know the situation here, I'm going to forgive you for saying that. But if you ever speak a word against my uncle again, I will throw your ass out of this cave myself. Do you understand me?"

Zeno sat back as well.

"So, you're planning to leave. You were hoping to persuade me to leave with you."

"And you weren't planning to convince me to stay?" Zeno struck back.

"I haven't, have I?"

Alexandra caught Zeno's eyes on her legs and breasts, the former of which glistened with water and blue light from the pool; the latter, although covered, were elevated and held tight by her brassiere. Zeno looked away again. "*Swimming?* Really?"

Alexandra grinned. "Not the naive boy you were when I left you at Dioskuria."

"You know, I've had no small number of lovers in the Woadlands."

"I don't doubt it." Alexandra smiled. "You're handsome."

"And you're beautiful," Zeno confessed without turning to look at her. "A few hours ago, I thought you were dead. I've lived the last eleven years of my life thinking you were dead. I know what my world looked like then, and I know what it looks like now. I don't want to leave you again. But I don't like what's happening here, Alex. You know you can't keep doing this forever," he finally said, turning back to her. Alexandra could see a deep tenderness and vulnerability in his eyes.

"Come here." Alexandra pulled Zeno to her and embraced him in a hug. "We don't have to work all of this out now. Just stay tonight. Walk by my side tomorrow and see how you feel. If you stay tomorrow night, do the same the day after. One day at a time."

"One day at a time," Zeno echoed her.

His arms made her feel safe. He made her feel. And she had felt so little for so long. At the same time, Zeno was right: things were not the same as they had been before. Zeno had changed. The fact of the change was not what bothered her. She had changed too. But the change was that he was distant, secretive in a way he had never been before. He seemed scared, existentially so. What happened to him while he was with her father?

CHAPTER X
ZENO

It had been ten years since Lysandros and Zeno fled from Dioskuria. Zeno was now twenty-six; Lysandros, fifty-five. After years of diplomacy and intertribal warfare when that failed, fourteen of the seventeen Woadish tribes fought under the tartan of the Chimmerians, the clan that had adopted the Brown Chieftain and Brown Warrior. They called themselves the Woadish League. Only three tribes held out: the Revetae, Angors, and Muldavī. The King of Jona, Phillip Monclair, an ally of the Vampire's, frustrated by his continued attempts to defeat the Brown Chieftain, formed these three tribes into an alliance. This was his last attempt to break up the League before having to turn to the Vampire for aid.

Zeno stood now with his troops on the border of the Revetae territory. Each warrior was armed slightly differently. Some had broadswords; others had battle axes; most had some type of firearm, either ion pistols, shotguns, or rifles. The most distinguished warriors had great claymore swords, massive two-handed blades that stretched over fifty inches long. All had armor: an ion-proof vest over a shirt or under a tartan and a shield. This armor did not provide the same protection as the ion-proof plate mail of knights or hoplites, but it did afford some protection and did not weigh the Woads down, freeing them to fight in their traditional way. They all wore war paint. Some had just a few symbols on their faces or chests. Others were covered from head to foot. The dyes were blue, lavender, and black. Zeno himself covered the upper half of his face, from the bridge of the nose to the hairline, with lavender paint. From noise to jawline was blue. Decked out in war paint, kilt, and carrying his great claymore, he looked like a demon from another world, a splendid image of the horror the Woads represented to the more civilized nations of the Republic while the Republic still stood.

It was an overcast day, as most were in the Woadish Highlands. It looked as if it might rain. Thunder rolled overhead. Before the Chimmerians and their allies was a field of green grass stretching for miles. Behind them was the Stirling Woads, to their left was Lake Tratonic, and to their right was a range of hills.

Directly in front of them was the only exit out of the valley. It lay open for now. But Zeno knew that the armies of the Revetae alliance would soon appear on the ridge. One could hear the war drums beating from miles away. Although Zeno controlled the larger coalition of tribes, the forces were about equal, with ten thousand men on each side. This was by design. Zeno commanded only a fraction of the league's forces in the valley. Two days prior, his troops had engaged with the Revetae alliance in a skirmish. Zeno had instructed his men to put up some fight and then break and run. A strategic tactic that no Woadish force would ever have considered before the Brown Chieftain and his warrior had taken command. The Woads were a people obsessed with manliness and honor. The proper way to fight a battle was for both sides to charge and let the champions hack at each other with their claymores. The last tribe standing won. The Woads would have found it beneath them to feign a retreat for some strategic advantage. But the Brown Chieftain had convinced them that there was far more honor to be had by the winning side for men who survived the war to enjoy it. Not all the Woads were swayed at first, but gradually they all came around.

The purpose of Zeno's retreat was to entice the Revetae

and their allies to attack him. He wasn't sure they would take the bait, but from their perspective, they had already beaten him back once, and they now had him trapped. Of course, the Revetae were unaware that the Brown Chieftain and his horsemen waited hidden in the hills to the north or that there were reinforcements who hid in the forest to the east. This was the generalship that had allowed Lysandros and Zeno to conquer tribe after tribe. They understood the gamesmanship of war.

"Will they attack?" asked Konan, a tall redheaded, grizzled leader among the Aesorians, Chimmerian allies.

"I doubt Dumnorix will be able to resist the temptation," Zeno replied. "The prideful fool doesn't know to be cautious. And he's spurred on by Joni money."

Then they appeared, as thunder and lightning appear in a clear sky, suddenly, shockingly: ten thousand Revetae, Angors, and Muldavī. It would be inaccurate to say they were in formation, but they did advance in some kind of loose order. Their faces were painted blue; their hair was long and matted. They barked and howled with bloodthirsty delight, each man holding aloft a sword or a firearm. They were a terrifying sight to behold. But Zeno had seen and fought the Rapti, centaurs, and great wolves. The Woads, as fearsome as they were, were nothing compared to them. He had also fought the Woads time and time again. He knew that their shouts of lust and fury would do little when swords on both sides carved into flesh. The Rangers used to call such displays fake courage.

Zeno himself let forth no battle cry, but his troops roared in return, as was the Woadish way, and despite Lysandros's and Zeno's Dioskurian influence, they were all still Woads. Woads, who collected the heads of fallen enemies and displayed them as decorations in their homes. Woads, whom many in the civilized nations believed drank the blood of the dead—in truth, this was done very rarely, only ceremonially. But to their credit, every warrior in Zeno's force maintained his discipline. That was the difference between the Woads under Lysandros and Zeno and the rest of the tribes. All Woads were courageous warriors, but it was the children of the egoga who had taught them military bearing and discipline. They had turned warriors into soldiers.

"Shields at the ready!" Zeno barked. Along the line, each lieutenant repeated the order. Zeno lifted his radio to his mouth. "You seeing this?" he asked.

"I see it," replied Lysandros. "You know the plan. Break under their fire. Draw them in. Our men in the woods will cover you when they pursue, and we'll sweep down with our horses and trap them in the valley."

"We'll do our part," Zeno answered. "Just don't leave us alone with these bastards for too long."

Up and down the Chimmerian line, men were now drawing their shields and pounding their ion rifles and swords against them. The noise grew deafening. The rumble reverberated throughout the valley floor.

"Here it comes." Konan smiled.

The battle lasted less than an hour. Once the Revetae and their allies broke formation and charged, they lost all hope of victory. The Brown Chieftain swept down with his cavalry attacking them in the flank, and the Brown Warrior led the infantry from the front, effectively trapping their enemies between them. Like a true Woadish chieftain, Dumnorix died fighting.

That night, the victorious force celebrated in the Woadish way. Zeno walked along tents pitched under the stars, opened barrels of honey wine, and groups of Woads toasting to their victory. To his left and right, warriors copulated with both women and men. Fires blazed, wine flowed, and music and drums echoed into the night.

"Are you celebrating with us, Brown Warrior?" one of Zeno's men called out to him as he passed.

Zeno lifted up a goblet of ale in response.

"Ah, but there are other fruits to taste?" The man grinned and nodded his head.

Zeno turned around to see two men penetrating a woman, one in her vagina, the other in her anus. The coordination of it impressed him.

Zeno shook his head. "I suppose it's the Elled in me," Zeno replied. "Orgies make me nervous."

"This isn't an orgy. It's a victory banquet. Orgies are far more violent!" the man laughed.

Zeno laughed in response and then found a place to sit under a tree. Two of his men were sitting there drinking. A Giorsal named Valaxian, and a Junton named Alcredik.

"Ah! These stratagems you brown men employ are boring," exclaimed Valaxian. "I miss the days when the men of the tribes fought it out with claymores in the center and the women and bitch boys fought on the flanks with pistols and knives. That way, you always knew the bravest warriors won. Today was hardly a battle at all."

"We won. Did we not, my friend?" Zeno smiled as he took a bite of roasted meat.

"Of course, we won. But it wasn't a fair fight. Dumnorix fought with his balls. We fought with our balls and our heads."

Alcredik laughed. "All the good it did him." He motioned to Dumnorix's severed head, which was mounted on a pike in the middle of the party.

Valaxian turned and looked at the severed head. Mucus and puss still oozed from the eyes, mouth, and nose. The severed head bore a mindless look as if he had just woken from sleep.

"Eh," Valaxian said, turning back to his friends. "He fought bravely. He died like a man and now lives in the other world. May I be so lucky."

"I still don't understand this *other world* thing," Zeno questioned.

"There are two parallel worlds," Alcredik began. "Whenever someone dies in this one, they are reborn in the other, with no memory of the previous life. When they die in the other world, they are reborn into this one. In this way, one never truly dies but remains in a state of perpetual life. This belief enables us to be bold in battle. A warrior doesn't actually lose anything when he dies."

Zeno smirked.

"You don't believe it," Alcredik asked.

"I do not want to disrespect your religious beliefs, brother. But it sounds too hopeful to me. It makes it sound like there is some kind of order to life."

"You don't believe there is?" Valaxian asked.

If there is any order, it should be ripped apart. It's a shitty order.

Zeno took a drink. "No. Tell me, Valaxian." He changed the subject. "You said in the old way the armies would just fight it out, hacking at each other until one party was left. And that such practices ensured the better men always won. But doesn't intellect make a man better?"

"Oh, fuck it!" Alcredik moaned. "Here we go again."

"No," Zeno asserted. "I'm serious. Isn't the warrior who uses his mind superior to the one who relies only on his sword?"

"Oh, the philosopher..." Valaxian mocked. "Tell us about how they taught you good civilized boys to fight in the Republic."

Zeno shook his head and smiled.

"They told you that shit because none of those men had cocks," Alcredik interjected.

"You seem to know a lot about Dioskurian cocks," Zeno joked. "Perhaps you're more civilized than I thought."

They all laughed and drank.

"If the Republic of Eighteen was so strong, why did it fall so easily to the Vampire?" Alcredik asked.

There was silence. Zeno just stared at his friend. Alcredik was drunk, and Zeno knew it. But the question burned him. His stare made Alcredik know that he should not ask such things again.

"What in Tartarus did y'all do to the Brown Warrior?" Konan yelled, approaching the group, his hand groping a brown-haired, naked woman on the butt. "He looks like he just drank ox piss." Konan bent over as if inspecting Zeno's face.

"We did nothing!" Valaxian claimed. "We were just talking politics."

"Ah!" Konan sighed. "Well, that sure will take the hard out of a man's cock. And on a night when we're supposed to be celebrating."

"I'm fine," Zeno was short.

"You don't look fine," Konan answered. "You look like you're ready to fight. But there's no one left to fight. All us Woads are united now. So you might as well do the next thing to fighting: fucking. Why don't you have a taste of my new girl?" Konan kissed the woman on the cheek.

"I'll pass," Zeno said, rising from under the tree.

"What do you mean *I'll pass*?" Konan shouted. "What kind of man says no to *that*?"

The woman turned and slightly bent over, exposing herself.

"Some men would say no," Valaxian rebutted.

Konan turned to him with a look of annoyance. "He's not one of those men." He turned back to Zeno. "I know."

"I'll pass." Zeno again stated, rising and taking his friend by the shoulders. "I'll see you all at the Great Fire." With that, Zeno disappeared into the crowd of revelers. In truth, he knew Konan was wrong. There was someone else to fight. First the Militae to force them to join Lysandros' alliance, then the Vampire. Only five other times in recorded history had all the Woadish tribes been united under one leader. Such alliances, while short-lived, brought about some of the bloodiest sacks of cities and the most destructive assaults on the civilized world. Five hundred years ago, under the High Chieftain Ralliam, the Woads made it as far south as Dioskuria and sacked the capital of the Republic. The Woads could be a great and terrible force to be reckoned with on the battlefield, more than an equal for any of the more advanced, mechanized armies of the Vampire's empire if they could be controlled.

But it would not be against mortal armies that the Woads would march. Lysandros meant for them to attack Yorland, which meant they would not only have to face the Joni but also the full force of the Vampire's unholy army; to say nothing of his own great prowess in battle, which no nation in Ninivon had any answer for. Perhaps the Woads, drunk and emboldened by battle and sex, did not understand these things, but Zeno did. He had fought the Rapti. He knew what his warriors were capable of and what they were up against. He feared for these people he had come to see as his countrymen, as well as for Lysandros.

CHAPTER XI
ZENO

Zeno awoke, with Lysandros' hand on his shoulder, dripping in sweat. He'd had another nightmare. He was walking over the rubble of what was once the eastern gate of Ying-Chau but was now a mound of stone debris. A hand burst forth from beneath the rock. Then another. A bloody, battered corpse was fighting to free itself from its grave. Then the head, and finally, the face. It was Alexandra. Purple eyes. Sharp teeth. She was a Rapti. Zeno turned over to face his mentor.

The Woad camp was still asleep. Few, if any, stirred. They slept out in the open under the stars. Zeno had found a myrtle tree under which to spread his bag for the night. He realized immediately that it was still very early. His first thought was that they might be under attack. But if that were the case, why did no one else stir? He wondered why Lysandros had awoken him so early.

"We have to leave," Lysandros finally said.

"Leave?" Zeno drowsily mumbled. "Where are we going?"

By the time Zeno finished the question, Lysandros had already handed him a pack full of provisions. Zeno took it but held it away from him and gawked at it as if he had never seen a rucksack before. The Woads did not bear their gear in kits. This was the Ranger way.

"Lysandros?" Zeno asked.

He rose from his work but did not make eye contact. He pulled out his ion pistol and checked it for ammunition. Zeno knew what that meant. What would he have to be nervous about?

"I can't really say where we are going." Lysandros looked up after putting away his handgun.

Zeno sat up. "What time is it?"

"It's early, very early," replied Lysandros as he slung his pack across his back and turned to walk away. "I'll give you a few moments to steady yourself and pack up your weapons. I'll be waiting on that ridge." He pointed off to the top of a hill, an eighth of a mile to the south.

"What?" Zeno squinted his eyes. "What about the army?"

"The Woads are in good hands, I can assure you. I left the chieftains in charge of their individual clans, and Konan in charge of the Woadish League until we return."

"Return from where?"

Lysandros looked annoyed. "I already told you. I can't say just yet. What I can tell you is that we'll be gone four months. Prepare accordingly."

"Four months?" Zeno looked even more perplexed. "No, God dammit! After ten years of alliances and fighting, we have finally consolidated all the clans under our leadership. And you want to leave now? You'll endanger everything we have won."

Lysandros turned and bent down to Zeno. "We have unified the Woads. But even with every tribe, we can't beat the Vampire through force of arms. We need sorcery, otherworldly sorcery. We're going to get it. Now get up."

Zeno's eyes widened, and his breath picked up. He was awake now. He leaped from his sleeping sack. Within twenty minutes, he had joined Lysandros on the ridge, both mounted on horses. They both looked back on the camp and the fires that were burning within it.

"Konan is a great fighter and natural leader. But he's not the most intelligent man. Are you sure you trust him with the Woadish League?" Zeno asked.

"No worries. The individual chieftains will assist him. They have been instructed to keep their warriors ready for mobilization."

"An ample opportunity for them to betray us. They may not see the value in the League or your leadership with you gone." Zeno smirked.

Lysandros laughed. "Let them try. When we return with this weapon when they see what it can do, not only will all the Woads follow us, but so will all the Militae, Yorish, Acheminids, Taedemaru, Vorse, everyone."

"All right," Zeno sighed, perplexed. "I hope whatever we are going after is worth it, for both of our sakes." They turned and rode side by side into the night.

After three months of travel, Lysandros and Zeno found themselves again mounted on horses at the southern border of the Sofia Forest. Lysandros dismounted.

"Tie up your horse. We go the rest of the way by foot."

Zeno obeyed, and the duo hiked on. They heard the owls in the trees and the crack of pine needles beneath bears' feet. They saw the starlight shine between the thick tree branches.

Lysandros was fully armed with an ion pistol and a Woadish broadsword at his side, and an assault rifle on his back. Zeno carried a fifty-three-inch claymore across his back and wore a revolver on his belt. They walked at a slow pace, but the trail was brief. It was dark. Zeno was reminded of how small he felt when he and Alexandra used to hike through these woods during the egoga. He began to feel small now. He had no idea where they were going. Then he saw it: a crashed, two-man fighter jet, Dioskurian first-class. It was the plane he and Lysandros had used to escape Dioskuria. Zeno stopped as he saw the jet, but Lysandros continued.

"Lysandros!" Zeno called. Lysandros didn't respond. He continued and checked his pistol for ammunition.

Zeno jogged up to meet Lysandros, and they continued in silence. The path began to look eerily familiar, even in the darkness. Could it be that they were on the exact same path he and Lysandros had taken ten years ago? He remembered the crash. He remembered the Osaerians chasing them. But that was all.

He could not recall how they had fled their pursuers that night. Had they fought and killed them? But there were so many. Did they outrun them or hide? Zeno had no memory whatsoever. He only recalled waking the following morning and heading with Lysandros to Ying-Chau. There was one other thing Zeno recalled: fear. Otherworldly fear. But fear of what?

After another quarter mile, they emerged from the thick brush into a clearing. Zeno froze with wonder and horror. Before them laid a spaceship, horrid and ancient, so ancient. Horrid because it was ancient.

"Zeno?" Lysandros asked.

Zeno gazed on in wonder and trepidation at the structure in front of him. A moment before, he had no recollection of this alien artifact. Now, his thoughts were filled with memories of this place. That they were here now shocked him, yet he was continually becoming more aware that, on a subconscious level, he always knew this was their destination. Zeno finally commanded enough of his senses to respond to Lysandros' address. "Yes?"

"Have you been here before?"

Without turning away from the vessel, Zeno said, "Once, the night we fled Dioskuria. We were being chased by a platoon of Osaerians. We fled to this place, and they followed. When we arrived, the doors were open. We ran in, took cover behind two columns, and... and the doors slammed shut. All was dark, and then a blue light arose. Creatures came out of the walls. Humanoid creatures, they moved like men but were made of steel. They..." Zeno's words began to sputter, recalling the unnatural terror of that night. "They grabbed the Osaerians in their arms, if they could be called arms, and walked back into the walls with them. The Osaerians fought back. But it didn't matter."

"You remember?"

"Parts of it are coming back to me, but not all of it. How could I have seen something like that and forgotten?"

"You didn't forget. She cast a spell on you. She didn't want you to remember."

"She?" Zeno asked, puzzled.

Lysandros never answered, but continued towards the spaceship.

"Lysandros! Lysandros!" Zeno shouted. Lysandros didn't turn around. He stopped about fifteen feet in front of the massive doorway. Zeno shook his head and rushed up to meet him again. As soon as Zeno reached Lysandros, the massive doors slowly began to open with a wailing screech, as if they had never opened before. Zeno could see nothing inside the spaceship but darkness. Lysandros never averted his eyes, nor did he flinch as if he expected the doors to open. He walked forward, disappearing inside the inner darkness.

Zeno stood there for a second, mouth slightly open in disbelief, breathing heavily.

"Come on," Lysandros called back. Zeno again ran to catch up with his mentor. Lysandros pulled out an ion-powered torch and lit it. The light chased the darkness into the far reaches of the hall, but the shadows remained. Zeno could see they were in a long, wide corridor, columns built into the walls on both sides with odd humanoid sculptures resting on top, supporting the weight of the ceiling, which was invisible in the blackness.

"Get out your torch," Lysandros instructed.

As soon as Zeno's torch was shining, Lysandros walked forward. He seemed to know exactly where he was going. Zeno followed, and before too long, the entrance by which they had entered was no longer visible. They walked for several minutes until Zeno saw a large set of double doors in front of them. Everything, everywhere, was alien and unsettling. Yet even more alarming was the fact that it all seemed familiar as well. Zeno now recalled every detail of the terrible night he and Lysandros had fled to this place to escape the Osaerians. Yet he was thoroughly convinced that his familiarity with this place was not from that night. Rather, it seemed as if it was from another life, as one reincarnated might recall. The Σ of Sofia was everywhere. This was both the most familiar symbol he saw and caused him the most distress.

The double doors opened before both he and Lysandros. They continued forward into what looked more like the throne room of a castle than the bridge of a ship. A primordial blue light softly shined, leading his eyes to the throne. There she sat, the woman whose face was etched in Zeno's mind and who he was sure could answer his questions. Lysandros had told them they had come for a weapon of great power. One capable of killing the Vampire. This woman was the key.

Zeno should have been terrified of her. Yet the moment he saw her, he felt at ease. He knew instinctively she meant him no harm. Yet at the same time, he understood he wasn't safe around her and, in fact, had perhaps never been in more danger in his life. Also, she reminded him of Alexandra.

Lysandros walked up to the base of the staircase and dropped to his knees.

"These twenty-six years, I have protected and prepared him. I have served you well, at great personal cost. Yet I bent to your will. Now, my lady, I present to you the vessel."

'The vessel?' Zeno thought. He didn't like that. He met Lysandros at the stairs and looked up at the mysterious woman.

The woman smiled, then slowly rose and began to descend the staircase. Lysandros grabbed Zeno's arm and pulled him down.

"Kneel!" he said under his breath. Zeno obeyed but could not take his eyes off the woman who was almost to the bottom of the stairs and would not take her eyes off of him.

"Welcome, Zenosthenes Andrea," she began. The woman had now reached the floor. Lysandros greeted her with a kiss on the hand. "May I call you Zeno, or would you prefer your full name?" she asked.

Zeno could not respond.

"I am the Priestess of the Light Goddess Sofia, goddess of wisdom, and keeper of this place. You must be wondering why Lysandros has brought you here."

Zeno eyed the Priestess uneasily. He could feel himself slouching. Her gaze weighed heavy on him. Zeno could barely nod in reply.

The Priestess reached out and took Zeno by the hand. Her touch was soft. But it was the touch of a woman who knew she completely owned the moment.

"There is no need to fear. I am on your side and want to do good for you, not ill. Walk with me, and I will tell you a story."

The Priestess took Zeno by the arm and guided him off to the side of the chamber. Lysandros followed a few steps behind, almost like an attentive servant. Zeno had never seen Lysandros so docile. They walked through a door and down a long hall of cyclopean stone. As they walked, the Priestess began.

"First, you must understand that there is much we don't know. Many are uncomfortable with this uncertainty. It scares them. In order to provide themselves with a false sense of security, they create answers where there are none. They pretend these answers are true and refuse to acknowledge any doubt or uncertainty. These people are like leaves, tossed by the winds of chance and their emotions, pretending to know things they don't know and, in the process, close themselves off to any real knowledge. Do not be like these men. Be comfortable with not knowing. That is the beginning of knowledge.

"What we do know is this: there is something. We are conscious, and that cannot be an illusion. Even if all the world around us is a dream, we are no less part of that dream; therefore, it is real to us. We believe that the All Fire is responsible for this. This All Fire which possessed both consciousness and will, is both the creator of the universe and the material of which it is made. All things were made from it. All things are it. And within it, all things reside.

"As you well know, Zeno, from fire comes light, and from

light, heat. As heat rises, the molecules move about more and more, causing expansion. But as heat decreases, the molecules slow, causing contraction. From the cooling of the All Fire, galaxies and worlds and the things which inhabit those worlds came to be. How many galaxies and how many worlds are within those galaxies? None can say. Mystics and holy men say that from this cooling came the first life, the Archaioi, great and horrific beings of terrible power. Then came the Light Gods: Sofia, the wise; Andrea, the brave; and Philos, the benevolent. As well as the Dark Gods: Achos, the sorrowful; Ultor, the avenger; and Furens, the mad. Then, other forms of life, ranging from sentient beings who possess consciousness down to single-cell creatures. Is any of this true? None can say.

"But the Stokians were real. Their civilization spread across the galaxy and lasted billions of years. For eons, the Stokians believed they were the only sentient race in the universe. Until the others came to them. We do not know where they came from. Or how old they were. We know only that they were much older than the Stokians. Through their science and technology, they discovered a new type of matter in the vastness of space. One not comprised of the All Fire. It was like the All Fire in all respects. But it was colder in comparison, darker. What the others called this, we do not know. But the Stokians called it Dark Fire. These others learned that by purging themselves of the All Fire and reconstituting themselves with the Dark Fire, they could prolong their lives; they could cheat death."

Zeno tried his best to listen to the Priestess' narrative as they walked down the long hall. But his mind was filled with wonder and terror at the same time. The hallway was lit by pale blue lights that tricked his eyes. Zeno could swear that there were more than three shadows bouncing around the wall. He felt his wonder give way to fear.

"But there was a terrible price. The more Dark Fire was within them, the longer they lived, but the less human they became. If they re-engineered themselves with only the Dark Fire, they lived eternally but became animals, devoid of consciousness. Thus, they learned that the Dark Fire had to be tempered with All Fire. This limited how long they lived but allowed them to retain consciousness. It was the perfect compromise between longevity and viability. The one who unlocked this secret for them was a scientist, Erīel. She became the one who would govern the delicate mixture of Dark Fire and All Fire within each body. First, she became their de facto queen, then their god. As eons passed, the created thing became the creator. Their society, ancient and advanced, abandoned their reason and clung to the religious dogma that grew around their discovery: the gospel of Erīel. Whoever they were before, they forgot. They became the Erīeds.

"Erīel and her followers would invade a world and kill all who did not convert to their cult of immortality. The Stokians waged war against Erīel and her armies for centuries. Finally, they won, but at great cost."

Zeno grew increasingly uncomfortable. He was certain now that something, and not just one but many somethings, was walking with them, invisible to the eye but whose forms were captured briefly in the flickering light.

"Listen, Zeno." The Priestess sensed his mind speed up and his thoughts wander.

"The shadows..." Zeno said.

"They long to hear the story. They listen, as should you. The Stokians defeated the Erīeds. But their planet was destroyed in the conflict. They then set out to all corners of the galaxy in search of a new home. This ship crash-landed here on Ninivon some ninety million years ago, when the race of men was still young, before we lived in cities or had writing.

"There were few survivors. But those who did survive intermarried with Ninivonians. In time, this ship, this artifact of a far more ancient and advanced people, was forgotten. The forest grew around it. The ship and the Stokians passed from history to legend, from legend to mythology, then were lost. But not all forgot. For this ship is special. In this ship, there is a chamber, the only one of its kind throughout the thousands of universes: the Theomorphosis Chamber. Built for one purpose: to join the All Fire with the one whom it chose."

"What do you mean *the one whom it chose?*" Zeno asked.

"It's as I told you before. The All Fire is conscious. Indeed, what in the universe could be more conscious? This was the great weapon the Stokians used against the Erīeds. It was the All Fire itself. They found a way to bind a piece of the infinite inside a finite being. It is difficult to say exactly how this came to be. We know only what was passed down to our ancestors. The All Fire brought great light, which in turn brought heat. Heat is power. This power was passed on to a man called Thumos, the Stokian the All Fire chose to be its host.

"Thumos became a god-man. Capable of great wonders. His flesh became armor unto itself. He was practically impossible to kill. His strength was that of a god, as was his mind. He could manipulate matter at the atomic level.

"Imbued with this power, Thumos broke Erīel's army and stopped the spread of her faith across the universe, although he was not able to save the worlds it had already ravaged, or restore the souls it had claimed. Thumos shut off the worlds and galaxies already lost to Erīel from the rest of the cosmos. They became known as the dark realm, animated not by the All Fire, but by Dark Fire. We call them collectively Tartarus. It is something analogous to a real-life hell, like the ones priests and prophets of every religious sect preach to scare children. In reality, it is a quarantine zone, one that spans galaxies, one in which everyone and everything living is infected by the madness of Erīel."

They reached a great door at the end of the hall. The Priestess opened the door and led Zeno down a dark spiral staircase. As they stepped in, flickering lights on both sides of the wall illuminated the dark. Zeno was relieved at first to leave the hall, but after a few steps, the staircase terrified him even more. He now thought he was hearing voices. He couldn't distinguish what they said. But they whispered many words in many different languages. His senses became his enemies. Zeno had no idea what he would see or hear next in this horrid place.

It seemed as if the staircase went down forever. They passed many doors on the way down, some of which knocked from the inside. Had he been alone, or even were it just him and Lysandros, Zeno would have run back by now. Many times, it crossed his mind to reach for his gun or sword.

The Priestess slid her arm down and took Zeno by the hand. She then raised their united hands and cupped them in her free hand.

She knows she's the only thing helping me maintain my sanity and discipline in this place, which straddles the boundary between worlds.

She clearly had mastery over this alien ship. Nothing happened within its walls expect by her will. Zeno believed that as long as he was with her, he was safe. He still felt that he was but a moment away from being assaulted by supernatural and other-worldly forces against which he had no defense.

"As you well know, Zeno, this ship has a spirit of its own. It hides from those by whom it does not wish to be seen, and even if found, it has a way of defending itself. Over time, the tales of terror spread. Only the bravest or the most foolish would ever come looking for Thumos' power. But the surviving Stokians who found a new home on this planet formed an order, the Order of Sofia, dedicated to protect the Theomorphosis Chamber throughout the ages. Century after century, one priestess of our order would pass on their guard to the next.

"I took over this role from my mistress and another will take it after me. For Sofia must always have a voice among men, even if a quiet and hidden one. It is our role to guard this sacred place, and to wait."

"Wait for what?" Zeno tepidly asked.

"The Stokians promised that another host would come one day. An heir of their line, who, like Thumos before him, would be imbued with the All Fire."

They came to the bottom of the staircase and entered another hall. As the doors parted, hot light flooded the dark room they were exiting and illuminated the huge room in which they stood. The hall was massive, with a single aisle extending from the doorway up to a staircase. The aisle was flanked on both sides by pillars of fire that almost touched the celling with their flames. At the top of the staircase was a great statue of a warrior. Like the reliefs decorating the halls of the ship, he was nude. Beneath the statue was a stone sarcophagus, decorated with ancient alien symbols. Most notably, the Σ.

"This is the Theomorphosis Chamber," the Priestess informed Zeno, leading him to the base of the mighty statue. "It is you, Zeno. You, Zenosthenes Andrea, whose name means courage, raised in the poverty of Limnae, were born to become one with the All Fire. Indeed, you are the Power of Thumos. You are the love song of the Dark Gods below. You are the vengeful ghost of the night. You are the last heir of the Stokians. You can defeat the one known as the Vampire and avenge this world. Will you except this great honor offered?"

Zeno's heart raced, his breath quickened and became shallow. His muscles tensed up but he could feel himself lightly shaking. His chest grew heavy, his stomach dropped, he felt as if he could vomit right there. He was terrified beyond reason. Zeno opened his mouth, but no words came out. He looked to Lysandros whose eyes were fixed on him and then turned back to the Priestess. He could feel the fear building inside of him, fighting, clawing its way to the surface. He kept expecting to wake up, but with every moment that passed he became more acutely aware that this was reality.

"I can't do this," Zeno stammered. "I don't want this responsibility. I absolutely don't want this power."

"Neither did Thumos. Those who are worthy of great power seldom want it. And those who seek it are seldom worthy of it. It is a curious paradox."

"I won't take it!" Zeno yelled. "I don't want to be here anymore!"

"Zeno," Lysandros stepped in. "Please calm..."

"No! Get me out of here!"

"It's not that easy, Zeno," Lysandros said.

"No! You lied to me. I want to leave." Zeno stepped in front of Lysandros. Fight or flight had already set in. He would leave this place and attack anyone or anything that got in his way.

Lysandros sighed.

"It is all right, Lysandros," the Priestess interjected. "There is no need to run, Zeno. You are as much the master of this ship as I. Thumos is your father; Sofia is your mother. This ship, and the ghosts that dwell within, will never harm you. If you wish to leave, I will escort you to the door."

The Priestess stepped past both Zeno and Lysandros and began walking the way they had come. After a few steps, she turned to them both, neither of which had moved. "Are you coming?" she asked.

Zeno eyed her with great suspicion. Lysandros stared at Zeno grimly. Zeno then stepped past Lysandros. He turned to give his mentor a cold stare and then continued after her. Lysandros too followed them back the way they had come.

The outer doors slowly opened when they reached them. The dark forest looked as welcome to Zeno as a lighthouse to a ship tossed at sea on a dark night. The Priestess stopped at the threshold of the doors. Zeno did not stop or acknowledge her. He just kept walking.

"When you change your mind Zeno, Thumos will be waiting for you. I will be waiting for you."

"I won't," Zeno replied without turning.

"You will. You're just not ready right now. You won't be ready when you return either. But the goddess does not call those who are ready. She makes ready whom she calls. She will call your name until you answer."

CHAPTER XII
ZENO

By the time Lysandros caught up to Zeno he had already pitched camp for the night. The young Dioskurian, dressed and armed like a Woad, sat there peering into the small fire he had made. His horse was tied to a tree behind him.

Lysandros dismounted, tied his horse up as well, and sat on the other side of the fire, being careful to leave plenty of distance between him and Zeno.

"We shall not speak of it," Zeno sternly said.

"Very well."

Zeno continued in a harsher tone. "Do you still plan to lead the Woads over the Casildel Mountains?"

"Not just the Woads. The Militae. Yorish. All the north."

"They won't unify."

"They will. When they realize they have to."

"I can't be part of that." Zeno looked down at the earth, and then, after listening for a moment to the crackle of the flame covered wood, spoke. "I was my mother's only child. She adored me. When I was older, I found out from an uncle that my father had offered to take her away with him, if she only gave me up. He was already married, see? He'd had enough of his wife and family. He wanted to run away with his mistress. A baby boy didn't fit into his plan. I asked my mother once why she didn't expose me, as so many other unwanted babies are. She could have left me at someone's door. Or just taken me to the temple of Misericordia the Merciful. She told me she thought about it. But whenever she seriously considered it, her heart just broke. She couldn't do it. She just couldn't let me go. As far as I know, she never took another lover after my father left. She died loving him. I think she always secretly hoped he would come back to her. Her life ended the day she decided to keep me."

"I never knew that."

"When I passed the Trials to enter the egoga, she was excited at first. We all were. I was to be the great hope for our entire family. But then the realization sat in. She knew that she would essentially lose her child. The sun around which her entire universe revolved would set. You know that generally neither parents nor children have the right to refuse entry into the egoga if they pass the Trials. But there is one exception."

"If the boy or girl is an only child to a single mother," Lysandros stated the exception. "The family has the choice. The egoga never demanded a mother's only child."

"I wanted to go," Zeno continued. "I knew it would break my mom's heart. I knew, even though she never said so, that she secretly wished I would turn down entry. But she never tried to hold me back. Gods, that must have taken such discipline. The only time I ever saw any weakness was when I told her that I had decided to enter. She just stared at me for seconds. She began to cry. She asked me, 'are you sure?' I said I was. She nodded and hugged me. She held me so tight I thought she might suffocate me. She held me as if all hell were trying to take me away from her. It might as well have been. I saw her occasionally on holidays and each winter and summer for the yearly breaks. I knew she was proud of me. Every time I left, she would stand in the doorpost and watch me as I disappeared down the streets. She cried each time I walked out of her sight. I never felt guilty until she died. I was released from training to spend her last month with her. I slept by her bedside. Alexandra was there with me the day she died. I held her hand as she expired."

"I remember signing the release papers to let you go." Lysandros nodded. "Most parents would kill to have their children by their sides during their last seconds. Most don't have the luxury, Zeno."

"I know you're right. But I still felt guilty. Guilty that I had left to begin with. Guilty I had taken her son from her. But I was a to be a Ranger. I was progressing in the egoga. I would defend our great republic. Yes, the sacrifice was great. But I had counted the cost. What demands can one mother make, even on her only child, against the interest of the people?"

Lysandros leaned back against a fallen log behind him. "Say what you mean, son."

"What are we fighting for Lysandros? Alexandra is dead. You are asking me to give up my soul. Why? So we can have our revenge? So you can rule as Archon in a new Republic?"

"Come now, Zeno. You know well I don't give a shit about being Archon. But as Archon, it is my responsibility to liberate Ninivon from that tyrant. Revenge against the man who buried my daughter alive is just a bonus."

"Don't you play that game with me either, Lysandros." Zeno's eyes flared. "I loved her. I loved her."

Lysandros looked down. "I know. I have never doubted that."

"Tell me the truth. Did you send Alexandra away so you could protect me? So I could have this *Power of Thumos*?"

"I was told that a great and terrible enemy would come from beyond the stars and that only you could save our planet. I was told I would have to make sacrifices I didn't want to and that if I did not obey our entire world would be lost."

"Sacrifices..."

Lysandros lowered his head and sighed.

"You scarified your own daughter for that witch. She's just as responsible for Alexandra's death as the Vampire, and so are you. And maybe I am, too. If I am this Vessel of Thumos, then everything that Alexandra suffered was indirectly because of me."

Zeno's self-guilt was matched only by his rage at Lysandros. He could not bear the thought that Alexandra had died because of him. He let his guilt find outlet through his anger at Lysandros.

Lysandros' face contorted. Zeno had struck a nerve.

"That *witch* has sacrificed more than you can possibly know."

"Goddamn you." Zeno stared back with a look of defiance on his face. He was not some young lad of eighteen. He was a grown man of twenty-six, and because most of his life had either been spent in war or training for war, a hard twenty-six at that.

"Now you defend the Priestess? You were her slave, Lysandros. You want me to be her slave as well."

"She wants to make you a demigod, Zeno."

"Don't you get it? I'm never going back there. I'm not going back there, ever. It was all in vain. You sacrificed your daughter for nothing."

"If it is for nothing it is because you are deciding it so!" Lysandros shot back.

"Don't make me the scapegoat for your sins!"

Lysandros looked down and then raised his eyes again to Zeno. Zeno knew his mentor well enough to see that he was desperately trying to hold in his own grief and frustration. The Rangers were not ones to let their emotions run so freely.

"I understand you're hurt," Lysandros began. "I'm sorry I had to manipulate you. Believe me, Zeno, no one misses my daughter more than I. You don't have to lecture me on loss, no more than I do you. But I did it for a reason. You are special. You can accomplish wonders. You can set right what has been wrong for so long. You Zeno, if only you can find the courage."

"You think this is about courage?" Zeno asked.

"In part, yes. You're scared, son. I don't blame you. I'd be scared too. This is a terrible responsibility to lay at any man's feet. But the All Fire chose you for a reason. You are the great hope who shall unite all peoples against their common enemy. You must find something in yourself to make you venture into the unknown."

Zeno shook his head. Utter dejection on his face.

Lysandros forced a smile and rose. "Then perhaps this is where our journey must end my friend."

"Really? That simple? You don't mean to follow me?"

"The Priestess advised against it."

"Of course." Zeno nodded.

"Can I ask where you plan to go now?"

"Don't know. Head east maybe."

"I'm sure there is work for an educated man in Zutaera or Sarpedon." Lysandros walked over to Zeno. "I won't push any more. Gods know I have pushed too much already. I know you blamed me ten years ago when I sent Alexandra to Ying Chau. At the time, I had to feint ignorance. But I always knew what would happen. I'm not looking for sympathy, but it was a terrible burden to bear. There is more you don't know, Zeno. And I cannot tell you. But when you discover it, it will change everything. I don't know exactly how it will happen, but one day you will know everything that I have been forbidden to tell you. I pray when you do, that you'll think better of me and that you'll return to Thumos."

"The only thing that matters, the only thing that could make a difference is Alexandra, and she is dead Lysandros. Dead because of the choices you made. Now I'm making a choice. You will never see me again. You'll die knowing you sacrificed her to a false god. You were supposed to protect her. That's what a father does. You failed. If I could, I'd kill you right now."

Zeno knew Lysandros well enough to know his words cut him. Lysandros did consider himself a failure as a father. Zeno wished to affirm in his last words with Lysandros that his deepest insecurity was true. It was all he could do to take vengeance. Lysandros was a better fighter. Zeno couldn't kill Lysandros and Lysandros wouldn't kill him.

Lysandros frowned, melancholy. "Good bye, Zeno." Simple, yet so final. Lysandros turned and disappeared into the darkness of night and the wall of trees.

Zeno stood there, his hands shaking. He had never felt more alone.

CHAPTER XIII
LYSANDROS

Lysandros made it to the entrance of the Blue Order's cave undetected, even though Nikolaus had sentries posted every quarter mile.

They might make good terrorist and thugs, but they're shit guards.

Lysandros now stood within striking distance of all the guards who were on duty at the main entrance, two on the ground, two above perched at the side of the waterfall. Lysandros had himself climbed down the waterfall to reach this point. Having progressed so far in secrecy, he was now ready to make himself known. He walked away from the rock face. It was night, but he was as visible in the ion torch light as if it were day.

The sentries seemed shocked that he had snuck up on them; embarrassed even. They made up for this embarrassment with force.

"Down!" several shouted. "Hands up!"

Lysandros put his hands above his head and dropped to his knees.

"No need for concern, my brave revolutionaries. I'm just here to talk with your leader."

The shouts attracted no small amount of attention from those just inside the cavern. Five more guards now held their rifles to Lysandros, in addition to the first four. Two approached. One pulled him up while the other frisked him.

"How did you find us? Are you armed? Did Glaucon send you?" A barrage of questions from another approaching guerilla.

"I found you by looking," Lysandros mocked. "It wasn't hard. And no, I'm not a spy for the Sarpedonain Emperor, nor am I armed, except for a dagger on the left side of my belt."

The soldier performing the frisk found a short, flat blade, with a red jewel in the hilt. On the pommel was the emblem of a bear.

That'll get my brother's attention.

"What are you doing here?" the lead inquisitor barked another question.

"Take that dagger to the one you call Ghost. He'll want to speak to me."

The soldier who held the dagger looked to the lead soldier, who nodded in turn. The man carrying the dagger disappeared into the cave.

"What do you want with Ghost?" again, the lead soldier asked.

"I just want to talk," Lysandros replied.

The soldier barked some more orders, and they pushed Lysandros around a bit, which he let them do. He could easily have killed this group, but he was not here to fight, not with them, anyway. Nor were they much of a threat to him.

A few moments later, the sentry who had taken the dagger returned. "The strategos says it's okay. Bring him."

A few moments later, Lysandros was led into Nikolaus' quarters. "Leave us," Ghost ordered. Then the sons of Polymaxes were alone. For a while the brothers stood there in silence, eyeing each other, as if to see if the person they saw was real, or a specter of their memory.

"Father's dagger," Ghost began. "Passed down to the first-born son of the House of Polymaxes." He smiled. But Lysandros could tell he was not happy. Again, silence followed.

Finally, Lysandros spoke, "It's good to see you brother. I heard about what happened at Ying-Chau. I'm glad you made it out. What of my daughter?"

"What are you wearing?" Ghost laughed.

Lysandros looked about his attire. "Clothes," he responded. "What of my daughter? Where's Alexandra?"

"I can see you're wearing clothes." Ghost still refused to answer the question. "Whose family tartan is that? You're not a damned Woad, even if you're wearing a kilt."

"Brother." Lysandros tried to keep his frustration at bay.

"Calm down, Lysandros," Ghost balked in reply "Do you think I would have left my niece to die in that hell hole? She's alive, and well, here. I'll call for her now if you like."

"I would appreciate that."

Ghost spoke through his wrist radio, "Alexandra, report to my quarters. Bring Zeno with you." He looked up to Lysandros. "How did you know Zeno was here?"

"An owl told me," Lysandros smirked.

Ghost did not seem amused. "Why aren't you dead? I thought you were dead," he hissed, almost as if disappointed.

Lysandros raised his eyebrows. He did not expect a warm welcome. He walked to the table off to the side of the chamber, took a goblet and filled it with wine. He then motioned to Ghost to see if he wanted a cup. Ghost shook his head. Lysandros pulled out a chair and sat down.

"I should be dead. I wanted to die. More than you can ever know." Lysandros saw his brother's eyes flare upon hearing those last words. "Or perhaps you can relate." He took a drink.

"I know what happened at Dioskuria," Ghost began. "The Vampire killed all the survivors and you wouldn't have abandoned the Rangers or Asha. Why aren't you dead?"

"Hasn't Zeno told you?"

Ghost responded with a cold stare, realizing some pivotal piece of information had been held from him.

"In her last act as Archon, Asha anointed me co-Archon of the Republic."

Nikolaus' eyes widened. His face contorted in mock reverence. "*Archon*, really? Well, why did you not come to your subjects at Ying-Chau, Archon?"

"The Vampire buried the city before I had a chance to come," Lysandros replied.

Ghost laughed. "Bull shit! I know you. Even if you thought Alex was dead, you'd have dug up the entire city to find her body. Why did you truly not come to us?"

"Why do you always have to be so combative?" Lysandros asked, leaning forward in the chair. "It's always like wrestling a wild boar with you. When I walked in, you looked almost disappointed that I was alive. Why do you hate me so much?"

Ghost glared at his older brother.

"By Sofia, Nikolaus." Lysandros leaned back. "You still blame me that you lost your lands and titles?"

"I never gave a damn about the titles." Ghost spat. "You know that. But those were father's lands. The last thing I had from him."

"You took up arms against the Republic you swore to protect, that our father protected. You're lucky the land and titles were all the Archons took."

"The Baroquista Uprising is another matter. You always wanted those lands. It wasn't enough that you were the oldest and always had the lion's share of glory as well as father's attention. You had to take even what he did give to me."

"All the other leaders in the Baroquista Uprising were put to death, save you, and Tarquinia. And we should have killed her. I saved your head. You couldn't just be grateful though. You always were an entitled shit."

"Gods of Tartarus, you're so damn self-righteous!" Ghost roared as he turned away from Lysandros.

"And you're still as cantankerous as ever. You and I are two old to change our ways, little brother. Although I never saw you as a rebel. I'm assuming you're planning to attack Sarpedon. Do you think you can take the city?"

"Yes," Ghost answered, turning back to Lysandros.

"Then you're a fool." Lysandros took another drink. "Don't

get me wrong. Your troops are good. In fact, I'm quite impressed by what you've done here. You've taken every thief, gutter rat, and brawler in Sarpedon and turned them into a well-disciplined and cohesive guerilla unit. You've managed to bring the city to the brink of anarchy through brutality and unpredictability. But sending kamikazes into packs of Joni knights is one thing. Capturing a walled and garrisoned city and holding it is quite another.

"Let's just say you do take the city. What then? What happens when the Vampire unleashes the Rapti. Do you think your boys are ready for that?" Lysandros now arose and looked Ghost in the eyes. "Let us get to it, little brother. You've done an admirable job with these cut throats and thugs. But you know what the Vampire is capable of. You'll need an army, a well-trained one at that, you'll need alliances, equipment, an answer for his aerial armada, and magic as well, and that's just to stand a chance."

"Do you think I haven't thought of that?"

"Yet you lead these people on."

"You're leading your savages on. You can't beat the Vampire either. I don't judge you for how you lead your rebellion. Don't judge me for how I lead mine. I'm doing the best job I can in the circumstances I have been given."

"Be that as it may, I don't want Zeno and Alexandra here when the hammer falls."

"They made a choice to be here."

"Zeno made that choice because Alexandra was here."

"She was here because you abandoned her," Nikolaus jeered.

Alexandra burst from behind the curtain with Zeno behind her. As she crossed the threshold, her pace slowed. She slowly walked up to her father.

It had been twelve years since Lysandros had seen his daughter. And though he had lied so much to conceal his true mission which the Priestess had commanded of him, the truth overwhelmed him now like a tidal wave. He had always known his daughter was alive. In this regard, his fate was far crueler than that of Zeno. For Zeno, having thought Alexandra dead, had something of closure. But he had to endure the last twelve years with the burden of knowing his daughter was alive, constantly in danger for her life, and that the safest place for her was as far away from him and Zeno as she could be. Furthermore, he had no one to share this with. His one solace, the Priestess, having abandoned even his dreams. Now Alexandra was a woman. He hardly recognized the woman who stood before him. Lysandros had always known what he had lost, but now he felt it. His discipline was close to breaking. He wanted to throw himself at his daughter's knees and explain everything to her and beg her forgiveness. But He knew he had another role and that he must carry that role out if he was to save Alexandra, and all of Ninivon.

It seemed Alexandra had a much simpler understanding of the moment. When Lysandros looked in her eyes, all he saw was rage and betrayal.

Zeno did not seem surprised to see him, but he did seem tense. Lysandros knew that Zeno had good reason to be scared. But worried that what he most feared was losing Alexandra again; not the awesome responsibility that had been laid at his feet.

"Alex," Lysandros broke the silence. "Not a day has gone by..." He took a step towards his daughter, but she took a step back, not letting him shorten the distance between them.

This stung him. More than he expected it would, given that he had expected this reaction. Then, Lysandros' eyes cleared, his posture straightened. He looked to Nikolaus and then back to Alexandra. "Come with me."

At first, Alexandra seemed moved, as if she might cry. But then her eyes turned cruel. A grimace came across her face.

"I've spent the last twelve years with Uncle Nikolaus. I will remain with him."

Lysandros bowed his dead in dejection. He raised it again;

his eyes desperate. "Alex…"

"Nikolaus was good enough for me twelve years ago, he's good enough for me now."

"Alex, your anger makes sense. But you must move past it. *Your feelings are real but they're not reality:* The Ranger mantra. There were extenuating circumstances that you don't know about. I had to send you to Ying-Chau."

"Like what?"

Lysandros looked briefly to Zeno, then back to his daughter. "You wouldn't believe me if I told you. But if you come with me, I can show you."

"Ah," Alexandra sighed. "Trust first and explanation later. No thanks, Father. I don't want to know what your *reasons* were. I don't want you. I'm staying right here."

"You heard her answer, brother," Ghost thundered.

"Alexandra," Lysandros pleaded. "This has been an emotional night for all of us. But I beg you to consider the facts, not just your feelings. If for no other reason than for your own safety. You know enough of violence to know what will happen to everyone here. The egoga taught you that. I taught you that. What happens when the Vampire sends his Equitati Knights or worse, the Rapti? You will be overrun and you know it. Also, you know in your heart; child smugglers and suicide bombers are not the way. Under the Republic of Eighteen, he could be tried and convicted of war crimes for what he has already done." He pointed to Nikolaus. "Alex, do you really want to be a part of this?"

"Still telling everyone else how to live their lives, I see. Lives that are just fine before you interfere with them. Like mine among the Militae before you took me away from my sisters. Or mine with you and Zeno before you sent me away. All for my protection. But as it turned out no protection was needed. I could have just fled the city when you did," Alexandra interjected.

Desperate, Lysandros turned to Zeno. "Zeno?"

"He doesn't make my decisions for me," Alexandra snapped.

"I didn't think he did," Lysandros shot back in frustration. "But maybe he has the sense to see what is happening here."

"You just want him to go back to the Woadlands so you can use him as your lieutenant. But you've got no more chance against the Vampire with your Woads and Militae than we do here with the Order," Alexandra reposed. "If Zeno's going to die, he might as well do it here, with me."

Lysandros shook his head. That sounded like something Nikolaus would say. He feared the influence his brother had had on her over these past twelve years. In truth, he sensed much of his brother's animosity towards him in her rejection. Who knows what Nikolaus had said to her about him? He wanted to reach out to her. But he knew to do so would only drive her farther away. She saw him as an enemy now.

But now Lysandros was worried about Zeno. Zeno was the Vessel of Thumos. He could not die a martyr in this cave or in the streets of Sarpedon. He had to get him out. Lysandros felt confident that were it just the three men, he could convince Zeno to leave with him. But he worried about Alexandra's sway on Zeno. He sensed that she was the only reason he had agreed to join the Blue Order at all. Perhaps he had even talked with Alexandra independently about leaving with him. But she wouldn't leave and Zeno never could tell her *no*.

"We all should be dead already," Zeno finally spoke, keeping his eyes down. "We've all seen battles, war, genocide. We've seen people transformed into monsters who rise up and attack their loved ones. Perhaps we'd be better off if we were dead." He raised his eyes to Alexandra. "But we're not dead. We're alive. So it falls to us to take what life we have left and live it well."

Zeno turned now to Ghost. "I understand why you have done what you have done, Nikolaus. When the Vampire threw down the Republic, he destroyed the greatest dynasty the world has ever known. I don't think any of us, all of us even, can beat him. Even if every possible variable turned in our favor, I don't think we could kill him. But we are all Rangers. It is our part to protect the people, not use them, not hurt them."

Lysandros smiled. He had known Zeno since he was a boy. He had seen him grow both physically and emotionally in the egoga. He developed into a fine commander and leader among the Woads, not an easy people to lead. But he had never been prouder of him than he was in that moment.

Ghost looked to Alexandra and then back to Zeno. His eyes fired with rage. "You self-righteous shit. I saved your life. You'd be dead were it not for me." He spit out the last word with contempt.

"Zeno, you've been with us a month. How many kamikaze attacks have you seen?" Alexandra interrupted, hoping to calm the tension.

"None."

"Yes, none. It's true we used suicide bombers in the past, but that was only when we had no other choice. When there's a better option, we have always chosen it. And we take care of their families when they're gone, most of which are starving without our aid."

"It's not enough, Alex," Zeno said. "No army, society, or even tribe has ever thrived by asking the weakest among them to sacrifice the most."

"So what then?" Alexandra continued. "Would you prefer I strap a bomb to my back and run into a Joni garrison? Or should we all die fighting them in an open battle where we are outnumbered and outgunned?"

"You don't owe him an explanation, Alexandra!" spit Ghost. "The poor children run the guns for us because they know the streets of the city and can get them out. The beggars sacrifice their lives for the Order because their lives are shit anyway and they have no hope. We give them purpose. We make them heroes and martyrs. Furthermore, because they make that sacrifice, I don't have to commit and lose my troops on objectives we need but can't accomplish through either guerilla or conventional military tactics. But I don't want to have to explain that to you,

Zeno, because when you question my decisions, you tell me you don't think I know what I'm doing!"

"You're using them as human shields to carry out your military operations. You care nothing about their lives and families. You only see them as a means to an end. How does this make you different from the Vampire?"

Everyone was silent. Lysandros knew that last question would get no answer, nor would there be another. Nikolaus did not appreciate criticism, particularly in regards to his leadership. Lysandros stood ready in case Nikolaus attacked. He hoped his brother would not order his troops to attack. He had come to this cave hoping to leave with both his daughter and Zeno. But if that was not possible, he had to leave with Zeno. The fate of all Ninivon hung in the balance. One thing was certain, Zeno couldn't possibly stay with the Blue Order after what he said.

Lysandros studied Alexandra's face. She looked forlorn, both frustrated and disappointed. His daughter was no fool. He knew that she understood as well that Zeno's time with the Blue Order had come to an end. Now the question was, would Zeno break through her stone heart? Would she follow him?

Ghost just stood there, square, bearded chin extended, jaw clinched, as if he had just been shot. At last, he turned to Lysandros. "They say a good teacher reproduces himself in his pupils. You must be an excellent teacher, brother, because this prick is just like you. Take this whelp and get out of my camp before I pummel him."

Lysandros walked to the exit. Zeno and Alexandra stood with eyes fixed on each other. Lysandros turned and said, "Zeno, come."

Zeno didn't move. He opened his mouth to speak. But Alexandra but cut him off before the words left his mouth.

"My place is here. You should go."

Pitiless rejection erupted across Zeno's face. Lysandros could not imagine how those words must have stung. He knew how Alexandra's rejection had wounded him. He had considered himself a failure as a father for not taking Alexandra with him, although it was not his decision. *You swore to obey me. Before house and nation. Before even your family.* Lysandros remembered her words, sharp to the heart. He knew what he was doing when he had sent Alexandra to Ying-Chau. All to serve the cosmic plan of the Priestess of Sofia. It was the greatest sacrifice he had ever made. But Alexandra didn't know any of that. All she saw in him was a father who had taken her from one home and exiled her from another. He deserved her scorn.

But Zeno loved Alexandra as he loved his own soul. Zeno had never abandoned her and he did not have the advantage of the foreknowledge the Priestess had afforded him. Zeno actually believed that Alexandra had died at Ying-Chau. To have received her back from the dead, only to lose her again, must have cut to his heart.

Then, as if the fog parted and he could finally see clearly, it struck Lysandros that this must have been her plan all along. What could make Zeno return to the Stokian ship of his own free will? What other than to save Alexandra from the destruction that was surely coming for her, and the entire Blue Order?

Alex was the key all along. He'll do it to save her. The Priestess knew it. She knew it before Alexandra was ever born. Gods! We're all just puppets on strings. She is the only one who cans see the strings. Even the ones controlling her.

It made Lysandros' head hurt too much to contemplate it. He let his mind come back to the present. If he survived this war, he would one day say this was the moment that changed Zeno's mind. *We humans are such fragile things.*

Zeno stood there for several more seconds. Then, he turned and followed Lysandros out.

"Just keep walking," Lysandros whispered. "There's nothing you can do right now."

Lysandros and Zeno exited the cave and walked onto the banks of the river. The moon shined beautifully off the river and the waterfall.

"How'd you know?" Zeno asked.

"How do you think?"

"I won't bother asking how you found the camp."

"I had spies in Sarpedon as well," Lysandros said. "I had to keep some eyes on you."

"You must have known this would be the outcome. And even if you didn't, your witch would have told you. You could have waited a few more weeks. You could have given us more time."

"There is no more time. When I passed through Sarpedon, I learned that the Vampire has had enough of Glaucon's incompetence. He is sending a force of Karthagoi mercenaries into the Sofia Forest to flush out and destroy the Blue Order. The Karthagoi are excellent at forest and woodland combat."

"The men who live in trees." Zeno mused the well-known epitaph of the Karthagoi people from the nation of Tyra.

"The Joni and Sarpedonians are augmenting them. I'm not sure how many they'll be. Besides, you and I both know you won't be away from her long."

"Did you know this was her plan? Did she tell you?"

"She tells me only what I am to do. And flatters me with enough honey words to keep me doing it."

"You always told me, that a good leader takes the emotion out of his decisions, and does what is best for everyone," Zeno replied.

Lysandros sensed the great weight that bore down on Zeno's heart. He wished he could help him carry it.

"I'm scared, Lysandros."

Lysandros stopped and put his hand on Zeno's shoulder. Zeno turned from the river and looked to his mentor. "Were you not scared; you wouldn't be worthy of the great power that has been offered to you."

Zeno's eyes cleared, and a resoluteness came over his face. He no longer looked sorrowful and frightened, but rather like a man set on his course and determined to hold it to whatever end.

CHAPTER XIV
ALEXANDRA

It was a mid-spring morning, but it was still cold. The morning mists rose off the Xor River, creating a deep fog.

Alexandra awoke to the sound of shouts and screams throughout the cavern and artillery falling on the rock above. For a second, she gathered her wits. She knew exactly what was happening. She jumped from her cot on the cave floor and immediately armed herself. Before she could finish, a guerrilla ran to her.

"Ghost needs you, now!"

She burst out into the main cavern to a scene of complete chaos. The support staff was panicked. A soldier was yelling instructions at them.

"You'll divide into groups of forty. A scout will lead you through the different caverns out into the Sofia Forest."

Evacuation protocol. This isn't just an attack; we're trapped. Alexandra's first reaction was the injustice of it all. But not for the non-combatants for whom she felt responsible. *My life has mostly been shit. I was happy under the Red Sky until I was taken away. Zeno made me whole again, and, my damn father.* She loathed to admit it even to herself. *Then my father betrayed me and I lost Zeno again. I thought I had moved on. But I didn't. I just used my anger and this revolt to mask my pain. Maybe that was why I had said yes to child smugglers and suicide attacks. Maybe that's why I've been so hostile to uncle since Zeno left, arguing with him in front of everyone. Uncle thinks it's because I saw my father. But father was never my moral compass, Zeno was. When I left him at Dioskuria, I left that part of me behind. But I thought he was dead. That helped. When Zeno left me, he took it with him. But now I know he's out there, somewhere. That's what really stings. That's why the last two months have been harder than the previous twelve years. It's not fair. I never had a choice. I lived like an animal all this time: only surviving, not truly living. Now I'm going to die. I should have left with him.*

These thoughts rocketed through her mind as Alexandra ran to Ghost's chamber where he was discussing last minute preparations with leadership.

"They've been flooding the forest with hoplites ever since the riot outside the walls." Ghost referred to the Sarpedonians. Firefights broke out in the woods; they happened almost daily since what had come to be known as the 'Riot Outside the Walls.'

"We've already lost a lot of troops. This was not how or where I hoped to fight his rebellion. I envisioned the streets of Sarpedon being our battle ground. The woods were to be our refuge."

At first, it was. But as the Vampire's military presence grew, the fighting shifted more and more into the wilderness. Ghost's troops were well trained and they could hold their own in skirmishes or safely and stealthfully find their way back to the cave if they were beaten. But with so many loyalist troops in the forest, eventually Glaucon would find the cave and when he did, where could the insurgents flee?

Father was right. Our increased aggression caught the attention of the Vampire himself and we were not ready to take on the Vampire. We were barely holding our own against Glaucon.

"The force now attacking are Karthagoi mercenaries under the command of an experienced and particularly brutal officer named Hashdrubal," Ghost continued the brief. "We don't have exact numbers, but it must be sizable indeed for Hashdrubal to be in command."

"How many deserters last night?" another officer asked.

"The same as we have seen every night for the last few weeks," a second answered.

"They won't get far with the Karthagoi out there." Ghost shook his head.

He feels responsible. I do too.

"The best chance we all have now is to dig in and hold out together," Ghost continued. "We all knew this day might come. We have to give the non-combatants as much time as possible to escape, just as our sentries are holding them off now in the forest to give us time to prepare.

"They'll hit us with artillery and try to collapse the cave. I doubt they have anything with them that can do it, but it will sound like the walls are going to cave in. It'll scare our men to death. But we must remain within the cave. If we leave the cave, they'll mow us down. When they see they can't scare us into coming out, they'll try to come in. That's when the real battle will begin. I want the troops broken up into companies. Hit the Karthagoi at every point. We can't let them have anything uncontested. We hit, hold ground for as long as possible and then fall back into the caverns and do the same thing from there. Our only hope is to wear them out and force them to withdraw long enough for our main body to escape. Now, go."

With that, Ghost dismissed his council. They left, urgency and anxiety in every step. Ghost motioned for Alexandra to stay behind in the chamber with him.

"Hashdrubal has cut off some of the escape tunnels. I don't know which ones."

"So we may be evacuating our people into a trap," Alexandra hissed.

"Yes," Ghost answered. "Which is why I'm sending soldiers with them. We still have no choice but to try and get them out. Some will die. But if we keep them here, all will die. At least this way, some have a chance to survive. If reports are true of his numbers, Hashdrubal has enough men to keep us trapped in here for months. It looks like we're about to go into a bloody siege, an underground siege at that. That's the same shit that you and I fled Ying-Chau to avoid. That's the best-case scenario. That assumes we can hold them back when they advance. Alexandra, do you recognize the name of their commander, Hashdrubal?"

"Wasn't he the Karthagoi who sacked the Zan city Tsao-Lo during the Great Terror?"

"Yes. He buried entire groups of civilians alive and personally raped women in front of their families."

"Andrea the Brave, the noncombatants."

Ghost nodded. "The Vampire personally chose Hashdrubal to lead this attack on account of his brutality. Like all cruel men, he is eager to display his cruelty. We have to hold his forces back. Short of that, we have to kill him. It will be far better for the ones the Karthagoi capture if he is dead. He's nearly seven feet tall. Shouldn't be hard to find."

"Understood."

"One more thing. I know you're angry with me. For sending Zeno away. For the way I have led this rebellion. For all of this." Ghost motioned to the panicked activity happening in the cave. "But second to myself, you're the best fighter here. More than killing the enemy, I need you to help me lead these men. If you are disciplined, hold when I say hold, and charge when I say charge, so will they. War is in the details of doing little things right when it matters most. Your prick of a father taught me that. Today, I need the best of you. If you give me that, you might just get the best of every soul in this cave." Ghost's eyes radiated an intensity Alexandra hadn't seen since their escape from among the Katanas. She understood they had become cornered animals. They were to fight off the hunters as long as they could.

Niece and uncle clasped hands and then embraced. "I'm sorry I haven't done better for you, my girl," Ghost whispered.

Alexandra's heart melted a bit. In many ways, Nikolaus

had been a father to her, certainly the last twelve years. He was a flawed man given to his passions. But he had shown her loyalty. In his very fallible way, she knew that he loved her.

"You have been the one constant in my life, uncle. You have done all that you could. I'm grateful." They released and Alexandra looked Ghost in the eye. "I will do all I can for you today. *Iva alloi zosi.*" The Ranger creed, in the Elledic tongue. *That others may live.*

Everyone took their positions. The shelling continued for another hour. The walls rocked and creaked. There were times Alexandra knew they would be crushed by falling stone or buried alive beneath it. She thought of the days underground at Ying Chau. Here she was again, surrounded by stone and hoping to not be buried alive. The Dark Gods had a sense of humor. But the walls held. She was scared. But she didn't move. She held her position on Ghost's left. Ghost was right, as they held strong, others held strong around them. Despite the fear that welled up in her like an ocean, two thoughts swam to the surface in that hour: first, she was so proud of the men and women beside her, proud of their courage and willingness to die rather than betray one another. The men were divided into companies and stationed at various points in the cave. Some hid behind stalagmite and inside dark corridors, others laid on their bellies, rifles pointed up to fire at whatever came through the entrance. There were several ion machine gun bunkers. Others still were perched on the ledges along the walls of the cave. No matter who or what came through the water fall, the first regiment would pay a heavy price. As the minutes passed, as no one broke, no one tried to escape, the bravery of the group gave bravery to the one and he in turn back to the whole. Bravery was infectious. They might all die today, but Alexandra knew their line would hold to the last man. Second, she desperately wanted to see Zeno.

Outside the cave, the Karthagoi detonated mortars on the rock face. The explosions blazed fabulous and deadly in the reflection of the waterfall, illuminating the mist rising from the river like lighting illuminates the clouds.

The Karthagoi hailed from Tyra, a heavily wooded country to the far east. Part of the Great Enkadu Jungle fell within their borders. But much of their homeland was covered by the giant sequoia trees, massive trees that stretched hundreds of feet into the sky. The Karthagoi built their cities in these trees. Much of their capital, Dido, sat fifty feet above the forest floor. For these reasons, the Karthagoi were the premiere woodland fighters in Ninivon. They were armed as such: generally carrying short ion rifles, short javelins, ovular shields, and falcata swords: short, twenty-five-inch, single edged blades with slight forward curves. Ideal for hacking off arms and legs. Their armor was similar to that of the Remani, ion proof breastplates, over tunics, and battle skirts over trousers.

The bombardment stopped. Seconds passed like hours. The men looked around. Why did it stop? Alexandra knew. Ghost had told the others what to expect. Had they remembered what he told them would follow the bombing? Seconds turned into minutes, one, five, even ten. Even she, for a moment allowed herself to feel the hope that was now infiltrating the Blue Order. The enemy, for whatever reason had decided not to attack and no one would die today. Alexandra looked to Ghost with questioning eyes. He just shook his head and mouthed the word "wait."

The Karthagoi burst through the waterfall.

"Fire!" Ghost ordered.

The cavern blazed with ion and fission fire. It filled with the smoke of burning flesh and the cries of dying men raised to its rafters. The Blue Order fired on the advancing Karthagoi at point blank range from dug in positions. Dozens fell. But more poured in. They stumbled over the bodies of their own dead, got up, and continued on. In seconds, Alexandra could no longer distinguish the enemy living from the dead. Rather, they all seemed to be one terrible organism; a monstrous form of flesh with hundreds of arms, legs, and eyes, awkwardly advancing through sheer weight at the rebels. They returned fire when they could. Alexandra felt the heat of an ion blast singe her skin. She saw blood and soft tissue erupt from the head of the woman who was next to her.

But the Karthagoi were too many. Despite heavy casualties they pushed forward, adorned with ion proof helms and breastplates and carrying ion proof shields. Alexandra knew that within seconds the fighting would be hand to hand and they would lose their advantage. Everywhere was chaos.

"Fall back to the second point!" Ghost shouted through his comm.

Alexandra relayed the order to smaller unit commanders and the entire Blue Order retreated further back in the cave.

Alexandra saw a Karthagoi charge her head on. She fired her rifle and put an ion blast through his head. The furens took her. She was out of ammunition. The enemy was upon her anyway. She threw down her rifle and drew her short sword and pistol, then threw herself headlong into hell.

She saw the giant Hashdrubal hacking through one insurgent after another with his falcata. Arms, legs, and occasionally heads, flew into the air with a bloody train behind them. None wished to fight him man to man. Each rebel of the Blue Order, when Hashdrubal charged them, either ran, or, if they had any rounds left, fired in his direction. But Hashdrubal was deceptively quick for a man his size. When the former, he would run them down and hack them to death. When the latter, he would duck under his shield to negate the ion blasts and then charge his prey before they were able to get off another aimed shot. Such a large target in such small confines could not go completely untouched. Several rebels had put ion rounds into him from afar. But none could get a killing shot. These were shallow wounds, which even collectively could not slow the giant down.

Alexandra turned to see her uncle hit. *How bad?* He fell

to the ground and lifted his head. Hashdrubal, the mad giant, ran towards him. Twenty Karthagoi soldiers ran behind their commander. Hashdrubal kicked Ghost in the head and drove him to his back. Hashdrubal lifted his falcata to take the head of the infamous Ghost, a prize for the Vampire no doubt.

Alexandra aimed her pistol at Hashdrubal but had to duck to avoid being decapitated by an ion blast. She reset and prepared to fire.

Then, a man emerged from the waterfall. Although not as tall as Hashdrubal, he was a giant in his own right, heavily muscled in the shoulders, chest, and back. He wore black boots and black trousers, overlaid by mail grieves and footguards, like those of a hoplite. A battle belt stretched across his waist. He wore no breastplate or mail shirt at all. He had steel wrist bands on both wrists that stretched up his forearms. Other than these and his girdle belt, he wore no armor. His hair was long, black. He was armed with one sword only, a Dioskurian bastard sword with a small semi-circle hilt, and a flat heavy blade which was drawn and slicing in lethal precision.

Before Hashdrubal could lower his blow, the man charged the group of Karthagoi surrounding their commander. The mercenaries fired. Alexandra swore the man had been hit, several times in fact, but he didn't fall. Rather, he accelerated. He plowed into them swinging his sword. They scattered before him as a herd of antelope would scatter before a lion. He severed Hashdrubal's right hand and slammed the blade into his side. The Tyrian giant gave a godless scream. The man shoved the commander of the Karthagoi aside as if he weighted nothing. Hashdrubal flew ten yards. Alexandra doubted that he had ever been manhandled like that before.

The mercenaries reformed around their wounded commander. The warrior drove into them, slicing through head and neck and loins. No one could catch him. His swing smashed right through the weapons and armor of all others. Alexandra had never seen anyone move like this. As water flowed, he killed.

The other Karthagoi now turned their attention to the warrior. Like a magnet he attracted the enemy. They couldn't fire with their guns because there were too many of their own in close proximity. They pressed on the man with spears and falcatas. Parries, blows, parries, and strikes. Alexandra couldn't see what was happening. But she knew one thing: This one man was pushing back a group of over a hundred soldiers.

The Blue Order, once hard pressed, now not the object of their enemy's attack, countered. Ghost rose to his feet, wounded but able to fight. For a moment, he was mesmerized by this mysterious warrior who had single handedly turned the tide of the battle. The second past. Ghost picked up his sword and waded into the ocean of Karthagoi with the warrior in the center.

Alexandra too joined her uncle in support of the lone warrior, not that he needed the help. Within a breath, it seemed there were only a handful of Karthagoi still fighting. Most were dead or wounded beyond capacity. The wise ones were in full retreat. No one thought to offer pursuit.

Hashdrubal, in agony crawled to his feet and pulled a long dagger from the still living body of one of his own men. There was still a small group of Karthagoi who were bravely standing against the warrior who had broken their force. He was distracted. Hashdrubal lunged at the warrior, dagger aimed at the back of his neck.

What followed burned a hole in Alexandra's mind. Hashdrubal came down on the warrior like a mountain, with all the strength and force his hulking bulk could muster. The blade buried itself less than a quarter inch into the warriors bare back and slid down, slicing him for sure, but just barely. It was as if Hashdrubal had driven the dagger into a stone statue. The warrior didn't even turn to look at Hashdrubal, who had collapsed to the ground under the incredible force of his own blow. Rather, the warrior slammed his sword in the chest of another Karthagoi to his left and left it there. He turned and slammed his hand into Hashdrubal's face. The force of the blow was so great that it collapsed the Tyrian general's head like a mace.

CHAPTER IX
ALEXANDRA

Seeing their commander manhandled so easily and in such a gruesome way, must have demoralized the remaining Karthagoi. Within minutes the signal for retreat was given, and they all fled the cave. What was a force of well over three hundred had been reduced to a few paltry dozen. With the enemy in full retreat, the Blue Order gave a deafening shout of victory which echoed through the caverns.

Alexandra was completely oblivious to all this activity. Her eyes were lazier focused on the strange warrior. He seemed so alien, literally. He didn't seem human. At the same time, he reminded her of someone.

No. He couldn't be him.

She wanted to move closer to him, but felt paralyzed. Alexandra saw Ghost approach the man. He stopped a few feet in front of the warrior who had saved his entire force. A few men, having vented their screams of triumph or uttered their prayers of thanks or reproach to the gods, focused on their strategos and gathered behind him, also looking at the stranger.

The warrior withdrew his sword from the warm corpse of the Karthagoi in whom he had deposited it. He pulled a rag from his belt and wiped the blood and fatty tissue from the blade. The weapon dripped of guts and gore, as did his hair and arms. He would need water. He lifted his eyes to meet Ghost, for a long while they stared at each other.

"Vultus!" Ghost finally ordered to his lieutenant, not taking his eyes of the stranger. "Take forty men and secure the escape tunnels. Make sure they haven't been compromised, but finding the non-combatants is your first priority."

"The old ones and children are fine. Just a little shaken up," the stranger said.

"What? How do you know that?" Ghost asked.

"I made an alternate tunnel and got them out before the fighting started. They're in a small grove a quarter mile north west of here."

"You made another tunnel?" Ghost asked, as if the stranger had just told him he could fly.

"Yes," the stranger answered.

"That's impossible!" Vultus yelled out.

"Then don't believe me. Go see for yourself."

Ghost nodded. Vultus sighed. With that, he collected his men and went out in search of the grove.

The stranger took the first step toward Ghost. "I know you have questions and I will give you what answers I can. But right now, your men are dying. They need their general. Immediately following a battle, people think of two things: the first, that they have survived and can still be counted among the living. The second, sorrow for their brothers and sisters who have been severely wounded or killed. There are wounded to be tended to, last goodbyes to be said, dead to be burned or buried, loved ones to hold dear, and furens to be shed. We should both look to those things now."

He's right. Don't argue, Uncle.

Ghost suspiciously eyed the stranger. He finally nodded, and the men parted ways.

The stranger threw himself into the mending of the troops as recklessly as he had thrown himself into battle. He bandaged wounds, reset fractures, and carried away bodies. He talked to everyone. He listened to the young embellish their tales of foes they had fallen and asked the old questions about other battles they had fought while young. He drank and laughed with the lucky ones. He cried and mourned with those who were not so lucky, who had lost someone dear to them. Out of the hundred and fifty or so fighters of the Blue Order, thirty-seven had been killed, another eighteen of the wounded would join them within days, and twenty-eight more were wounded. Ghost had indeed turned the poor and angry of Sarpedon into quite the guerrilla force, but they were no army and when they met a real army the results were shattering. Alexandra watched. It was as if this stranger knew the force. He seemed genuinely interested in all of them and they seemed to welcome him in turn.

Alexandra went about her own work. But she rarely let the stranger out of her sight. When she did, she strained to hear some details about him. Where had he come from? How had he known about the attack? Who taught him to fight like that? What was his name? Yet for all her effort she could not distinguish any details. It wasn't that she couldn't hear them. The stranger didn't share any information about himself. He just kept asking them questions, and they kept talking. At one point, Alexandra wanted to shout *his name, damn you! Ask him his name!* Then she realized this was all quite intentional. Whoever this man was, he understood human nature. People love to talk about themselves. As long as he kept asking questions, they would keep talking, which meant he wouldn't have to.

Hours later, the soldiers, exhausted from the physical and emotional trauma of the day, began to retire. Others, formed in groups around a dozen camp fires. Few words were spoken; the mood was solemn.

Alexandra stood back with Ghost and twenty other guerillas. They found the stranger sitting on a rock at the entrance of the cave overlooking the waterfall. He had cleaned his sword and himself. The blade now sat flat across his legs and he gazed into the sheets of water pouring down a few feet in front of him.

"I'll approach him first," Ghost instructed. "Find out who and what he is. Be ready if he's a threat."

"Uncle, he saved the entire Blue Order and mended the

wounded. If he were a threat, I think we'd know it by now," Alexandra protested.

"This isn't time for your backtalk Alex! He saved the Blue Order by cutting through a small army singlehandedly. If there is the slightest chance he could pose a threat, we have to take it as an absolute."

"And do what, strategos?" another asked. "Kill him. Arrest him?"

"Let me worry about that. Just follow my lead and support me."

"No." Alexandra grabbed Ghost's shoulder. "You let me talk to him."

Ghost glared at his niece. "Fine. But I'll be watching you."

Alexandra walked forward and stopped behind the stranger. She felt nervous. But not nervous as one walking into danger. Rather as a school girl, wondering whether or not a boy would like her.

"We found the others," she began. "In the grove, as you said."

The stranger didn't move.

"They said the rock just split open, and you were waiting on the outside."

"Doesn't that sound ridiculous?" the stranger replied.

"They all said it. The old, the young, everyone. And after what I saw today..." Her voice broke off. "Who are you?"

"I told you Alexandra. I told you what would happen if you kept using civilians, children to run your guns, beggars to blow up temples and markets. I told you they would eventually track you here."

"How do you know my name?" Alexandra asked, beaming bewilderment.

"I know much about you. I know you are a daughter of the Women of the Red Sky. I know that you were taken from your home to train in the egoga under your father. And I know I have missed you like the winter misses the heat ever since I left this camp with him." The stranger sheathed his sword and rose to his feet, turning to address her.

Alexandra's eyes widened, her jaw dropped. In some ways he looked nothing like him, this man was far larger and more muscular than he was. Yet in some ways they were identical, the stranger's cheek bones and jaw structure were the same, his hair was the same jet black, and his eyes were the same dark brown, as was his skin. More telling than all this, she felt that feeling rise within her, the same as when she was last with...

"Zeno..."

"I told you I wasn't leaving you again."

Alexandra dropped her rifle and walked right in front of the man claiming to be her best friend. She put her right hand on his cheek. She looked into his eyes, deep in his eyes, as if she could see his soul.

"Sofia... Zeno, It's you."

Ghost and the others now emerged from the shadows. "What sorcery is this?" the commander of the Blue Order asked.

Alexandra could read her uncle's body language. He was tense. Ready to strike. The troops behind him all stood with their rifles pointed at Zeno.

"Are you scared of me, Nikolaus?" Zeno broke the silence.

"Should I be?"

"No. But I understand if you are. That is to be expected. But I must ask you work through this quickly. We have defeated the Karthagoi, but the Vampire will send an even more powerful force against us. If we don't work together, if you don't trust me, we will all die."

"Trust you to do what?" Ghost barked.

"To lead you."

The men looked at Ghost, as if for some clue as how to receive Zeno's words.

"Look, boy," Ghost began. "I don't know what sorcery you used to gain this power. But you're still no member of the Blue Order. I formed this force. I trained it myself. I have forgotten more battles than you have ever fought. These men will not fight for you."

"I'm not asking them to fight for me. I'm asking them to fight with me, for the rightful Archon of the Republic of Eighteen, your brother, Lysandros."

"The Republic is dead," a soldier yelled.

"Then why are we fighting?" Zeno asked. "Even if we slay the Vampire and the Rapti, even if we overturn his government, we have to replace it with something. As long as we fight for the Republic, the Republic lives. If we are going to go to war, if we are going to sacrifice our lives and those of the people around us, it will not be for some suicidal delusion, or for hate's sake, to kill our enemy only. It will be for the only thing worth the sacrifice of war: liberty."

"Liberty is a tall order," Ghost growled. "Revenge is a much more tangible goal."

"Can you give them revenge Nikolaus?" Zeno responded.

"How would you give it?" another woman asked.

"Whether liberty or vengeance is our goal, we will need more men. I will start by growing this force. Even now, Lysandros is mobilizing his forces in the Woadlands and the Militian Plains."

"Barbarians!" shouted another onlooker.

"Barbarians whose swords and guns kill as well as ours. They hate the Vampire just as much as we do. They are willing to fight and die alongside us. He is coming with these men and women. And not only these. He is rallying forces among the angels in Achemenidos, knights in Yorland, and warriors in Zutaera. In the meantime, I will attack Sarpedon, liberate the Elledic villages and towns under her control, and take control of the isthmus."

"Attacking Sarpedon would be suicide," Ghost solemnly said.

"Not for me, or anyone who follows me."

"Zeno, we have no way to offset the city walls," Alexandra protested from behind.

"I'll take care of that," Zeno replied.

"You're mad as the day is long, boy," Ghost balked.

"Oh Nikolaus, if you knew what I know, if you had seen what I have seen, you would know that I am far beyond madness. But madness or no, I will take Sarpedon. Tomorrow, at sun rise, I will set out for the city. I want Glaucon and his sycophants to be gripped by terror when they arise in the morning and see us at their gates, knowing they're helpless to defend themselves, just as our Archon felt when the Vampire took Dioskuria. Spread the word: Anyone who wants to join me can meet me here at that time. I compel no man to follow me except by his own rational choice. I will go alone if I have to."

With that, Zeno walked towards the crowd of men who were already parting in his wake.

Ghost grabbed him by the shoulder. "It's one thing to make a sneak attack on an enemy already engaged in combat. It's quite another to attack a walled city."

"You haven't seen half of what I can do," Zeno responded. "Tomorrow, Sarpedon falls. All you have to decide is whether or not you want to be a part of it." Zeno walked back into the cave and was gone.

Alexandra walked the familiar corridor she had walked dozens of times before. As she approached the opening to the pool to which she often came to collect herself, she could see the blue light, transcendent, glowing on the walls, and she knew that Zeno was waiting for her there.

"That was quite a show," she said to Zeno as she sat beside him. "I knew you would come here. Uncle made the troops swear to silence about what you said. But it's no use. Such things can't be kept secret. Your words are spreading through the camp. Rumor flies on eagle's wings. Uncle also ordered Vultus to take his ten strongest fighters and kill you during the night. They won't find you here of course. There's already a group of us that have pledged to meet you at the waterfall tomorrow morning."

"*Us?*"

"Of course, I'm coming. Someone has to protect you," Alexandra laughed.

Zeno turned to look at her. His eyes seemed heavy, as if he were on the brink of tears.

He's still human. He has to shed the furens too.

"Can you not be killed?" Alexandra asked.

"I can be killed; but it will take a lot more than ten of Nikolaus' *strongest fighters*," Zeno mocked.

"Zeno," Alexandra whispered with an affection that surprised even her. "What happened to you?"

CHAPTER IX
ZENO

Zeno stood with Lysandros peering across the open field. Across from them was the Stokian Starship.

The sun was starting to rise in the east. The forest seemed alive with activity as the creatures of night hurried to their hiding places.

And I'm trying to get inside the one place I can't hide.

Zeno sighed deeply and took a few steps. He stopped and turned to his mentor. "Are you coming?"

"I'm not." Lysandros stood planted. "This is your time. You must go alone."

"I'd prefer if you came."

Lysandros smiled. "I'm glad to hear that. Truly. Yet my answer remains the same. Surrender Zeno. Trust the Light Gods. Trust yourself."

Zeno frowned and nodded. He turned and approached the ship. The doors again opened before him, anticipating his arrival. Zeno didn't slow down, but continued his pace as he entered the starship.

The lights came on as soon as Zeno entered. This did not happen when Lysandros first brought him to the ship. This shocked him. He could see clearly. Then he felt a burst of wind hit him. His head hurt. Zeno closed his eyes and looked down for a moment. Then opened his eyes. The ship had changed yet again. The lights were on, and the walls were resplendent. Men and women in blue uniforms, each with silver capes hanging from them, stood along the walls at attention. They held something that looked like spears but the blades were transparent crystal.

Zeno stopped. He circled around, his breathing having picked up due to fear.

What am I seeing?

When he finally turned around, he saw a man standing in front of him. The man was bare chested and wore a silver loincloth. He held some type of bowl in his hands.

Thumos.

Zeno wasn't sure how he knew. But somehow, he knew this man was his forebearer. He also knew that he was watching Thumos unifying with the All Fire and that he must follow.

Some of the Stokians standing along the halls held some kind of trumpet-like instrument. They now raised these and blew them. Zeno had never heard such a sound before. It was neither pleasant or unpleasant. It just was, and was otherworldly. It was a sound from outer space. The tone was low, but not mournful. More than anything, it evoked in him a sense of responsibility. The melody was more of a call than a song. A call from eons of dead Stokians, stretching back to time immemorial, all calling him fourth to do his duty.

Thumos began walking forward and Zeno followed.

Zeno was hardly conscious that the path on which he now followed Thumos was not the path he had taken with the Priestess eighteen months before. Yet he knew where they were going.

They came to two great doors which opened before them. When Zeno walked in, he saw the Theomorphosis Chamber, but not as it had been. The walls and causeways glistened a blue green light. Fires shot forth from beneath the causeway and extended up, as tall as trees. Zeno looked up and now saw they extended out into the blackness of space. The ship had no ceiling in this room.

The room was also filled with spectators, several thousand by Zeno's estimation. Each wearing some variety of gown that stretched to their feet. These all looked on in silence.

Zeno looked forward and saw the stone sarcophagus. It looked mysterious and new. The alien runes that had long been faded when he first saw them were now exquisite in their sharpness. Most clear was the Σ that rested on the center of the lid. The great statue of Thumos was not standing over it. Next to the sarcophagus stood a woman. She wore the exact same gown and headdress as the Priestess of Sofia. This woman wore an additional breastplate which also bore the Σ.

Zeno followed Thumos to the sarcophagus. There, Thumos stopped.

"Have you come to offer yourself as a sacrifice?" the woman asked.

Zeno wasn't sure what to say. He felt the woman was speaking just to him. He started to respond but then Thumos spoke.

"I have come as a living sacrifice to that which constitutes life."

"Know that you must understand the cost." The woman walked towards Thumos. "For once you have been made one with the All Fire, you can never truly be human again. Are you willing to look into the void?"

"I am."

I'm not.

The woman was now in front of Thumos who bowed before her. Zeno stood there, looking on. The woman placed her hands on his head.

"See now. See as the All Fire sees."

Zeno screamed out and fell to the ground. Searing pain shot through his head. He rolled over onto his back. Before his eyes, he saw change. Not someone lone or something changing, rather the action of change itself. He saw time. He saw measurement. He saw order and beauty. He saw connectedness. He heard the voices of living things both so small to hardly be said to exist, and gargantuan things, so large they were worlds unto themselves. He heard them all distinctly, yet they were one. He saw creatures striking out against others. Yet they were hurt, not those they struck. Zeno understood that they could not understand why they were hurt, or that they were the authors of their own pain. He also saw creatures reaching into the bodies of other living things and touching their minds. Yet when they touched the minds of others, they were the ones who felt the warmth. Zeno knew deep in his bones all things are one thing, that each life is every life.

"It's true..." He murmured. "It's true... its truth... it's Truth."

Then he saw the face of a child. A boy, perhaps ten years by Ninivonian accounting. Zeno knew the boy was the child of Thumos. Thumos approached the child and wrapped his arms around him.

"What I do now, I do it for you," Thumos told the boy.

Zeno looked to his left. There sat a beast with twelve heads coming from space. On top of the beast sat a woman, naked, her face joyous and in her hand a cup. In the cup was blood. Behind her were untold trillions, purple, pupilless eyes, hungry and ravenous.

The diseased beast... The whore of her decadence... Techno-theocracy.

Zeno felt what Thumos felt: isolation, loneliness, fear. He knew this was due to the great horde coming against him.

Thumos rose. He put his child behind him and raised his hand to the coming creatures. There was a flash of light.

Zeno opened his eyes. He was indeed in the Theomorphosis Chamber, but it was as he had first seen it when Lysandros had brough him to the Stokian Ship. Zeno sat up, breathing heavy.

"You will not understand until later," the Priestess said.

Zeno turned to her and stood. He shook his head. "A ship of truth."

"Yes. That you do understand. That is the first thing but not the last. That is what you must embrace to begin. Man with his burning soul has but a moment to build a ship of truth in which to sail upon the sea of death. For death conquers all; love, hate, youth, courage, all but truth."

"The creatures?"

"The Erīeds."

"They didn't believe in truth."

"They don't believe in death. But death is coming for them. It's coming for us all. Unless you take up the Power of Thumos."

Zeno shook his head. He gasped his hair with both hands. "I don't think I can. I... I want to. I don't want to. I only want this power to save her."

"I know, Zeno."

"Will it even save her? Is anyone ever saved?"

"Saved from death. No. Alexandra will die. It is not the role of the Vessel to save life from death. It is its' role to bring life truth."

"I don't think I can, Priestess. I'm too small to let the void look into me. What will the All Fire find?"

"It will find itself. But shaped in your image." The Priestess walked towards him. "You're wondering if it is right for you to have this power. You're thinking that all you care about is Alexandra. You're scared you will lose her. Know that you must understand the cost. For once you have been made one with the All Fire, you can never truly be human again. Are you willing to look into the void?"

"Will I save her?"

The Priestess said nothing.

"Will I?" Zeno shouted.

"No. If you accept the Power of Thumos, she will die. If you do not, she will live for thousands of years. But it will not be her. She will lose her soul. In life, death will conquer. In death, life will be preserved."

"What does that mean?" Zeno screamed in desperation.

"I can't tell you, Zeno. I don't know myself. I can't know. It is beyond me. The only one who can understand is you. But you will not understand until later. If you take the first step now, when these things come to pass, you will look back on this conversation and you will know why you did what you did. You will know that you had to do what you did. There will be pain and tears. But in the end, you will have a peace that passes understanding, as will Alexandra when her time comes."

There's pain now! There are tears now! And there has been too many of both already. Not just for Alexandra and me. For everyone, for everything.

"It is not death that torments consciousness. It's lack of truth. Deliver them Zeno. Bring it to them."

Zeno understood that it didn't matter that he did not understand. It didn't matter if he did, and it was not the answer he wanted. All he could do was get in the sarcophagus.

The heavy lid raised up as if lifted by invisible hands. Zeno looked inside. Steam rose from within. He looked back to the Priestess who still stood there stone-faced.

Zeno took off his clothes and placed himself inside. As the lid closed, he thought, *I'm following you Thumos, wherever we shall go.* He felt a kinship with this alien whom he did not know. Whatever awaited him on the other side of this, Zeno deeply felt that he would come to know him more. He took great comfort in knowing that he would not walk this road alone.

The last vestiges of fire light were extinguished as the lid of the stone sarcophagus closed. But it was dark for only a moment. Blue light sprung fourth. Zeno couldn't distinguish the source. He couldn't even sense that there was a source. Zeno felt he had been transported to another place; another vision perhaps. He felt he was floating through space. He tried to reach out to test this theory, but he could not move his hand. He tried to move the other arm, his legs, his feet. He tried to turn his head. His body remained immobile. He was paralyzed.

Fear now sat in. The blue light grew increasingly bright. Blinding. He tried to close his eyes. They would not respond. His eyes began to burn. Was this *the void* the woman and the Priestess speak of? He grew warm, then hot, too hot. His temperature seemed to be rising from within him. It burned. Zeno tried to scream out in pain. Again, his mouth and tongue did not obey.

The pain grew unbearable. He now saw blue flames dancing in his periphery. Not coming towards him; coming from within him. He was burning. The flames spread over his entire body. Zeno sensed his extremities had burned to ash, yet he still felt the agony of the fire consuming him. His eyes burned, yet he could still see. The pain was such that he could not even contemplate escape. It was the type of pain that so demanded attention as to keep one bound in the present. There was no tracking time. All his consciousness was filled with suffering.

Do not resist. He heard a voice in his mind that was not his. *Surrender to the pain. Let yourself burn.* It was Thumos. *You did not choose the All Fire. It chose you. You would not feel this were you not capable of bearing it. Let go. Follow it. Follow me.*

How do I know that is true?

You can't. You have no choice but to trust. You are not your feelings. You are not your sufferings. You are not your consciousness. You are not. Not really. Embrace it. Embrace us. Embrace truth.

The heat began to cool. Fire still remained, but lessened, and the pain with it. Given the torment he had already endured, this pain seemed bearable by comparison. Had this process reached a plateau? Was this now a downward trajectory? Everything slowed.

Movement decreases with heat loss. A basic principle of physics. For the well-trained warrior, the battle slows down. It does not overwhelm him. A well-known tenet of soldiery.

Zeno began to breathe slower. The pain decreased, as did the light. All pain and light faded. His tactile sensations returned. He could now distinguish hand from chest from foot. The last sparkle of light shrank and then went dark. The lid of the sarcophagus opened. Zeno could see with what he knew were his eyes. He saw the ceiling of the chamber. Yet he saw so much more. He could distinguish the smallest participles of the stone that made up the chamber ceiling. It all came in and out of focus, as if his eyes had become some kind of microscope gone made. But he could see individual atoms, neutrons, electrons. He saw everything. He could hear cellular activity, his own, and that of the Priestess. He could smell a million different scents.

Zeno rose from the sarcophagus. He knew he was taller. He looked at his arms and chest, all of which were much larger and more muscled than they had been. He stared for a moment at his hands, as if they were strange things he had not seen before. He looked to the priestess.

"Your new body will seem strange at first. You must learn it anew. You must stay with me until you are ready to enter the world again."

"What have I become?"

"You have become Truth, the salvation of men."

CHAPTER XVII
THE VAMPIRE

The Tower of the Sphinx was alive with activity. Generals, soldiers, support staff, slaves, and emissaries from every kingdom were present. The Vampire: Terror and Woe of Ninivon, had ordered a council of all rulers who served under him. The council consisted of the rulers of the ten nations who sided with the Vampire during the Great Terror. Every other kingdom was a vassal state ruled through regents. These were the rulers of the world.

They met in the council chamber on the highest floor of the tower. It was a room designed for military deliberations between the Archons of the Republic and their most trusted generals. An iron throne rested in the back of the room, elevated on steps, overlooking a rectangular oaken table, and at the opposite wall, oval windows from which one could look out on the city below.

All the expected delegates had arrived and taken their seats. There was the Emperor of Rema: Tarquinius Augustus, the High Warden of the cyclopes of the Grey Peaks: Tyanus, the Pharaoh of Osaeria: Akmoses, the Consul of Tyra: Hanno, the Sultan of the Hipperi: Iban Alzared, the Queen of Bramhas: Ravi of house Zachaves, the Queen of the angels of Dimron: Elliana Zid. And the King of Jona: Phillip Monclair. Only Glaucon, Emperor of Sarpedon, and Ahuatzi, queen of the mermen of Itzel were absent.

Two guards were posted at the double iron doors. As the doors opened every delegate rose from their seats and dropped to their knees. The Vampire entered the room. He wore black pants and boots and a crimson leather cuirass over a white shirt. A long purple cape hung from his shoulders. His body was lean, but well-muscled. His grey hair flung about, as if carelessly. His purple eyes, stern, yet slightly inviting. His skin was smooth and hairless, not just fair, but snow white, as if he had no blood running through his veins. A Joni broad sword hung at his side.

The Vampire promptly mounted the steps and sat on the throne, clutching the armrests as he leaned back.

"Rise and be seated," the Vampire said in a soft voice. All the rulers of Ninivon rose from their knees and sat down. "By now you must all know why I have summoned you," the Vampire began. "A rebellion has begun. This is neither unusual nor unexpected since virtually all of you have had uprisings in your nations and territories since we overthrew the Republic. Until now, I have let you deal with them individually as best you saw fit. But this rebellion is different. A terrorist organization calling itself the Blue Order harassed Sarpedon for months. Due to Glaucon's incompetence, I assigned a regiment of Karthagoi to Sarpedon to deal with the matter. Not only were they slaughtered, but now the rebels have sacked Sarpedon itself. We have lost the isthmus. Furthermore, there are reports that additional rebellions have ignited in Acheminidos, and Zutaera, to add to those already afoot in Yorland and among the northern savages. All these nations are sending additional troops to Sarpedon to swell the rebels' numbers which already include the Sarpedonian regular army. They have massacred our garrisons and taken control of the airfield. I do not have to remind any of you how pivotal the isthmus is for logistics and transport. Now, my lords, how shall we deal with this?"

Akmoses spoke first, "My Lord, the Sarpedonians have always been lukewarm allies. They are a city of cowards that have preserved themselves through alliance rather than war for thousands of years. It is no great thing that they have been conquered. Nor should we concern ourselves that the Karthagoi have been defeated. As for the other cities, when we burn their homes and throw their children from the city walls, they will fall back in line. Let Osaeria mobilize our forces, give us the honor of slaying your enemies."

"We don't know how many of them there are," interjected Elliana. "Our Lord has brought us together precisely because individual attacks have already failed. I think it would be unwise to blindly send in more troops before we have an idea what we are up against."

"We know what we're up against. A band of murderous rebels," Akmoses replied.

"The assault was led by Hashdrubal of Dido," interjected Hanno. "He was one of the finest commanders in Tyra."

"He was a giant and a killer," Elliana countered. "But he was also a fool. He knows only one means of attack, always forward, always head on. He has the tactical sense of a rock. Easily outsmarted."

Hanno seemed annoyed but held his peace.

"We have heard many wild stories about what happened in Sarpedon," spoke Tarquinius. "Do any of us know the truth?"

"There were six Joni regiments in Sarpedon when the city fell but not one man survived," said Phillip. "The reports we received were incoherent, unbelievable. But we have seen surveillance footage from the city. It was not an army that attacked Sarpedon but a man, one man, accompanied by a few paltry dozen. The footage shows him walking up to the city and shouting that if Glaucon surrendered and gave himself over to be tried for war crimes, he would spare the aristocrats. If not, he said, he would kill any who resisted. Glaucon sent a contingent of troops to apprehend the man and his allies. But he slaughtered them all. Then he ran up to the gates through artillery fire. The gates burst open before him on their own, as if some magical force preceded him that battered them open as he reached them. But the man did not need to recover from using magic as all sorcerers do. He kept attacking. Our men poured around him like water around a stone. Some say they saw him shot and stabbed but he never fell. He kept fighting."

"Many of us have already seen this footage, it's unbelievable, and choppy. It could have been altered," Tarquinius exclaimed. "Do you have something new to tell?"

"Only that this man killed everyone, everyone my Lord," he looked to the Vampire. "By himself. Even his own companions were horrified by the display of his power. Word of his exploits has incited the other rebellions. Everywhere in Yorland, our garrisons are finding this." Phillip pulled a brown cloth with an "Σ" from his tunic. "The totem of Sofia, my Lord. They are calling him *the Demigod*."

"That is the stuff of fantasy and children's stories. Likely propaganda put out by this Blue Order to recruit," yelled Tyanus. "It can't be true."

"That's what the Dioskurians said when Vorsehelgda fell, remember?" Tarquinius rebutted. "By the time people accepted the truth it was too late."

"That was different," said Ravi.

"How?" asked Tarquinius.

"There is more," continued Phillip. "This man, whoever he is, claims that Lysandros, of the House of Polymaxes, was crowned Archon and keeper of the Republic by Asha before she died." Phillip turned to look at the Vampire as he whispered those final words. "He says that Lysandros is this *Brown Chieftain* we have heard so much about among the Woads and is marching to join him at Sarpedon."

"We never found a body," Iban added. They had all long hoped that Lysandros was dead, but feared the contrary. If alive, Lysandros would have been the greatest threat to their power.

"I'm not sure it matters," added Hanno. "What matters is what the people believe, and they believe this man. They believe that an Archon of the Republic still lives and they believe this man, this *Demigod*, possesses powers equal to those of you, my Lord."

The Vampire half smiled and tilted his head.

"A lie to be certain," Hanno immediately modified his words. "But the common people are prone to believe lies. Some even believe that he is an incarnation of Ultor the Avenger sent to throw back your power. Such belief is irrational, but it is contagious. Such belief is a threat to us."

"Belief may be a threat to you, Hanno." The Vampire silenced the room. "But not to me, nor is Lysandros, if he indeed still lives. This man, on the other hand, this *Demigod* could prove problematic, if he can actually do the things they say he can do."

"My Lord, I volunteer our army to put down this rebellion," Akmoses said. "I will lead them myself. By the next moon you will have the head of this Demigod and, if he does still live, Lysandros."

There was an intermission of silence. Anxious looks were passed about between each of the leaders as the Vampire glared at each of them.

"My lord," Tarquinius began. "Pharaoh Akmoses is a foolish man who would make the same mistakes for which he criticizes others. I do not believe these wild claims. But when you came to Ninivon, none of our enemies believed your power. Your power was great. But equally important, particularly in those first few weeks of campaign, was the willful ignorance of our foes. It gave us time to plan and move freely, consolidating our resources, and calculating each move to the finest detail. This was a gift from our enemy. We should not return the favor."

Akmoses rose, fire erupting from his eyes.

He was cut off as the iron doors flung open. In came Lana Tarquinia, adorned in dark purple robes, senator of Rema, daughter of Tarquinius and the Vampire's de facto queen. She removed her hood. She was beautiful, but not in a natural way. Lana reeked of an evil that was foreign and disturbing. Hers was not the evil of primitive men, who kill and rape and steal according to their needs and opportunity. No, Lana's evil was something darker, not born of the passions, but of the mind. As daughter of the Emperor of Rema, there were rumors that, as a teenage girl, Lana tortured prisoners and criminals for sport. She would order them chained outside during the winter snow. They were given a coat to make sure hypothermia did not prematurely kill them. But they were barefoot. Cold water was poured on their feet and she would watch, day after day, until gangrene rotted their exposed limbs right before her eyes. Sometimes, their feet even exploded. Another of Lana's favorite torments was to strip down young women whom her guards had kidnapped, cover their bodies with honey and then chain them up in her garden. Insects would flock to the victims and slowly devour their flesh. There was even a rumor that she created the Vampire through her sorceries. She instantly commanded the attention of everyone, even the Vampire.

"Sit down, Pharaoh," she began as she walked to the steps leading up to the Vampire's throne. "Save your strength for the battle ahead. For a terrible power is rising against us.

"As you all know, I have my own spies. As well as my own methods of extracting information. Lord Phillip is correct. It was one man who sacked Sarpedon, the same man who broke Hashdrubal's forces in the Sofia Forest. The Blue Order is nothing. The other rebellions are nothing. Even Lysandros, although he lives and is the last living Archon of the Republic, is nothing. This Demigod is everything. If we strike him down, we have nothing to fear from the others. But he by himself can destroy us; all of us. He must die. No effort should be spared until we have his head," Lana raised her voice for emphasis.

"My lady," Tyanus began. "Are you then suggesting we make a full-force attack to deal with one man?"

"No," Lana replied. "I suggest we make three. We should mobilize two full armies, one to attack from the east and another from the south to trap the Demigod at the isthmus. We will also need a third for our protection here at Dioskuria."

The delegates, even those who had argued for caution such

as Phillip and Elliana arose in protest. Shouts filled the room. That Lana, who knew their fighting strength better than any, thought three full armies were needed to deal with one man was not only illogical but insulting. Only the Vampire and her father, Emperor Tarquinius, remained seated and quiet. The Vampire knew his consort well and sensed Lana's anxiety; he knew she wound not suggest such measures lightly. Suggesting such a show of strength only meant one thing, she was scared. The Vampire wondered what could scare a woman who herself terrified so many?

Lana held her peace. The Vampire rose from his throne, ending all protest. Not a man dared to utter another word.

"Leave," the Vampire commanded. "All of you. The council is dismissed. I will tell you what we shall do when I emerge."

Lana stood still. He wanted to talk with her alone. The delegates filed out of the council room. Once the other kings and leaders had left, the Vampire came down from his throne and stared at Lana.

"You know me better than any of them. You know what I'm capable of. Why should I deploy three armies to deal with one man?"

Lana took some seconds to choose her words and tone carefully, then spoke. "It is not just the testimony of the Karthagoi survivors or the footage from Sarpedon. I have consulted my magics; he has found the Theomorphosis chamber."

Within minutes, the Vampire erupted into the command center with Lana behind. His purple eyes blazed with an even more intense fire than normal. The command center was filled with kings and delegates, soldiers and slaves, intelligence officers and support staff, all subservient to the Vampire. Practically every wall of the massive room was covered with computers and monitors displaying various tracking systems and communication devices. The command center was just that, it was designed to be the command-and-control fortress of the Archons of the Republic. From within these walls, they could have instantaneous intelligence and command a battlefield anywhere on the planet. It was clear that whatever Lana had said to him, disturbed the Vampire greatly. There was little doubt what his orders would be.

"I want every kingdom mobilized for battle," the Vampire roared, walking up to the edge of a small staircase leading to the main area of the command center "The Dimronians and Bramhai will consolidate here at Dioskuria to augment our defenses. The Hipperi will ride east and join with the Joni, who will land on the northern coast of the isthmus. Phillip and Iban, you will retake the Isthmus of Sarpedon. You will be augmented by ten thousand Rapti and share joint command. Sir Le Flor of my personal knights will accompany you in an advisory role, along with a hundred Equitati. Rema, Osaeria, and Tyra will mobilize their full armies in the east. The Xhiputzec navy, as well as our air carriers, will transport them north of the Sofia Forest, where you will cut the rebels off from the south. I want this demigod and his army surrounded on all sides. I will take no chances, and if you do, it will be at the risk of your lives. It will not be hard to force him out of Sarpedon; he will want an open battle. Invite him into the valley of Drisdos. Wait until our eastern allies have all landed to support you, then attack in bulk. Close him in and slaughter all of them. Destroy any villages and settlements you pass on the way. Let them see the price of their rebellion. Bring only the Demigod back to me alive."

The Vampire now turned to an old Dioskurian general, Gregorios, commander of his air armada. "Alert Altus Mons. I want a full contingent of bombers over Sarpedon within twelve hours."

CHAPTER IX
ALEXANDRA

It had been nearly nine days since Zeno sacked Sarpedon. Technically, he was not alone. Alexandra and thirty-four others had met him in the cave the morning he set off. They all seemed trepidatious; Alexandra couldn't blame them. By noon, they had made it to the city. The battle that ensued, if it can be called that, lasted a few hours. The Joni and Sarpedonians threw themselves at Zeno in droves. They broke against him like waves on a cliff. Thousands fell.

Alexandra and the members of the Blue Order who followed took positions along the walls and shot point blank into the mob of soldiers that came at Zeno. Hardly anyone noticed them, so preoccupied were the defenders with the Demigod among them. At times Alexandra caught herself just watching as a spectator. From such a high vantage point, she could see all that Zeno had become. Her best friend looked like a giant among children. There was such elegance in his movements; it was almost like a dance, well-rehearsed, every step memorized and precise, having been practiced a thousand times. Yet everywhere, men were screaming, bleeding, running away deprived of arms, crawling away deprived of legs. Others were run through or completely sliced in half. It was like watching a terrible storm, both awe-inspiring and fearful. There could be no mistake; Zeno was to be feared, like a tempest, not malevolent in any way because his nature was above benevolence and malevolence, yet supremely lethal.

Before too long, half the army of Sarpedon mutinied, taking up arms against the occupying Joni and even their own troops who remained loyal to Glaucon. Perhaps reports of the city's prosperity under Glaucon had been greatly exaggerated, or maybe they were just saving their own skins. At any rate, they were now rising up in arms against Glaucon and his government. Zeno welcomed their change of heart. Other Sarpedonian soldiers threw down their arms and begged for mercy, which Zeno granted.

After the battle, the first order was to completely stamp out pockets of resistance. In this endeavor, it was truly fortuitous that half the Sarpedonian army had changed their allegiances, and that Zeno had been wise enough to show mercy to those who had surrendered. As powerful as Zeno was, he could not be in two places at once and in order to take and hold an occupied city, soldiers were needed to search out the enemy, seize buildings and neighborhoods which the enemy had previously occupied, and maintain that territory, gradually driving the opposition from the city. This redeemed Sarpedonian army was all too happy to go about this dangerous and grueling labor. Zeno went out daily on patrol to aid them in their task. Within a week, Zeno, Alexandra, the Blue Order, and the now liberated Sarpedonian army had pushed hostile troops out of the city and had rounded up the aristocrats who funded them.

The second order was to deal with the aristocracy, all of which were loyal to the Vampire. This group, some two hundred in number, included not just high-ranking government officials but the richest citizens in the city and the Emperor of Sarpedon, Glaucon himself. Zeno called them into the council hall in the imperial palace. They were packed in the large room under an armed escort led by Alexandra and the Blue Order. When they entered the hall, Zeno rose to meet them. He wore black trousers with a blue shirt. A grey belt stretched across his waist, and steel wristbands hung on his arms. He was unarmed save for a large, high-caliber ion pistol that hung on his belt. His black hair flowed wild, unkempt, and his eyes shone with dignity but also blazed with fury. He was an intimidating sight, particularly considering the horrors the aristocrats had just seen him do.

When they entered, Zeno ordered them to stand against the wall. Some looked at him and shivered in terror, others with pure hatred, all knew they had no choice but to listen.

"My lords, I have much work to do so I will make this quick. Your city has been liberated. But I know to you, the former rulers of Sarpedon, it must seem more like it is occupied. Regardless of your view, this much is fact, and surely you will agree, my forces and I are now in possession of the city, and the isthmus. Your Joni knights are dead and your native Sarpedonian hoplites have all sworn allegiance to me, partly out of fear, partly because I am actually paying them respectable wages. It was truly arrogant on your part to pay the men who protect your power so little. But I digress. You all betrayed the Republic of Eighteen during the Great Terror. I could legally kill you all right here in this chamber, confiscate your property, redistribute it to the poor, and I would be not only justified, but loved by the citizens of this city, whom you have abused these past twelve years."

"Those citizens would all be dead had we not sided with the Vampire," a noble whimpered.

Zeno looked at the man and then looked around the room. He wanted to see the looks on everyone's face, hear their gasps. And gasp they did; each unsure if they would see the outside of the chamber again.

"You are right," Zeno replied. "Because of the importance of the isthmus every invading army hits Sarpedon first. It's hard to be loyal when you're the punching bag of the world. Because of that fact, I will not kill you." As soon as the words left Zeno's mouth, there was a universal sigh of relief in the room. "In return for my generosity you will free all your slaves and donate fifty percent of your liquid assets and land holding to the state to be redistributed to those in need and hasten the rebuilding of the city."

The mood immediately changed from gratefulness to disbelief and even rage. The hall erupted in screams and curses. Zeno slammed his left hand into the solid stone table before him with a deafening thud and broke off a piece that easily weighed fifty pounds. All shouts ceased.

"Calm yourselves, my lords," Zeno said with indignation in his voice. All obeyed. "Additionally, your city will be used as the staging point for our rebellion. In a few days, a great army will come here, an army loyal to Lysandros, of the House of Polymaxes, the one true Archon of the Republic."

"You're a fool!" Glaucon blurted out. All eyes turned to the Emperor of the city, a tall and slender man. "You're a damn fool!"

"My lord, please be silent!" another aristocrat urged.

"I will not be silent. I will not cower under this madman," Glaucon boasted back.

"You will cost us our lives!" another bellowed.

"Coward!" Glaucon pushed the fat old aristocrat down to the floor. "He's lying to you. He's going to kill you anyway." He turned to Zeno. "You may have taken this city, and you may hold it for some weeks or even months. But you know whom we serve. You know who will be coming for you. Whatever power you think you have, he will beat you, and not just beat you, he will humiliate you, torment you, torment those dear to you. You will live just long enough to see his agents of hell ripping at the throats of the same people you have *liberated*. You will feel the guilt of their slaughter as they cry for the mercy of death, knowing you failed to protect them. And if any do survive, they will be returned to the very chains you..."

Zeno rose to his feet, cutting the emperor off. His first step seemed slow as if his foot weighed hundreds of pounds. But then his pace quickened. He did not walk faster with each step but more purposefully, more intentionally, as if the few steps between him and Glaucon were all that separated him from his heart's desire. The look of indignation on Glaucon's face morphed into anxiety. His breath quickened. He was scared. As were the other aristocrats about him. They all stepped aside as the man who had taken their city singlehandedly approached.

Zeno stopped in front of the emperor. "My parents were born in Limnae. Do you know it? Of course not. Why would you? It's a gutter in the north sector of Dioskuria. I spent my childhood watching roaches climb out of our bathtub, just like some of the poor boys whom you flayed alive for running weapons. And yes, I know exactly who is coming for me. But he doesn't know who is coming for him."

There was silence in the hall. Zeno stared at Glaucon. Then, as if he heard some vital secret spoken behind a closed door, Zeno tilted his head to the right. A look of worry came over his face. He turned to Alexandra. "Alter the Sarpedonian air armada, tell them to get their ships in the air. Fire the city alarm system and get the men to the anti-aircraft guns. We're under attack." With that he burst from council hall and out onto a large pavilion overlooking the central sector of the city, leaving both the Blue Order and the Sarpedonian aristocracy behind.

There, Zeno stood, staring off into the east. After a few seconds, Alexandra joined him on the pavilion along with some members of the Blue Order. "I altered Theodotius," she began. "He's getting the piolets to their fighters now and the Sarpedonian gunners are at their stations. What is it? Our radar systems haven't picked up any incoming aircraft."

"They will."

Below, the city streets exploded with activity. All were frantically running to bomb shelters constructed deep beneath the surface. Shouts and screams of terror rose like smoke from a fire. Many of the very old and very young were overrun trying to reach safety. The Sarpedonian military tried to restore some order and safely guide the citizenry to the shelters but they were undermanned following Zeno's slaughter of some half of their number and taken by surprise. On the ramparts, the gunners sat at their stations, fission turret guns armed and ready, the necessary support personnel, re-loaders and machinists, flanking the guns on both sides.

High above, the first Sarpedonian fighters took to the air. Almost as soon as they were visible, Dioskurian fighters and heavy bombers came into view. There were dozens of the former and easily twelve of the latter. The Vampire meant to pulverize the city with an air raid. If he was aware that Zeno held the old aristocrats, all of whom were loyal to him, the Vampire didn't care. As the opposing ships drew closer, both prepared for the oncoming air battle. Fighters on both sides let loose a barrage of ion fire as individual piolets took evasive maneuvers, leaving formation. The gunners began to fire from the Sarpedonian ramparts.

Inside the council hall, the aristocrats began to panic and scatter. The members of the order still inside with them, unsure of what to do, opened fire. Having heard the ions, Zeno and Alexandra rushed back into the hall.

"Cease fire!" Zeno roared. "Cease fire!" Some thirty were already either dead or wounded. "See to the wounded," Zeno ordered some of the Order. He then reached down and grabbed Glaucon, who had been shot in the leg and laid on the floor whimpering. "The rest of you, come with me," Zeno commanded.

Zeno brought Glaucon out onto the pavilion. In the eastern sky, the air battle was in full motion. The Sarpedonian fighters were heavily outnumbered. Several planes had already been shot down. With the numerical advantage, the first bombers had broken through and were now making a pass over the city to drop their payload.

The anti-aircraft guns unleashed a barrage of ion fire in the direction of the bombers. One of the Dioskurian fighters broke off and fired down on the outer walls, igniting the gun positions and killing the men manning them.

"We must seek shelter!" Glaucon panicked, twitching like a wounded squirrel in Zeno's mighty right hand.

"We're not going anywhere," Zeno replied.

Alexandra, receiving updates regarding the air battle through her comm, followed with many of the Blue Order, their rifles all pointed at the Sarpedonian aristocrats, herding them out onto the pavilion.

The lead bomber lowered its elevation. It fired its payload at the air field north of the palace. Neither Alexandra nor those with her could see from the pavilion but they heard a colossal explosion behind them. The airfield was destroyed.

A second bomber lowered, this one heading right for the palace. It seemed to fly straight towards the pavilion. It let loose its payload which slammed into the western sector of the imperial palace. The Sarpedonian palace had been reinforced with ion resistant Ninivonium. Nevertheless, under such a heavy assault, the walls began to quake.

Down below, the rest of the city had no such protections. Several missiles and bombs fell. Fighters fired on the city streets as well, which were full of panicked civilians. Everywhere was fire and death.

Another bomber lowered their altitude and seemed to head straight for the pavilion on which Zeno, Alexandra, and the aristocrats of Sarpedon now stood. The aristocrats were terrified. They began to scream and protest. But they did not try to force their way out. The Blue Order had already demonstrated that they would kill them if they tried to flee. Rather, they fell to their knees and begged their captors to deliver them to safety.

For their part, the Blue Order was also rattled. Two other bombers lowered altitude.

"Zeno..." Alexandra said. Her voice was panicked.

"I can hear your heartbeat speed up," Zeno said.

"Why aren't we heading for shelter?"

"Trust me, Alex," Zeno replied. "They need to see this. You need to see this."

The lead bomber released two missiles; both screaming

towards the imperial palace. The aristocrats and the Blue Order guarding them on the pavilion now began to break and flee. Only Alexandra held firm but her eyes were growing, fear rising up within her and struggling with discipline for supremacy. It was a true testament to her bravery that she still stood there with Zeno in the missiles' path. Glaucon was flailing his arms and legs and struggling to get away. But Zeno held him suspended by the collar of his fine shirt.

The missiles neared. Zeno's eyes closed. His brow furrowed. A look of struggle appeared on his face, as if he had a demon fighting to break through his skull. Suddenly, he opened his eyes. He raised his free hand. The missiles both exploded in midair.

Alexandra's mouth fell open. Glaucon stopped his struggling and looked on in wonder. All the civilians and military, both in the palace and on the streets below, ceased their terror-stricken strivings.

A thunderous explosion ignited across the sky as the very bomber that fired the missiles drove through their combustion, and itself exploded. The crowds looking from below roared in both relief and shock. Another three bombers lowered to let lose their payload. Zeno closed his eyes and roared like a wounded lion. He was in deep pain. He stumbled a bit, but then steadied himself, straightened his posture, and again opened his eyes and extended his hand. The munitions within ignited; each of the bombers burst into flames.

This must have rattled the other Dioskurian aircraft. Three Sarpedonian fighters came up behind another bomber and shot it down. The anti-aircraft guns brought down another two bombers.

Meanwhile, in Sarpedon, the Dioskurian fighters pulled up as well and disengaged from the Sarpedonian defensive squadron. The battle was over.

Zeno fell to his knees, breathing heavily. He had long since dropped Glaucon to the ground who still sat there. A member of the Blue Order put his rifle in the former emperor's face and escorted him back into the council hall with the other aristocrats. Alexandra rushed to Zeno's side and propped him up on her shoulder.

"Zeno? Zeno! God damnit! Wake up." Alexandra shook him violently. Zeno appeared to be in a deep trance. Finally, he bobbed his head twice and raised it for good before turning to his friend.

"It was harder than I thought," Zeno whispered. "I'm not sure how much longer I could have done that."

Five minutes later, Zeno came storming back into the council hall with Alexandra close behind. The other aristocrats had not seen the great toll destroying the bombers had taken on him. But whatever such a deed had cost him in stamina and energy, he had clearly regained now. Magic always extracted a heavy toll on its users. But no single sorcerer could have done what Zeno had. It even took the Vampire an entire platoon of sorcerers to bring the walls down at Ying-Chau. Zeno walked in front of the men who only minutes earlier, were certain they would be ignited by the missiles of the very dictator they served. They all knew what Zeno had done. As he came into the room, his countenance fiery like that of a lion fresh from the kill, they all shivered.

"Make no mistake, change is coming for you, my lords. But you should not fear." Zeno reassured the aristocracy, many of whom had openly cried when they saw the missiles heading for them. "The Vampire would kill his own friends the moment they are an obstacle to them. I, on the other hand, spare my enemies, so long as they swear to never raise arms against me again. You will keep your lives, and fifty percent of your personal wealth which will be more than enough to relocate to another city, which I will allow. This, is my mercy to you. You have all done very well for yourselves serving the Vampire. You will be allowed to enjoy the fruits of your conquests," Zeno looked around the room with a cold stare, careful to make eye contact with as many as he could, "so long as you don't get in my way."

The nobility of Sarpedon was then escorted out by the Blue Order. Only Zeno and Alexandra remained in the room. With the others gone, Zeno's strength again failed. He practically passed out. But Alexandra was there to catch him and she walked him over to the chair at the head of the council table where she sat him down.

"Hey, look at me," she said, grasping Zeno's face into her hands. "Are you all right? Shall I find a doctor?"

"No. No one can see me like this," Zeno protested. "I just need a few minutes. I'll be fine."

Alexandra was unconvinced. Nevertheless, she obeyed. She sighed deeply. "How the hell did you do that? Even witches and warlocks have to use spells. You just...stood there."

"I concentrated hard. It was as if I could see and control the individual molecules in the bombs if I concentrated hard enough." He shook his head. "But I feel as if my head is about to burst." He looked deep into Alexandra's eyes. She slowly shook her head in disbelief.

"What kind of wizard have you become, Zenosthenes Andrea?"

So, you're not untouchable. You have weaknesses and limitations. You probably don't know what they are any more than I. There will be times when you are vulnerable. You can fight the world, and win. But you will need someone to watch your back, to stand guard over you in times like these. I can do that.

In that moment, Alexandra felt she had a sense of purpose that had been denied her all her life. She had always been a warrior; but she had always been told for whom and what to fight by those over her. First her grandmother among the Militae, then Lysandros, then Ghost. When she left with Zeno from the Blue Order's cave, she thought this role would be transferred to him. Now she understood she would have a very different role. She was the soul mate, the *phile*, to the Demigod.

She would be closer to him than anyone. He would show his weakness to her alone. She would be with him when he was most vulnerable. She would defend him when he could not defend himself. Ninivon needed him; but he needed her. This was her purpose. She could not save Ninivon herself, but she could save the man who could save Ninivon.

All the Light Gods and Dark, they will not take you away from me. I swear, I will cross Tartarus itself to defend you even if I must stand alone between you and death. There is no gulf I would not close to fight at your side.

CHAPTER XIX
ZENO

"Zeno!" Alexandra shouted from atop the ramparts at the Sarpedonian air field. "An army is approaching!"

Zeno was rebuilding an air control tower that had been destroyed in the bombing. The tower was almost complete, but the air field was still mostly in ruins. Once the political and economic structure of the city was rebuilt, with leaders in place loyal to him, Zeno began rebuilding this and other parts of the city with its citizens. They welcomed him as one of their own. They followed his orders and honored his wishes without being told. He in turn was tireless in his efforts to rebuild what they had lost. The people marveled as he put roads and bridges back together. With the power at Zeno's disposal; the city began to function again within days.

Zeno walked to the high wall atop which Alexandra stood. "Who rides at their head?"

Alexandra looked down with a scowl, rageful as a lioness. "Who do you think rides at their fucking head?" she yelled back.

Zeno smiled. "Open the gates."

In they poured mounted on steeds and on foot. Riding at point was Lysandros. Behind him were the Militae, the Women of the Red Sky.

Behind these marched the Woads, wearing their clan tartans and leather armor, their wild hair blowing in the wind and their rifles and mighty claymores on their backs. Some were mounted but most were on foot.

As the allied army poured in, Zeno was amazed. Lysandros had exceeded everything he could have possibly hoped for. Once the entire force was within the gate, Lysandros dismounted and Zeno ran to embrace him with a hug.

"Wha... how?" Zeno mumbled releasing the embrace.

"I told you, the Vampire has many enemies and I can be very persuasive." Lysandros smiled and turned back to the gates through which three more nations entered.

The first were Yorish mounted knights in full plate mail. They carried lances, pistols, and bastard swords at their sides. The infantry came next, wearing less plate armor but more ion resistant chain mail and leather cuirasses. These carried longer shields, broadswords or battle axes, and rifles. These men hailed from the north country, where the sun seldom shined and the wind always blew. They were one of the two Angolid peoples of Ninivon. The other were the Joni who lived on their island in the middle of the Lumen Ocean. These two cousin nations had long been hostile to each other. When the Vampire came, the Joni saw it as an opportunity to conquer their Yorish brothers and did so.

The ebony skinned warriors of Zutaera followed. They wore breastplates, shoulder guards, leg guards, and greaves. But beneath the armor they wore no clothing save for a long battle skirt under utility belts. Daggers rested on their right shoulders and Ida broadswords rested on their waists. Forty-inch, leaf cut blades, with a long handle and no hilt. They carried ion shotguns on their backs. Some were bald, others had dreadlocks.

The final army was that of Acheminidos: angels. These flew over the walls and landed around the others. The Angelic peoples were divided into two nations: Acheminidos and Dimron. Both rested in the Sky Piercer Mountains. As with the Joni and the Yorish, these two nations shared a common ancestor, but they had hated each other longer than anyone could remember, each trying to drive the other out of the mountains.

While both were angel nations, Acheminidos and Dimron could not be more different in culture; the former building great cathedrals and palaces in the Sky Piercer Mountains that stretched into the heaves, the later building pyramids. Before they both joined the Republic, they often waged war on each other. During the Great Terror, Dimron sided with the Vampire. Acheminidos was overwhelmed and conquered. Each angel wore their traditional red battle helmets and carried long range rifles and throwing lances on their backs with pistols at their sides, decked out in light chain mail armor. Their armor was light so as not to impede their powers of flight, but more susceptible to gun fire. The Acheminids flew on two massive wings which protruded from their lower shoulders. Each wing was between six and eight feet long when fully extended.

"Actually, it was easy," Lysandros replied. "Acheminidos was itching to rebel. They just needed someone to give them a push. When we came back south through Zutaera, they had already thrown out the occupying Dioskurian and Remani garrisons. The Yorish, Zutaerae, and Acheminids number about forty-three hundred collectively. And I brought another eight thousand Woads and three thousand Militae. There are also three supply planes hidden eighty miles to the southeast. They're full of food, weapons, ammunition, medical supplies, and money. Contributions from Yorland, Zutaera, and Acheminidos. They are all fully behind us in this war."

Zeno shook his head in disbelief. "How did you get them to give so much?"

"They heard about how you sliced through a small army of Karthagoi, took Sarpedon singlehandedly, and brought down warplanes with your mind."

"He had help!" shouted Alexandra from behind, having climbed down from the ramparts.

"Yes," Lysandros said turning. "I'm sure you played an indispensable role. It is good to see you again, Alex."

"Go fuck yourself!" Alexandra angrily hissed in response.

But as she turned away from Lysandros, Alexandra saw the five leaders of their respective peoples walking toward them. One of which she recognized immediately, Diana of the Militae, her childhood friend. The two were practically inseparable before Alexandra left the Militae to endure the egoga. She immediately ran towards her. Diana, when she recognized Alexandra did the same. They met halfway, throwing themselves in each other's embrace.

"Did you have much trouble with the aerial blockade?" Zeno inquired.

"Us? No. We landed on a small Zutaeran air field forty miles east of the Chalendria River. We made the rest of the journey on foot. The Vampire's armada is patrolling the skies like ants all over Dioskuria and Sarpedon. But there are holes in the no-fly zone over Zutaera. We marched at night and used signal jammers to block their infrared cameras. But the bastard is hitting the other nations hard. Every day, bombers make runs over Yorland and Zutaera, and he's already sending Dimron to besiege Acheminidos. No site is safe. Hospitals, temples, schools. All the same. The civilians have taken to underground shelters or sewers. Some have taken their chances in the country side. But the Vampire's thugs are rounding them up into the feeding camps, and that's when they don't gun them down outright. Those who aren't captured are starving. The death toll is nearing catastrophic proportions. We have to win this war quickly, Zeno."

Zeno nodded. It pained him to hear of the price so many others were paying for his actions. But he knew, even with his great power, he could do nothing to help them at the moment. All he could do was try and break the Vampire's power as soon as possible. "What of Grey Peaks?"

"I sent spies. They confirmed that he's alive."

"I understand," Zeno replied.

Lysandros turned to introduce the various leaders who now stood behind him: A stocky Yorishman with tight cut hair and soft eyes, a tall, bald headed Zutaeran, a long bearded, tan skinned Acheminid with a red felt cap on his head, and Konan of the Woads. "Zeno, may I present Sir Ranold of Yorland, Lord Ngozi of Zutaera, and Lord Cyrus of Acheminidos." Lysandros turned to the Woad. "And of course, you remember Konan."

"It's good to see you again, Zeno," Konan said in Woadish. "Looks like the Brown Warrior has moved up in the world." He smirked.

Zeno replied in the Woadish tongue. "I can't tell you how good it is to see you, old friend."

"And..." Lysandros began but could not finish

"This is Diana!" Alexandra joyfully roared, releasing her embrace and turning back to Zeno. "War Mother of the Militae and the deadliest woman in all Ninivon! Well, second." Alexandra grinned as Diana playfully jabbed her in the ribs. Diana had large, enchanting brown eyes and long, black hair pulled back in a ponytail in the Militian style.

Lysandros smiled. "Every leader here, be they chief or lord, is a hardened battle commander with the trust and backing of their people."

Zeno had an immense amount of respect for them all. Sir Ranold, Cyrus, and Ngozi were Rangers who had fought in the Great Terror. That they now stood ready to serve under him, made his heart beam with pride.

"My friends," Lysandros continued. "This is Zeno, our great equalizer in this war."

Zeno immediately stepped forward and clasped each leader individually by the hand. He could not have been more grateful for their support and faith.

"Thank you all for coming. I know you are taking a great risk to be here. Lysandros has told me about how your people are suffering in your own lands. Yet you have come to support us here rather than stay to protect your homes and families. I cannot express how honored I am to fight by your side."

"It is us who are honored, Lord Zeno," Ranold replied. "If

rumors of your power are not exaggerated," Ranold looked about the city for a moment, "and they appear not to be. You represent the first real chance we have had against the Vampire."

"I am no noble, Sir Ranold. But I appreciate your respect."

"Lord Ranold is more optimistic and patient than Zutaera," interrupted Ngozi. "You are right that we have all risked a great deal to be here. If you want the warriors of Zutaera to stay, you had better convince us our families are safer with us here than with them, and fast."

"Rest assured, my Lord Ngozi, I know full well the cost you could pay for supporting me. You have given me a down payment of good faith; I will repay you back tenfold."

"Well, he speaks like a commander," Diana said to Alexandra in Militian.

"I am eager to show you what kind of commander I am, War Mother," Zeno answered in her tongue.

Diana smiled and laughed. She was clearly impressed that Zeno knew her language.

"Yes," Alexandra added. "He was always a bit of a linguist. But since he received his powers, Zeno has become a true polyglot. He can decipher any language within seconds of hearing it."

Diana laughed as a school girl might. Zeno could tell she liked him and suspected she was thankful to know he understood her before she made some raunchy comment about him to Alexandra in their mother tongue.

Lysandros interjected. "It looks like your exploits have attracted other admirers."

Everyone turned to look at the gate. A little over a hundred armed guerillas were walking through the threshold. Ghost was in front.

Ghost walked among the leaders, many of whom he had fought alongside of as a Ranger during the Great Terror. He eyed them all before stopping in front of Zeno. Ghost looked at the man he had kicked out of his camp two months earlier. He turned to his brother who stood by Zeno's side, giving him a look of reluctant submission.

"A fucked-up world this is," Ghost began. "In order to fight against the Vampire, I have to put my own brother on the throne." He turned back to Lysandros. "And after you've been such a self-righteous ass."

Lysandros just grinned in reply.

Ghost turned back to Zeno. "I received your invitation Zeno." Zeno had indeed sent word to the Blue Order immediately after he had taken Sarpedon. He invited Nikolaus and his guerillas to fight with him, under Lysandros. Zeno hoped Ghost would accept the invitation; but he knew the man's pride and expected to be rebuffed. "I'm a proud man. But when I'm wrong, I admit it. I don't know if what they say about you is true. But you have done more in a few weeks than the Blue Order has done in a year and a half. If our planet is to have a future outside of the Vampire, you will have to lead them. You have my sword and my men."

With that, Ghost reached out his right arm and clasped that of Zeno's. There were cheers and claps. The men's eyes met for some seconds.

Zeno and Ghost finally released each other's arms. Ghost turned to Lysandros and clasped his arm as well. "See that your boy doesn't fuck it up," he said to his brother, motioning to Zeno. The sons of Polymaxes smiled and then all set about quartering the soldiers in the large estates which the Sarpedonian aristocrats had left behind.

CHAPTER XX

LYSANDROS

There were several small to moderate air battles over the next few weeks. Sarpedonians fighters took to the skies to defend Acheminidos, Yorland, and Zutaera, who themselves fought back with both their fighter aircraft as well as anti-aircraft artillery. They were always outnumbered. But Zeno often took to the air with them in his own fighter, or did what he could from the ground, both of which were awe inspiring. The rebels were able to carve some holes in the no-fly zone, as well as ease the blow of the Vampire's bombers over allied states.

But Zeno was able to help in other matters besides military. He liberated tens of thousands of refugees fleeing the Vampire's feeding camps and brought them to Sarpedon. Many of the native Sarpedonians worried that food and water would become scarce. But Zeno used his supernatural strength to divert the Xor River, providing fresh water to the city. He was able to rearrange molecules turning stones into food.

Aside from keeping his followers alive, these miracles spread his fame throughout all Ninivon, which prompted even more to make the journey to fight alongside the god-man. In turn, everyone in Sarpedon, be they an immigrant child, soldier, or a wealthy lord, all sought to contribute to the war effort in whatever way they could. They refurbished warplanes, made weapons in factories, seen to the wounded, and prepared meals. The entire city had turned into a large and highly efficient military camp.

But there was a limit. Using his uncanny abilities took its toll on Zeno. Exploits such as manipulating matter with his mind often left Zeno incapacitated for hours, in some cases, even days. They had to pick their miracles sparingly. Also, the defenders were only partially successful. Zeno could not be in two places at once and the Vampire's air armada attacked multiple nations and cities within those nations simultaneously. When the Vampire's fighters and bombers were able to penetrate the defenses, some sector of the city paid dearly, and people died, both civilians and military.

When they were not fighting in the skies, or caring for refugees, Zeno gave the individual commanders full rein over their troops, the commanders reported directly to him and he reported to Lysandros. He actively conversed and engaged with the lowest ranking men and women; he knew their names and their stories. Yet he was always careful not to give the impression that he was micromanaging his officers. He wanted to inspire, not control.

"Zeno!" Lysandros found Zeno with Alexandra atop the western wall, overlooking the sunset. The two had been inseparable. On one hand, Lysandros was happy because the two people he loved most in the world had the support of each other, and they both needed support. On the other hand, he feared Zeno might become too reliant on Alexandra, and that she might be hurt through being too close to the Demigod. Lysandros knew well the heartache of loving a servant of the All Fire.

Zeno and Alexandra immediately separated.

Lysandros stopped a few steps before them. "Did I interrupt something?"

"It's nice to have you around to interrupt, father. It's quite a change," Alexandra snapped.

"Alex..." Lysandros wanted to talk with his daughter.

"Archon," Zeno cut him off. "How can I be of service?"

Lysandros straightened his posture. "There have been two more air attacks on Yorland and another in the Militian Plains.

Our allies are paying dearly for supporting us. Something must be done about the Vampire's air armada."

"I know," Zeno replied. "Should I go now?"

"Go where?" Alexandra asked.

Zeno looked at Lysandros for approval. Lysandros glared back at him.

"What?" Alexandra asked. "You don't want to tell me?" Alexandra looked back and forth between the two men. "You don't trust me. Or maybe you just don't have a plan and you're embarrassed."

"We have a plan," Lysandros answered.

"Then you can share it with me," Alexandra firmly said. "I followed you." Alexandra turned to Zeno. "When my uncle whom I trust with my life wanted you dead, I followed you. I encouraged others to do the same. Do you think Nikolaus would have joined us so easily were it not for me? I helped you secure this city right after you took it. I think I've earned your trust."

There were a few seconds of silence and assuming glances between the men.

"Dragons," Zeno said. "We are going to enlist the aid of the Dragons of Grey Peaks and attack Altus Mons directly."

Altus Mons was the aerial battle station which the Vampire built to patrol the dragon homeland and protect his own air assets. It was huge, housed thousands of personnel, mostly Remani and Dioskurian traitors, was heavily defended, and hovered fifty-five hundred feet above the mountains of Grey Peaks. It was also where over eighty percent of the air craft in Ninivon were docked. Strategically, it was paramount. Taking it would all but eliminate the Vampire's air force, save for the few aircraft he had on hand at urban airfields. It would also simultaneously give the rebels an air force. The rebels would never take back Ninivon unless Altus Mons fell. But the rebel force had limited air assets with which to mount an assault.

Alexandra laughed. "That's your plan? Truly? There are no

more dragons. The Vampire killed them all."

"There are," Lysandros answered. "I sent Woads to Grey Peaks myself. Likavitos lives, but Zeno will need to go to him in person."

"Hmm." Alexandra looked at her father. "There you go sending people away again." She turned back to Zeno, "if that's your plan, then it's insane. Since it is insane, I'm going with you." Alexandra turned and walked away.

Lysandros and Zeno stood there for a moment. Then Lysandros turned to go after her.

"It would be best to let her be, Archon," Zeno said.

"Being a leader means having uncomfortable conversations, Zeno. I've avoided this one long enough." Lysandros took off behind his daughter.

Lysandros found Alexandra in the palestra, sparing with padded tomahawks with one of the Militae. The girl Alexandra was fighting was young. She could not have been older than seventeen. But she was clearly someone of some importance within the tribe because the bout took place under the watchful gaze of Diana and a number of other tribal leaders. They wanted to see what the child was made of and asked Alexandra to test her. A great compliment among the Women of the Red Sky.

Lysandros had not really had an opportunity to watch his daughter fight since he had arrived at Sarpedon. In fact, he had had few opportunities to see her at all. They were busy and he was sure that Alexandra was avoiding him.

Alexandra brought the fight to an end with an overhead strike that knocked the young girl to the ground. The Militae roared and jeered, as was their way. They gave tips to the girl and complemented Alexandra.

After a few moments the women began to disperse. Diana saw Lysandros and said a few words to Alexandra, who now looked and saw her father as well. Her expression immediately turned cold. Alexandra crossed her arms and turned off in the distance, but she did not walk away. The other Militae left and Alexandra was alone with her estranged father in the palestra.

So twelve years have come to this? I wonder if this was how she felt when she asked me.

The *she* was Alexandra's mother, the Priestess of Sofia.

"This cannot be the way?" Lysandros argued in the throne room of the Stokian starship.

"You swore an oath, Lysandros," the Priestess replied.

"Even oaths have their limit! If I send her to Ying Chau she'll die. There's no way out of the underground city. The only reason it has survived until now is because the Vampire didn't want to waist the time to besiege it."

"Yet your Archon has ordered that millions evacuate there."

"She hasn't."

"She will."

"She doesn't have a choice. She is trying to protect millions. We're talking about one person, our daughter! One person who can be hidden and smuggled. She should stay with me."

The Priestess was silent for a moment. Lysandros knew her well enough to know silence often preceded some revelation he didn't like.

"You are an experienced warrior, my love. High Strategos of the armies of the Republic of Eighteen. How do you see this war ending?"

Lysandros didn't want to think about that.

"Humans often believe communication is the key to resolving conflict. Yet when asked, they are so reticent to speak."

"Are you not human then?"

"Is that what you think of me? That I am some alien devoid of emotion? You know where I come from. You know I wasn't always like this. She's my daughter too."

"Then compromise with me," Lysandros pleaded. "Please. I have served you all these years. I bowed to your words and worshiped at your alter. I've protected and trained Zeno. Have I not been faithful?"

"You have."

"Is this then the reward for my fidelity? Alexandra is all I have. I never took a wife. I was always faithful to you. I lived without her for eleven years. Don't ask me to give her up again."

"You know the ways of the Women of the Red Sky. As a girl, she always belonged to the tribe. To her mother, and that is me. You had more time with her than you otherwise would have. More than I have had. You were given that time as a reward for your fidelity, as a respite for your service. But more importantly, I did not arrange for Alexandra to leave my people and come to Dioskuria so she could have a relationship with you. I did it so she could have a relationship with Zeno. Zeno needed her to become who he has to become. Now, he needs her to leave for that same reason. Likewise, Alexandra has a great role to play. She must go with your brother to Ying-Chau for them both to fulfill their destinies."

"Why can I not at least send her back to the Militae?"

"Because that is not where she needs to be. Ying- Chau is where she needs to be. Just like Dioskuria is where you and Zeno need to be. And you both must stay there until you are released by the Archon. If you stray from this path, but a little, all will be lost, including the very people you are trying to protect by holding onto them."

Lysandros felt a sorrow rise from deep within. This was the worst day of his life. This strategos, this warrior, covered his face with his hands and cried without any thought to hold back.

"Kallista." A cry for help and affection.

The Priestess walked to Lysandros and pulled his hands from his face. She then cupped his cheek with her left hand and placed her right hand on his heart.

"Oh, my love. She will live. I swear it. She will escape the coming siege. She will have to fight, and run, no less than you and Zeno. She will have your brother to look after her. She will grow hard, strong. And one day, you will see her again."

Lysandros rose his head to look at the Priestess. "She'll

hate me. She won't understand. I don't understand."

"She will hate you. But before the end, she will understand and she will know that you love her. She will confess her love for you. And you will be proud to see the woman she will become. Trust me, Lysandros. Will you trust me?"

"Why are you just standing there?" Alexandra's voice brought Lysandros back to the present moment.

Lysandros shook his head, as if he were shaking the painful memories away. "You really are a gifted fighter," he began.

"I have areas to improve. Jenesia is still learning. Beating her really isn't that impressive," Alexandra said, arms still crossed and staring at her father.

"Perhaps," Lysandros responded. "But all of the Militae respect you. Even Diana. They would not give away their admiration so easily unless you had earned it."

"I grew up with many of them. They respect me and I them. They support me and I them. Most of all, they don't abandon each other on the brink of war. That's how it is supposed to work."

"Alexandra, I know you are still angry. You have a right to be. But I had no choice."

"This again? There is always a choice," Alexandra hissed as she turned and walked away.

"But sometimes they are all bad choices. Sometimes all one can do is choose the lesser of two evils."

Alexandra turned. "You know what massacres are like? Of course, you do. You have both committed and survived them. We fought with the Katanas against the Vampire for four years. Four years of constant warfare, never having enough sleep or food to eat. Constantly freezing or burning under the hot sun. Always having to be on guard for the roar of gunships or tanks. We held out. For four years, we held out until the Atoloi centaurs rounded us up in the Dokajo Ravine and wiped us out.

"You know, I understand why you didn't come after me.

You thought me dead. You had to protect Zeno above all, I understand why now. But you didn't have to send me away to begin with. Had you not, we would have all been together."

"I was trying to save you from certain death."

"All death is certain. I made my choice. I wanted to stay with Zeno, with you. I was prepared to die with you. That was the level of my devotion to the Rangers, to you. But you took my choice from me by sending me away. That is what was most hurtful. Twelve years, *father*. We would have had to live on the run, fighting as we went, but we would have had each other. But instead, I had to fight to survive without the two people I most loved. Thinking they had been slaughtered! I'll never forgive you for that." Alexandra again started to walk away.

Lysandros thought long before he said his next words.

Is now the time? Should I tell her the truth? I can't tell her everything. It's not my story to tell. But I can share my part in it.

"Sending you to Ying-Chau didn't just save you from certain death. It guaranteed your life," Lysandros said, stopping her in her tracks. "The Priestess of Sofia. She commanded that I send you to Ying-Chau. She swore it was the only way you would live, and Zeno."

Alexandra turned; questioning in her eyes.

"She said you would go through hell. But she said you would live. Moreover, she said I couldn't take you with us."

"Why would she ask you to do that? What am I to her? More importantly, how could you listen to her over your own daughter?"

"Because there was more on the line than either of our lives. Because I knew you actually would be safe at Ying-Chau. Perhaps safer than anyone else in Ninivon." Lysandros took a step towards Alexandra. "She doesn't get things wrong, Alex. She sees shadows of the future. She does not perceive time as you and I do. She sees the end from the beginning. As much as it hurt, as much pain as it caused you, sending you to Ying-Chau was the most loving thing I could have done for you."

"Some say it would be hard to know the future," Alexandra snarled. "But I think it would have its advantages. For one, you would never have to take responsibility for your actions."

"I do not blame the Priestess. The choice was mine. But I want you to know I have regretted it. I knew I would regret it even before I did it. You're probably thinking that doesn't make sense. You're right. But you've done things you knew you'd regret. I do love you. I pray to Misericordia the Merciful that one day you will forgive me. I will wait for you, with open arms. I will always be waiting to hold you. If I die in that state, please think better of me."

Lysandros turned and left the palestra. He felt he had planted a seed. He wanted to say more. But he knew that time was on his side, and that she would, one day, come back to him. Then it struck him, the promise of the Priestess was that she would forgive him, and that they would win the war. She never promised that either of them would live to see it. That meant that as soon as she did forgive him, he might lose his daughter again.

CHAPTER XXI
ZENO

As reports of the Vampire's movements flooded in, Lysandros called a meeting of his generals in the Sarpedonian council hall.

"The army coming from the east consists of twenty-five thousand Joni, five thousand of which are heavy cavalry. The Hipperi number another ten thousand, all light cav. They will have ten thousand Rapti with them. And some Equitati as well," said Theodotius, a Sarpedonian noble who had willingly surrendered to Zeno when he took the city. He now served as general for the Sarpedonian contingent of the rebel army. "The Remani, Karthagoi, and Osaerians are mobilizing as well. Easily a hundred thousand between the three. The Remani and Osaerians are bringing their mechanized cavalry. C-380 and 240 troop carriers as well as the mermen navy are transporting them to our southern shore."

"Mechanized cavalry takes time to transport," Sir Ranold added. "The tanks take up all the room in the planes which means they can't transport as many troops. If they opt to transport the troops first, they can't bring all their tanks."

"They can fit tanks and men on their naval ships," Ngozi countered.

"Yes," Alexandra said. "But ships take longer than planes. How much time until they land?"

"Weeks. Possibly a month. Invasions of this scale take time. But the Joni and Hipperi will be here much sooner," Theodotius answered.

"How long until they arrive?" Zeno asked.

"Ten days," Theodotius replied in a dry and grave voice.

"As we thought," Lysandros nodded. "The Joni and Hipperi are the vanguard. They don't have to move armored tanks half way across the world. They will hold us here until the rest of the Vampire's army lands. Then they will strike in bulk and destroy us. All while we will be collecting refugees and non-combatants here."

"What about aircraft?" Ghost asked.

"Our reports say that the Vampire is sending no air support." Theodotius shook his head.

"He must be tired of your little tricks." Ghost smiled at Zeno. "I don't suppose you could wave your hand and make the Rapti disintegrate." He sarcastically smirked.

Zeno shook his head.

Theodotius returned to his report. "You haven't heard the worst of it, Archon. It is whispered the Vampire is filling the dungeons at Dioskuria with men, women, and children, and unleashing Rapti among them to feed." Everyone knew exactly what Theodotius meant. "Two hundred thousand Dioskurians have been rounded up in Dikaiosune Tower. In days, they will all be *taken*."

The chiefs and generals looked about. Many shook their heads, others whispered curses. The Vampire was taking no chances. Such a force would easily overwhelm their army of just over thirty-two thousand men.

"Sofia!" Ghost yelled rising from the table. "I told you this would happen! They'll outnumber us ten to one. It would be suicide to attack a force that large, even with Zeno. Most of them will be Rapti!"

"We fought against them before," Cyrus answered.

"Yes! And were nearly wiped out! And that was with a larger, better trained, and better supplied army," Ngozi replied.

"You are right to be so concerned Lord Ngozi," Lysandros said. "As are the rest of you," he turned to his generals. "My brother is right; they have ten for every one of ours. I need not remind you all how fearsome the Rapti are; many of you fought against them during the Great Terror. But I assure you my lords, they will not be a factor in this battle because they will not get close enough to our men to hurt them. Nor will we have to fight against such suicidal odds. The force we face will be forty-five thousand at most and only ten thousand Rapti. Still larger than ours by over ten thousand, but don't let that alarm you either. All is going according to plan. The Vampire is doing exactly what we thought he would do. He is egotistical, and like all frightening creatures, is himself driven by fear. He is scared of us, of you. That is why he is emptying his kingdoms against us. By hitting us with everything he has, he is betraying how terrified he is."

Zeno rose from his seat and placed a map of the Valley of Drisdos on the table. Everyone leaned in to hear his plan.

"First we must engage the Joni and Hipperi before the eastern forces arrive," Zeno began. "We will pitch camp in the valley of Drisdos to offer battle. We will set up our infantry in the center, Woads and Sarpedonians on the inside, Zutaerae and Yorish on the outside. Militae cav on the left wing, Sarpedonian and Yorish cav on the right. With no air support, Phillip will lead with artillery. When they open fire, the infantry will feint a breakdown and retreat."

"You want us to break our formations before the battle even starts?" Diana asked in the best common tongue she could muster.

"We do," Zeno continued. "As soon as our lines break, Phillip will unleash the Rapti. I will go out to them and I will fight them, alone. When our men see me cut through them like water, they will forget their fear. By seeing courage, they will find their courage. After I have broken their charge, the Acheminids, who until this point will be formed up behind the infantry, will take to the skies and fire on them from above, further depleting their numbers. Then our infantry will reform just beyond the tree line, and gun down any Rapti still charging at them."

"Ha!" Ghost laughed and sat back down, shaking his head.

"Zeno, they are not of this world," Alexandra protested. "You can't fight them by yourself, not that many. Even if you can fight them off, you want our men to fire on you?"

"It will be a grueling feat," Zeno answered. "Far more grueling than anything I have attempted before. It will be my greatest test since assuming the Power of Thumos and I will be at risk. But no more than the common soldier behind me." His eyes now blazed with an otherworldly intensity. "Phillip and Iban think the Rapti are unstoppable. The strength of their force is the *taken*. They will think nothing of unleashing them on fleeing men. When they see me go out to meet their ten thousand by myself, they will think I am a suicidal fool. They all have heard about my power. But they don't understand it. By the time Phillip and Iban do understand, it will be too late. The Rapti I don't kill will have to sprint across a two-hundred-yard field with no cover under heavy ion fire. Our men will easily mow down the few who do make it through to our lines. More importantly, that will buy us the time we need."

"Time for what?" Konan asked.

"For our cavalry on both flanks to put the enemy cavalry to flight." Lysandros again took command. "When the Zutaeran infantry break they will reform and support the Militae from the left flank. The Yorish infantry will likewise reform and support theirs and the Sarpedonian cav on the right. The Hipperi and Joni cavalry won't expect the wings of the infantry to hit them. Once we put their cavalry to flight, our cav will advance and attack the Joni infantry in the rear in a pincer move, forcing them forward. Then the infantry will charge. If it works right, we will have them completely surrounded."

"It will be a circle of death with the Joni trapped in the center." Alexandra nodded.

"That's right." Zeno smiled.

Ngozi began "This plan requires multiple armies to break

formation, then reform under fire. It also requires that our cavalries, which are outnumbered, beat the Hipperi who have the best light cavalry in the world..."

"Second best," Alexandra interrupted.

"Second best," Ngozi corrected himself, eyeing Alexandra. "But still outnumbered. Most of all, we are counting on one man to stop the charge of ten thousand Rapti. It would take a god to accomplish such a thing. Even if he does do it, if either of the other parts of the plan fail, we are doomed."

"It's damn near impossible," Cyrus said. "We'd have to drill for ten hours a day every day for a month to get something like that perfect." Cyrus paused for a second. As if he were in thought. "But we don't have to execute it perfectly, we just have to fuck up our plan less than the Joni fuck up theirs."

"Yes. But their plan is much simpler so it's harder to fuck up," Ghost countered. "And they have more men so they can afford to fuck up more."

"They don't have more men," Zeno answered. "They have more fighters. Ten thousand of them are monsters who can't think or move in formation. They only know to charge without any thought for their own protection. When we kill them, our armies will be virtually even. Besides, you all remember the affect it had on our armies when we first saw the Vampire lead the Rapti onto the battlefield. Our lines often broke and ran before the Rapti even reached them. The *taken* terrified even our bravest soldiers. They were supernatural and foreign. It's been almost fourteen years since the Vampire took Vorsehelgda with his daemonic army. No one has dared stand up to his creatures. Can you imagine how terrified the Joni will be when they see me destroy them? The fear alone might cause them to break."

Both Zeno and Ghost looked at each other for a brief second, before they meet with the eyes of others around the table.

"Most of you have not seen Zeno fight on the battlefield. But you have all seen him fight beside you in the skies," Lysandros said. "Do any of you still doubt what he can do?"

"This is different," Ngozi replied. "The Rapti are different."

"All of you came here voluntarily," Lysandros answered. "You are free to go if you think our cause in vain. But before you walk away from our best chance to throw down the Vampire, ask one who has seen Zeno fight up close with his own eyes." Lysandros gestured to his brother.

Every eye rested on Ghost. Months before he was ready to kill Zeno. Seconds before he openly criticized their strategy. Now both Zeno and Lysandros conceded to him. If he endorsed the strategy, the other lords and chiefs would follow. If he struck it down the alliance, still forming, might fall apart. Did he truly believe that one man could halt the unforgiving onslaught of the taken?

"We have been living under the Vampire for nearly fourteen years now," Ghost spoke. "Many have died and many more are still to die before we can be free. But at some point, we have to take our chances. I've seen the Rapti put myriads of a hundred thousand to flight. I've never seen a force that can stand up to the taken. But to Tartarus with it. If any man can stand alone against the Rapti, it's Zeno. My men and I will follow him, perhaps to hell, but we will follow all the same."

"Good. Because we have you and the Blue Order leading the Sarpedonian phalanx." Lysandros smiled.

Ghost looked to Theodotius who returned a disgruntled stare.

"The Blue Order and Sarpedonian regulars have shed much of each other's blood." Zeno nodded. "It's time you all finally made peace. No better way than to shed the blood of a common enemy."

"Hmmm..." Ghost sighed. "Bastards."

There were some wry smiles and laughter. "I'll be right beside you brother." Lysandros smiled. "I'll be leading the Woads, along with Konan." Lysandros slapped the Woadish commander on the shoulder. "Outside of Zeno this battle will rest on our shoulders. You and I, Nikolaus. Like old times."

Alexandra smiled. Ghost nodded. All around the room there was consent. The plan was adopted, and the generals left to make their final preparations and check on their troops. Zeno started to leave as well.

"Zeno, stop," Lysandros ordered without raising his eyes from the map. "You know, some ten thousand men will be firing on you. Or at least in your direction. That's a lot of ion fire. All while fighting off the Rapti. You're sure the blasts won't hurt you?"

"No," Zeno answered, walking to a window overlooking the city square. "But I'm pretty sure they won't. Besides the Priestess told me I should push myself."

"Charging ten thousand Rapti and having your own troops shoot at you is a damned way to *push yourself*," Lysandros said. "You're risking more than just your life you know. You are risking the whole rebellion. If you fall, we will never be free from the Vampire."

"We are asking these men to risk their lives for the Republic. I can do no less."

"But Zeno..."

"Come, Archon," Zeno cut him off. "The generals have accepted the plan. It gives us the best possible chance to win. Besides, the Dark Gods would be offended if I left the battle without a scratch."

CHAPTER XXII
THE BATTLE OF DRISDOS

Zeno

The Valley of Drisdos is perfect for war: a flat grassy plain approximately two hundred yards long and roughly eighty yards wide, it rests on the final narrow strip of the Isthmus of Sarpedon before opening into the Sofia Forest to the south and the Tempus Desert to the east. Any ground force invading the western hemisphere from the east had to pass through it.

The rebel army, or Republican army, as they were now calling themselves, marched into the field of Drisdos on a cloudy day, the eleventh day of the ninth month in the twelfth year of the reign of the Vampire: Terror and Woe of Ninivon. They were thirty-five thousand strong. As he led his troops into the open field, Zeno could feel his stomach quake. He was nervous. And if he was nervous, what must the others be feeling?

The Republican army had formed fifty yards from the tree line in plain sight—they wanted to be seen. The Woads wore their traditional kilts and were covered in blue war paint. No two warriors had the same design. But all looked equally fierce and monstrous; a stark contrast to the standardization of the Sarpedonian hoplites who all covered their faces behind identical helmets. The Yorish infantry were on the right flank, and the Zutaeran infantry on the left, with the Acheminids lined up behind them all. The burden of faking a disorganized retreat under artillery fire, then reforming a firing line would fall to the Woads and Sarpedonians. The Zutaeran and Yorish infantry would have to feign a retreat and then reform to support the cavalry units. It would be challenging. But they had drilled the feint tirelessly over the last few days, and Zeno believed they could do it.

If I believe they can do it, they will believe as well.

At the far-left flank were the Militae, led by Diana with Alexandra as her second. Like the Woads, the warrior women of the plains wore little armor, but were covered in war paint: black on their faces, with streaks of white and red. They looked fierce and primal, like warrior-goddesses. At the far-right flank were the Yorish and Sarpedonian cavalry, with Sir Ranold and Theodotius at their heads. The former armored in full plate mail and the latter in a combination of hardened leather and chain mail, all ion proof. Their job was far simpler, but not easy. They would be asked to rout the cavalry units across from them, both of which had them outnumbered, and then ride around the infantry and push them forward into the trap.

Then there was Zeno, atop a fantastic black mare, wearing a hoplite mail breastplate with a large blue Σ in the center. He wore a sleeveless tunic beneath the armor. His was a short crimson battle skirt. Steel greaves wrapped about his calves and covered his boots. A blue cape with a gold border hung from his shoulders. It was a Ranger cape. A Dioskurian bastard sword rested in a sheath on his back, as did a *hoplon* shield. Zeno had no firearm. He wouldn't need one. His work would be up close. His was the most important role in the battle. He must occupy ten thousand Rapti, alone. That he had the Power of Thumos at his disposal did little to calm his nerves. Men always fear when confronted with the truly terrifying, and the Rapti were terrifying. Some of his force had never seen one before, but they had heard the horror stories from those who had. If Zeno failed to break their charge, fear alone would break the lines of his force, and the soulless taken would gorge themselves on the blood of the men and women who had trusted him with their lives.

Then again, the Rapti were not the only terrifying force on the field that day. He would be just as alien to the eyes of their enemies. The question was, which alien power would win: the taken, or Thumos.

Between stints of intense focus on the tactics and maneuvers that had to be executed today for his army to win, and his own personal feelings of fear—fear not for his own safety but that he would fail those who had wagered their lives on his sword—Zeno thought about one person above all: Alexandra. He feared for her safety and wished he could fight alongside her. But she was an accomplished warrioress in her own right; the proud daughter of a double military heritage, that of the egoga and the Militae. And like he among the Woads, she had cut her warrior's teeth among the Katanas. An impressive resume. Besides, the army needed him against the Rapti in the center. Zeno could best protect her by wiping out the taken. Alexandra would have to fight her own battle today.

Lysandros was also mounted and sat atop his horse to Zeno's right, wearing an ion-proof leather cuirass and a Woadish kilt. He had an ion rife and a claymore strapped across his back, and a pistol at his side. To Zeno's left was Ghost, also mounted, covered in a highly polished hoplite breastplate, with both a blue cape and a hoplite helmet. An Elledic short sword hung from his side, a hoplon shield was on his back, and an eight-foot spear rested in his right hand. A handgun hung on his belt.

Across the field, a few hours before noon, the enemy marched into view. The Hipperi cavalry rode first into view, armed with short rifles, cavalry spears, and scimitars, wearing their traditional tan battle helms over felt caps. Both their horses and horsemanship were things to behold. The beasts were of the most exquisite quality, tall and strong. Their riders commanded perfect mastery over them, all trotting in cadence onto the field.

Zeno's thoughts wandered to his fifth year in the egoga. One of his history instructors was teaching about the various nations that made up the Republic of Eighteen.

"The Hipperi are a desert people, but they are not nomadic, like the great Attolian centaurs with whom they share the Tempus Desert," the teacher lectured. "They live in walled cities made of sun brick. The cruelty of their environment and the prowess of their cavalry protect them from attack from the outside."

"Why don't they use motor vehicles?" one student asked.

"Because the large war jeeps are too unwieldy in battles against centaurs. And desert bikes are too small," Alexandra chimed in. "Horses allow the Hipperi to meet the centaurs as equals. Plus, they have a magic with their horses, like what my people call the Bond."

"The girl who talks to horses would know." Another initiate laughed.

Alexandra shot a glare of disdain at them.

"The horses probably have smarter things to say than you do, Janiska." Zeno stood up for his friend. "Hipperi horsemanship is the key to their independence. It's allowed them to build a thriving civilization in the presence of monsters in a grueling environment. They are a powerful people."

That power was arrayed against him now.

It had long been a topic of debate throughout Ninivon, which was the better light cavalry, that of the Militae or the Hipperi. The Hipperi's national unity and industrialization provided them the advantage of logistics and sure supply lines. The Militae were wild; they fought as wolves in a great pack. A terrible foe. As to which people were the better horsemen, the result of today's battle would surely provide something of an answer.

Next came the Joni cavalry. They were armed and armored

in much the same way as the Yorish knights, both being Angol-id in race. Lances in their gloved hands and bastard swords at their sides, all were mounted on armored horses and carrying pistols as tertiary weapons.

Behind them came the infantry. This made up the bulk of the force; twenty thousand men, all with open-face helmets and either chain mail or leather cuirasses, boots, and trousers. These carried shields, rifles, broadswords, and either pikes or spears.

Then came the Equitati Knights. There were but a hundred of these, but they stood out for their distinct arms and armor, which was a mix of that of a Remani legionary and an An-golid knight. They wore visored helmets with synthetic horse hair plumes. Their breastplates were hardened leather etched with pectoral and abdominal muscles. These rested over long-sleeve tunics. On their legs were dark-red trousers. They carried Joni bastard swords and ion rifles on their backs and wore pistols and gladius swords at their sides. They were the Vampire's new Rangers, and like the Rangers, their strength was versatility. Rather than specialize in one type of combat, they could duel hand-to-hand or fight as a unit in a battle line, in multiple different styles.

Following these was the heavy artillery unit. There were not many of them. Such units slow down armies over chal-lenging terrain, and this force was meant to respond to the rebels with speed. But there were some fifty motorized vehi-cles with guns ranging in caliber and strength mounted atop.

Then, the Rapti, devil spawn of another world. It was said that the Vampire had drawn these from hordes of the taken he collected in his feeding camps. There were men, women, and children among them. Some could not have been older than five when they were taken. Their flesh was a ghastly white. They wore various garments, whatever they had been wearing when transformed, now tattered from constant wear. Their mouths were filled with rows of razor-sharp teeth. They were dirty and reeked of excrement. Their arms and feet were bound in ion chains that held them secure: metal cuffs, united by an ion ener-gy link which could be dispersed at the touch of a button. They had just enough mobility to march with the army. Were it not for the chains, they would have turned on the Hipperi and Joni who now marshaled them. With the Vampire not present, there was no one who could control them, and their thirst for blood did not discriminate between friend and foe.

On the other side of the field, Zeno began to dismount, but Lysandros stopped him.

"You should probably say something to them," he said, mo-tioning to the army.

"You always said professional soldiers don't require speech-es."

"Ha! Yes, but we aren't paying them very much," Lysandros joked. "You should say something to them. Perhaps something from the poets, some Remoh or Ligriv."

"You're their commander," Zeno urged.

Lysandros just laughed in response. "Yes, all these soldiers have left their homes and families behind and are now risking their lives against the taken, because of me. It had nothing to do with you pulling fighters from the sky or turning stones into food with the All Fire."

Zeno rolled his eyes. He reseated himself atop his horse and rode forward so the entire force could see him. All were silent. As Zeno scanned the faces of each man and woman in the line, he could see trepidation. They all looked so young to him now, even the old ones.

"My brothers and sisters," Zeno began, "I know you are all scared. I'm scared, and I'm the *Demigod*, so you must be scared. It's all right to be scared. It would be surprising if you were not. We are about to go to war with monsters." Zeno pointed to the army across the field. "But I'm not talking about the Rapti. They kill and drink blood out of hunger. I'm talking about the humans that stand behind them, who have used them to terrorize you, to make themselves rich by enslaving your sons, and to gorge their lusts by raping your daughters. These men, who have set themselves up as your lords and masters and under whose yoke you have suffered these twelve years, they have done so not on their own strength, but on that of the Vampire and his Rapti. How shall we treat our masters?"

Zeno spurred his horse and rode up and down the line. All the while, shouts of "revenge," and "kill them," as well as other curses and threats, boomed from the army. Someone even yelled, "fuck them in the ass," to the laughter of all.

"Today, you will learn what you would do to them," Zeno began again. "Today they will be able to hide behind their taken hordes no longer. They think they are untouchable behind the Rapti. They think they are going to unleash the taken and you will break and run. They probably think they can win this battle without even unsheathing their swords. But they are going to learn today as well. They are going to learn that there is a new monster in Ninivon. I am that monster. I am your monster, when you want vengeance. I am your monster when you want justice. I am your monster when you want freedom. I am going to kill the taken monsters. Will you kill the monsters behind them?"

A mighty roar erupted from the rebel army.

Whatever devils or monsters there are, they'll have to deal with this: so many men and women willing die so that others may live. We're all Rangers today.

Zeno and the sons Polymaxes could see the artillery operators of the enemy hurry to their stations. All three dismounted and handed their horses' reins over to attendants. The Jonish King and Hipperi Sultan were responding how Zeno had expected they would; as arrogant men who thought they knew how this battle would go.

They'll soften us up with their heavy guns first. When we send out our cavalry, they'll match us. When they see us retreat, they'll think we're running and send the Rapti.

The air was thick with tension. Zeno turned to Lysandros,

and the two locked eyes. Throughout the ranks, no one said a word. This was the eternal moment before a battle in which humans on the verge of death searched their souls. Every man and woman, up and down the line, waited in breathless anticipation, all fighting back fear, not just the fear of death and the death of loved ones, but also fear of fear itself.

"The one thing all warriors fear most is to fail the man next to him in the line when it matters and to live to endure the shame." Lysandros once told Zeno this. No one felt this fear more than Zeno, who was confident that nothing across the field could kill him—although he was concerned about wounds that would slow him down—but who worried greatly that he would not be able to do enough, quickly enough, to win the battle.

Finally, he spoke to Lysandros. "May Andrea protect you, Archon."

"And you, Ranger of the Republic." Lysandros smiled.

Everyone now hurried to their posts: Ghost at the center of the Sarpedonian infantry, Lysandros beside Konan among the Woads.

The heavy guns roared in horrific disorder, sending forth both shockwaves of sound and brilliant flashes of light as the steel-encased fusion bursts fired from the barrels. The shells soared toward the sky before turning downward and rushing toward the Republican Army.

"Shields up!" Zeno yelled.

The command was repeated. Every infantryman who had a shield raised it. Those who had none dug in behind those who did. The Sarpedonian shields were fifty inches in diameter and could easily protect two men. The ions shells fell like deadly rain. Men fell dead or howled in pain or from nerves. But most shields held; their Ninivonium coating dissipating the energy of the blasts. The first volley was done. Zeno raised his head above the rim of his shield just enough to see but not so far as not to be able to cover up quickly. Just as he had learned in the egoga. He looked to the flanks first; he was mainly concerned about the cavalry, which were larger targets due to their horses. The Militae had smaller and weaker shields. But then again, the infantry was the main focus of the artillery barrage.

Zeno looked back to his infantry. For a moment, he lost himself. There were few casualties, but each man fallen was a brother, a sister, a friend, someone with whom Zeno had broken bread, shared stories, or worked beside in the past few weeks. Zeno stood up tall. Everything slowed, all he could hear were the cries of his wounded troops. The emotion was welling within him. Each life lost was one too many. He felt each one.

Lysandros yelled at him through the microscopic radio attached to his breastplate. "Are you trying to show off? Cover up!"

The heavy ion guns fired again. Zeno heard the cry of a man directly behind him and felt the heat rise from his now goo-like flesh.

"Lysandros!" came Ranold's voice through the radio. "Theodotius is dead! The Sarpedonian cavalry is about to break and run!" All the commanders were on the same frequency, and Zeno could hear through his radio as well.

"Ranold! Take your cavalry and attack! Diana, you as well!" Lysandros commanded through the communicator.

The cavalry units on the wings broke from the main body and rode toward the sides of the enemy. The Hipperi cavalry fanned out to meet the Militae, and the Joni cavalry, with some Hipperi augmenting them, did the same to meet the Yorish and Sarpedonians.

This was sooner than Zeno wanted, but he understood that Lysandros had no choice. If the cavalry broke under aerial fire, the entire plan would fail. If this hurt them later, they would have to deal with the consequences then.

Meanwhile, the heavy guns again fired. The cries of the dying could be heard among the roars of artillery. That was enough.

Zeno rose as the last round fell. "Now! Fall back!" he roared through the radio. The Republican infantry, twenty-seven thousand strong, took to their feet and broke into an all-out run.

Everywhere was madness, and that was exactly the way it was supposed to look. Zeno grabbed hold of two wounded Woads and dragged them back with him.

Alexandra

The cavalries clashed on the wings. Militae verses Hipperi to the left of the Republicans. The Militae immediately fanned out. This was their way: use their horses and their speed as their primary weapon, fire on the enemy from a distance, then close the gap and finish them off once they broke formation.

Diana led the formation and Alexandra was right beside her. The other warrioresses rode in a crescent moon behind them. The Hipperi tried to block them off. A rush of adrenaline rushed through Alexandra as they closed with the enemy. In a split second it occurred to her that she had never actually fought as a Militae in battle; she had never fully developed the Bond. But she had spent the first eleven years of her life riding and shooting with these women.

Once of the Way, always of the Way. A familiar Militae saying. They believed that the Way of the people, including the Bond, was passed down through the bloodline.

You're scared. The animal spoke to Alexandra.

I am. Alexandra replied. *The ones riding against us, they're horse warriors too. Even have their own magic; like the Bond. It has allowed them to survive against the centaurs for centuries.*

Like what you and I have. But not the same. There was a pride in the creature's response. It wanted to fight. It wanted the challenge. *Run with me. I will take care of you.*

Alexandra's nerves calmed. There, with Diana beside her, with the warrioresses behind her, with her horse beneath her, and knowing that Zeno would soon be somewhere in the center chopping down the Rapti, it was as if she had never left the

Women of the Red Sky. Her legs hugged the belly of her steed. She released its back. She raised her rifle in unison with her sisters.

"Fire!" Diana roared through the comms each woman had in their ears. The Militae fired their ion short rifles into the Hipperi, who then returned fire. Alexandra launched ion rounds from her short rifle at breakneck speed and with deadly accuracy. The two formations danced around each other firing; the Hipperi employed the same tactics as the Militae. It was not all that different from a battle between two warring Militae tribes, which the Women of the Red Sky were well accustomed to. Alexandra hoped they could maintain their distance. For if the Hipperi closed on them, they would have to fight hand to hand, and unlike the Militae's battles against each other, and the Hipperi's battles against the centaurs, the men would have the size and strength advantage.

Zeno

The infantry retreated to just in front of the tree line and re-formed. Commanders barked orders, curses, and encouragements up and down the line. This would be the hard part. Could soldiers who had never fought together before as a unit perform at peak level under duress?

The Dark Gods smiled on the rebels. They executed the maneuver perfectly.

Far better than they had in any of the countless hours of drills leading up to the day. They turned just in time to see the Rapti sprinting across the Valley of Drisdos. The Vampire's hellish demon hive gave a gruesome cry. Their mouths opened wide, purple tongues hanging out. They charged like mad dogs.

Zeno could hear the gasps escape his soldiers' lips. "Gods, help us," he heard one Woad whisper. They were terrified. Lysandros looked to Zeno, as did Ghost. This was his moment. But he didn't move. He just looked across the field at the horde of taken charging his army. Zeno seemed frozen.

"Commander!" a Sarpedonian behind Zeno brought him back to reality. Zeno turned his head. The look in his eyes startled the man. The furens had taken him.

Zeno threw down his shield and drew the sword from the sheath on his back. He walked like a man prepared for what lay ahead of him. And what lay ahead of him, Zeno knew, was butchery. The fate of his men rested on his sword. If his rebel army saw him break the Rapti, what force could stand against them? His steps quickened. His breath picked up. Zeno ran forward. Within a second, he had covered some two hundred yards and was in the center of the battlefield. The Rapti narrowed their run to focus on Zeno, like an army of ants, intent on attacking the closest insect in their path. Zeno raised his sword.

The Rapti came upon Zeno like a mighty ocean wave on a rock. At first no one could see anything, only the sea of vampiric monsters. But as long seconds passed, it became clear. The Rapti came at Zeno like demons, but Zeno came at them like a wrathful god, rejoicing in his destructive power. His sword danced among fountains of blood and mounds of carved flesh. Unquenchable, alien, sovereign power seemed to animate the blade, which served as a conduit for all the hurt and remorse that Zeno had absorbed over the years, both his own and that of others, now refined into hate. He unleashed that hate onto the bodies of the taken. His sword severed the head of one, blood erupting from the neck. He plunged his sword into the gut of another. The taken howled, as much in frustration as in pain. They grabbed Zeno's legs but could not hold him. So mighty were his muscles and the power that moved them that with every step, he freed himself. They bit into the flesh of his arms and legs, but their fangs, accustomed to shredding human flesh, could not pierce his tough skin. Before they could separate themselves, Zeno was upon them, hacking. This was indeed not a battle, but butcher's work. The two great alien forces in Ninivon had met, it was now obvious: The Rapti were as ineffective against the Vessel of Thumos as the Sarpedonians and the Joni and the Karthagoi had been, less so, for the former had not the reason to fall back seeing they could not hurt him. The Rapti continued to offer themselves before him, and Zeno, effortlessly, cut them down. They were as dull sheep among a ravenous lion.

Lysandros

Lysandros was amazed. The sight was awe inspiring. The slaughter was epic. Zeno was hindered only by the lack of room as hundreds of lifeless corpses fell about his feet. The rebel forces were inspired as they watched the man in whom they had placed all their hope throw himself so completely into the midst of those whom they had feared for so long. As his sword consumed Rapti, valor rose within the army. The melee excited them as chum would a shark. The furens was upon them all. But their courage would soon be tested. For thousands of the taken were now sprinting around Zeno and running towards the infantry.

"Ngozi, Edgard, support the cav," Lysandros roared through his radio. "Gunners out!"

The Zutaeran and Yorish infantries re-formed and threw themselves at the cavalry battles on the wings. The Republican cavalry was still outnumbered, but they now had fresh support.

The Acheminid angels took to the skies. They swooped down in formation just outside of the Rapti's grasp and fired their long rifles at the sea of taken closing in on the Republican infantry. The Rapti were utterly defenseless. Those who rushed Zeno were butchered. Those who ran on to the infantry had to sprint a hundred yards in open terrain as the Acheminids rained down sniper rounds from above. Yet the taken ran on.

The heavy artillery again opened fire. Groups of five and six Acheminids fell from the sky, some dead, others wounded. As soon as the Acheminids hit the ground, the Rapti closest to them broke their charge and leapt upon them, satiating themselves on their blood. Once they had drained the fallen Acheminids, the Rapti resumed their charge. Within seconds, the Acheminids, now taken, rose and took to the skies to attack the others. A second, smaller battle now erupted between the angels and the taken angels in the sky.

Other bodies that fell from the sky were so charred from the ion blast that the Rapti's hands and mouths were burned from clawing and biting them. Nevertheless, they continued to sink their teeth into bodies of the fallen angels, even as the flesh around their mouths and hands grew white-pink and softened from the heat.

"Pull the Acheminids out! We can't risk them becoming Rapti!" Lysandros ordered.

The winged warriors drew up, firing at their taken counterparts as they retreated. The Acheminids flew over the Hipperi cavalry, already engaged in a death match with the Militae and Zutaerans and sniped the enemy from above.

The Republican army would not leave Zeno alone for long. The Woadish infantry readied their ion rifles. "Ready," Lysandros commanded.

"Aim, fire!" Ghost did the same with the Sarpedonians. They proceeded in rank and file: the first line took a knee, and the second line stood, all firing. Twenty-three thousand men opened fire on the taken some of whom were only twenty feet away from them. Hundreds of Rapti fell. Some made it to the infantry line, but these were quickly overwhelmed by the numerous swords and spears that carved up their bodies. No one was bitten. The line had held.

The Republicans fired a second time, and a third. The first rank of Sarpedonians came to their feet. Lysandros now marched the Woads forward, and they fired at point blank range into the sea of Rapti. The Sarpedonians followed. There could not have been more than four thousand Rapti left, so complete had been Zeno's massacre of them, so efficient had been the aid, first of the angels, and then of the Woads and Sarpedonians. Even the enemy had aided in killing some of the taken when they fired their heavy artillery. This had been Lysandros' plan: to minimize the hand-to-hand combat between the Rapti and the Republican army as much as possible because every bite of the Rapti ensured the assaulted soldier would be taken.

"Nikolaus, bring up the Sarpedonians!" Lysandros yelled through the communicator. The men had exhausted their rounds. They could no longer safely kill the taken from a distance. They would have to engage face-to-face. But few of the demons remained, and those who did seemed all too vulnerable; many were wounded.

Lysandros drew his great two-handed claymore from his back and screamed, "Andrea, deliverer, and Ultor, avenger!" A brief, half prayer, half salute to the Light God of courage and the Dark God of vengeance. With a war cry worthy of the Archon of the Republic of Eighteen, and the undisputed chieftain of the Woads, Lysandros charged the taken. The Woads followed, their fear having dissipated and their ferocity having taken preeminence. No longer did they cower under the monstrous things but rather sought to satiate their own barbaric bloodlust and live up to their reputation as being the fiercest people of Ninivon.

Ghost

The Sarpedonians had a different way. They were hoplites, like the Dioskurians, and they fought in formation to maximize the killing capacity of, and minimize the threat to, each soldier. They hoisted their shields and spears and huddled into a great phalanx, each solidly tucked behind the shield of the one to their right, spears raised overhead by the right hand and pointing down. Ghost was in their center. "Do the sons of

Sarpedon fear the taken?" he bellowed.

"No!" The sound vibrated like a mighty gale through the ranks.

"Fuck them!" Ghost replied and surged forward.

They pushed forward behind him, methodically, professionally, engaging the Rapti who were now beset with the Woads to one side, the Sarpedonians to the other, and Zeno in their center, still hacking away atop a growing mountain of now inanimate corpses. The few remaining Rapti were chopped down by barbarian claymores and stabbed through by Sarpedonian spears. The phalanx was losing cohesiveness, but it didn't matter. The taken were trapped.

Zeno

"Ranold is bogged down! The Joni are shifting to our right!" Lysandros yelled to Zeno via radio.

"We have to cut them off and help the cavalry!" Zeno responded. He sheathed his sword as he took off to the right where the enemy cavalry was killing his men. Zeno sprinted across the battlefield with the speed of a stallion, and a fast one at that. Without breaking stride, Zeno leapt atop a horse, knocking off the dead Joni knight atop it. In a flash, he looked back to the center of the battle. His eyes, quickened by the All Fire, could make sense of the chaos of war. He saw that Lysandros, Nikolaus, and the infantry had finished off the Rapti and were charging the main body of Joni infantry, who were now practically sprinting to their left to form up with their cavalry. The Zutaerans further rushed in on foot. Zeno looked to the left. He saw the Militae on horseback, Alexandra among them, also pressing his direction on horseback, the Acheminids from the air. Now that the Rapti, half the cavalry, and the heavy artillery were nullified, the Republican Army had a numeric edge. But it was slight, only a few hundred in a mixed battle of about twenty-six thousand souls on each side. There would be no strategy or generalship now—only bravery, individual soldiership, and chaos. Zeno took the reins of the horse and bolted farther across the battlefield.

Alexandra

The Militae were the first to reach the Joni infantry on the right. They fired their short rifles with both hands, thundering across the field on horseback without holding the reins. They came close enough to fire, then fell back. The Joni were in no position to chase. They were on foot and already engaged with the Sarpedonians and Woads. The best they could do was huddle under their shields when they saw the warrior women riding in to deal death through their riffle muzzles.

Alexandra's horse was shot out from under her. She crashed to the ground; The dead bodies that carpeted the earth broke her fall. Her arm throbbed, and she saw flashing lights in her eyes, but only for a second. Alexandra leapt to her feet and stabbed and slashed at the Joni with a knife in one hand and a hatchet in the other, the former weaving through flesh and armor like a needle, stabbing through chests and bellies, the latter colliding into shoulders and legs like a hammer, tenderizing whatever meat it struck.

Zeno

Within seconds, Zeno had ridden to the right flank of the battle field. The Zutaeran infantry, as well as the Acheminids, now threw themselves into the Joni as well, the Zutaerans on the ground, the angels in the sky, swooping down to fire aimed shots at the Joni with their rifles. The final phase of the battle ensued. Ranold and the Yorish and Sarpedonians were surrounded and were slowly giving ground. Ranold was in the thick of it. He had already been wounded in half a dozen places and had been thrown from his mount, but was holding as best he could, hacking and slashing with his sword. Zeno dove right into the fray. He charged his horse into a group of ten Joni knights who were at the point of attack. Zeno gripped the reins with his right and fought with his left. He cleaved the arm from one Joni and slashed open the back of another. Blood both sprayed and oozed from various openings in each body. Even the horses sensed that Zeno was not like the other combatants and threw their riders rather than charge against him. What Joni managed to stay atop their mounts had Zeno to deal with. All broke before him—with every strike, he crushed both body and will. Cries of agony and torment were met with bursts of fear. The mounted Yorish and Sarpedonians re-formed and rallied behind Zeno, and the ones who had lost their horses finished off the wounded Joni and Hipperi who lay on the earth groaning in the throes of mutilation and death. Zeno slaughtered large groups of the Joni at once. He single-handedly turned the tide of the only part of the battle that was not going in the rebels' favor.

The Joni infantry and Equitati were all that was left of the Vampire's army. Zeno drove through large groups of them, breaking them up and making them more vulnerable. Victory was close! He sensed it. He sensed that his army sensed it. What was considered impossible four months earlier was now becoming reality. The furens was as a god that day, the Republican army its frantic worshippers. Those mortally wounded fought on until they gave out, pouring out every last drop of blood and life to bring down just one more of the enemy. Others fought through crippling wounds, and mere stabs or broken bones were completely ignored. None grew weary. For when they grew tired, the maniacal fever of their comrades and the gravity of the moment spurred them on to further exertion. Zeno leapt from his horse and swung his sword with both hands. He ripped open chests and throats. As more and more of the Equitati died, the ones remaining found themselves fighting off not one, but two, and then three rebels.

As Zeno noticed the scarcity of enemy troops, he stayed his hand from slaying the Joni whom he had knocked to the ground. He wanted some survivors. His eyes picked up movements across the battlefield becoming smaller. The cries of rage decreased; the cries of agony increased. All surviving Joni and Equitati now fought to break through the army and escape. But it was too late. The ground was littered with warriors wallowing or dead in a pool of blood and urine, thickened with human organs and body parts. For the first time ever, a united Ninivonian army had defeated the forces of the Vampire.

CHAPTER XXIII
THE VAMPIRE

The Vampire stood in the throne room of Ninivon Tower alone, staring out the great window that overlooked the city. It was night and a foul chill was in the air.

He had followed the battle from the Tower of the Sphinx. From a tactical standpoint, he understood why Phillip and Iban had been defeated. The Demigod was a sound strategist. He baited them into engaging before the other allies had arrived, surrounded them, and forced them to fight on two fronts.

What troubled him the most was the accounts of how the Demigod had dealt with the Rapti. When he had taken Ninivon fourteen years ago, the Rapti were his greatest weapon, not just for their ferocity and relentlessness on the battlefield, but also for the terror they struck in the hearts of his enemies. The Rapti were considered virtually unstoppable by all. Would his allies now come to fear this Demigod as his enemies once feared the Rapti?

As the Vampire looked out over the city, he recalled another battle, many years ago, a galaxy away.

You will never see her again...

The words haunted him. Drove him. They were why he had come to this planet to begin with, to have his revenge.

The wind blew through the window, bringing the Vampire back to the present. He had come to Ninivon in search of the one weapon he knew could give him the revenge he so longed for against the woman who had taken everything from him and her religion. Whatever his losses were at Drisdos today, the Vampire felt he had won far more. The Theomorphosis Chamber, and thus the Power of Thumos, was within his reach. Once he had it, he would finish what the Stokians started so many billions of years ago.

220

CHAPTER XXIV
ZENO

The night and the following two days were a blur. There were graves to be dug, wounds to be dressed, friends to be consoled. Lysandros let his generals lead their respective peoples as they felt best. He made it his business to actively be about the dirty work. Whatever job no one else wanted to do he jumped to complete, and Zeno was right behind him.

The following night a great celebration was planned. All forces consolidated at Sarpedon. As the sun set, the city lit up with festive lights. Zeno did not see the point of such displays but Lysandros assured him that his generals would expect a feast and the common soldiers needed such celebrations following great victories to converse together with a belly full of food and a glass full of wine in order to ease the great emotional burden of being in such close proximity to death for so long. In a sense, it was all part of the process of shedding the furens. Now, with not only the wealth of the Sarpedonian elite who were loyal to the Vampire, but also with the fortune captured in the baggage train of the Joni and Hipperi, Lysandros had the resources to fund a grand feast. Tables were set up along the city agora and through streets surrounding the capital buildings. Every tavern owner and brew master was employed. Lights were strung around stone towers and hung from trees. There was song and dance. They dined in the open air. Generals sat with their men. Unspoken for women flirted with men and vice-a-versa. Everyone was laughing, drinking, living life to the fullest, if only for a night. Even the shy ones came out of their shells. So thankful they were to have survived the battle, so desperate they were to be consoled for the brothers and sisters in arms who were lost. Sarpedonians drank with the Blue Order. Woads had sex with Militae. Everyone smiled; except Zeno.

He was truly happy that the people had this moment to rejoice. But Zeno had learned quite a bit about himself in the last few months. He was stoic; even more so than the Elleds who had invented the philosophy. This was not uncommon for graduates of the egoga, for the harsh taskmaster demanded such discipline. But Zeno was exceptionally so. He wasn't happy unless he was completely committed to an endeavor and working tirelessly towards it. He had trouble relaxing and didn't understand the military concept of recovery. He knew his troops needed it, but such liberties were not for him. He was a leader and with leadership came a burden. Furthermore, he hurt, not physically, but spiritually, he ached. Why did so many have to die? He had saved so many, why could he not save then all? Zeno simulated gladness on his face while he suppressed deep pain in his heart. He played the part of joyful reveler. Lysandros had always told him a general must be as good an actor as a leader. Most were so drunk they couldn't perceive his halfhearted smile. The only two who noticed it were the two who best knew him: Lysandros and Alexandra.

Ranold, Diana, Cyrus, Konan, and Ngozi all offered toasts, to their troops, to each other, to Lysandros and Zeno, and to the Republic for which they fought. But most of all, to their honored dead. All lifted their chalices. All drank.

"Well said, my Archon," Zeno said, once Lysandros had given the closing speech.

"The victory was more yours than anyone's. You should at least try to relax."

"I am trying," Zeno answered.

"No. You're not trying. You're trying to act like you're trying. It's not the same."

Zeno just shook his head. He didn't look up.

"Come on," Lysandros said, getting up and motioning for Zeno to follow him. They left the table and entered the imperial palace building. They walked out on a patio, four stories high, overlooking the agora.

"Do you want to talk about it, son?" Lysandros asked.

"When the Vampire first attacked, I was a *Ursae*. I had studied war most of my life, but didn't understand it. Not really. War is like love, you can commit your life to studying it, but until you are in the middle of it, you never really understand. I was too young to fight when the Great Terror happened. But when we fled to the Woadlands, I was expected to not just fight, but lead. I had always thought fighting was the hardest thing. But I was wrong. Worrying about other men, men beneath your rank, men for whom you are responsible: That was much harder. The funny thing is, I worried so much for my men that I didn't worry for myself at all. It was as if I only had so much emotional energy to give. I spent it all trying to ensure my men came back alive. I had none left to ensure I came back."

"That's the crucible of battlefield leadership," Lysandros replied. "It is the hardest thing. To assume the responsibility for someone else's survival."

"I thought the same thing, Lysandros. When I was out there on the battlefield, I felt a consciousness that I have never felt before. A consciousness of the moment, of everything happening within it, from microcosm to macrocosm. I could sense every active process happening on that battlefield. I could feel inside the soldiers in our army. I could feel inside the Joni and Hipperi as well, but not just them. I could feel inside the grass and trees, the skies, and wind. I even had an acute sense of what was not happening. I could feel everything, expect the Rapti. I was lost in the vastness of life, how much happens beneath and even above the conscious level that everyone else is completely unaware of; that I was unaware of until I took up the Power of Thumos. It is such a terrible responsibility.

"I have to save these people. I must. I'm not just talking about saving them from the Vampire; I must do that as well. But I must save them from everything else. From earthquakes, and famines. From diseases and accidents. All of existence is a great battle now, and they are the troops for whom I am responsible. To not save them, to not ache to save them, would make me a terrible, terrible thing. Not human."

Lysandros tried hard to understand. He knew that he couldn't fully understand. Outside of Zeno, no one knew the weight of Thumos more than he. But he felt uncomfortable with what Zeno was saying.

"You can't save everyone from everything, son. Not even the gods do that. The struggle against the monsters at our door, both alien and familiar, both natural and supernatural, that is what makes us human."

Zeno turned and looked out over the balcony onto the people below. How happy they were. He should be happy too, even if only happy for them. But he couldn't. All Zeno could feel was a deep existential dread for the mockery eternity makes of conscious existence.

"The gods aren't human, Lysandros," he finally said. "If they were, they could not look on the vastness of suffering and do nothing." Zeno paused now. This was the first time he realized that he had eclipsed Lysandros, this man who had mentored and guided him for practically all his life, who was like a surrogate father to him, this man who would rule the new world Zeno sought to build. Zeno could no longer look to him for much practical wisdom. He knew more than Lysandros did. "With respect, Archon, you haven't seen what I have seen."

Lysandros lowered his head and sighed before lifting it again. "I know you are right. I know I can't understand what it's like. But you're no god Zeno, not yet. Don't assume their responsibility without their power. Do what you can for the living. Don't trouble yourself with what you can't do. Don't trouble yourself with the dead. Not much bothers them."

"Do you require more of me tonight, Archon?"

"No," Lysandros answered.

"Then I can retire?"

Lysandros smiled. "I will be addressing the generals tomorrow at first light. All of them. We will need your voice at the meeting."

"Then my voice will be present," Zeno replied.

In the first few weeks of the occupation, Zeno insisted that he sleep in a storage shack in an alley of the forum. He was expressly against luxury. But as the other allies poured into the cities, the generals convinced him to take a bed chamber in the ambassadors' wing. They said it looked bad to the troops to see their commander sleeping in the streets. They said the common soldiers would expect some separation between them and him. Zeno didn't agree, but he obeyed.

Zeno entered the dark room. It was large, with couches and tables in the center and a huge bed and elaborate bedframe against the far wall. Against the near wall were bookshelves filled with texts. There was a great window to the far right. It was the full width of the wall and overlooked the city. Below, he could still hear the revelers. Zeno turned on no lights, but only a single ion candle on a night stand and hung his sword by his sheath on a rack next to the bed and undressed. He crawled underneath the covers and closed his eyes. When he heard the slightest sound of breathing from behind the floor-length window curtains in the corner of the right wall, He sat up in bed.

There, walking from behind the curtain towards the bed, was Alexandra. Zeno had seen little of her earlier that evening. She had been wearing green trousers and a cotton blouse, but not now. Now she was dressed in a night gown. Zeno could tell it was silk, and thin, he could see right through it. It stretched down to the floor and hung off her right shoulder, revealing her hard olive flesh. Her black hair, which she normally tied up, flowed freely from her head. Her brown eyes pierced him. They screamed of desire. As she drew closer, Zeno could see details of her body beneath the gown; her naval and the curve of her breast. The perfect ovular shape of her hips. Her mighty leg muscles tensing slightly with each step. At that moment, she was the most glorious sight he had ever seen. She radiated like a goddess in the moonlight which came through the window.

"I'm surprised you didn't realize I was here," Alexandra said.

"As am I," Zeno answered, trying not to stare at her body too much.

"You didn't look like you were enjoying the party. In truth I wasn't either. I thought we could console each other."

"And... and that?" Zeno muttered, referring to her gown.

"I bought it yesterday from a vendor. It makes me look like a woman, yes?" Alexandra smiled. "I am a woman sometimes, you know."

"You're a woman all the time." Zeno gasped.

"I know you haven't been with a woman since this rebellion began," Alexandra began as she sat on the bed beside him.

Zeno cut her off "I... I don't need your pity."

"It's not pity, Zeno." Her voice cut deep within him. She began caressing Zeno's hair and ear with her left hand. "I am free and can give myself to whomever I chose. Now, I am choosing to give myself to you." She pressed her pointer finger on his right temple and drew it down his cheek. "Do you want me like the other boys do?"

Zeno said nothing. He closed his eyes and relished in the sensation her touch created. His lips quivered and his head slightly shook as Alexandra moved her finger along, affectionately caressing his face. The Power of Thumos offered no bulwark against this sensation. In fact, it only heightened it. He felt her touch more closely than he had ever felt anything in his life.

Alexandra leaned close. Zeno could see down into her cleavage now. Alexandra smiled and leaned in for the kiss.

"Wait," Zeno stopped her. He closed his eyes. He wanted this more than anything. But he had to ask. "You don't just want me..." He struggled to find the words to express himself. He didn't know if he even knew the words. Finally, he blurted something out. "Because of this." He gestured to his entire body. He meant because of the Power of Thumos.

"I would prefer the Zeno that swam with me in the cave that night and couldn't keep his eyes off my legs. Is he available?"

"I can put down the power, yes." He nervously smiled. "But I can't re-assume it on my own. I would have to go back to the ship and enter the Theomorphosis chamber."

"Then I'll take you as you are."

They embraced. Their eyes met, and the kiss. A kiss which Zeno had waited his whole life to taste. Not like the kiss she had given him outside the gates of Dioskuria long ago. No, this was the kiss of a woman who wanted him. Alexandra's lips were soft and wet. As he gently pressed down, the sweet juice of her mouth poured over his tongue. The warmth of her skin engulfed him. Her smell flooded his senses. She wore perfume, extracted from the elderberry no doubt, but beneath it she still smelled of the woods and sun and wind. The mixture was intoxicating, exaggerating his hunger to taste her flesh. Zeno could feel Alexandra's breasts pressed against him through her blouse and his shirt.

Zeno turned and laid Alexandra on the bed. He threw off his night shirt before he crawled on top of her. Again, he threw himself into the kiss, excitedly sucking, and slightly nibbling, lips and tongue and juice and flesh all rolled into one; a delicious and maddening taste that demanded to be savored.

Alexandra dug her fingers deep into his back and Zeno's hands danced through her hair. He pulled it back just slightly, tilting her head and exposing her neck. He could practically see her pulse jump through her skin. Zeno plunged his mouth into Alexandra's exposed brown flesh and began working his way down her collarbone to her breasts while his right hand slipped underneath her dress.

Alexandra's breathing picked up. Zeno could feel her heartbeat rage beneath him. His was no slower. Alexandra began to gasp, as one would who struggled to keep their head above water.

Zeno raised up just enough. Alexandra tore off her nightgown. She was now naked and exposed beneath him, save only for her underwear. For a few seconds Zeno just gazed at her body. Every inch of her captivated and delighted him. Something told him not to rush, that these moments were rare, and to take the time to appreciate everything she offered him, to relish the beauty of the sight before him. His eyes went up and down her body, spellbound by the simplest and most powerful magic. Finally, their eyes met again. Both grinned. Zeno bowed low before the temple of her body, and worshiped her as one would a goddess.

CHAPTER XXV
ZENO

The rising sun spread rays of light into the window of Zeno's chamber. Zeno slowly opened his eyes. His first thought was that last night must have been a dream. In that awkward place between sleep and wake, before one has full control of their senses, he wasn't sure if what he remembered was real or not. Then he felt her. Alexandra was nuzzled up in his left arm. Her head laid on his chest and her body was molded around his. She was naked. He could feel the warmth of her skin against his. Zeno looked at the woman who laid next to him. *She is so beautiful.* Zeno had had lovers, but that moment was the happiest of his life.

They made love joyously, with a sincerity neither had felt before. They had thrown themselves into each other, over and over. When their eyes met, Zeno seemed to be in a trance. He held her tightly, as if in preparation for the inevitable morning that would surely carry her away. He kissed her hungrily. He kissed her with the full weight of his desire and the complete existence of his soul.

Alexandra breathed deep without opening her eyes. She let forth a yawn and turned over on her back. Zeno turned on his side and studied her, trying to memorize every fine detail about her. He wasn't sure how many more mornings there would be like this. He wanted to remember everything.

Alexandra opened her eyes and turned over again. She glared at Zeno. "What are you doing?" she asked.

"Watching you breathe."

"That's creepy."

"Sorry." Zeno sighed. "I, I couldn't help it."

"By Sofia, Zeno, you act as if you've never slept with a girl before. How long have you been awake?"

"Not long."

"How long were you going to watch me?"

"As long as I could. Is that all right?"

Alexandra laughed. She put her hand on his check and kissed him. "You're the Vessel of Thumos," she said without pulling her face away; practically speaking the words into him. "You can do what you like." Alexandra laid back in the bed. "Did I meet your expectations?"

"Is that a serious question?" Zeno grinned.

"Well, I've never had any complaints. But only the gods know how long you've been fantasizing about me. Sometimes unrealistic expectations can form in the head," Alexandra teased.

"You were like a goddess," Zeno admonished her. "But I don't want to hear about what other men have told you in bed."

Alexandra laughed. Then her look grew thoughtful. "I don't think I've ever been kissed like that before. You delighted in me in a way no other man ever has. Not just the act, not just my body, but me. Being kissed like that gives a girl permission to kiss like that in return."

"I just want to remember what this was like, always," Zeno said.

"Zeno, last night was just the first time. You and I will have many nights like that and mornings like this. Unless you want to bed every woman in the army." Alexandra cringed.

"I thought the Women of the Red Sky freely bedded whomever they liked and allowed their lovers to do the same."

"That's only true for bedding women. With men, a warrioress makes a claim and the rest of us have to respect it."

"Ah. Because with men you can have babies. It's not just good clean fun. It's tribal business."

"It's never very clean." Alexandra grinned. "It's powerful,

creating life. You have to be responsible with it."

"I don't ever want to be with anyone else but you."

"And I you." Alexandra smiled, raising up again for another kiss. "What do you say we have another go before our meeting with the generals?" Alexandra playfully caressed Zeno's hair and licked his lips.

Now Zeno was the one who laid back, creating distance.

"What's wrong?" Alexandra was confused.

"I have to go," Zeno said, staring straight up at the carved ornamentation on the ceiling: rose petals and hyacinths.

"What do you mean *you have to go?*"

"I have to go to Grey Peaks. I have to seek Likavitos. An alliance with the dragons is our only hope to have long-term success in this war. I can negate some of the Vampire's air armada, but I can't bring down an entire air fleet. Eventually the Vampire will realize that and he'll unleash all his bombers on us simultaneously."

"You were serious when you and my father told me that you planned to recruit Likavitos to our cause?"

"Yes," Zeno answered.

"Then I will go with you," Alexandra said, again seeking to curl up in Zeno's arms.

"No." Zeno pushed her back. "You can't. The road will be too hard. Even if the dragons agree to help us, attacking Altus Mons is too dangerous."

"Too hard?" Alexandra barked, her eyes piercing through Zeno like daggers. *"Too dangerous!"* She immediately turned and jumped out of bed.

Zeno knew that he had said the wrong thing. Alexandra's emotions could change on a whim. She was like her uncle in that regard. And Zeno, more like Lysandros. Alexandra was a stark contrast to his stoic nature. Perhaps that was why he found her so irresistible. He didn't know what to say and was mesmerized by her naked body, which she was now hastily dressing.

"*Too dangerous?* Really? I'm glad you're looking out for me," Alexandra said, sliding on her undergarments and the gown. "I mean, it's not like I spent years training in the same military program you did. Or escaped a siege at Ying-Chau, or fought alongside the Katanas for years, or started an organized crime cell, the only one that stood up to the Blood Sucker's totalitarianism, from the ground up with a gang of cut throats and orphans in a goddamned cave, or built a rebellion from that crime cell. I haven't done any of that. I'm a fine lady who can't ride more than an hour before I need my ass powdered. I just don't think I could bear the journey!" Alexandra raised her hand to her head and fake swooned, mocking the fine ladies of royal courts.

"Alexandra..." Zeno got up and walked towards her.

"Oh yes." She cut him off, tightening her corset around her chest. "What was I thinking? I'm not even remotely qualified to accompany you in the attack. I only followed you when you attacked Sarpedon by yourself, when everyone else thought you were insane and that I was a fool for going with you. I merely led the left wing of your army in a major battle, a battle that we won, by the way."

"Alexandra, please listen." Zeno reached out to wrap his arms around her.

Alexandra slapped his arms away and stepped back, a hateful stare beaming from her face. "Careful Zeno. You can touch me when I say so."

"You know I love you," Zeno patiently said. "You *know* I love you. And you know exactly why I don't want you to come. It's not because I don't think you are brave enough, or strong enough, or a good enough fighter. It's because if I lost you, it would destroy me. And this mission has a high probability of death for those who accompany me."

"In war, people die. I may die, or you may. It's not your job to protect me. If anything, it's the other way around. I've seen how weak you can become when you manipulate matter with the All Fire. There have been times you have almost passed out. Who's going to defend you if that happens at Altus Mons? I'm a daughter of the Red Sky, women who have held off larger and more technologically advanced armies, made up mostly of men who are bigger and stronger, for centuries. I am a Ranger: bearer of a sacred charge and guardian of an ancient tradition. I fought for years with the Katanas. Widely regarded as the best swordsmen in Ninivon. I'm not just the equal, I'm the superior of every man out there except for my father and uncle." Alexandra pointed out the window, through which the sun was invading. "I'm a better fighter than you and would beat some sense into you right now if it were not for the fact that I love you and you have superhuman powers. I won't endanger you or the mission, Zeno. I can more than take care of myself." Alexandra strapped her belt around her waist. "If our little love affair is going to make you act like this, then perhaps this *should* be our only time."

Zeno sharpened his eyes. He worshipped her but was far too experienced with women to submit to that primitive type of manipulation. "You can't use sex as a weapon against me, Alexandra."

"I'm not using it against you. I'm using it against your cock. Maybe your sense will intercede on its behalf."

"You never listen to reason," Zeno soberly said, shaking his head.

"You don't have any reasons! Not any good ones anyway. Is it just because I have a cunt or is it because you want it so bad that you won't allow me to go with you?"

Zeno sighed and dropped his head. Part of him was angry, part of him wanted to yell back. Another part was frustrated and wished to just walk away. But then he considered the brevity of life, how much he cherished this woman, and that either of them might be killed at any moment, and his anger and frustration abated. Rather, a sadness filled him. He sat back down on the bed. "I just want to protect the person that means most to me."

Alexandra calmed. "Your intentions were pure, if misplaced. You are not my enemy. In fact, I've never had one who is more on my side. Zeno, all my life, I have lacked the autonomy to fight for the people that I love. My father took that from me, twice. He says he had to. Says the Priestess commanded him and that she knows everything and that only by following her orders blindly can any of us avoid the apocalypse that awaits. I don't know about any of that. I do know you have never treated me as a means to an end. I have always felt that you have always seen me, for me. You've always respected me enough to let me make my own choices."

"Sometimes that meant letting you go to hell the way you wanted to." Zeno looked up.

"Fair. But that's what freedom is." Alexandra sat beside him. "You're my *commander*. If you order me to stay, I will. But as your friend, it will hurt. Especially coming from you. I guess I'm trying to say, don't treat me like that."

Zeno looked at her. "You're right. I'm sorry."

Alexandra leaned back. "How do you even plan to communicate with the dragon anyway? You're not going to use those damn phonographic scrolls, are you? The ones we learned about in the egoga, that our early zoologists and sorcerers developed for communicating with dragons?"

"Don't really have a choice. Dragons can't talk."

"They take forever."

"It will go faster through the All Fire. I can process information much quicker."

"It's a shame your power didn't give you something like the Bond my people have with horses."

Zeno's face grew curious.

"What?"

"Why shouldn't it have? What is magic except mutation of the All Fire we can't explain, but can predict?"

"Just like science is mutation of the All Fire we can predict and explain." Alexandra slapped his back. "You're making my head hurt with your philosophizing."

"I'm serious. I think I can communicate with Likavitos through the All Fire directly. But I don't know exactly how. Can you teach me how you communicate with horses through the Bond?"

"I'm not the best teacher. There are other warrioresses who would be far more qualified to teach that."

"But they're not going to spend weeks traveling with me to Grey Peaks." Zeno chortled.

Alexandra smiled. "So, I'm going with you then?"

"I need you. Part of me is ashamed to admit it. It feels vulnerable. But the road will be so hard without you. I don't want to go without you."

"It's vulnerable for me too. Who knows what lies ahead for any of us? I know it would break my heart to watch you leave again and not be able to go with you. I know I took a vow not to leave your side again." Alexandra began to untie the corset and tilted Zeno's face down to her breasts. "Go ahead. We've got time."

CHAPTER XXVI
LYSANDROS

Later that morning Zeno and Alexandra entered the Sarpedonian council chamber. The generals were all there. They looked beat up and hung over, but they were there. Lysandros had always said that a leader must comfort his men after losses and push them after victories.

Lysandros' eyes studied Zeno first and then followed his daughter. Ghost grinned at them both with the lewd and sarcastic grin of a soldier. Diana's face lit up.

"I want to hear about it later," she said to Alexandra in Militian. Most of the people in the room did not understand their language, but Lysandros did.

Alexandra smiled and took her seat beside Diana who playfully nudged her. Alexandra brushed her hand away and smiled without turning to acknowledge her.

"My friends," Lysandros began. "I trust you feasted and drank your fill last night. As was deserved, we have won a great victory. But one victory does not win a war. In fact, our position is only slightly improved. We still have a colossal army marching to besiege us from the east and the Dimronians and Dioskurians are coming to attack your families and homes from the north."

"The Archon is right," Cyrus interjected. "I received word earlier this morning that the Dimronian angels are on the offensive. They will be at Acheminidos in a matter of days."

"The Dioskurians are attacking Yorland," Sir Ranold added.

"There is another matter even more grave," Lysandros continued. "We still have no answer for the Vampire's air armada. Although Zeno's abilities have warded off offensive air assaults, the Vampire can and has still used his armada in a defensive posture. We have to break his aerial blockade or time will soon be our enemy and logistics our conqueror. We must eliminate the Vampire's air superiority once and for all."

"How shall we do that?" asked Diana through her interpreter.

Lysandros' eyes turned to Zeno, as did those of the other generals at the meeting.

"Can you bring the flying fortress down with your powers?" Diana asked Zeno.

"I can't do that," Zeno sighed. "At least I don't think I can. It's too big and would take too much time and concentration. Besides, I would have to be close enough and Altus Mons would counter with their fighters. We'd be blown out of the sky if we sent one ship and we don't have the air support to even try an aerial battle."

"Then how do we destroy it?" Ghost inquired.

"Why destroy it when we can capture it?" Lysandros countered. "There is an entire fleet of bombers onboard Altus Mons. We didn't have bombers when the Rapti first attacked. If we had, the war might have turned out differently. But the Archons feared developing such war machines because of the dragons. We already have the Vessel of Thumos, but he can only be on one battlefield at a time and eventually the Vampire will send the Rapti against us on multiple fronts. But if we had those bombers, we could wipe them out from above, without ever endangering our troops. Plus, the Vampire has used his fleet to attack your homes and families in your respective countries. I know the cost has been great. It is a moral imperative that we nullify those aircraft as soon as possible."

"All the same," Ghost barked. "How do you suggest we capture it then?"

"I will take a small strike force and capture the battle station," Zeno spoke up. "Eighty percent of the warships on the planet are docked in that aerial fortress. If we can capture it, not only will we eliminate the Vampire's air force, we'll have one of our own."

All over the room the generals looked puzzled.

"But you just said we don't have the ships to fight an air battle," Sir Ranold replied.

"We don't," Lysandros answered. "But if we had dragons, not one or two, but many, they could distract the Vampire's air force while a small strike force, led by Zeno, infiltrated and took the air base."

"Dragons?" Ngozi yelled, his face disgruntled with disbelief.

"There are no more dragons," Ghost said.

"There are," Lysandros replied. "My spies have confirmed Likavitos himself still lives, hidden deep within the mountains."

"Nikolaus, unless we take Altus Mons, all of our labors will be in vain," Zeno added. "We can't do it on our own. We need the dragons' help. If Likavitos sides with us, the surviving dragons will follow. I will go to Grey Peaks to find him myself. The dragons can't defeat the base, but they can keep the defenses busy long enough for my team and I to board. I will do the heavy fighting while my team takes the bridge. Once we have the control bridge, we control the base's defenses. We can then bring our forces up one ship at a time and take the station as we would a hostile city."

"It's a great risk for those who follow you, Zeno," Ngozi said.

"In war people die, my Lord Ngozi," Alexandra interjected. "If dying fifty-five hundred feet in the air terrifies you, stay here."

Ngozi turned to Alexandra and began to stand, but Ghost put his hand on his shoulder. "Don't take it personally, my lord," he said to him. "She's a bitch." Ghost smirked at Alexandra.

"In the meantime," Lysandros sought to move the meeting along. "Sir Ranold, Lord Ngozi, and Lord Cyrus, you will mobilize your forces and return home to defend your respective peoples. The Remani and Osaerians will have some weeks before they arrive. Zeno, will lead the assault on Altus Mons with five others. I want only volunteers. I will remain here, in command of the remaining force, to defend Sarpedon from the Remani and Osaerians coming to besiege us. If the attack on Altus Mons is successful, Zeno will return to lift the siege with warplanes."

"Zeno, what makes you think the dragons will help us?" Cyrus asked. "Even if Likavitos still lives, they are raving beasts."

"Dragons are among the most intelligent creatures in Ninivon," Zeno replied. "They behaved so savagely during the Great Terror because of the Vampire's magic."

"Even so," Sir Ranold asked. "Why would they help us?"

"The primary reason the Vampire built Altus Mons was to take the skies from the dragons. I believe my power, along with some coaching, will allow me to communicate with them." Zeno looked to Alexandra. "But the journey will take time. Since we have control of neither the sky nor the sea, we will have to make some of the journey on foot. Resist the siege. Defend the north. Give me three months and you shall never have another enemy bomber soaring over your homes again."

"Zeno's right," said Ranold. "We have gone too far. My people will hold Yorland. We can withstand not only the Dioskurians, but the Rapti as well if needs be, for three months. If Archon Lysandros can hold the city here, and you other generals can hold your cities," He nodded to Cyrus and Ngozi. "We have to give the Demigod a chance to take Altus Mons."

The room was silent. As in the council before the Battle of Drisdos, Lysandros' strategy was sound and had been thought out meticulously. Much of it depended on Zeno's supernatural power. But now there were few who didn't believe in him. Even Lord Ngozi had to admit that if Zeno could stop the charge of ten thousand Rapti, he could likely take Altus Mons with five men, if the dragons agreed to help them. The respective leaders of their peoples looked around at each other.

"Well," Ghost began as he rose. "May the gods damn it all to Tartarus! One more siege in a walled city and I'll shoot myself in the head. I will accompany you Zeno. I request the honor of being the first of the five."

"Second," Alexandra shot back.

Lysandros' eyes flared and he began to speak.

"Save it, Father. I already had this discussion with *him* this morning," Alexandra cut Lysandros off, pointing to Zeno. "I'm going."

CHAPTER XXVII
LYSANDROS

The journey to Grey Peaks would take sixty-seven days. They would fly through Zutaera, Acheminidos, and into western Yorland, a great deal out of their way, but such inconvenience was necessary to avoid the Vampire's aerial blockade, and was still faster than traveling the entire way by horse. They would then take a Yorish vessel over the Lumen Ocean, too far north to be detected by the Jonish navy, to the borders of troll territory. From there, they would travel the rest of the way on foot. The journey alone would be arduous—Troll territory was one of the deadliest and most unforgiving places in Ninivon—and that was assuming they had no setbacks.

In addition to Alexandra and Ghost, Zeno was accompanied Perseos, a member of the Blue Order, Galaxian, a Woad, and Aspia of the Militae. They all knew the risk. Theirs was a crack mission. They would, assuming the dragons agreed to help, break into the aerial fortress via fighter plane and take the control room. Once the other five were in control of the battle station, Zeno would single-handedly defend them from assault while they sent the signal to request more of their troops be brought up to take Altus Mons. Normally an undertaking such as this would be considered a suicide mission but with the Demigod, they all believed they could do it.

The night before the six travelers were to leave Sarpedon, Zeno and Lysandros were alone. They were playing *strategos*, a game of generalship. They played on a small wooden board with twenty-four hand carved pieces. Each piece was a member in the players' 'army' and had their own strengths and weaknesses. They had played often when they lived among the Woads. It helped them both feel civilized. Lysandros had always told Zeno that the game taught one how to think like a general.

"I hate leaving the army for so long," Zeno said

"Taking the long way gives you the best chance to arrive at your destination and escape should you be discovered. Do you not think I can hold Sarpedon against a siege for three months?"

"I'm more worried about the Acheminids against the Dimronians, and the Yorish against the Joni, particularly if the Vampire deploys the Rapti."

"The angels will fight in the heavens as they always have. The Rapti can't fly. As for the Yorish," Lysandros sighed. "I'm concerned too. But we have no choice but to have faith in them. Part of being a leader is believing in your troops; they will often pleasantly surprise the commander who believes in them and gives them opportunity to validate that belief. How much more time do we have?" Lysandros changed the subject, while moving his lion into attack position. "I know she will be coming later tonight." He looked up at Zeno.

"You disapprove?" Zeno asked while moving his dragon to defend Lysandros' attack.

"You are both adults. You can do what you want. No man will treat her better than you and no woman will be more loyal to you than her," Lysandros said, moving another piece into play.

Zeno smiled. "If you don't have a problem with our relationship, then there is only one other thing that could be bothering you."

"We are leading a rebel uprising against a superhuman monster. There are a million things that could bother me right now."

Zeno nodded. "She will be here soon."

"I don't want her going to Grey Peaks with you," Lysandros said.

"I knew that. I also knew we'd have to have this conversation before we left. I need her Lysandros."

"You need her, but not to teach you the Bond. You could learn that from any Militae in an afternoon at most. You rely on her too much Zeno. You're the Vessel of Thumos. You can order her to stay."

"You're the Archon of the Republic; you can order her to stay. But she'll tell you to go to hell as she did me. Your daughter is like a wild horse. She can't be controlled, merely guided, and even that only when she feels like it."

"She would hate you for it. Curse you. But you *could* make her stay. How do you hope to be a good leader if you fear upsetting one woman?" Lysandros leaned back in his chair and gave Zeno a rebuking stare.

"That was uncalled for," Zeno responded.

"It needs to be said. This would be an excellent time for you to develop some boundaries with her. Instead, you are packing her up with you and traveling with her half way across the world."

"*Boundaries*?" Zeno rose from his seat and stared for a few frustrating moments at the paintings on the far wall before he turned to his mentor. "Like the boundaries you set with the Priestess of Sofia? You know she brough that up. When I told her I didn't want her going the morning after the banquet. Maybe if you hadn't done that, her wound wouldn't still be so sore."

That stung. Lysandros grew angry with Zeno, as angry as he ever had been. "I already have to deal with her contempt for that choice. I will not tolerate yours. I won't allow it. Had I not followed my orders neither of us would be here to have this argument now."

"Maybe you're right. But I'm not you. I will not push her away for some abstract greater good that no one has bothered to explain to me."

Lysandros rose from his seat. "Then you're not ready for the great responsibility that has fallen to you. You know how dangerous this mission is. She could easily be killed. Why would you lead her into that kind of danger?"

"She could be killed here in the siege. What's the difference?"

"The difference is she will not be a target if she remains here. You are the beating heart of this rebellion. The Vampire knows that. At Drisdos his underlings underestimated you, but he will not make that mistake. From here on out, you and you alone will be the object of his ire. He will send everything he has against you, and that puts anyone with you at great risk."

"She also won't have a godman protecting her if she stays here," Zeno roared.

Lysandros just stared at Zeno.

"You don't think I can protect her?" Zeno's face contorted in confusion and disbelief. He shook his head. "I don't understand. More than anyone else in this army, you know what I am. You know what I can do. Yet you doubt me?"

"I have no doubt that you will take the battle station," Lysandros claimed.

"That wasn't my question," Zeno said stepping forward.

"You are the Vessel of Thumos. But you are also young. You have been given great power, the limits of which are still unknown to you. You think you are invincible. But the Vampire is wise. Your love for Alex is your greatest weakness, your unshaking confidence in your power is your second. The Vampire has spies everywhere. He will find those weaknesses and use them against you. You don't know enough to be cautious. You don't know enough to be afraid. Zeno, please." Lysandros' eyes were those not of a responsible general or statesman, but rather of a concerned father. They pleaded. "I just recently received my daughter back from the dead. Don't take her away again. I am asking you to leave her here as a personal favor, to me."

"I'm sorry Lysandros," Zeno said after a few seconds. "But you don't get to make that decision for me, or her." Then he turned, opened the great oak door, and disappeared into the hallway.

The next morning, the company of travelers met at the

eastern sector of the Sarpedonian airfield at sunrise. Their rucksacks were packed and their pockets full of currency to buy provisions along the way. A few of the generals and a handful of soldiers were there to see them off. This was how Lysandros wanted it. No parades. He wanted to keep their movements and intentions as much of a secret as possible. When the sun rose, the individual generals would take control of their forces and carry out his orders. The Acheminids and Yorish would head north to defend their homelands. The others would remain in Sarpedon and hold the isthmus.

Alexandra was dressed in a mail battle skirt and simple leather breastplate over a blouse. She was dressed lightly but had packed warm pants and furs to combat the cold they would inevitably face as they moved into Grey Peaks. Her pistol was strapped to her right hip, her Militian tomahawk to her left, and her rifle was lodged in its sleeve in the plane. She was ready.

As she tied her pack into the cargo compartments, Lysandros walked up behind her. Alexandra lifted her head from her work. When she saw her father, she sighed once and returned her attention to the double knot she was tying.

"The last time I watched you go away with Nikolaus was at Dioskuria," Lysandros began.

Alexandra raised her head and looked into her father's eyes. Then she turned and began to walk away.

"Alex," Lysandros called as Alexandra stepped from the troop compartment of the aircraft.

Alexandra stopped and turned.

"I told Zeno not to take you. I don't want you go. But that's because I'm your father. And because," Lysandros looked down, as if the words he sought were hidden on the metal floor beneath him. "Seeing you leave again reminds me of how much time we have lost over the years. I'm not sure Zeno's reasons for taking you are completely uncomplicated. But I do think you are the smart choice. In order for this mission to succeed he will need the best crack troops with him. That's you. You give this mission the best chance to succeed. Were I not your father, you're the first soldier I would choose. You're younger than me, and far more refined than that one." Lysandros motioned over to Ghost who was barking at one of the plane's crew chiefs.

"These fig cakes smell like mermaid pussy." Ghost could be overheard. "Have you ever sniffed Xhiputzec pussy, boy? It's putrid. But I'll eat these cakes anyway."

Alexandra chuckled and Lysandros smiled. "You are," Lysandros again began, "who you always wanted to become." Lysandros stood there for some seconds studying his daughter's face. He could tell his words had touched her. He had affirmed her. He had affirmed that he saw her as she wanted to be seen, by him specifically.

Lysandros didn't want to pressure her to open up more than she felt comfortable. He had hoped they could make some strides before she left though, he knew the danger she was walking into. Suddenly he felt an incredible sense of inadequacy come over him; as if although he had been so successful in so many other aspects of life, he had completely failed as a father, and that was the one area by which his whole life would be judged. Lysandros nodded and walked away.

"Father," Alexandra called out. Lysandros turned. "May Sofia preserve you."

"And you, my brave daughter."

The six took their seats in the aircraft. The vertical engines fired, lifting the machine off the ground. It climbed, ten feet, thirty feet, sixty feet. When it reached proper altitude, the main engines kicked on and the vertical thrusters turned off. The jet rocketed away in the northern sky, carrying the great hope of freedom for Ninivon with it.

CHAPTER XXVIII
ALEXANDRA

On the forty first day after leaving Sarpedon, the company reached the fabled mountain range of Grey Peaks. This stretch of mountains, spanning some five hundred miles, was once the home to thousands of dragons.

"Just like I remember them," Alexandra said to Zeno, but loud enough for everyone to hear. "Remember the last time we saw the mountains?"

"During our third year of the egoga," Zeno responded. "We spent two weeks training and studying the animals, from afar. Those were good times." Zeno smiled.

"I went on that trip as an initiate," Ghost interrupted. "Twenty years before either of you were born. I thought it was shit. These mountains were hell then. They were even more hell the other two times I was deployed here as a Ranger. If its not the dragons it's the goddamned cyclopes. Their settlements are on the far side of the mountains," Ghost warned the others. "Our presence should go unnoticed until we reach the Great Pit. But be on your guard."

They climbed. They pitched camp when night fell and ate what berries and nuts they had foraged from their journey. No one slept well that night. So haunting was the mountain range. They continued the hike for several days.

As they traveled, the company grew very close. Zeno stood the first two watches every night, and the others rotated taking the third. When Alexandra did not have watch, she and

Zeno shared a small tent. They kept each other warm. When before the others, they were respectful and reserved with their affections. But within the tent at night, they reveled in each other's arms, making love and conversing, and trying not to make too much noise. Both considered themselves equally blessed to have been chosen by the other and ardently strived to shower each other with their affections. As miserable as the conditions were, their love gave them both strength. It was the happiest Alexandra had ever been.

One such night, Alexandra lay curled up in Zeno's arms. Zeno laid there but could not sleep. He stared at the moonlight, faded but still visible through the opening at the top of the tent.

"You should really try and sleep you know," Alexandra said softly. "You need *some* sleep."

"I know," Zeno answered. "Alex?"

"Yes?"

"I don't know if I'm going to live through this. I don't know if any of us will. But if we do, if we win this war and survive, I want you to marry me."

Alexandra's body tensed up beneath him.

"What?" Zeno asked. "What is it? You don't feel the same way about me as I do you?"

"That's a stupid question. I'd die for you."

"But do you love me?"

Alexandra raised her head from Zeno's chest and propped herself up on her elbow. "During the summers, when we were released from our age grades in the egoga, I got a taste of life at the court of the Archons. My father was the third most powerful man in the Republic. His daughter was expected to be visible, and lady like, even if she was the half breed child of some Militae bitch. I never got along with the highborn daughters of the aristocrats. They were attending preparatory schools, learning how to be respected, proper ladies. While I was getting my ass beaten in training, learning how to defend their freedom so they could be those dainty ladies who never had to touch weapons or think about violence. They didn't understand me, nor I them. But I do remember them running around the city giggling whenever they kissed a boy. They would say they loved this one or that. Made grand plans for their futures, complete with glistening wedding dresses in the great Chapel of Charis the Matriarch. I was always so obsessed with training, even then, so I never talked with them or played their amorous games. But I remember thinking they shouldn't use the word 'love' to describe an infatuation for a boy whom they would drop in a second if an even more handsome, or higher status one became available. Love isn't like that. I was so young, I didn't know myself what love was, but I knew that wasn't it. They were childish games. But as I got older, I noticed the childish games never stopped, they just became more sophisticated. I always said I would never be part of that.

"When I lived among the Militae, I saw a very different model for love. Among them, a woman does not pursue a man for his status, land, or titles. When they venture to the Entitled nations to find mates during the genion, they don't base their selection on a man's wealth, status, or even his looks. There has to be a strong attraction and energy, of course. But the Militae are not obsessed with finding the most handsome man available. When they choose a man, they choose him for himself, for who he is, and who she is when she is with him, not for any other reason. Half the men they bed are married anyway. It is not, as the Entitled people of Ninivon used to say, that they are a nation of deviants and whores. When a Militae warrioress chooses a man, she loves him, and lets him love her in return for as long as they can; for as long as their souls meld together. She returns to her partner every year during her mating season to spend that week with him, then returns to her people, hopefully with his baby inside her.

"But people grow and change, or they don't grow but still change. Life pounds them like a blacksmith would hot metal and shapes them into something else. When their lovers change, or they do, to the point where there is too much distance between their souls, the Militae let their lovers go and find new ones. It is hard at first, but they believe this is actually the humane thing to do. They believe they should never hold their lovers back from becoming the people they are meant to be. They don't believe their lovers should expect them to hold themselves back. And that's it. No marriages. No commitments. Just two humans freely giving, taking what is given, and giving in return. No one owns or has exclusive rights to anyone, but it is everyone's responsibility to help each other grow as people and treat their lovers as they would hope their lovers would treat them."

Zeno rose up and looked Alexandra in the eyes. "So you're not interested in being my wife? You don't want me to *own* you and you're not interested in *owning* me."

Alexandra cupped Zeno's right cheek in her hand. "It's not that. You are more than just the leader of this rebellion. You are the Vessel of Thumos, you belong to the goddess."

"What sacrifices you make," Zeno smirked.

"Zeno..." Alexandra knew she had hurt him.

"I love you with my whole heart," Zeno replied, looking away. "I love you beyond sanity. If I had my way, once this war was over, I'd take you away and we'd make a life together, far away from all of this, all the power, all the responsibility. So, what will happen, assuming we live, when you decide you can't *hold me back anymore*? What will be left for me? What do I do then?"

"You worry too much about things you can't control, Zeno, and ignore the beauty that is in front of you. We are both wine for the gods, you and I, poured out as a libation on their altars and then gone. You know me. You don't judge me. You make me laugh. You're my best friend. You delight in me, and every day I am learning more about you, and it captivates me. I love you and will love you forever. I can't promise I will be in love with you forever. But I am in love with you now, and we may die tomorrow. Let's enjoy this precious thing while we have it. But if you want me to be your wife, ask me when this is all over. Ask me again; you know I'll say 'yes.'"

Zeno smiled. "Now that's how every man dreams his proposal will be accepted."

"You haven't actually proposed yet," Alexandra teased. They kissed. Alexandra turned around and curled up for sleep.

As they hiked deeper into Grey Peaks, the evidence of war became more visible: cyclops skeletons, long ago decomposed, but whose identity was unmistakable due to the large, singular eye socket in the forehead, wrecked machinery, and the skeletal remains of dragons.

"So how do we know any are still alive?" asked Aspia, looking at the skeleton of a great dragon. "How do we know this Likavitos still lives?"

"We don't," responded Alexandra, reaching the bottom of the steps. "But the Archon thinks he does and my father has ways of knowing these things. If Likavitos is still alive, he's hiding somewhere in the caverns beneath the Great Pit, so that is where we're going."

The following day, they reached a great open expanse leading into the earth: The Great Pit. As they came closer to the pit, a curious smell filled the air. It was not a bad smell, but different, unlike anything the less well traveled members of the party had smelled before. But Zeno felt it intuitively.

"This is it," he reported to his companions.

"So now what?" Ghost asked. "We go down there?"

"No," Zeno answered. "I want you all to stay here. I'm going down there alone."

"Zeno..." Alexandra protested.

"You have followed me this far, Alex," Zeno responded. "But these last few steps, I must make alone."

CHAPTER XXIX
ZENO

Zeno hiked down for nearly half an hour. Then he came to a straight vertical drop. The hole in the earth was easily forty feet in diameter. Zeno squinted but could see nothing beyond the entrance, only darkness.

Then, all of Zeno's senses were assaulted at the same time. He smelled fire. He heard the rumble of the earth beneath him. He saw the darkness flee as brilliant flames ignited in the cave, small, and far away at first, but they grew, and were coming towards him fast. He tasted the saliva thickening in his mouth. He felt the heat increase, and with it, his fear, an overwhelming fear. But this was not the same fear he felt at Drisdos. This was like the fear he felt at the Stokian spacecraft. The fear of being confronted with a powerful and alien force. He could now see a shape moving in the darkness, it was large, but still undistinguishable.

Zeno closed his eyes. He was surprised how frightening it was for him to do so. He concentrated. Mages had once used the old phonographic scrolls to communicate with these creatures. He would use the Bond, powered by the All Fire.

I don't blame you for not trusting me. Zeno thought. His thoughts were as words to the dragon. *I know how the Vampire used you and then betrayed you. I can't imagine the hurt, the rage. I won't pretend that I can. I am here to ask for your help.*

The dragon growled, low and menacing. Zeno instinctually opened his eyes. He saw eyes large as full shields staring back at him. They flashed with fire in the darkness and then turned away. He again heard a low grumble, almost a laugh. Zeno saw the mighty nostrils of the dragon protrude from the darkness and then submerge within it again. Zeno could feel the temperature rise and fall slightly with each breath from the dragon's nostrils. It was already laboriously hot. The dragon pit was dug deep in the earth, and radiated a subterranean heat.

There was once a pact between dragons and men. Zeno continued. *Our species shared the skies. I know it has been long broken. But my people are fighting a war against the one who destroyed your kind. I am here to ask you to join us.*

A mighty roar exploded form the cavern. It shook the very walls of stone. Zeno felt his pulse quicken. He sensed the dragon was angry and bitter. Zeno knew he couldn't show any signs of aggression. If he did, the dragon would surely attack. But he also could not show fear. For Likavitos would not follow one he intimidated.

I know. I know. There are a million reasons why you should not trust men. Men, who are vain, greedy, war-like, and untruthful, who barge into other's homes and demand aid, then when it is given, are often ungrateful. Who speak at length about peace when they are in want of allies, then betray those same allies when they see the opportunity for gain. Zeno's eyes widened. He had to fight to push down his fear.

But we are not only those things. We can be charitable, humble, trustworthy. There is no shortage of examples of the kind of men who betrayed you, great dragon. I have fought them myself. But there are also many who would gladly lay down their lives for their brothers and sisters, for Ninivon, even for dragons. I have fought beside them too. They fight for you now, whether you know it or not. Now is the time to join them. Together we can avenge both our species. I know you have laid in this pit these last fourteen years, yearning to fly, desperate to strike out against the devil who damned you and your kind to such an unworthy existence. Will you now, when the moment has arrived to fight, still cower in your pit?

Zeno regretted the words as soon as he thought them. He knew the dragon would perceive his words as an insult.

The earth rumbled. Likavitos, last *drakōn basileus* of Grey Peaks, leader of his genus and nightmare of his foes, sprung forth with a bellowing roar that shook the rock around him. His front legs slammed into the earth before Zeno, four toes from which protruded claws as thick as shields and as long as cutlasses. Dark brown scales covered his hide and opaque scales his underbelly. His face was as hard and unforgiving as time. His eyes blared crimson red. His mouth, now fully open was lined with rows of razor-sharp teeth. His wings, though not fully extended, easily spanned sixty feet, and at his full height he stretched forty-five feet tall. For a moment the man called by many the Demigod was again a child, paralyzed by both wonder and terror. The creature let forth a roar, low and rageful. It was the sound of unmet justice and vengeance unanswered, crying out for innocent, spilled blood. Again, Zeno sensed his rage. But it was rage against Zeno for reminding him of the injustice rather than against the Vampire for committing the injustice in the first place.

I have come to you as a suppliant. I will not fight you. I am not your enemy. Attack if you will, great dragon. I will not raise one finger to either defend myself or flee. If my bruised body is what you must have to trust me, then so be it.

The old dragon emerged fully from the pit now and slowly walked around Zeno, his eyes fixated on the lone warrior. A long, thick tail followed, covered in dark brown scales; the tail stretched for at least seventy meters. The dragon's advanced age had done nothing to diminish his grandeur.

Zeno stood frozen and did not as much as turn around. This was the pivotal moment. Everything in him screamed to both fight and run at the same time. His hands quivered and his breathing was heavy and deep. He concentrated on breathing through his nose to try and regain some control of the physiological functions he felt were wrestling away control over his body.

But he also knew that Likavitos wanted a closer look at him, and he would let him have it. Zeno could not let his fear compromise his behavior in these next few moments. He needed Likavitos to side with him. The Republic needed Likavitos to side with him. Could he unseat the Vampire from the throne of Ninivon without the dragons' help? Yes. But it would be a far harder fight, with far heavier casualties. The egoga had taught Zeno that fear always lived within a man, but could be kept at bay. The Rangers believed that bravery was the highest virtue, precisely because it was the one virtue which could not be faked. To act brave, was in fact to be brave. Zeno remembered this and saw beyond his fear. His breathing slowed.

The dragon snapped his tail like a giant whip, driving Zeno into the earthen walls of the pit.

Zeno, shook his head. There is no question that such a blow would have pulverized a strong man. Zeno felt his body ache, but he was alive, and well. He slowly rose to one knee, and then stood.

Likavitos again roared, mighty and terrible. He raised his front claw and slammed it down onto the man. The claw was easily four feet in length. It came down on Zeno like a ballista. Such a strike would have shorn an armored knight in two.

The force of the blow again drove Zeno to the ground. He had not felt pain like this since he had ignited the bombers above Sarpedon. Nevertheless, he again struggled to his feet.

The dragon bellowed. Once, twice. He was as much shocked as enraged. What kind of man could stand up to this? The dragon thrashed his tail about the pit and slammed both front claws into the earth before Zeno several times. Zeno felt the ground quake beneath him. Yet he did not move.

Likavitos now held nothing back. He opened his mouth and unleashed fire, hot and unforgiving on Zeno. Zeno stood there. When the dragon relented, all of Zeno's clothes and his weapons and gear were melted. His skin was charged; he was clearly burned. Yet even before Likavitos' very eyes, his wounds began to heal. The entire time, Zeno did not move a muscle.

Likavitos stopped long enough to inspect his victim.

Zeno could see the look in the dragon's eyes turn from hatred, to disbelief, to fear.

Likavitos again poured fire onto the man. This time, not for a few moments, but for long seconds. The dragon emptied his pyro-glands. Once the glands were empty, the dragon finally stopped, winded and gasping for breath.

When the smoke lifted, there was Zeno, on one knee, but he lived. He raised his head. A look of agony met the dragons face, yet there was no judgement. Rather, the look communicated sympathy. *I understand. I am prepared to endure your wrath. But I will not strike out against you, not even in self-preservation, nor will I flee. I'm sorry for all you have suffered. Please help us.*

I know you're in pain. Likavitos thought. *I know you're scared. What kind of man are you?*

Come and see.

CHAPTER XXX
ZENO

The sight would have been terrifying had it not been so marvelous. Against the calm backdrop of the night sky was the awesome sight of a brood of one hundred dragons soaring in flight. The beasts came in varying colors and sizes. Some were little larger than a fighter aircraft, others were large as the heavy troop and supply carriers. They flew in unison with their wings pounding the air around them, they sounded like a mighty ocean tide crashing against the rocks off the coast; their roars and bellows carried on the winds. The sound was deafening and humbling. It was equal in magnitude to that of jet engines and cannon fire. Never before in history had there been an allied assault of both human aircraft and dragons. Flying with so many of these majestic creatures, each member of the company couldn't help but feel privileged to be there. They all sensed that their actions this night, either for good or ill, would seal the fate of the rebellion.

Zeno and his company flew among the dragons in a Class D cruiser vessel. They acquired it from a Zan smuggler. It was old, and lightly armored, the vessel was made to transport small groups of people, five to ten, at high speeds. It had no weapons. Their speed, along with the diversion the dragons created, as well as Zeno's godlike powers, would be their defense. Nikolaus flew. Everyone else sat, buckled into their seats.

"This is our plan," Zeno told his colleagues around a camp fire three nights prior. "Likavitos and his dragons will create a diversion. Altus Mons will counter with fighter jets and defensive guns. The dragons can't keep up with the jets in terms of speed. But the fighters' guns can't pierce the dragons' scales. At least not easily. It will take concentrated fire from either fighters or artillery to bring any one dragon down."

"They seemed to bring them down pretty easy during the Battle of Grey Peaks," Galaxian said.

"Yes," Alexandra answered. "But most of the dragons were in or around the Great Pit when the cyclopes attacked. They didn't have time to take to the skies. Our dragons will already be airborne. It's a lot harder to concentrate fire on a moving target."

All nodded. Zeno continued. "Likavitos himself will escort us to the royal landing bay." He pointed to a bay door on a blueprint of the battle station. "This is where the Vampire's personal ship docks when he visits Altus Mons. It is also the closest bay to the control room. I will see to the bay door. All of this will have to be done under a barrage of enemy fire. Fighters and gunships will fire on us from all sides and once we land in the bay, guards will attack. Likavitos can provide cover with his fire in the bay but once we enter the stairwell we will be on our own." Zeno's finger traced a line on the blueprint. "We make our way to the control bridge and take it. Nikolaus has the override codes that should give us access to the main computer."

"How did we acquire the codes?" Aspia asked.

"Sexual favors, of course," Ghost grinned.

All jeered. Zeno grinned and continued.

"From there we can control every door, elevator, engine, and automated gun in the facility. Once we have the control room, we can use the battle station itself as a weapon against its guards and staff. We will own Altus Mons and all the aircraft within it. A complete sweep. The Vampire will lose all of his aircraft and we will have an air force for ourselves."

"In case we cannot take the bridge," Alexandra interjected. "This is our contingency plan. We've marked eight different escape routes along our path. If we get bogged down, we make for the nearest bay. Highjack a cruiser and escape with the dragons as our cover."

"But not before we deposit this." Ghost pulled a device from a satchel. It was round and silver with a jungle of wires protruding from the top only to disappear again into the device. It looked like it would bring down an entire mountain. "This beauty will destroy anything within a quarter mile. It's on a ten-minute timer. If we can't complete the mission, we stash it as close to the control bridge as we can and look to Zeno to get us the hell out of there."

"With respect strategos, you make it sound easy. It would be hard to execute such an escape in such tight confines, under fire, in only ten minutes," Perseos said.

"It will, my friend," Zeno confirmed. "Which is why it will be far better for us to take the control room."

They had flown for fifty minutes before they began to see Altus Mons on the horizon in front of them. It looked like an arrow head hovering in the sky. They were still several miles away but the battle station was already visible.

Altus Mons was, in many ways, a marvel of modern technology and engineering. An aerial battle station perpetually maintained in the air by thrusters and hover engines, large enough to dock almost every air craft in the Vampire's fleet, nearly five thousand various ships. Over two-hundred thousand personal were required to run the battle station and had living quarters on board. Roughly half of those living and working in Altus Mons were Dioskurians. The rest were a mix of the Vampire's privileged populations.

Aside from housing over a thousand fighter aircraft and gunships that could be quickly launched in defense, Altus Mons was defended by a battery of artillery guns stationed at various levels. Zeno knew Likavitos had lost many of his kind at this accursed place and that he would likely lose many more today, even if the attack was successful. He could not help but feel humbled by the bravery and nobility of the dragons.

Tonight the last of the dragons would go to war against an enemy that had hunted them almost to extinction.

Zeno flew the cruiser high and tight behind Likavitos, who himself led the first rank. They were only ten miles away now. The battle station was huge. Even the largest of the dragons looked tiny before it. Undaunted, Likavitos bellowed a war cry, and the dragons charged forward.

The seven hundred and twenty-eight bay doors of Altus Mons opened. From the retracted doors, hundreds of fighter aircraft and gunships flooded the night sky. The aircraft formed up immediately and rocketed towards the flock of dragons. As the two battle lines came closer, they picked up speed. Zeno looked to Likavitos who flew directly ahead of them. This was the dragon's battle; he would be in command. Zeno's primary job was to get his cruiser safely to the royal bay and take the control room as soon as possible. But he would help the battle in whatever way he could. Seeing the leader of the dragons fly so boldly, and command his forces with such intensity, galvanized Zeno's will. The dragons flew as if they were on a suicide mission to hell.

The lines clashed. The dragons roared. Fire, both from dragons and ion cannons, lit up the night sky. The dragons were larger and stronger. They held formation and broke through the line of aircraft. The dragons shot dozens of fighters from the sky with their fire or pulverized them with wings and claws on the initial clash, sending the wreckage of the planes crashing to the earth in violent flame. The fighters and gunships looped around and reformed, again placing themselves between the dragons and Altus Mons. They were faster than the dragons, and more agile. Again, the lines clashed. This time both shattered. There was no strategy or formation. Just beast against machine, ion guns slicing and burning into reptilian flesh, filling the air with a repugnant scent, and dragon fire likewise igniting metal and ion munitions into flying billows of light blue fire.

"Gods of Tartarus!" Ghost yelled, observing from the window of the cruiser. "There must be a thousand of those damn fighters! They'll overwhelm the beasts!"

There were too many aircraft. They laid into the dragons, emptying their missiles and ion guns, then moving out of the way before the dragons could counter. But it took many such attacks to bring one dragon down, whereas one dragon could easily destroy multiple fighters with one blast of fire or whip of tail or claw. They fought back tenaciously. One dragon smashed a fighter in his talons. Another shot two down with a blast of fire. The whole time, the dragons moved as quickly as they could and still propelled themselves toward their objective: Altus Mons.

Zeno closed his eyes and entered the trance those of the company had all seen several times before. Two enemy fighters appeared behind them firing. Zeno opened his eyes. His pupils had rolled into his head. He raised both hands back in fists and punched forward. Both aircraft ignited in the sky. Another fighter appeared to their left bow. Zeno shot his hand forward in an arch. The pursuing fighter fluttered before crashing to the earth.

They were only a half mile out now and the ion cannons mounted on the outside of the battle stations began to fire into the fray. They were as likely to hit their own as they were the dragons. But many of the fighters were drone piloted and even the ones that were manned by humans were seen as acceptable casualties. One blast found its mark on the side of the neck of a dragon, piercing straight through its hide and out the other side. The beast let loose a monstrous roar and fell to the earth. The cannon was quickly destroyed by another dragon who in turn was attacked by four gunships simultaneously. One wing was seared off, and it fell.

Land battles were chaotic but aerial battles made them look organized. Dragons swooped in and out, firing at the battle station, doing what damage they could and then retreated before cannon fire. A cannon decapitated one dragon. Fighters scattered before another and then converged behind her firing. Explosions marked the destruction of fighters and gunships. Roars and blood marked the death of dragons. The dragons of Grey Peaks fought like angles of death, but they were outnumbered and suffered heavy casualties. Every roar of agony pierced Zeno's soul. These brave creatures were dying to give him and his five companions a chance to take the battle station. But he had to focus on Likavitos, who himself had suffered wounds but flew ever faster as he approached the royal bay doors.

Likavitos dropped altitude with three fighters behind him. He wanted to fly below the heavy fighting but was attracting attention from the enemy. The flames bursting from his mouth annihilated a dozen fighters and another two gunships. Zeno couldn't keep count. All he knew was that were it not for the dragon, the cruiser would have been shot from the sky. He moved so gracefully for a creature so large. He flew like an eagle and attacked like a lion, powerful, erasing from existence anything in his path. He was receiving wounds but flew on without losing speed or agility. Even with Likavitos paving the way they were receiving heavy fire. Three ion rounds screamed towards the great dragon. But before they could reach him, Zeno ignited them all with his power. They banked and turned.

"Bellos the bloody! They're everywhere!" yelled Galaxian.

"We're almost there," Ghost responded; his mind focused on flying.

They could now see the royal bay doors. As they approached, more and more of the fighters focused on Likavitos. This brought the dragons as well and cannon fire pursuing them. This is not what Zeno wanted. An ion blast cut into Likavitos' shoulder. The mighty dragon roared and for a moment dropped altitude. But almost as soon as he began to fall, he rebounded in his course, like a runner who stumbles, but rather than falling to the earth catches himself with a long stride and continues to sprint.

They were racing now to the bay doors, racing with war and fire and death all around them. Likavitos picked up speed. The dragon's resolve was iron. He dodged fire, hit on target when retaliating, leaving a trail of wrecked ships falling from the sky behind him in flames.

Zeno spread his arms apart and the bay doors folded like paper before them. Likavitos plowed into the bay at full speed. Nikolaus reduced speed, but they were too close. The cruiser burst through after Likavitos. The cruiser slammed into the steel floor and began to skid. Zeno closed his eyes and concentrated. He focused all of his energy on slowing the ship down. The cruiser skid eighty yards before it slammed into the far wall. Zeno's powers had slowed it down just enough to prevent it from colliding in the wall at suicidal speed. All the passengers were tossed about, their security belts only keeping them from being thrown around the aircraft like balls inside a metal box.

Likavitos was instantly on his feet. The bay was filled with maintenance personnel who were running back and forth, trying to escape. Dioskurian guards were pouring in with ion rifles at the ready. Likavitos snarled, glorifying in his strength and the promise of blood wetting the steel floors beneath his claws, and unleashed hell fire on dozens of them.

Zeno looked first to Alexandra. She didn't speak but nodded. She was unharmed. He meant to check on the others but Ghost beat him to it. "Any of you pussies hurt?"

No.

"Let's go!" Zeno commanded.

They were up, and had their rifles ready. This was the calm before the storm. The dragons' bravery and Zeno's power had landed them inside Altus Mons. That was the hardest and most perilous part; for Zeno's abilities were somewhat nullified while flying through the skies. Now he was on solid ground, and the fight would not be machine against machine, but rather man against man. Or in Zeno's case, man against god.

Zeno kicked the door free from the cruise ship, and the soldiers leapt forth into an already raging battle. Death erupted from Likavitos' jaws. He was covering the cruiser, giving the heroes a chance to gather themselves and form up. A few Dioskurians broke through Likavitos' blockade of flame. They sprinted towards the cruiser. Likavitos turned and lit them ablaze. Their shouts were horrifying. The scent of putrid, burning flesh filled the bay. Zeno caught glimpses only. One fell a few feet in front of him. He cried maniacally. His face melted off, revealing only a skull caked with globs of muscle tissue, sinew, all of which turned to ash.

Likavitos swung around again and knocked a dozen hoplites back to certain maiming or death with one swing of his mighty tail. Still, they poured in. Zeno opened fire. He shot with deadly accuracy. Every round fired killed or crippled a foe.

Alexandra, Ghost, Perseos, Aspia, and Galaxian fell in behind Zeno and followed his lead; firing their rifles on anyone who happened to escape Likavitos' fire.

"Head for the stair well at the east side of the bay!" Zeno barked. "I'll cover you!" Even with Likavitos and Zeno, guards were flooding into the bay. Several hundred were already dead but many more hundred were rushing in. The interior defensive guns began to fire on Likavitos. This is where things became dangerous for him. The small, ion rifles of the guards were not a high enough caliber to even phase the powerful dragon. But the interior cannons could wound or even kill him, if they hit him enough times in the same area, which was likely, given the fact that his mobility was nonexistent inside the bay. Likavitos could not remain much longer and Zeno knew it. His job was to give the company a fighting chance once they were in the bay and he had done that. The others ran for the elevator, receiving heavy fire. One round blew through Galaxian's shoulder knocking him to the floor. Zeno placed a shot between the eyes of the hoplite who fired the blast.

Perseos pulled Galaxian to his feet and carried him behind

the others. They hurled themselves into the stair well.

"Fuck!" Aspia roared, seeing Galaxian bleed out. The wound was large and bleeding fast. Alexandra was already putting gauze over the wound when Zeno burst through the door.

"Brown Warrior," Galaxian stuttered. "Leave me. I'm bleeding to death. Leave me here. Give me a grenade."

Everyone understood. There was no time to morn. Outside in the bay, Likavitos had already taken off into the night sky to organize his army's retreat. The dragons had served their role beautifully. How many of them had died? Zeno had no way to know. He knew he had already lost one of his own. The dragons would now retreat. Galaxian would remain here to kill however many more guards he could with an ion grenade. It was all on him and the others now.

The company flew up the stairs. None looked back, but all felt the heat, and heard the explosion as two ion grenades went off, sealing the entry to the stair well. No enemies would be following them that way.

They sprinted up the stairs. No one uttered a word. Zeno stood out front. He wore the traditional armor of a Dioskurian hoplite, including a helmet, as did Ghost and Perseos. Alexandra and Aspia were lightly armored in the Militae way. But Zeno would be the great human shield for all. They, in turn, had their guns at the ready behind him as they climbed.

They burst through the double doors two stories up and into a long black hallway. The red emergency lights were already flashing above and sirens were calling all personnel to arms. Each side was lined with guards of various races who fired in unison as soon as the doors burst open.

"Stay behind me!" Zeno barked to the others without turning around. He threw down his rifle and drew his sword from his back. He charged the guards head-on. They fired. Zeno dodged one round only to walk into two others. The smell of burning flesh lit up the hall. But the Demigod continued his charge. He slammed his blade into the guts of one. The next second, he sliced through another and then hacked the torso of a third. He moved like a demon. With each half second, another guard fell in a bloody, mangled heap. It made no difference if they were Bramhai or Dioskurian, Remani or Joni. Alexandra, Ghost, Aspia, and Perseos followed, firing at any Zeno might have let live behind and trying to kill a few before him. More than a shield, Zeno was their human battering ram. The hall was just wide enough for him to have full range of motion to swing his sword but too narrow for the guards to avoid the blade. The guards fired on them. Some particularly brave ones even drew their swords and charged. It didn't matter. All died before him. Several guards tossed grenades Zeno's way. One grenade stopped in mid-air and flew back towards the guard who threw it before igniting. The other, Zeno caught in his hand, a blinding light and deadly heat radiated from his closed fist, before it dissipated.

By the time Zeno reached the end of the hall, the surviving guards threw down their weapons and tried to get through the great double doors at the end of the hall, but they were locked. Zeno was out of mercy to give. Nor could he afford to leave living hostiles behind him. He hacked through them in seconds. The others were sprinting behind him, almost slipping several times on the blood and piss that covered the floor under them. By the time they joined Zeno at the far end of the hall, almost all the guards were either dead or dying.

Zeno kicked the double doors open as if they weighed mere ounces. The doors led into a two-story atrium. The room was filled with columns and eerie blue light from the lamps behind the columns. At the far end was a staircase that led to the control room on the next level. Much to their surprise, there was only one defender in the atrium, standing halfway between the elevator and the staircase. He was covered in a dark purple hood and cloak that hung to the floor. Underneath, they could see he wore an Angolid chain mail shirt under a crimson red leather cuirass, all over a white silk shirt. He wore dark red pants and held a Joni bastard sword in his right hand. His face was angled down, but not so much that he could not see what was directly ahead of him.

Zeno strode forward, and the others fanned out behind him, rifles up, their points moving from the sole inhabitant of the room to the columns. They were sure guards were behind the columns lying in wait.

"War against men is easy for gods and monsters," the cloaked man said in an ominous voice. "The real challenge comes when you face an equal."

The man looked up. His purple, pupilless eyes could be seen beneath his grey hair. Under his upper lip, Zeno could see the very tip of two inhuman fangs protruding.

Zeno

Zeno was torn between fear and exultation. Fear for his companions; for Alexandra most of all. The fact that the Vampire was here was proof that he knew about their attack, and so this was certainly a trap. But exultation because he had an opportunity to kill the Vampire here and now, ending the war.

The egoga had taught Zeno that war was, stripped to its most basic elements, just problem-solving with the highest of consequences under the greatest of pressures. One of those pressures was the element of time. Zeno had to make a command decision. He knew that he would have to deal with the Vampire. The question was, did he now order his friends to fight to the nearest aircraft and escape, or should they press on to the control room? Either way, they would have to do it without him, and they would be virtually defenseless against the army of troops who were surely coming. Which was the least dangerous route?

"Nikolaus," Zeno said. "Take the others and make for the control bridge. When you get there, set the blast doors and hack into the computer. Don't open them until I join you. I will deal with *him*."

"I'm not leaving you!" Alexandra roared like a lioness.

"No, Alex. This is my fight. Obey my orders."

Ghost tugged at Alexandra's arm. "The best thing we can

do for him now is take the bridge."

Alexandra growled. Her eyes glossed over with anxiety and rage. Then, she took off with the others to the stairs and disappeared behind another set of doors. Zeno was alone with the Vampire: Terror and Woe of Ninivon.

Lysandros always said duels were odd things. More like a dance than a fight, every step choreographed, predestined by some omnipotent force. It was for the combatants only to dance their steps and let the swords fall where they may.

The Vampire threw down his purple cloak. "The *Demigod*," he jeered. "That is what the people call you, yes? Vessel of Thumos, wrath of the Stokians, defender of Sofia. Are you ready for me, Zenosthenes Andrea?"

"How do you know about Thumos and the Stokians?"

The Vampire laughed. "I know more of them than you, boy. I know you gained your powers through the Theomorphosis chamber."

"Then you know what I'm capable of."

"What I do not know is whether you have the resolve to use your power to its fullest extent. Demons always make men see the good in evil actions as if the actions were themselves good. To kill demons, you must become a terrible thing, worse, perhaps, than the demons themselves. I ask you, Zenosthenes of Limnae, are you ready to slay demons?"

"Even if I die tonight," Zeno's voice dripped with conviction.

"How very noble, *Demigod*, that you are willing to die to save your people. How unfortunate that I am also willing to die to watch them burn. And to what gods will you call on to help you? Seeing how it is so much easier to destroy than to save?"

Zeno gritted his teeth. He did not anticipate that the Vampire himself would be there. Ever since he had been driven from his home like a fugitive, he had dreamt about this moment but it was not until he was given the Power of Thumos that he knew he would one day be face to face with the Vampire, the author of so much misery for Ninivon and her people. He often wondered how he would feel when he finally beheld the man who had taken so much, not just from him, but from his entire world. He raised his sword and the dance began.

Zeno opened with a downward, two-handed strike. The Vampire raised his blade to parry and countered with a swing for the side. Zeno knocked the strike away and swung. The Vampire blocked again and, with his right hand, grabbed Zeno's forearm and pulled him past him, making a final swing that Zeno avoided.

There was a break in the dance. Both combatants paced the floor and eyed each other. Zeno had not felt power like that before. The Vampire possessed superhuman strength as he did. The pull alone would have propelled a normal man across the room.

The Vampire stepped forward and brought his blade through. Zeno blocked, but he struck again, this time across the belly. Zeno jumped back only to see the blade come screaming at his side. He blocked and blocked again as the Vampire countered with a swipe at his back. The Vampire drove his foot into the back of Zeno's knee, forcing him to the ground. He struck from above, but Zeno rolled out of the way and burst to his feet. Zeno's helmet rolled off. Again, a pause. Both panted.

Zeno snarled and hurled himself at the Vampire, thrusting his sword. The Vampire sidestepped the attack and struck down. Zeno stepped into the attack and threw him over his back. The Vampire crashed to the ground. Zeno was upon him, blade firing down. The Vampire moved and recovered his blade, which he had lost. Zeno planted his sword's edge into the floor where the Vampire had laid a fraction of a second earlier. Now the Vampire sought to create distance. Again, both combatants stalked each other like sharks in the shallows.

Alexandra

Alexandra, Ghost, Aspia, and Perseos ran down a less well-lit hall that opened into yet another atrium whose back wall was decorated with a low-relief sculpture of the Vampire's conquest of Grey Peaks. Down a short flight of stairs were the double doors that opened into the control room. It bothered Alexandra that they had met no resistance since encountering the Vampire in the hall. She suspected a trap. But they had come too far; if a trap was behind those doors, they would have to spring it. If they could hold out long enough for Zeno to kill the Vampire and join them, it wouldn't matter. Even if Zeno could not aid them, they were so close to their goal. If the guardians of Altus Mons were close enough to slay them, then they were close enough to slay the guards as well. They just had to take the control bridge, and she and her uncle were Rangers, easily worth five guards apiece.

Perseos threw an ion grenade, and the doors exploded into the control room. The four rushed in and fanned out, firing, not so much with the intent to hit anyone so as to force everyone in the room to take cover. As the smoke cleared, they realized that no one else was there. No engineers, no officers, no slaves, no guards. No one. The Vampire had left the control bridge completely unguarded. Alexandra looked to Ghost, worry across her face.

"Fuck it!" Ghost roared. "This *is* the goddamned bridge. Trap or not, if we can hack into this computer, the fight is over."

Zeno

Zeno caught his breath and pressed again, slicing from right to left. The Vampire parried the blows, but they were so powerful he couldn't gain his feet to counter. It took all he had to block. Zeno fired an uppercut. The Vampire blocked, but the force of the blow picked him off his feet and drove him in the air before he came crashing down.

The Vampire was on his feet almost as soon as he hit the marble floor. Zeno pressed his advantage. The Vampire blocked an attack across his chest and another at his right leg, then across his side. He thrust through, but Zeno moved. The Vampire struck across Zeno's chest again. Zeno parried, but the Vampire brought his sword crashing down into Zeno's exposed right thigh.

Zeno wobbled back, but did not fall. The blow would have cleaved through the leg of a mortal man. The wound leaked blood, but he was still mobile. That the blow had broken skin and drew blood was a testament to the Vampire's godlike strength. He thrust forward. Zeno spun to the ground and swung his Dioskurian bastardsword, cutting into the Vampire's back. The blow didn't penetrate the leather armor, but it did drive him to a knee. The Vampire jumped to his feet, setting himself for another attack.

Alexandra

"Guard the door," Ghost ordered his three companions. Ghost stood at the bridge master computer. It controlled every automated system on board. He began imputing information into the keyboard. A series of displays came up on the clear screen before him. Then the computer completely crashed. Fear surged through Alexandra's heart.

Before any of the company had a chance to react, nitrous oxide began to fill the room.

"Gas!" Ghost yelled. "Get out!"

Perseos was the first out. No sooner had he exited than three ion rounds blew through his chest. He fell dead. At least one hundred Remani centurions were flooding the atrium, cutting off their only route of escape.

Alexandra, Aspia, and Ghost retreated back into the control bridge. The gas had yet to completely fill the room. They still had some visibility, but the gas was strong. If they stayed inside the control room long, they would certainly pass out. If they fled into the atrium, they would be shot. Alexandra and Ghost both had the same thought. They looked for the source of the gas. There were four tanks secured in the ceiling. They aimed and fired. They hit two tanks. Both exploded. The force of the blast was enough to cave part of the ceiling in and knock the defenders down. But it also gave pause to the guards advancing from the atrium, on whom Aspia was firing. Alexandra and Ghost were up in a flash, thankful the blasts had not claimed their lives. They fired at the other two gas tanks, which were further away. Again, two violent explosions. The control bridge was now a chaotic mess of debris. But the tanks were destroyed. The gas cleared. The three defenders now took their positions behind the door, Ghost on the right with Alexandra on one knee beneath him, Aspia on the left, and fired into the sea of enemies working their way towards them.

The three fired on the oncoming Remani, the nearest of which fell to the bottom of the steps leading to the bridge. They all tossed what grenades they had. But the guards were pressing in, each hulking between the wall and his shield to lessen his vulnerability. They proceeded in quick bursts from cover point to cover point, as cautiously as they could, stepping over the bodies of those already fallen, which were piling up in clusters along the narrow path. But the guards were in the open, and the company was well protected by the doorway. They could hold this position, at least until they ran out of ammunition. The Remani fell under their rifles amidst a cacophony of gunfire and screams of the dying.

"Alex," Ghost cried over the din of gunfire. "If you make it out alive, you should forgive your father. Tell that prick he should forgive me as well."

Zeno

Zeno charged and thrust his blade forward. The Vampire side-stepped and slammed his elbow into Zeno's jaw. Zeno felt the sting and blood running from his nose. The Vampire buried the edge of his blade into Zeno's side, under the breastplate, once, twice. The blow cut deep enough to bleed dark red. Zeno was in trouble. He punched the Vampire and swung across the side again, slicing through the cuirass and piercing the flesh. The Vampire shoved Zeno away and leaped back to create distance.

The dance grew sloppy. They were both tired and wounded. Nevertheless, like two bulls trying to break each other, both men raised their swords. They rushed. Swords clashed together in the center of the room. It was the final stages of the dance. Both knew it. Like runners who, when they see the finish line in the distance, double their speed, each emptied all their hate, hope, malice, and souls in the blows, trying to find that one opening that would bring the dance to an end, or force such an opening through brute force. Block and parry, counter-step, again and again.

Finally, the Vampire's blade bit deep into Zeno's sternum. Zeno was stunned. The Vampire swung across his back and sliced into his deltoids. Zeno roared like a wounded tiger and crashed to the ground.

Zeno instantly began to sit up, but the Vampire slammed his boot into his jaw, sending him back to the floor, and placed his blade at Zeno's throat. Zeno lay there, his body screaming from the pain, looking up at his enemy, who had conquered.

"Zeno!" Alexandra shouted.

Zeno looked. At the top of the staircase, pouring from the doors through which his friends had disappeared, were at least fifty Dioskurian hoplites and Remani centurions, with Alexandra in ion chains. Soot and blood covered her body.

Zeno could tell she was wounded in more than a few places. The guard holding her pressed a knife to her throat.

Zeno's eyes grew wide, like those of a lunatic. The Vampire pushed the tip of the blade a little deeper into Zeno's throat, forcing him to turn to him.

"Yes, Vessel of Thumos, I knew you were coming. And that you were bringing your greatest weakness with you; your love for this woman," the Vampire said. "Which is why I stationed a full squadron of guards in the passageways outside of the control room and rigged the ceiling of the bridge with gas. You and your dragon allies were never the objective; your woman was. I knew even if I failed to beat you, you would surrender willingly to save her life. So to capture her, I gladly sacrificed a fraction of my fleet and a handful of men."

Zeno stared at Alexandra. He could see the rage and terror in her expression. Her face was hard, but the hurt written all over it was easy to read. Nikolaus was dead, as were Aspia and Perseos.

"Relinquish the Power of Thumos," the Vampire commanded. "Return to your mortal form. Or she dies."

Zeno looked at the Vampire and then back to Alexandra. So many thoughts flashed through Zeno's mind: rage, hatred, fear. The moment sped up. He wanted to lash out at everything. At that moment, if he could have slain the Light Gods, he would have torn them apart bone by bone.

Alexandra's face was hard as stone. She looked directly at Zeno. Her intent was clear. Zeno was not to surrender the All Fire, no matter what happened to her.

"I'll surrender the power," Zeno said.

"Zeno, don't!" Alexandra barked. But her lover just shook his head in reply.

The Vampire nodded to the guard, who slightly lowered the knife.

The Vampire pulled back his sword. Zeno climbed to one knee and then stood. His eyes met with Alexandra's again. Her head tilted slightly; there was such sorrow and regret in her eyes. Zeno opened his mouth to speak the chant, the chant that would again render him mortal and effectively end the rebellion.

Alexandra struggled to free herself. "He'll kill me anyway! He'll kill me anyway! Zeno, don't do it," She roared like a lioness, watching her beloved mate surrender to the hunters.

Zeno lowered his head and began to recite the chant in old Stokian. The words were alien to all in the room, save the Vampire, who knew well the old language and magics of alien worlds.

"...again to the great flame shall the spark return... again to the great flame shall the spark return..."

Zeno let fourth a monstrous cry. There was a blinding flash of blue light. All had to look away. When the light dissipated, they saw Zeno, again driven to his knees, his face planted in the floor. His wounds seemed all the more severe. He was smaller, frailer, mortal. He slowly raised his head. Again, his eyes met Alexandra's. He was again that young man who had swum with her in their secret pool. That had been a mere seven months ago, but it seemed like a lifetime.

Then they saw a flash of light from the corridor leading to the bridge. They heard the blast and felt the heat. The entire wall and upper level on which Alexandra and the guards stood incinerated. They were all thrown onto the lower level on which the Vampire and Zeno were. Everyone crashed to the ground. Zeno knew the source of the explosion the second he felt the blast. It was Ghost. He had planted the bomb in the control bridge.

Before they even landed, the floor beneath Zeno ripped open, dividing the room into halves. Zeno rolled back to avoid falling through the floor. The Vampire stumbled back and fell backwards. The battle station rendered itself straight through to the outside. Air pressure now set in, further tearing that section of Altus Mons apart. Power lines exploded. The evacuation alarm went off.

Zeno looked around to locate Alexandra. He was now on his feet and prepared to jump across the chiasm. This was their opportunity to escape. He had to get to Alexandra. He could see her. She had survived the blast. But she was weak, wobbly. A hoplite grabbed her left leg. She drove her right foot into his temple, breaking his grip. Another tremor rocked the battle station. The floor beneath Alexandra tore away. She fell through several stories before she passed into an ocean of open sky.

CHAPTER XXXII
ALEXANDRA

Alexandra opened her eyes. She was lying in a bed; her wounds were dressed. Her body throbbed; she was sore everywhere; but she was alive. At least, she thought she was alive. The last thing she remembered was being in free fall from Altus Mons. There was no way she could have survived such a fall. She did recall something large and fast moving towards her in the air. But she was too seized with terror at the time and it all happened so quickly that she couldn't distinguish any details. With great pain, she sat up in bed.

Alexandra was set back by her location. She had been in ancient buildings made of cyclopean stone; she had been in high tech buildings with the most modern amenities; but this room seemed to be an uncanny mixture of both. The walls were constructed of what appeared to be dark blue marble. But there were lights shining from inside the stone, making the room seem like it was submerged in a glittering pond of water. It was a bedroom. The bed she laid in was large, but simple. There was a stand to the right of the bed with a pitcher of water. Other than the light emitted by the walls, the only light was a dim blue glow that shined down directly over her head. There was a large oaken door at the far end of the room. The entire environment made her feel uneasy. It seemed alien. She felt as if she should not be here.

The door opened and Lysandros entered, followed by a woman with long black hair and soft eyes. She wore a simple blue gown.

Alexandra lit up the moment she saw her father. Her first instinct was to get out of the bed and run to him. She didn't remember that she still harbored so much resentment. Then her pain reminded her she would not be running anywhere. Lysandros and the woman stopped in front of her bed. Alexandra just sat now and stared at her father, not sure where to begin.

"We heard about what happened at Altus Mons," Lysandros began, a deep well of pity building in his eyes. "I'm so..."

"Zeno?" Alexandra blurted out. "Is he...?"

"No," Lysandros answered. "Not yet. But he is in the Vampire's custody, being held in the dungeon of Dikaiosune Tower. He is to be executed nineteen days from now in Acropolis Square, for all Ninivon to see."

Alexandra bowed her head. "He was waiting for us, father. The Vampire was waiting for him. It was a trap and I led him right into it. I was the trap. He meant to capture me because he knew Zeno would surrender his power to save my life."

Lysandros nodded his head. "Sarpedon has been destroyed," he replied. "The Remani and Osaerians came through the western gate. Suddenly, they were everywhere. Yorland fell. As did Zutaera. We waited for you at the Balena but could not stay any longer. As we speak, the Militae and Woads are escorting the Sarpedonian refugees here."

"*Here?*" Alexandra looked puzzled.

"You are inside an alien starship, Alexandra," the woman said, in a soft tone that would coax the demons of hell into peaceful sleep.

"*An alien starship...* By Sofia. You are the Priestess."

"I am. When you fell from the sky, a dragon caught you and brought you here by my bidding. I then notified your father of your survival." The Priestess motioned to Lysandros.

Alexandra continued to look unsure. Then she looked down.

"You told me what would happen. You told both of us. But I didn't listen."

"Alexandra..." Lysandros tried to interrupt her.

"I did this." She looked up.

"You made a choice," Lysandros replied. "You couldn't have seen the unintended consequences at the time, none of us could. All the intelligence we received said the Vampire knew nothing of the attack."

"You saw them, the unintended consequences."

Lysandros lowered his eyes.

"You would have had me stay with you at Sarpedon," Alexandra continued. "If I had done so, Zeno would have taken Altus Mons, Sarpedon and Zutaera would not have been sacked…"

"You're right," Lysandros authoritatively cut her off. "I would have had you stay with me. But that might not have saved Zeno, or our allies. What if you had stayed and Zeno had been captured or killed anyway. You would have never been able to live with yourself for not going."

"No less than you lived with yourself for sending me to Ying-Chau."

Lysandros looked at his daughter. He gave no response, but the gleam in his eye let her know that he recognized that she saw the parallel between her choice to accompany Zeno to Altus Mons, and his decision to send her to Ying-Chau. They made opposite choices, Lysandros choosing to let the one he loved go to protect Zeno from danger, Alexandra choosing to accompany Zeno despite the danger it posed to him. Neither choice had worked out the way they had hoped. Finally, Lysandros spoke.

"That was a lifetime ago, Alex."

"I was a fool," Alexandra replied. "A fool for going with Zeno, and a fool for holding your choice against you for so many years."

"It wasn't Lysandros' choice to send you to Ying-Chau," the Priestess inserted. "Which he told you."

Alexandra turned to the Priestess. "He did," Alexandra began to ball up in the bed, making herself more compact, as if she were preparing to receive a blow.

"Don't you want to know why I did that, child?"

Alexandra's heart throbbed. Perhaps before she had awoken, before she accompanied Zeno to Altus Mons, perhaps every second of her life leading up to this one, she would have screamed 'yes.' But now, her soul was leaping to find a place to hide. All she could do was shake her head. "No…"

The Priestess tilted her head. "You do. But you're scared. You feel the answer will be the final key that unlocks the mystery of your life. A mystery you have long wished could be solved. Yet you know that this knowledge comes at a price. You have already lost so much. But could it be that the one thing that has always been outside your grasp, lies behind the words you fear to hear?"

Alexandra turned away, saying nothing.

The Priestess began. "During the Baroquista Uprising, Lysandros commanded a regiment deep within this forest. He was a younger Ranger then. Outside of this starship, I have almost no power. I needed him to come to me of his own free will. So I prepared Lysandros for months through dreams and visions.

"He awoke one night, troubled by dreams. That's when he saw me, in the form of the great owl. As in the dream, I flew and he followed. I led him here, to this ship and brought him into these walls." The Priestess now looked at Lysandros, who returned a gaze ripe with yearning and memory. "You must have been so scared," she said to him.

"Terrified. But I knew I had to follow you," Lysandros replied.

"I easily recruited him to my cause. He swore to forsake all if needs be, his house, name, rank, family, even the Republic, if that's what it took to defend Zeno.

"When Lysandros first came to me thirty years ago, something else happened. I fell in love with him and bore him a daughter. We high priestesses of Sofia are forbidden to leave this place in human form. Nor, are we permitted to have children, or any attachment of any kind. I could not care for the girl. I entrusted her to the Militae, the Women of the Red Sky, the people from whom I came. When she came of age, they entrusted her to Lysandros, as per my wishes."

Alexandra's eyes grew large with shock and surprise. Also something else; a great sorrow, a nameless loss.

"I am your mother, Alexandra," the Priestess said. "I commanded your father to send you to Ying Chau. I told him to leave you there. I wanted to make sure Lysandros was free and undistracted to look over Zeno, and to see that he grew into a man worthy of his calling. I knew you would go through hell. I knew Zeno would as well. I knew it would break your father's heart to let you go. I knew you would hate him for it. I knew that you and Zeno would eventually find each other, and I knew that we all would eventually arrive her, at this moment."

Alexandra just sat there; her eyes sorrowful. Her face bitter and confused "My grandmother?" She asked.

"A distant relative of mine from another life. I am much older than I appear."

"A lie." Alexandra whispered.

The Priestess sighed. "I have never been a good high priestess. I knew I would fail my order when I fell in love with Lysandros and had his child."

"Yet you did it anyway," Alexandra said. "You knew how much pain and regret we would all suffer. You knew Zeno would eventually end up in chains. Yet you took no steps to alter our paths. Why?" Alexandra began, shaking her head. "You played with our lives as if they were pieces in some cosmic game. Not just me and Zeno, but the thousands who have died in this conflict. You're a monster."

"Alex..." Lysandros spoke up.

"Lysandros," the Priestess interrupted her one-time lover. "Leave us. Alexandra and I must speak alone now."

Lysandros looked frustrated, but he obeyed.

The Priestess walked to Alexandra's bed and sat down. She lifted Alexandra's face by the chin. Her touch soothed Alexandra's raging soul. Alexandra wanted to push her away, but she could not. Something about this woman, her mother, who she now knew abandoned her in the name of some greater plan, captured her attention and would not let it go. The Priestess had the same calming effect on Alexandra that Zeno did.

"You are right to hate me. I withheld a great deal of information and put the people I love most in harm's way. When the Vampire came, you have no idea how badly I wanted to ask your father to bring both you and Zeno here, to this starship, where I could protect you. But protection was not what you needed. You needed to feel the pain of this world. You needed to grow strong and wrathful against it. Just because a puppet can see its strings, does not make it any less a puppet. I had a sacred charge. I never chose for that charge to mean more to me than anything in this world, more than my daughter, my lover, my own life. It just did. I had no control over how I felt any more than you did when you fell in love with Zeno, or all those years you were angry with your father. That charge was to make sure Zeno was ready for the ancient power of the Stokians, and then endow him with it. I was a slave to my charge. But tell me, Alexandra of the Red Sky, Alexandra, Ranger of the Republic, Alexandra, rebel of the Blue Order, who is not a slave? One man is a slave to lust, another to greed. The Vampire is a slave to his own sadism and pain. Zeno was a slave to you when he took up the Power of Thumos to save you, and when he abdicated his power to save you again at Altus Mons. All men are slaves to fear; all men are slaves to hope. We do well if we can at least understand the masters who rule over us. But none of us choose them. I understood that Zeno would never become the Vessel of Thumos unless it was the only way he could save you. I also knew that Zeno would never escape the Vampire, unless you saved him."

"*Save him?*" Alexandra asked.

"Lysandros is planning a rescue mission," the Priestess continued. "He will fly into Dioskuria on the backs of dragons and pull Zeno down from the cross. He will ask you to join him."

Alexandra looked the Priestess in the eye. She felt that she was telling her future plans that Lysandros had not even worked out yet.

"You will recommend the dragons to him." The Priestess nodded. "I already have Likavitos' consent."

"Will we save him?" Alexandra asked.

The Priestess stood. "Even if you knew you would not, you would attack anyway. It is who you are, my child. It is a fearful thing to tell someone their future, even if it is what they think they want. But you are my daughter and I have been such a cruel mother to you. I have kept such secrets from you for so long. I will tell you your fate, and the fate of the raid, if you wish to know."

"I do."

"Yes, if you accompany Lysandros on this attack. Zeno will live. You will be the difference that makes the difference. And one day, he will liberate this planet from the tyranny of the Vampire. But the cost will be great, Alexandra, so great."

Alexandra looked up to the Priestess. Her eyes now welled. She made no attempt to hold back the sorrow. "It's not fair. All my life, my purpose has been to lay down my life for those I loved. And all my life, I have been denied that choice. I never had the autonomy to stand in the gap. By saving Zeno, I can save the world. My life is a small price to pay in comparison. What's waiting for me in Acropolis Square, is the fulfillment of my life's purpose. I'll win everything I have always wanted. But what's waiting for Zeno is heartbreak. He'll lose everything he ever wanted: me. It's not fair to Zeno."

"You see with more than your eyes, Alexandra. But now look further. Zeno was chosen by the All Fire to be the Vessel of Thumos. Just as you were chosen to be the one who made him worthy of such power. You know now that the All Fire chose well with you. Do you truly believe it poorly chose Zeno?"

Alexandra's posture straightened. Her eyes beamed a glimmer of hope, frail, yet long suffering, and, so sweet and long absent, understanding. "Lady, will you tell me your name?"

"Kallista Orthia."

"Kallista Orthia, you are a hard woman. I hate it all." She

sobbed. "I want Zeno. I want a life. More than that I want him to have a life, and me." Then, as the calm after the breaking storm clouds, peace and determination grew across Alexandra's face. "But I understand. I finally understand. And I can forgive, myself as well as others. For that, I do thank you."

The Priestess smiled. Her face radiated gratitude, as if every sin she had ever committed had been forgiven. She sat back down beside her daughter and held Alexandra close for the first time in her life, and Alexandra let her, wrapping her arms around the priestess as well.

"And you are an honor to both your mother and father's people, Alexandra, of the House of Polymaxes. Alexandra, of the Red Sky."

CHAPTER XXXIII
ZENO

Water trickled down the stones and formed a small puddle in the south corner of the cell. Zeno occupied the cell known as "the oven." It was called this on account of its shape and size. It looked like a long, wood burning oven. It was seven feet long but not more than three feet wide or tall. Zeno laid down flat on his back. He could not sit up, he had enough room to turn on one side. He was not chained. No chains were needed. There was one entryway directly behind his head. It was locked from the outside. The oven would have been completely dark had it not been for a small opening, about the size of a small plate, over his face. Light poured in from a window about forty feet above that. The Vampire had this cell constructed following his conquest of Dioskuria; such barbarism would have been anathema during the reign of the Archons. They had not fed Zeno at all and the only water he had to drink was from the puddle up by his head. He had just enough room to turn over and cup the water up with his hands. Zeno had been there, as best as he could tell, eighteen days. He had seen no one all that time. He laid, during night in complete dark, on the cold stone, warmed only by his own urine which was minimal due to the scarcity of water.

Occasionally, he caught an insect or rodent. He had easily lost twenty pounds. He was segregated from other prisoners and even guards, but he could hear chains rattling and men and women screaming and crying in the distance. More than once, he was certain he heard voices speaking to him.

One evening he saw Alexandra. She bent down over him, staring down into the small hole through which he looked. She wore a soft blue dress, looking not like a warrior, but a woman in love, charmed by spring time.

"Alex?"

Alexandra smiled back but did not speak.

"Alex?" Zeno sobbed.

She got up and walked into the darkness. Was she a dream, a hallucination, or some other mind game concocted by the Vampire's sorcery? Zeno had no way to know.

His mind played odd tricks on him. He could not sleep. Every time he closed his eyes, he sensed an evil presence come over him. Tall, with pale white skin and silver long hair. It had no nose or mouth but seven eyes across its face. He never looked at Zeno while he was awake. But when Zeno's eyes surrendered in drowsiness, it looked down through the hole over his face. Something about the monster's glare horrified Zeno beyond reason. Therefore, he resolved not to sleep. Zeno was quite certain he was losing his mind. Although he believed all these visions to be nightmares and hallucinations, in a place with so much dark magic and human suffering, who could be sure?

He tried to think of places and people with whom his heart had been glad. He recited the poetry of Remoh and Ligriv. He considered the philosophy of Olto and Elowen. Often, he would chant their words, almost as a liturgy.

"So shall the gods give end to these times of toll,
It is appointed to man once to die,
And from that time, forever in silence to lie.
Each day brings death closer, ever fading the All Fire
  within,
We are here for but a little while and then are no more."

He thought of Lysandros, Nikolaus, all his childhood friends he had been through hell with from the egoga, his brothers in arms among the Woads, the Priestess, and above all, Alexandra.

On the nineteenth day, a jailer came and gave him food. It was bread with old ham and cheese, covered in fish pulp. Zeno immediately knew two things: this was a manipulation of the Vampire and the food was not poisoned. The Vampire would not kill him in a dark dungeon, but publicly, for all Ninivon to see. He didn't care about either. He was starving and devoured it in an instant. He was fed twice the following day as well.

On the twenty-seventh day, Dioskurian guards pulled Zeno from the oven and took him to another chamber. This one was large and tall, the ceiling stretching twenty feet at least. A small window sat high in the wall. Zeno could not stand on his legs. So atrophied were they from nearly four weeks in the oven. The guards chained him to the wall to hold him upright, then left.

The Vampire: Terror and Woe of Ninivon, entered the cell. This did not surprise Zeno. He knew the Vampire would want to talk with him before he killed him. The Vampire's great hubris demanded that he be recognized as the conqueror by those he had conquered. Zeno found this petty. If the Vampire were truly wise, he would have already slain him.

"I was thirty-three by your years when their first ships appeared in the skies above my home," the Vampire began. "My planet was not nearly as advanced as Ninivon is now. We had no plumbing, or motorized vehicles, much less starships. When the Erīeds came to us with their great technology from beyond the stars, many took them for gods.

"Moreover, my people had been brutally enslaved. When the Erīeds arrived and promised the annihilation of our overlords, many took them for saviors. I always knew what they were. Not gods, not saviors. Just a cult of extremists. But I didn't care. All I knew was that this cult of fanatics would eat my masters. There is a saying among the Zutaerae: A child who isn't given the love of a village will burn it down to feel its warmth. That was me. I was happy to give myself over to them, but I always knew what they were."

The Vampire turned away and stared intently at the window in the upper wall, almost as if he wanted to distance himself from his enemy while reliving his most vulnerable moment.

"I have always been fascinated by the naivety of the religious mind." He turned back to Zeno. "The Erīeds had long traveled the universe for untold eons preaching their gospel of immortality. The gospel of anti-death. My world was just the next one in their path. Many converted; the rest were food for the converts. They said their goddess could make us live for thousands of years. But there was a price: If we accepted their goddess, we would crave human blood, but not as a thirsty man craves water. Rather, how an addict craves a drug, or a drunk, wine."

"Ignorant fools. It's a virus. A virus, plain and simple. Of course, they don't realize it. For all their great knowledge and technology, the Erīeds are blinded by their zealotry. They think it is the spirit of their goddess indwelling them that allows them to live for so long. But it's really just the *ignis obscura*, the Dark Fire, which slows cellular aging but requires a certain protein found only in human blood. The younger the specimen, the more of the protein is present. Thus, by consuming blood we prolong our lives." His smile turned sadistic. "Many who convert struggle with this craving. Many don't feed for months. Even those who are most devout in the faith. Of course, eventually, everyone comes around.

"I, on the other hand, took well to my new life. I never bought into their dogma, but their faith is obsessed with growing, both through child birth and conversion. It is one of the most deeply held Erīed beliefs that all sentient life in the universe must bow before Erīel. Death must be eradicated from existence. I was happy with the conquest, if not the religion. I did well in their army. In time, I built a new life for myself. I took a wife and even had a daughter.

"But there was also something else. I was unique among my peers. I could transfer the Dark Fire through my bite, the same virus that the Erīeds had passed to me through their machines."

"Their *machines*?" Zeno inquired.

"Yes. That is how the Erīeds transform new converts. They transfer the virus to them technologically. Techno-theocracy is what your Stokians called it. The Erīeds call it *the baptism*. What it really is, is parabiosis. In me, the virus mutated, like it never had before in Erīed history. Not only could I transfer the Dark Fire through my bite, but those whom I bit could transfer it as well. But the strand I passed down was stronger, less tempered. This was not the mixture of Dark Fire and All Fire that had made the Erīeds the most powerful creatures in the universe. No, this was pure Dark Fire. It does not bond with the host, it overtakes them, making them lesser creatures, more primal, base. With the All Fire within them completely extinguished, they become the living dead, their consciousness erased. Their only thought is always to sustain the Dark Fire within them on blood. Unlike the Erīeds in whom only a small portion of Dark Fire is mixed with All Fire, who can go weeks or even months without consuming human blood, and must still drink water and eat food to sustain their bodies, these creatures feed only on human blood and must have it often. But by doing so, they extend their life indefinitely, if you can call such an existence life.

"With such unique gifts, I quickly rose in the ranks of the Erīeds. I became what you Rangers would call their strategos. For over two hundred years I served them. I served the Elder Council. I led their armies in campaign after campaign. I conquered empires, converted millions, killed billions.

"But such things are not meant to last. Many within the cult envied me for my gifts. They thought one as sacrilegious as me unworthy; questioned the plan of their goddess to grant me such powers. Others feared me. They said my powers and those I created were an abomination. A personification of death; and nothing is more hateful to the Erīeds than death. Still, others were looking to break away from the cult. They saw in me someone who might lead them."

Zeno studied the Vampire's demeanor. He seemed to drift in and out of a forest of memories.

"With such power, I could not be controlled by their Elder Council. I grew tired of taking orders from fools who thought trusting in their goddess's will was a military strategy. It was just a matter of time before I rebelled.

"We fought the Erīeds for years. Pushed them further than anyone had since the Stokians. With my ability to create what you call the Rapti, and control them, and their ability to quickly reproduce, and with my intimate knowledge of how the Erīed army fights, its strengths and weaknesses, we almost won."

"But you didn't," replied Zeno.

"I was betrayed," the Vampire snarled. He turned parallel to Zeno and let his eyes fixate upon him. "Because of their dogma, those who have already been either batized or born into the faith can never be executed. They killed many of those who followed me in battle, of course. But those who were captured or surrendered, were allowed to live, and sentenced to a hundred years of reconditioning in their re-education camps. I was banished. Condemned to an eternal living death. I found my way here in a battered starship.

"The crash nearly killed me. I was incapacitated for days. I awoke in a bed, in a shack in the Darklands, my wounds dressed and beginning to mend. Lana Tarquinia sat at my bedside, with a bowl of her own blood to offer me."

"Why are you telling me this?"

The Vampire took a few steps toward Zeno, his eyes sharpened.

"Because I want you to see just how alike we are. Like you, I saw my world conquered by an alien force. Like you, I fought against them. Like you, I lost."

"We are nothing alike!" Zeno exclaimed. "You committed a genocide. You killed millions. Enslaved millions. You allied yourself with devils!"

"What you say is true. I did serve devils, but then again, I also slew many of them. I hated my goddamned world so much, that I was willing to deal with religious fanatics and alien monsters, to watch my enemies die. They were all devils; my enemies. Horrible men and women who did horrible things. They deserved to die. But that's not why I killed them. I killed them because I could, and because I wanted to. I deserved to die as well. But they did not have the power to kill me. When I found the devils with whom I dealt were no longer useful to me, I struck out against them as quickly as I had allied myself with them. Now, I kill whom I will. I drink from whom I will. I make death out of life where I will. All for the same reason, because I can. This makes me a monster, I know."

The Vampire now drew close. "But let me tell you something else." He reached out and shoved his pointer and index finger into Zeno's face, forcing him to face him. "When I made myself known to this world, they came to me. The Joni nobles, Rema, Osaeria, the angels in Qarek, they came to me. Just as the Woads and Sarpedonians came to you, they begged me to lead them. So anxious were they to throw off the oppressive and prejudiced rule of your precious Archons. They hated the Republic as much as your supporters hate me. Your high and mighty Archons: who called the Remani deplorable, who demanded Osaeria pay higher taxes because of her wealth, who presumed to dictate terms between Acheminidos and Dimron, who had been fighting each other for hundreds of years before the Republic came to be, who outlawed slavery in Jona, yet abandoned the cyclopes to servitude among the dragons. Your precious Republic. It is the arrogance of youth to see one's enemies as absolute evil. But there are heroes and villains on both sides in every war. Even heroes can act like monsters, and monsters like heroes.

"You see, one man's hero is another's villain. You yourself serve as evidence of this? That Jonish and Hipperi army you butchered, do you think them all eunuchs without wives and children? In Fluer d'Mar and Tahira they call you the '*hated one.*' A whole generation will grow up without fathers because of you. I shall be hailed an avenging hero when I kill you."

"What of all the fathers you killed?" was all Zeno could think to say. He yelled it to as great an extent as his weakened state permitted.

"Countless? Yes. I admit it. But how many wars have there been since I claimed the thrown? A few uprisings, easily discouraged, but that is all. Did you know, that Archon Godfry once suspended all cattle shipments to Tahira, because he was offended at the wine they served him at a banquet? You condemn me as a murderer, and do not consider that you might have made the same choices were you in my shoes. You condemn the nations that followed me as greedy and power hungry. Some certainly were. But were the Xhiputzec mermen ever known for their greed? Their kingdom is beneath the sea. What use do they have for the riches of land dwellers? Hard as it may be for you to hear, they saw me as your followers see you: a welcome savior. I made the trains arrive on time. I fed people whom your Republic let starve. I gave security to those whom your Republic had bullied. So, when I massacred your armies and massed your citizens into feeding camps, enslaving some and killing others, everyone turned the other cheek. Because they were prospering. I conquered all; some by the sword, others by luxury."

"*Luxury?* They are as much your slaves as the peoples you conquered."

"You are a smart boy, Zeno. You see the inner workings of human systems. Your mistake is that you fundamentally misunderstand human nature. You think they care. How do you think my troops retook Sarpedon so fast? As inspiring as it was that you took the city singlehandedly, you practically handed it back to me as soon as you won it. You seized the wealth of the aristocrats and redistributed it to the peasants, and then you let the aristocrats live, confounding your mistake! I led a slave rebellion. If you wish to free slaves, you must kill the masters, not one or two, but all of them. Otherwise, they will always seek to re-enslave the ones you liberate, and ask who you are that you should hinder their freedom to enslave others. Did you not think the Sarpedonian elite would return to their city and rise up against your forces once you left to recruit the dragons? You stole their wealth."

Zeno ragefully roared. "They gained that gold on the backs of their own people! They stole from their own!"

"It doesn't matter. There will always be men willing to watch others suffer if it lines their pockets. They think they earned their great wealth through great intellect and effort. They think themselves better than the lower orders. They see their wealth as power. You came and made them feel helpless. You showed them what real power is. You made their great wealth seem irrelevant. You showed them how small they, and their banks, truly were; and they hated you for it. I, I affirm the lie, and they serve me. They pay their taxes and lament. Occasionally, they talk of rebellion, of seizing more power. But they never will. Because in their hearts they know: their wealth is worthless. There is only one power: the power to kill, and that is mine. They will not risk the lesser treasure they now have for the greater which will always be beyond their reach. I give them just enough room to live, but not enough room to think. I astound them with mystery and magic not of this world. Awe, fear, and distraction are powerful allies to the ruler."

Zeno turned away and shook his head. "You can't continue this forever. If you rule the people through fear, eventually they will rise up against you because they will realize they have nothing to lose. And even if you beat them back, of who will you then be king?"

"Now, you would tell me how to rule?" the Vampire snickered. "You are willing to die for freedom, not just your own but that of others. That's what makes you heroic. But heroes seldom make good rulers. That is the difference between you and me. I deal with humanity as it is. You deal with it as you wish it to be.

Most men aren't willing to die for their own freedom much less another's. Now, I will tell you the secret that I learned subjugating worlds for two-hundred years for the Erīeds. Men, all men, secretly, in the deep places in their souls that not even the poets touch, hate freedom, and yearn to be slaves. Freedom confuses them. It forces them to think. It demands that they be responsible, responsible!" the Vampire spat the word. "Could the race of men ever be responsible? Slavery is easy. They are told what to think and how to believe. Why do you think so many millions bow down and pray to gods they cannot see, hear, or touch? They wish to be slaves, creating imaginary masters where there are none. Slavery lets them focus on other pursuits. It allows them to distract themselves from what really terrifies them. Do you know what that is?"

Zeno still looked away. He had lost all interest in the conversation.

"Death. What really terrorizes every man is death. We are waiting to die. All of us stand with our head already in the noose, just waiting for the executioner to kick the stand from beneath us. Men are powerless to stop it, so they seek to distract themselves from it. Slavery distracts men from their cursed fate. Freedom enslaves their minds and compels them to give account of what they have done with their finite number of days. It is such a burden for their childlike intellects. Look at yourself. You offered them freedom, but in doing so demanded the best of them; that they always be brave, that they always be selfless, putting the welfare of others before their own. Such a burden. And did you offer to lift one finger to lighten their load? No. Rather you sought additional burdens to pile on your own back. You asked too much of them. You are a false god. But I, I ask so little of them. Only that they turn their heads when I burn the bodies, and not question me when their neighbors disappear in the night. In return, I offer them safety and prosperity." The Vampire stopped. For a few seconds there was silence.

"It would take very little to make you like me, Zenosthenes Andrea," the Vampire began again. "Which is why I'm prepared to offer you mercy."

Zeno turned to face his captor. He knew the Vampire had no mercy in him. He must want something.

"Although I should kill you, I am prepared to let you live. And not just let you live, but give you what you want most in this life. Guards! Bring her in."

The cell door opened. In walked Alexandra. She looked battered and bruised. But her eyes blazed with love and hope when they saw Zeno. She rushed to him and wrapped her arms around his neck.

"Zeno... Zeno!" she gasped.

Zeno was overtaken by a tidal wave of emotions. Had he not seen Alexandra fall from Altus Mons? Surely, she could not have survived such a fall.

"Alex..." he incoherently mumbled. "How?"

"I fell one story. Nothing more. I left in chains on the same aircraft you did."

"But..."

"It doesn't matter, Zeno," Alexandra cut him off. "*He* has already spoken to me." She nodded at the Vampire. "He is a killer, and a liar. But knowing what I know now about his past; about the Erīeds, I believe he speaks the truth now. He is willing to free us, you and I. We can live, together, if you tell him what he wants to know."

What does he want to know? Zeno felt so confused. He was no longer sure any of this was real.

"The Theomorphosis chamber Zeno, the Stokian ship. He wants it. He wants to assume the Power of Thumos as you have so he can have his revenge against the Erīeds. That was the reason he came to this planet in the first place. He came in search of the one weapon he knew could destroy them. But that is not all." Alexandra looked back to the Vampire, as if for reassurance that what she was about to tell Zeno was truth.

She turned back to Zeno. "Once he has been imbued with the All Fire, he has sworn to leave Ninivon, forever."

The Vampire stepped forward. "When the Erīeds exiled me, they took the last and only real thing I ever cared about in this life. When I came to this planet, I did so to find the Theomorphosis Chamber. When I could not find it, I sought to subjugate Ninivon, knowing that eventually Thumos would find me. That if I brutalized these people enough, an heir of the Stokian would rise to fulfill their age-old prophecy. It took twelve years. But then came you. I don't care about your planet. I know the source of your power is Stokian Thumos. I know about the Theomorphosis chamber. The Erīeds still live in fear of it. It was the weapon that took their goddess from them. It was the only weapon that ever stopped them. Give me that power. If you give me the power to destroy them, I will leave you, your woman, Lysandros, your whole goddamned world alone. I swear it on the one name I hold sacred."

Zeno's eyes were clouded. He was tired and his senses began to fail him. He looked at Alexandra.

"Kiss me," he softly asked.

Alexandra slowly took his face in her hands and lifted his head to touch her lips. They kissed, slowly and deeply. Then Zeno began to bite down on her lip. Alexandra winced. Zeno now put all of his strength into the bite. He had her lower lip trapped between his teeth. Before Alexandra could let forth a scream and pull back, Zeno had bitten through her lower lip.

Alexandra reeled back and screamed, both hands clasped to the wound. Zeno spat out the limp, blood-soaked piece of flesh.

"You didn't think I could tell you were an imposter? You thought you could fool me?" Zeno wailed. "You thought you could pass for her? I know Alexandra like I know my own soul! I can tell her mood by how she breathes."

Before Zeno's eyes, Alexandra's face and hair, skin and figure, all melted away. Beneath the illusion the image of Lana

Tarquinia came into view. No sooner did the metamorphosis stop than Lana rushed to the door, which was opened for her by a guard standing on the outside, her hands still pressed tight to her lower lip, bleeding freely.

The Vampire again stepped into Zeno's view, his eyes following his lover. Then he turned back to Zeno.

"The deception aside," he spoke. "I meant what I said. Tell me where the ship is, and I will go away."

"You think the Theomorphosis chamber is magical," Zeno replied. "But there is no magic in the world. It's just an alien artifact. Unless the All Fire chooses you, it will give you no power."

"You lie."

"You know I speak the truth, but your great hubris prevents you from accepting it. There are some things in this world beyond the reach of even the most violent men. The Power of Thumos is not like an inanimate thing that a thief can steal. No, the All Fire is alive. Like a capricious woman, it chooses whom it joins with. It has a will just as you do. It chose me as its host."

The Vampire's eyes flared with rage.

"What? What will you do to me, Erīed?" Zeno shook his head in defiance. "She's dead. You are powerless to hurt me." He meant Alexandra.

The Vampire clutched Zeno by the throat and slammed him into the wall. "I will crucify you in Acropolis Square. You will hang on a cross for all of Ninivon to see. Your silence will only delay me. It will not stop me. I will find the ship. Sooner or later, the Power of Thumos will be mine."

Zeno shook his head as if in pity for his tormentor's disillusionment. "The All Fire won't join with you. The power of Thumos will never be yours. You know it. I know it. Thumos knows it."

The Vampire clinched his jaw in rage and stormed out of the cell.

Zeno was alone again with nothing but his thoughts. The Vampire had planned this interrogation very carefully. Days without food, then food, a visitation, and finally, his witch disguised as Alexandra. He meant to beat him down. But Zeno persevered. What's more, he did so by telling the truth. Knowing that the Vampire could spend a thousand years studying the Theomorphosis Chamber, and not be one step closer to the Power of Thumos, the object of his desire, perhaps the only thing in all Ninivon that he truly desired, gave him joy. But the feeling of victory quickly subsided. All resolve having left his soul, Zeno cried like a child and whispered "Alexandra…"

CHAPTER XXXIV
THE VAMPIRE

"Lana!" The Vampire stormed into the laboratory where Lana was already casting a spell to heal her lip.

"We will have to find the ship on our own. What progress have you made in your studies?" he demanded.

"Progress is slow, my Lord," Lana pleaded. "The ship is guarded by powers not of this world. The histories and sorcery books merely give legends and suggestions as to its location. They give even less regarding the ritual and the Theomorphosis chamber. None of the authors had ever seen the ship much less beheld the power within. None of my vision spells are working. And every time I think I am making progress..."

"What? Tell me."

"The data changes. It is as if the old Stokian secrets are alive and actively working to further hide themselves from us."

The Vampire threw Lana to the floor behind him and turned his back.

Lana looked up at him, shocked to find herself on the floor, breathing heavily. He rarely put his hands on her like that.

"I told you he would never help you," she spat, still laying on the ground but propped up on her elbows. "We should just kill him, forget the Theomorphosis chamber, and be done with this."

"I'm sure you would like that," the Vampire seethed, still not turning to acknowledge her. "The Theomorphosis chamber is the greatest source of power in the universe. Not even the Diseased Beast was immune to its sting. It is the only way I can fight them."

Lana picked herself up off the floor and dusted off her dark robes. "This has nothing to do with them," she responded. "This is about her. You want the Power of Thumos so that you can have her!"

"So that I can kill her," the Vampire roared back.

"But for her, nonetheless," Lana likewise bellowed with a wrathful tone she seldom took with her lover.

The Vampire turned and strode forward. He grabbed Lana and pulled her to him. He positioned his head right in the crux of her neck. He could feel her shaking. He breathed in her scent as his tongue lightly caressed the surface of her skin. Then he extended his tongue, slowly, and licked the blood from her cut lip.

"Do not think that you are so important to me that I will not turn you into one of *them*. You will never speak of *her* again."

"I have never spoken of her until now," Lana tepidly began. "Because I knew it would do *this* to you. But she has always been here, coming between us, keeping you from me."

"You will be silent," the Vampire demanded, his hands tightening around her lower jaw and head.

"If I do not hold my peace, will you kill me?" Lana coughed out. "Damn you! I have given you everything! My loyalty, my intellect, my body, my very life. If you had ordered me to kill my own father, I would have done it without ever asking why. I found you, and loved you, when you were an exile living in an alien world. When you were at the point of death, I feed you with bowls of my own blood and brought Darklanders and slaves for you to feed upon. When our allies would have rejected you as an alien or monster, I convinced them that you were their deliverer. I accepted you into my home, talked with you, studied with you, made plans with you, shed blood with you, challenged an empire with you, and put you on the throne of all Ninivon. Is this the reward for devotion, my Lord? She betrayed you! She chose *them* over you! She rebuffed you as your wife. I'd settle to be your whore! Was she so enchanting that her memory is more desirous to you than my warm flesh?"

The Vampire slammed Lana against the near wall and buried his fist into the stone mere cementers from her head. His eyes were wild. His sharp teeth were clinched. Despite his reputation for murder and savagery, he was not, nor ever had been, one prone to angry outbursts. The Vampire was level in his emotions. His was not the evil of so many brutal men who lacked the ability to conceal their brutality. Rather, the Vampire saw violence as a tool, nothing more. Never something to be exercised at the whim of feeling. He had too much respect for it to do that.

Yet, this topic, the one not even Lana had dared broach for twelve years, moved him to rage as no other could. He now stood ready to rip the body of his first and most essential benefactor limb from limb with his bare hands. The Vampire breathed fast and heavy like a lion about to pounce on his prey. His daemonic purple eyes rested fixated on Lana. After some seconds of silence, he let her go and walked to the doors of the chamber.

Lana came forward to watch him walk away. "You now have everything we sought out to attain so many years ago when I first found you in the ice of the south, except one thing," she called out behind him. "You are ruler of all Ninivon. Your glory reaches to the highest heavens. Many believe you to be a god. You have me."

The Vampire kept walking and burst through the heavy steel doors as violently as he had enterer.

"Why is it not enough for you? Why am *I* not enough for you?" the Vampire heard Lana bellow as the doors closed behind him.

CHAPTER XXXV
ZENO

It was the thirteenth day of the fourth month of the thirteenth year of the reign of the Vampire: Terror and Woe of Ninivon. Zeno could see from the inner gate of Dikaiosune Tower, where he was chained to a motorized cart. A wooden pavilion was built in Acropolis Square in front of Ninivon tower. Tens of thousands of people jammed in the courtyard between the Three Towers and the Great Gate leading from the acropolis down to the city proper. The aristocrats and nobles had rows of seats closest to the pavilion. Others stood.

Another million must be watching down in the lower city, even from Limnae.

There was light talk and chatter, but the mood was somber. Armed hoplites were stationed at various points along the wall and even within the crowd to ensure that order was maintained.

On the pavilion stood a regiment of the Vampire's elite knights, the Equitati. Next to these were a set of six men dressed in black cloaks and masks. These were the executioners whose job it was to carry out the sentence. In front of them, the kings and national rulers sat in cushioned chairs. There was Tarquinius Augustus, Emperor of Rema, Akmoses, Pharaoh of Osaeria, Hanno, Consul of Tyra, Saladin Alquhafi, new Sultan of the Hipperi, Ravi Zachaves, Queen of Bramhas, Elliana Zid, Queen of Dimron, and Edmŏnd, new King of Jona. Following Tarquinius, on the right side of the pavilion was a rise. There sat Lana. Two more steps up, was an empty seat.

Trumpets thundered. Drums echoed. Every citizen in the square and the thousands watching outside dropped to their knees and bowed low their heads. The monolithic doors to Ninivon Tower opened. Another half dozen Equitati came out first, followed by eight great wolves, and last of all, the Vampire: Terror and Woe of Ninivon. They walked through the forest of columns and towards the pavilion.

The Vampire anxiously walked up the stairs to his throne and sat. He wore his finest purple cape over a silver shirt and black pants and boots. From the highest point on the pavilion, he gazed over the crowd. They were both in awe and terrified of him. The trumpets stopped and the spectators all rose.

"Activate the holosphere!" the Vampire commanded. The cameras turned on. The Vampire's image was projected all across the planet.

"People of Ninivon," he began. "Now behold the awful price of insurrection. This man, this false god, threatened our common peace. He offered you freedom. But there is no freedom from me; only through me. You who have lived under my power and protection know this to be true. But this man questioned that, and encouraged you to do the same. He offered you freedom but what he gave you was death. But today my subjects, I stand before you to offer what only a true ruler can give. I offer order."

The violin began a funeral dirge. The gate to Dikaiosune Tower rose. The cart surrounded by armed guards slowly came into the street. Atop the car, with both hands chained together to a post behind him, was Zeno. What whispers there were instantly ceased. Everyone strained their necks to look over their neighbors. Zeno stared straight forward, without looking to the left or right. It had been years since he had been in Acropolis Square. As a young boy, his mother often brought him here to run and play, before he began his training in the egoga. He was here for the announcement of those who passed the trials, gaining admittance into the egoga. As an initiate, he was here often for ceremonies.

One of the spectators spat at Zeno. In an instant, practically the entire square began to hiss and curse and shout obscenities. Many in the front row of the road on which the cart traveled, threw rotten fruit or small stones. Zeno's hands were hoisted above him. He could not use them to defend himself. He turned his head and tried to avoid what he could. A rock slammed into his right temple and cut him. Blood began to stream from his head.

As the cart rolled closer to the pavilion, the insults and mockery grew more obscene. Zeno thought of Iocus the Martyr. He was a great philosopher of Tyra who was unjustly sentenced to death. According to his students, when the jailer gave him the poison hemlock to drink, he thanked the man. The dirge played on. While Zeno was struck with spit and mud and fruits and vegetables on all sides, he recalled the philosophy of the great man.

"Death, like birth, is one of nature's secrets. Those elements which first made up man are then dispersed. But the spirit returns to the All Fire. So that in no way should death trouble the philosopher."

And...

"That certain men should cause suffering for their fellow man is inevitable and should not be marveled at. To wish it otherwise would be to wish that the ocean were dry. But the wise man knows that in a short time both he and his tormentor will soon be dead, and all offenses will be ended."

And finally...

"Lead me, Andrea the Brave, and destiny. I will follow whithersoever thou shalt go. Though I turn coward and shriek back, I shall have to go nonetheless."

These words encouraged Zeno. He was not ready to die. He was terrified, defiant, bitter, and nervous all at the same time. Every second the cart carried him nearer to the cross. There he would be made a sacrifice to cruel gods. It wasn't death itself that bothered him. Zeno had reasoned that once he was dead, he would not know it. It was dying alone as a spectacle before his enemies that was so maddening: it was unjust. Zeno was not ready to die. He still had so much strength within him. He knew he would need all his strength, and pain, if he was to endure the day. The Vampire would not make this short. Zeno knew he would be tortured. It took time to die on a cross. Zeno could not let himself cry before his enemies. It was the only vengeance he had left.

The cart stopped at the base of the pavilion. Executioners came down and unlocked Zeno's chains. They lead him by each arm up the pavilion. They stopped before the Vampire, who still stood. Zeno looked to his left and could see the cross lying on the floor of the pavilion. Next to it was rope, a hammer, and three nails, all large, but one larger than the other two. All meant for him.

A magistrate stepped forward. Like the executioners, he wore a long black robe and a black pointed hat that covered his entire head and face. He raised his hands and the crowd grew silent.

"There can be no mercy without justice, or justice without mercy. Our Lord is rich in both. If the prisoner will publicly kneel and beg the forgiveness of our Lord, he shall be spared the long torments of the cross. He shall be shown another way." The magistrate pointed to a chopping block to his left, with a great ax buried in it. "Will you kneel?" the magistrate asked Zeno.

Zeno did not respond but stared at the Vampire, who wrathfully returned his gaze.

The magistrate looked to the Vampire who nodded back at him.

"Whip!" the magistrate yelled. Zeno was tied to a post in the center of the pavilion, and his shirt was ripped from his back. One of the executioners stepped forward and unwound his whip. Unlike the others, his hood was red. He was the torturer. Zeno looked straight ahead. He picked the face of a small child in the crowd to focus on. The egoga had taught him that the key to overcoming pain was to meditate on something else.

"Your mind is a powerful thing, Zeno," Dekaleon, a conditioning instructor during Zeno's fourth year, would say. "Use it to make the pain smaller."

The torturer lifted his tool. He twirled it around, once, twice, three times. Then the release. The barb of the lash sliced into Zeno's naked back. Zeno clenched his teeth. He would let no groan of agony escape his lips. The crowd erupted in approval. They cheered for the torturer to strike him harder so they might see him break. It was all a form of sadistic entertainment.

The torturer struck again and again. With every lash, raw flesh was sliced, ripped, and torn. After five lashes, Zeno's back looked like a highway grid drawn in blood. Every lash sapped his discipline a little more. He opened his mouth but did not cry out. He grimaced but did not groan. The agony reverberated throughout him. Gods, the pain! Each blow sought to drive him to his knees, and with each blow he sunk a little more, and after which, he rose a little less.

Zeno lost count, so numerous were the lashes at his back. The magistrate raised his hand, and the flagellation ceased. "Now *Demigod*, now will you kneel before your Lord?"

Zeno gasped for breath. The post was all that held him up. His mouth was dry and a white paste formed at the edges of his lips, as if he were a dog foaming at the mouth. In spite of all of this, Zeno found the wherewithal to defiantly shake his head.

The magistrate nodded at one of the executioners. He untied Zeno's left hand and pushed him over. Zeno fell like a brick. With his right hand still chained to the post, he lay half slouched, half sitting, his chest and stomach laid completely bare.

The torturer raised the whip again. The strike sliced across Zeno's chest. Bright red blood gurgled beneath the wound and dripped down his stomach. Zeno gasped at the contact. The torturer struck again and again. Zeno now had huge lacerations across his chest and ribcage. He tried to turn his body just slightly to protect the tenderest parts. But as a butcher tenderizes meat, lash upon lash made his whole-body ache. Zeno sat in a growing pool of his own blood. He began to sob ever so quietly. None could hear him over the roar of the crowd, who cheered more and more violently with each strike.

The torturer relented again.

"Will you kneel?" the magistrate questioned Zeno. There was no response. "Will, you, kneel?" roared the magistrate.

Zeno again shook his head, pouring forth what valor still laid within him as a libation to whatever Dark Gods had yet to abandon him. He knew he would not be asked again.

The executioners unchained Zeno's right hand and drug him to the cross. Two others joined them. They tied both arms and feet down. Then they reached for the hammer and nails. Zeno's mouth gaped open wide. The first nail pierced his lower right forearm and burst through the wood beneath. Zeno's eyes welled. A second nail was added through his left arm, and lastly one great nail for his legs, shattering both tibias.

The executioners stepped back and used the ropes to hoist the cross up. As the cross stood, Zeno could feel his flesh ripping apart from his own weight. The crowd cheered, louder, and louder, as the cross rose. When it stood almost vertical, the cross hit the critical angle and slid into the crevice built into the pavilion for that very purpose. The cross slid through the wooden scaffolding and slammed onto the marble floor of Acropolis Square. As the cross hit the ground, the weight of Zeno's body jerked down. The nails tore his tendons as they stopped his momentum.

The pain was immense. Zeno hung on the cross, dejected, alone. In that moment, he raised his head to look over the thousands who had filled the square. They had all come to watch him die. Zeno closed his eyes and let forth a groan of anguish. If he pushed down with his legs and up with his arms to raise his torso, the spikes suspending him on the cross caused excruciating pain. On the other hand, if he let his body slouch, he couldn't breathe. Zeno alternated from one to the other, lifting his torso until he could no longer endure the pain and slouching down until his lungs demanded a breath. His back burned, still dripping blood from dozens of open lacerations, yet tenderized even more by chaffing against the wood every time Zeno raised his body to get a breath. His throat was already starting to burn from thirst. This was utter agony.

In addition to the physical pain, which made it almost impossible to think, Zeno's mind was torn a million different ways by a million different thoughts. There were no cohesive thoughts; just flashes, a stream of consciousness. Had he been capable of cognitive thought, Zeno would have thought of the irony that he now died before the eyes of the very cheering people whom he wished to liberate. Brief glimpses of the people he loved sped through his mind; his mother, Lysandros, Nikolaus, the Priestess of Sofia, and most of all, Alexandra. Were he to have a monument to mark the place where his body would be laid in the ground, it would not say that he was the Vessel of Thumos, or even a Ranger. It would say he loved a woman, one woman, hard, and she loved him. But there would be no grave or monument. Only the time it would take to die of asphyxiation or thirst on the cross, and then no more. As he was actively being offered up as a sacrifice to the Dark Gods, Zeno silently prayed to Andrea the Brave, "Goddess, if anything of me or my service was pleasing to you, have mercy on me... hasten my death."

Zeno opened his eyes. It was a cloudy day. Faint in the

distance, he thought he saw something in the sky. It looked like an owl, black with white stripes along the wings. This comforted him. He knew he was seeing visions, and would soon be dead.

CHAPTER XXXVI
THE RAID ON ACROPOLIS SQUARE

Alexandra

Alexandra and Lysandros wiped the blood from their weapons. They had just had one of the bloodiest fights of their lives, and it was soon to be bloodier. Between the two of them, they had just killed both the operators and guards of the control tower. And that, after having infiltrated the tower and the control room itself, disguised in two communications officers' uniforms they had stolen days before. A testament to the martial skill the egoga instilled in its graduates, as well as to the combat talent each possessed. Both knew that if their mission was to have any chance of success, they would have to fight today, harder, and better, than either ever had in their lives. If they were artists and killing their medium, today they would create their magnum opus.

Alexandra was fine with this. When she first saw Zeno as the Demigod at the Balena, she marveled at how he fought. It was not the skill with which he had fought that so captivated her, rather it was the emotion. There was an energy, a rage, a hatred, and a love that animated every strike Zeno made that day. It was the most majestic thing Alexandra had ever seen. She didn't understand how Zeno did it at the time. But later she realized it was because he was fighting for someone he loved.

Now the tables had turned. The one man who could deliver her and her world from an ongoing genocide and tyranny was at death's door, he also happened to be the man she loved. She would fight today as Zeno had fought at the Balena, and for the same reasons. The furens had taken her completely. Today, nothing would stand between her and Zeno without paying a price.

Alexandra spoke through her radio in Militian. "The sphinx is blind. How far out are you?"

"Twelve miles," Diana replied. "I can see the city from here. Head to the square and get in position."

Alexandra and Lysandros pulled the hoods back over their heads and made for the exit. Soldiers would soon be all over the control room, but it was too late. Their mission was to prevent the controllers in the Tower of the Sphinx from alerting the city that it was under aerial attack. They had done that. With the control center in Altus Mons still inoperable, there was no other warning mechanism for the capital city. This was the first and most pivotal part of the assault. For if the Tower of the Sphinx detected the rebels flying in, they would alert the Dioskurian air defenses, and the attack would be over before it began.

The Vampire

In the square, everyone's eyes were focused on Zeno hanging on the cross. No one could hear due to the roar of the crowds. Then, the alarms rang out over the din of the spectators. The sirens resounded throughout the city. The Vampire was the first to hear them. He leapt up and looked above. In the distance, he could see dragons, easily forty, heading for the acropolis.

Others in the crowd now heard the alarms. Shouts of delight turned into screams of terror as soldiers and spectators one by one looked to the heavens. Like a contagious disease, fear spread from one to another until the entire crowd was in a full panic. Lana was now on her feet, as were the other kings on the podium and the aristocrats seated in the front row.

"How could a brood of dragons fly into Dioskuria unde-tected?" Lana asked the Vampire.

"Lysandros…"

The dragons opened fire on the artillery guns mounted on the city walls. The guns returned fire. In the streets, everyone ran in opposite directions, screaming. Anyone who fell or was shoved to the ground was trampled.

The Vampire looked to Gregorios, the admiral of his aerial armada, who was seated in the front row. "Launch our fight-ers and gunships."

Gregorios gave the command, his ear to the microscopic radio on his wrist. Within seconds drone fighters were in the skies and piolets were racing to their gunships. Once they were airborne, the attackers would lose their aerial advantage.

Just then, a dragon swooped into the middle of the acrop-olis. It was Likavitos, oldest and most powerful of the drag-ons of Grey Peaks. A series of harnesses hungover his back and fastened onto those harnesses were Konan, and twenty Woads. They leapt to the ground while the dragon was still in flight. Two other dragons dived inside the square bearing Di-ana, twenty Militae, and twenty of the Blue Order. In a matter of moments, the square was overrun with rebels. The dragons took off to destroy the anti-air guns and enough enemy air-craft to clear the escape.

Just then, a dragon swooped down and ignited the twenty-four Doric columns that held up the Great Gate, leading down into the city. The columns all exploded and collapsed, bringing the monolithic gate structure with it.

Seeing the explosions, the Vampire knew their intent. "They mean to seal off the acropolis and free him!" he yelled at his subordinate rulers. "Form up around the cross!"

Equitati Knights and hoplites poured from all three towers into Acropolis Square, which was now packed with soldiers. An all-out mealy broke out. The scene was complete chaos: The Vampire's Equitati formed a perimeter around the podi-um on which Zeno was dying. The Woads, Militae, and Blue

Order fought to break through the perimeter and free Zeno, and the Dioskurian hoplites in the square fought to form up enough to attack the rebels in the rear. All in the midst of fifty thousand civilians trying to avoid the blood and fire.

The Vampire drew his sword and rushed into the chaos. The great wolves were unleashed. Half the kings and their body guards all drew their arms and rushed into the fray. The other half rushed into the Three Towers either to hide or escape.

The rebels all pushed their way forward to the podium and clashed with the Equitati, who fought like devils around their master. The Vampire sliced one Militae in half at the torso. He ran through another.

Alexandra

Alexandra and Lysandros ran through the Tower of the Sphinx. They could see the disorder around them as soldiers hurried to the exit and could hear the battle already raging outside in the acropolis. Alexandra knew the Woads and Militae would fight with all their ferocity. Each had volunteered for this mission. Each expected to die. Each Woad had taken a blood oath to free the Brown Warrior. Each Militae had sworn to offer three kills each to their ancestors before they crossed death's door.

They emerged from the Tower of the Sphinx, and ran to the cross. Alexandra caught a glimpse of Konan swinging his massive two-handed claymore and caving in an Equitati's skull. He swung to his side and knocked another off his feet. Diana buried a tomahawk in one Equitati's chest and her dagger in another's. The rebels pushed their way forward in a cacophony of screams, gunfire, explosions, and war cries. Already the slick stones of Acropolis Square were soaked in blood, urine, spit, and tears.

There was but a second of hesitation. Alexandra then turned

her attention to the cross. She looked up and saw her lover and friend. He was unconscious, blood seeping from his wounds. He looked as if he might fall apart at any moment.

Alexandra sawed through the bottom of the cross with an ion saw and Lysandros lowered Zeno to the ground with the same ropes that hoisted him up. Then Alexandra began to pull the nail out of Zeno's right forearm as Lysandros did the left.

Alexandra extracted the first nail. A deep moan escaped Zeno's lips. This whole time he had not raised his head, even when the cross fell back. Zeno now looked up and saw Alexandra. His eyes beamed.

"How...?" he muttered.

"I told you I'd never leave you."

The Vampire

Other dragons attacked the army of soldiers now trying to climb over the rubble that was the Great Gate just moments before. The Vampire had only the forces on hand in the square which, although more numerous in total than those of the rebels, were divided, with himself and the Equitati defending the podium and the hoplites still fighting to get through the panicked crowd.

"My lord!" Lana yelled out over the din.

The Vampire heard and turned to see Lysandros and Alexandra desperately trying to free Zeno. He wheeled about. But the Woads had broken through the line of Equitati and were now heading to the cross as well, to defend Lysandros and Alexandra while they did their thwork.

The Vampire rushed the group like a tiger. He swung his bastardsword with deadly precision, knitting its tip and edge among the defenders as a skilled craftsman would a needle through a tapestry. Five Woads fought bravely but fell, one by one, in gushing fountains of blood. In a few moments, the Vampire had killed them all.

Lysandros

The Vampire was closing upon them. Lysandros, who was now helping Alexandra free the ropes, abandoned this work and pulled his rifle around. He emptied the clip, all rounds piercing the Vampire. The Vampire fell in a pool of blood. His face and body mangled. Other Equitati were now attacking Lysandros and Alexandra on the cross. He reloaded his weapon and brought them down as well.

Then, as if rising from the grave, the Vampire arose, his wounds closing right before Lysandros' eyes.

Lysandros threw down his rifle and drew his short sword. The two champions clashed weapons. Lysandros was the more skilled swordsman, but the Vampire had supernatural power and eternal youth. Lysandros came through with a thrust which the Vampire parried. The Vampire swung back around, but Lysandros ducked and drove his shoulder into his ribs. The Vampire took a few steps back but was already raising his sword for another blow. Lysandros countered that blow and then the next before swinging across his chest. The Vampire ducked and slammed his sword into Lysandros' gut. Only the breast plate preserved his life. The blow knocked Lysandros nearly ten yards back.

Alexandra

The Vampire went straight for Alexandra.

"Look out!" Zeno roared.

Alexandra did not stop or look up. She tore the final rope free. Zeno gasped in pain as he slid from the cross. Alexandra fell back. Both fell beyond the stretch of the Vampire's blade as it slammed into the cross where Alexandra's head and Zeno's legs had been a moment before.

The Vampire turned immediately to Zeno and raised his sword. But was stopped by the sting of a sword point piercing his back and bursting out of his chest. As quickly as the blade burst in, it was ripped out, creating an even larger wound. The Vampire coughed up blood and hissed in pain. He turned to see Alexandra, a look of murder on her face. She slammed her sword into his shoulder. Such a blow would have cleaved into the chest of a mortal man. It did not even sever the Vampire's arm. She stepped between him and Zeno and sliced him a third time across the head. The force of the blow knocked the Vampire off the podium and onto the blood wet stone of Acropolis Square.

Lysandros

Lysandros rushed to Zeno. "Likavitos, now! Everyone, get out!" he roared through the communicator.

All across the square, dragons lowered and blasted enemy troops with fire, creating a gap. They then landed, briefly. The Militae and Woads grabbed ahold of the ropes hanging from their backs before the beasts took to the skies.

Likavitos likewise dove down and opened his claws. Alexandra started to rush back to her father and Zeno. But as Likavitos lowered, a spear, propelled by a savage throw, pierced the beast's chest and punctured his heart. Such a weapon would, if thrown by even the strongest mortal's hand, never have pierced the dragon's thick hide. But propelled by the Vampire's godlike strength, it cut through Likavitos' chest as a knife would through cooked meat. The oldest and wisest of the dragons of Grey Peaks crashed between Ninivon Tower and the Tower of the Sphinx, dead.

Alexandra

Alexandra looked up. She saw the Vampire: Terror and Woe of Ninivon. His eyes were fixed on her, burning with the fires of hell. She turned back to her father.

"Call for another dragon! Get him out of here!"

"Alex, no!"

"Get him out of here!"

The numbers of the Vampire's troops were now beginning to take control of the brawl. In the instant before her sword clashed with the Vampire's, Alexandra looked up to see Konan cut down, fighting against three Equitati, a dozen Militae lying dead in front of the podium. This was the great sacrifice they all had made. Dragons were even falling from the skies under anti-aircraft fire outside the walls of the acropolis. They could not have hoped in their wildest dreams that they would have made it this far. Now, they were so close to achieving their object: Zeno's rescue, against all odds. But the cost had been great, as the Priestess said it would be. Most knew this to be a suicide mission, even if they managed to save Zeno. They knew they would not all be able to escape in such an unorthodox way in the heat of battle. Many were shot down from the harnesses on which they hung as their would-be dragon saviors flew away. So few would make it out.

Alexandra looked up and saw another dragon drop altitude. He was heading towards Zeno and her father. So much sacrifice. So much blood. She looked behind her and saw Lysandros yelling through his radio, and Zeno just conscious enough to understand what she was about to do, now using what strength he had left to fight his way out of Lysandros' grasp and to her side. The entire mission, and perhaps the fate of her world now rested on her. If she could but delay the Vampire a few moments, both Zeno and her father would go free.

The Vampire now threw himself at Alexandra, fuming with

rage. He struck down at her. She stepped back, avoiding the first blow and the second. She parried the third and struck back. The Vampire blocked and for a moment the two swords were locked against each other, strength against strength.

But the Vampire was far stronger. He pushed off, knocking Alexandra onto the wood of the podium. He struck down, but Alexandra skidded back and leapt to her feet. She struck over her head. Parried. She set herself and struck again, and again. She was on the offensive now, driving the Vampire back. The shadow of the dragon passed over them. The furens had taken her. She had settled into the dance. She fought now as Xaimera, the horse goddess of the Militae, with no thought for herself. She lived only for the next parry and strike, knowing well that if she could hold the Vampire off just a little longer, Zeno would live.

Lysandros

The dragon lowered to pick up the Archon and Demigod. Lysandros hoisted Zeno up. The hoplites and Equitati were now rushing the podium and were firing on both men and the dragon. Such weak shells would not puncture dragon scales, but Lysandros had to get Zeno out now. One more wound would kill him.

But Zeno fought back. His eyes focused only on a single duel before his eyes. Alexandra swung her blade, again and again. The Vampire parried, swung his blade around, and sliced into Alexandra's side.

"No!" Zeno thundered as a god. "Let me go! God damn you! Let me go!"

Lysandros turned back. He saw his wounded daughter steady herself. She still stood between them and the Vampire. She raised her sword in defiance. His heart strained with sorrow and pride.

The Vampire struck over. Alexandra avoided the blow and

swung herself. The Vampire blocked and countered, as did Alexandra. He caught her sword arm by the wrist and snapped her arm. Alexandra wailed in pain. The Vampire then buried his weapon through her chest.

"No!" Zeno fought against Lysandros as if he were completely whole, and Lysandros were his most hated enemy. The dragon lowered and opened his claws.

The Vampire

The Vampire had to be quick. His enemy was near escape. He started to pull his sword free from Alexandra's chest, but the young woman grabbed his hand. Their eyes met briefly. Alexandra's were glossed over, dazed. Her strength was so frail. The Vampire smiled slightly. He easily tore his hand away and the blade he grasped. Blood exploded from the wound in Alexandra's chest cavity, but she was not done. She fell to the ground, but with her good arm she reached up and clasped the Vampire's belt. It was a pathetic sight. She was so powerless against one so powerful. All she could do now was hold on in the hopes that she would slow him down just enough. Zeno and Lysandros were so near to escape.

The Vampire clasped Alexandra by her armor and lifted her up with one hand. He opened his mouth wide. His teeth receded back into his gums and fangs grew inside his jaws where none had been earlier. He now seemed more alien monster than human. The Vampire pulled Alexandra's head to the side with his free hand, exposing her neck, and plunged his teeth deep into her throat. But rather than drink, he tore out a chunk of flesh, taking half her esophagus with it. Alexandra fell instantly, blood bursting from the gaping hole in her throat as water from a broken dam.

The Vampire looked up. He still had time to reach Zeno. Then he heard the click. The daughter of the Red Sky had one more trick, even in death.

A delayed detonation. Well played...

A grenade ignited, blowing Alexandra's dead body into pieces, and blowing the Vampire and his warriors who were rushing behind him back twenty yards. The former rose, many of his clothes and much of his skin severely burned. But these wounds healed quickly. Again, he looked to the back of the podium. But Zeno was not there.

The dragon, with Zeno in one claw and Lysandros in the other, took off between Ninivon Tower and the Tower of the Sphinx. The beast turned and gained altitude. Every ion cannon fired at him, one connected. But it was not enough. The beast flapped its wings like a hurricane and flew away.

The Vampire roared through his radio to Lana. "Get every ship we have in the air! I want that dragon dead!"

"We have no operational vessels here, my Lord. All our aircraft were either damaged or destroyed in the fight," she answered. "I have sent word to Altus Mons to organize sorties and get them airborne. But it will take time with the bridge still inoperative. The dragons have all flown in different directions. It's impossible to guess which one has the Demigod."

The Vampire lowered his head. He considered Lana's words in her chamber. He should have killed Zeno when he had the chance. Now, he would have to beat Zeno on the battlefield. But not the same Zeno he had fought at Altus Mons, but a far more bitter and hateful version thereof. He himself had told Zeno how much easier it was to destroy than create. He himself had told Zeno that in order to free the slaves, he would have to kill the slave masters, all of them.

"His wrath will be terrible," the Vampire muttered. Then, an irony crept over the heart of the Vampire: Terror and Woe of Ninivon and clouded out the rage of having had his enemy snatched from him at the point of conquest. He smiled slightly. "To slay monsters, you must become a monster."

Zeno

Zeno laid back in the claws of a dragon flying south as fast as it could, crying. He drifted in and out of consciousness but he knew Alexandra was dead. The Vessel of Thumos felt the loss, and was tormented.

ABOUT ATMOSPHERE PRESS

Founded in 2015, Atmosphere Press was built on the principles of Honesty, Transparency, Professionalism, Kindness, and Making Your Book Awesome. As an ethical and author-friendly hybrid press, we stay true to that founding mission today.

If you're a reader, enter our giveaway for a free book here:

SCAN TO ENTER
BOOK GIVEAWAY

If you're a writer, submit your manuscript for consideration here:

SCAN TO SUBMIT
MANUSCRIPT

And always feel free to visit Atmosphere Press and our authors online at atmospherepress.com. See you there soon!

About the Author

DEMITRIOS LOPEZ lives in Texas with his daughter and puppy dog where he teaches Ancient Greek and Latin. The Classics saved his life, and it was from their seeds that the tree of the Σ series grew. Aside from being a daddy, writing, and teaching, he loves Zack Snyder movies (especially Man of Steel), Greece, and peanut butter.